continued . . .

Titles by Christine Feehan

Anthologies

Sea Storm

CHRISTINE FEEHAN

BERKLEY BOOKS, NEW YORK

THE BERKLEY PUBLISHING GROUP
Published by the Penguin Group
Penguin Group (USA) Inc.
375 Hudson Street, New York, New York 10014, USA
Penguin Group (Canada), 90 Eglinton Avenue East, Suite 700, Toronto, Ontario M4P 2Y3, Canada
(a division of Pearson Penguin Canada Inc.)
Penguin Books Ltd., 80 Strand, London WC2R 0RL, England
Penguin Group Ireland, 25 St. Stephen's Green, Dublin 2, Ireland (a division of Penguin Books Ltd.)
Penguin Group (Australia), 250 Camberwell Road, Camberwell, Victoria 3124, Australia
(a division of Pearson Australia Group Pty. Ltd.)
Penguin Books India Pvt. Ltd., 11 Community Centre, Panchsheel Park, New Delhi—110 017, India
Penguin Group (NZ), 67 Apollo Drive, Rosedale, North Shore 0632, New Zealand
 (a division of Pearson New Zealand Ltd.)
Penguin Books (South Africa) (Pty.) Ltd., 24 Sturdee Avenue, Rosebank, Johannesburg 2196,
South Africa

Penguin Books Ltd., Registered Offices: 80 Strand, London WC2R 0RL, England

"Magic in the Wind" was previously published in the anthology *Lover Beware,* published by The Berkley Publishing Group.

This is a work of fiction. Names, characters, places, and incidents either are the product of the author's imagination or are used fictitiously, and any resemblance to actual persons, living or dead, business establishments, events, or locales is entirely coincidental. The publisher does not have any control over and does not assume responsibility for author or third-party websites or their content.

PRINTING HISTORY
Berkley trade paperback edition / November 2010

Library of Congress Cataloging-in-Publication Data

Feehan, Christine.
  [Magic in the wind]
  Sea storm / Christine Feehan.
    p.   cm.
  ISBN 978-0-425-23677-2
  1. Witches—Fiction.   I. Feehan, Christine. Oceans of fire.   II. Title.
  PS3606.E36M34   2010
  813'.6—dc22   2010029321

PRINTED IN THE UNITED STATES OF AMERICA

10 9 8 7 6 5 4 3 2 1

CONTENTS

MAGIC IN THE WIND

For my sisters . . .
Thank you for the magic
and the love that has always been in my life.

1

"SARAH'S back. Sarah's come home." The whisper was overly loud and tinged with something close to fear. Or respect. Damon Wilder couldn't decide which. He'd been hearing the same small-town gossip for several hours and it was always said in the same hushed tones. He hated to admit to curiosity and he wasn't about to stoop to asking, not after he had made such a point of insisting on absolute privacy since he arrived last month.

As he walked down the quaint narrow sidewalk made of wood, the wind seemed to whisper, "Sarah's back." He heard it as he passed the gas station and burly Jeff Dockins waved to him. He heard it as he lingered in the small bakery. *Sarah*. The name shouldn't carry mystery, but it did.

He had no idea who Sarah was, but she commanded such interest and awe from the townspeople that he found himself totally intrigued. He knew from experience the people in the sleepy little coastal town were not easily impressed. No amount of money, fame, or title earned one deference. Everyone was treated the same, from the poorest to the richest, and there seemed to be no prejudice against religion or any other preferences. It was why he had chosen the town. A man could be anybody here and no one cared.

All day he had heard the whispers. He'd never once caught a glimpse of the mysterious Sarah. But he'd heard she'd once climbed the sheer cliffs above the sea to rescue a dog. An impossible task. He'd seen those crumbling cliffs and no one could climb them. He found himself smiling at the idea of anyone attempting such an impossible feat, and few things amused him or intrigued him.

The only grocery store was in the center of town and most of the gossip originated there and then spread like wildfire. Damon decided he needed a few things before he went home. He hadn't been in the store for more than two minutes when he heard it again. "Sarah's back." The same hushed whisper, the same awe and respect.

Inez Nelson, owner of the grocery store, held court, spilling out gossip as she normally did, instead of ringing up the groceries on the cash register. It usually drove him crazy to have to wait, but this time he lingered by the bread rack in the hope of learning more of the mysterious Sarah who had finally returned.

"Are you sure, Inez?" Trudy Garret asked, dragging her four-year-old closer to her and nearly strangling the child with her hug. "Are her sisters back, too?"

"Oh, I'm certain, all right. She came right into the store as real as you please and bought a ton of groceries. She was back at the cliff house, she said. She didn't say anything about the others, but if one shows up the others aren't far behind."

Trudy Garret looked around, lowered her voice another octave. "Was she still . . . Sarah?"

Damon rolled his eyes. Everyone always annoyed the hell out of him. He thought moving to a small town would allow him to find a way to get along to some extent but people were just plain idiots. Of course Sarah was still Sarah. Who the hell else would she be? Sarah was probably the only one with a brain within a fifty-mile radius so they thought she was different.

"What could it mean?" Trudy asked. "Sarah only comes back when something is going to happen."

"I asked her if everything was all right and she just smiled in that way she has and said yes. You wouldn't want me to pry into Sarah's business, now would you, dear," Inez said piously.

Damon let his breath out in a hissing rush of impatience. Inez made it her life's work to pry into everyone's business. Why should the absent Sarah be excluded?

"Last time she was here Dockins nearly died, do you remember that?" Trudy asked. "He fell from his roof and Sarah just happened to be walking by and . . ." She trailed off and glanced around the store and lowered her voice to a conspirator's whisper. "Old Mars at the fruit stand said Penny told him Sarah . . ."

"Trudy, dear, you know Mars is totally unreliable in the things he says. He's a dear, sweet man, but he sometimes makes things up," Inez pointed out.

Old man Mars was crotchety, mean, and known to throw fruit at cars if he was in a foul enough mood. Damon waited for lightning to strike Inez for her blatant lie, but nothing happened. The worst of it was, Damon wanted to know what old Mars had said about Sarah, even if it was a blatant lie. And that really irritated him.

Trudy leaned even closer, looked melodramatically to the right and left without even noticing he was there. Damon sighed heavily, wanting to shake the woman. "Do you remember the time little Paul Baily fell into that blowhole?"

"I remember that, now that you say. He was wedged in so tight and no one could get to him, he'd slipped down so far. The tide was coming in."

"I was there, Inez, I saw her get him out." Trudy straightened up. "Penny said she'd heard from her hairdresser that Sarah was working for a secret agency and she was sent to some foreign country under-cover to assassinate the leader of a terrorist group."

"Oh, I don't think so, Trudy. Sarah wouldn't kill anything." The store owner's hands fluttered to her throat in protest. "I just can't imagine."

Damon had had enough of gossip. If they weren't going to say anything worth hearing, he was going to get the hell out of there be-fore Inez turned her spotlight on him. He plunked his groceries down on the counter and looked as bored as he could manage. "I'm in a hurry, Inez," he said, hoping to facilitate matters and avoid Inez's usual attempts at matchmaking.

"Why, Damon Wilder, how lovely to see you. Have you met Trudy Garret? Trudy is a wonderful woman, a native of our town. She works over at the Salt Bar and Grill. Have you been there to eat yet? The salmon is very good."

"So I've heard," he muttered, barely glancing at Trudy to acknowledge the introduction. It didn't matter. They'd all made up their minds about him, making up the history he refused to provide. He felt a little sorry for the returning Sarah. They were making up things about her as well. "You might tell me about that beautiful old house on the cliffs," he said, shocking himself. Shocking Inez. He never gave anyone an opening for conversation. He wanted to be left alone. Damn Sarah for being so mysterious.

Inez looked as if she might faint and for once she was speechless.

"You must know the one I'm talking about," Damon persisted, in spite of himself. "Three stories, balconies everywhere, a round turret. It's grown over quite wild around the house, but there's a path leading to the old lighthouse. I was walking up there and with all the wild growth, I expected the house to be in bad shape, dilapidated like most of the abandoned homes around here, but it was in beautiful condition. I'd like to know what preservatives were used."

"That's private property, Mr. Wilder," Inez said. "The house has been in the same family for well over a hundred years. I don't know what they use in the paint, but it does weather well. No one lurks around that house." Inez was definitely issuing a reprimand to him.

"I was hardly lurking, Inez," he said, exasperated. "As you well know, the sea salt is hard on the paint and wood of the houses. That house is in remarkable condition. In fact, it looks newly built. I'm curious as to what was used. I'd like to preserve my house in the same way." He made an effort to sound reasonable instead of annoyed. "I'm a bit of a chemist and I can't figure out what would keep a house so pristine over the years. There's no sign of damage from the sea, from age, or even insects. Remarkable."

Inez pursed her lips, always a bad sign. "Well, I'm certain I have no idea." Her voice was stiff, as if she were highly offended. She rang up his groceries in remarkable time without saying another word.

Damon gathered the bags into one arm, his expression daring Inez to ask him if he needed help. Leaning heavily on his cane, he turned to Trudy. "The hairdresser's dog walker told the street cleaner that he saw Sarah walk on water."

Trudy's eyes widened in shock, but there was belief on her face.

Inez made some kind of noise he couldn't identify. Disgusted, Damon turned on his heel and stalked out. Ever since the first whisper of Sarah's name he had been unsettled. Disturbed. Agitated. There was something unfamiliar growing inside of him. Anticipation? Excitement? That was ridiculous. He muttered a curse under his breath at the absent Sarah.

He wanted to be left alone, didn't he? He had no interest in the woman the townspeople gossiped about. Sarah might not walk on water but her house was a mystery. He saw no reason why he shouldn't pay her a neighborly visit and ask what preservatives were used in the wood to achieve the nearly impossible results.

Damon Wilder was a man driven to the edge of sanity. Moving to this tiny town on the coast was his last effort to hang on to life. He had no idea how he was going to do it, or why he had chosen this particular town with all its resident eccentrics, but he had been drawn here. Nothing else would do. He had stepped on the rich soil and knew either this place would be home or he had none. It was hell trying to fit in, but the sea soothed him and the long walks over million-year-old rocks and cliffs occupied his mind.

Damon took his time putting his groceries away. The knowledge that this town, this place, was his last stand had been so strong he had actually purchased a house. His home was one of the few things that gave him pleasure. He loved working on it. He loved the wood. He could lose himself in the artistry of reshaping a room to suit his exact needs. For hours at a time the work occupied him such that nothing else could invade his brain and he was at peace for a time.

He stared out his large bay window, the one that looked out over the sea. The one that had an unobstructed view of the house on the cliff. Damon had spent more hours than he cared to think about staring up at the dark silent windows and the balconies and battlements. It was a unique house from another century, another time and place. There were lights on for the first time. The windows shone a bright welcome.

His leg hurt like hell. He needed to sit and rest, not go traipsing around the countryside. Damon stared at the house, drawn to the warmth of it. It seemed almost alive, begging him to come closer. He went outside onto his deck, intending to sit in the chair and enjoy his view of the sea. Instead he found himself limping his way steadily up the path toward the cliffs. It was nearly a compulsion. The path was narrow and steep and rocky in places, almost no more than a deer trail and overgrown at that. His cane slipped on the pebbles and twice he nearly fell. He was swearing by the time he made it to the edge of the private property.

He stood there staring in shock. Damon had been there not two days before, walking around the house and the grounds. It had been wildly overgrown, the bushes high and weeds everywhere. The shrubbery and trees had drooped with winter darkness on the leaves. A noticeable absence of sound had given the place an eerie, creepy feeling. Now there were flowers, as if everything had burst into blossom overnight. A riot of color met his eyes, a carpet of grass was beneath his feet. He could hear the insects buzzing, the sound of frogs calling merrily back and forth as if spring had come instantly.

The gate, which had been securely locked, stood open in welcome. Everything seemed to be welcoming him. A sense of peace began to steal into his heart. A part of him wanted to sit on one of the inviting benches and soak in the atmosphere.

Roses climbed the trellis and rhododendrons were everywhere, great forests of them. He'd never seen such towering plants. Damon started up the pathway, noting every single weed was gone. Stepping-stones led the way to the house. Each round of stone held a meticulously carved symbol. Great care had been taken to etch the symbol deep into the stone. Damon leaned down to feel the highly polished work. He admired the craftsmanship and detail. The artisans in the small town all had that trait, one he greatly respected.

As he neared the house, a wind rose off the sea and carried sea spray and a lilting melody. *"Sarah's back. Sarah's home."* The words sang across the land joyously. It was then he heard the birds and looked around him. They were everywhere, all kinds of birds, flitting from tree to tree, a flutter of wings overhead. Squirrels chattered as they rushed from branch to branch. The sun was sinking over the ocean, turning the sky into bright colors of pink and orange and red. The fog was on the far horizon, meeting the sea to give the impression of an island in the clouds. Damon had never seen anything so beautiful. He simply stood there, leaning on his cane and staring in wonder at the transformation around him.

Voices drifted from the house. One was soft and melodious. He couldn't catch the words but the tone worked its way through his skin into his very bones. Into his vital organs. He moved closer, drawn by the sound, and immediately saw two dogs on the front porch. Both were watching him alertly, heads down, hair up, neither making a sound.

Damon froze. The voices continued. One was weeping. He could hear the heartbreaking sound. A woman's voice. The melodious voice soothed. Damon shifted his weight and took a two-handed grip on his cane. If he had to use it as a weapon, that would give him more leverage. Concerned though he was with the dogs, he was more centered on the voice. He strained to listen.

"Please, Sarah, you have to be able to do something. I know you can. Please say you'll help me. I can't bear this," the crying voice said.

Her sorrow was so deep Damon ached for her. He couldn't remember the last time he'd felt someone's pain. He couldn't remember how to feel anything but bored or frustrated. The dogs both sniffed the air and, as if recognizing him, wagged their tails in greeting and sat down, hair settling to make them appear much more friendly. Keeping one eye on the dogs, he strained to catch the words spoken in that soft lilting tone.

"I know it's difficult, Irene, but this isn't something like putting a Band-Aid on a scraped knee. What do the doctors say?"

There was more sobbing. It shook him, hurt him, tore up his insides so that his gut churned and a terrible weight pressed on his chest. Damon forgot all about the dogs and pressed his hand over his heart. Irene Madison. Now he recognized the voice, knew from Inez at the grocery store that her fifteen-year-old son, Drew, was terminally ill.

"There's no hope, Sarah. They said to take him home and make him comfortable. You know you can find a way. Please do this for us, for me."

Damon edged closer to the house, wondering what the hell she thought Sarah could do. Work a miracle? There was a small silence. The window was open, the wind setting the white lacy curtains dancing. He waited, holding his breath. Waited for Sarah's answer. Waited for the sound of her voice.

"Irene, you know I don't do that sort of thing. I've only just come back. I haven't even unpacked. You're asking me . . ."

"Sarah, I'm begging you. I'll do anything, give you anything. I'm begging on my knees . . ." The sobs were choking Damon. The pain was so raw in the woman.

"Irene, get up! What are you doing? Stop it."

"You have to say you'll come to see him. Please, Sarah. Our mothers were best friends. If not for me, do it for my mother."

"I'll come by, Irene. I'm not promising anything, but I'll stop by." There was resignation in that gentle voice. Weariness. "My sisters will be coming in a day or so and as soon as we're all rested we'll stop by and see what we can do."

"I know you think I'm asking for a miracle, but I'm not, I just want more time with him. Come when you're rested, when the others have come and can help." The relief Irene felt spilled over to Damon and he had no clue why. Only that the weight pressing on his chest lifted and his heart soared for a moment.

"I'll see what I can do."

The voices were traveling toward him. Damon waited, his heart pounding in anticipation. He had no idea what to expect or even what he wanted, but everything in him stilled.

The door opened and two women emerged to stand in the shadow of the wide, columned porch. "Thank you, Sarah. Thank you so much," Irene said, clutching at Sarah's hands gratefully. "I knew you would come." She hurried down the stairs, straight past the dogs, who had rushed to their mistress. Irene managed a quick smile for Damon as she passed him, her tearstained face bright with hope.

Damon leaned on his cane and stared up at Sarah.

2

SARAH stood on the porch, her body in the shadows. Damon had no idea of her age. Her face seemed timeless. Her eyes were old eyes, filled with intelligence and power. Her skin was smooth and flawless, giving her the appearance of extreme youth, very much at odds with the knowledge in her direct gaze. She simply stood there quietly, her incredible eyes fixed on him.

"How did you get through the gate?"

It wasn't what he expected. Damon half turned to look back at the wrought-iron masterpiece of art. The gate was six feet high and an intricate piece of craftsmanship. He had studied it on more than one occasion, noting the symbols and depictions of various animals and stars and moons. A collage of creatures with raw power mixed with universal signs of the earth, water, fire, and wind. Always before when he had come to stare at the house and grounds the gate had been firmly locked.

"It was open," he replied simply.

Her eyebrow shot up and she looked from him to the gate and back again. There was interest in her gaze. "And the dogs?" Her hand dropped to one massive head as she absently scratched the ears.

"They gave me the once-over and decided I was friendly," he answered.

A faint frown touched her face, was gone in an instant. "Did they? You must get along well with animals."

"I don't get along well with anything," he blurted out before he could stop himself. He was so shocked and embarrassed at the admission he couldn't find a way to laugh it off, so it remained there between them.

Sarah simply studied his face for a long while. An eternity. She had a direct gaze that seemed to see past his physical body and delve straight to his soul. It made Damon uncomfortable and ashamed. "You'd better come in and sit down for a while," she said. "There's a blackness around your aura. I can tell you're in pain, although I can't see why you've come yet." She turned and went into the house, clearly expecting him to follow her. Both dogs did, hurrying after her, pacing at her heels.

Damon had been acting out of character ever since he heard that first whisper of gossip. He stood, leaning on his cane, wondering what had gotten into him. He'd seen the mighty Sarah. She was just a woman with incredible eyes. That was all. She couldn't walk on water or move mountains. She couldn't scale impossible cliffs or assassinate heads of terrorist organizations. She was just a woman. And probably as loony as hell. His aura was black? What the hell did that mean? She probably had voodoo dolls and dead chickens in her house.

He stared at the open door. She didn't come back or look to see if he was following. The house had swallowed her up. Mysterious Sarah. Damon lifted his eyes to the gathering darkness, to the first stars and the floating wisps of clouds. It irritated him but he knew he was going to follow her into that house. Just like her damn dogs.

Damon consoled himself with the fact that he was extremely interested in the preservation of wood and paint. He had been interested in her house long before she arrived back in town. He couldn't pass up a genuine opportunity to study it up close, even if it meant trying to make small talk with a crazy stranger. He raked his hand through his dark hair and glared at the empty doorway. Muttering curses beneath his breath, he stalked after her as best he could with his cane and his damaged hip and leg.

The porch stairs were as solid as a rock. The verandah itself was wide and beautiful, wrapping around the house, an invitation to sit in the shade and enjoy the view of the pounding sea. Damon wanted to linger there and continue to feel the peace of Sarah's home, but he stepped inside. The air seemed cool and scented, smelling of some fragrance that reminded him of the forests and flowers. The entryway was wide, tiled with a mosaic design, and it opened into a huge room.

With a sense of awe, Damon stared down at the artwork on the floor. There was a feeling of falling into another world when he looked at it. The deep blue of the sea was really the ocean in the sky. Stars burst and flared into life. The moon was a shining ball of silver. He stood transfixed, wanting to get on his knees and examine every inch of the floor. "I like this floor. It's a shame to walk on it," he announced loudly.

"I'm glad you like it. I think it's beautiful," she said. Her voice was velvet soft, but it carried through the house back to him. "My grandmother and her sisters made that together. It took them a very long time to get it just right. Tell me what you see when you look into the midnight sky there."

He hesitated but the pull of the floor was too much to resist. He examined it carefully. "There are dark shadows in the clouds across the moon. And behind the clouds, a ring of red surrounds the moon. The stars connect and make a bizarre pattern. The body of a man is floating on the sea of clouds and something has pierced his heart." He looked up at her, a challenge on his face.

Sarah merely smiled. "I was about to have tea; would you care for a cup?" She walked away from him into the open kitchen.

Damon could hear the sound of water as she filled the teakettle. "Yes, thank you, that sounds good." And it did, which was crazy. He never drank tea. Not a single cup. He was losing his mind.

"The pictures of my grandmother and her sisters are to your left, if you'd like to see them."

He had always considered looking at pictures of people he didn't know utterly ridiculous, but he couldn't resist looking at the photographs of the women who had managed to create such beauty on a floor. He wandered over to the wall of memories. There were many photographs of women, some black-and-white, others in color. Some of the pictures were obviously very old, but he could easily see the resemblance among the women. Damon cleared his throat. He frowned when he noticed a strange pattern running through every grouping. "Why are there seven women in each family picture?"

"There seems to be a strange phenomenon in our family," Sarah answered readily. "Every generation, someone produces seven daughters."

Startled, Damon leaned on his cane and studied each group of faces. "One out of the seven girls has always given birth to seven daughters? On purpose?"

Sarah laughed and came around the corner to join him in front of the wall of photographs. "Every generation."

He looked from her to the faces of her sisters in a picture near the center of the wall. "Which one carries the strain of insanity?"

"Good question. No one's ever thought to ask it before. My sister Elle is the seventh daughter so she inherits the mantle of responsibility. Or insanity, if you prefer." Sarah pointed to a girl with a young face, vivid green eyes, and a wealth of red hair pulled carelessly into a ponytail.

"And where is poor Elle right now?" Damon asked.

Sarah inhaled, then let her breath out slowly, her long lashes fluttering down. At once her face was in repose. She looked tranquil, radiant. Watching her did something funny to Damon's heart, a curious melting sensation that was utterly terrifying. He couldn't take his fascinated gaze off of her. Strangely, for just one moment, he felt as if Sarah was no longer in the room with him. As if her physical body had separated from her spirit, allowing her to travel across time and space. Damon shook himself, trying to get rid of the crazy impression. He wasn't an imaginative person, yet he was certain Sarah had somehow touched her sister Elle.

"Elle is in a cave of gems, deep under the ground where she can hear the heartbeat of the earth." Sarah opened her eyes and looked at him. "I'm Sarah Drake."

"Damon Wilder." He gestured toward his house. "Your new neighbor." He was staring at her, drinking her in. It didn't make sense. He was certain she wasn't the most beautiful woman in the world but his heart and lungs were insisting she was. Sarah was average height, with a woman's figure. She wore faded, worn blue jeans and a plaid flannel shirt. She certainly was not at all glamorous, yet his lungs burned for air and his heart accelerated. His body hardened painfully when she wasn't even trying to be a sexy siren, simply standing there in her comfortable old clothes with her wealth of dark hair pulled back from her pale face. It was the most infuriating and humiliating thing it was his misfortune to endure.

"You bought the old Hanover place. The view is fantastic. How did you come to find our little town?" Her cool blue gaze was direct and far too assessing. "You look like a man who would be far more comfortable in a big city."

Damon's fist tightened around his cane. Sarah could see his knuckles were white. "I saw it on a map and just knew it was the place I wanted to live in when I retired." She studied his face, the lines of suffering etched into his face, the too old eyes. He was surrounded with the mark of Death, and he read Death in the midnight sky, yet she was strangely drawn to him.

Her eyebrow went up, a perfect arch. "You're a little young to retire, I would have thought. There's not a lot of excitement here."

"I'll have to disagree with that. Have you hung out around the grocery store lately? Inez provides amazing entertainment." There was a wealth of sarcasm mixed with contempt in his voice.

Sarah turned away from him, her shoulders stiffening visibly. "What do you actually know about Inez to have managed to form an opinion in your month of living here?" She sounded sweet and interested but he had the feeling he had just stepped hard on her toes.

Damon limped after her like a puppy dog, trying not to mutter foul curses under his breath. It never mattered to him what other people thought. Everyone had opinions and few actually had educated ones. Why the hell did Sarah's opinion of him matter? And why did her hips have to sway with mesmerizing invitation?

The kitchen was tiled with the same midnight blue that had formed the sky in the mosaic. A long bank of windows looked out over a garden of flowers and herbs. He could see a three-tiered fountain in the middle of the courtyard. Sarah waved him toward the long table while she fixed the tea. Damon couldn't see a speck of dust or dirt anywhere in the house. "When did you arrive?"

"Late last night. It feels wonderful to be home again. It's been a couple of years since my last visit. My parents are in Europe at the moment. They own several homes and love Italy. My grandmother is with them, so the cliff house has been empty."

"So this is your parents' home?" When she shook her head with her slight, mysterious smile he asked, "Do you own this house?"

"With my sisters. It was given to us through our mother." She brought a steaming mug of tea and placed it on the table beside his hand. "I think you'll like this. It's soothing and will help take away the pain."

"I didn't say I was in pain." Damon could have kicked himself. Even to his own ears he sounded ridiculous, a defiant child denying the truth. "Thank you," he managed to mutter, trying to smell the tea without offending her.

Sarah sat across from him, cradling a teacup between her palms. "How can I help you, Mr. Wilder?"

"Call me Damon," he said.

"Damon then," she acknowledged with a small smile. "I'm just Sarah."

Damon could feel her penetrating gaze. "I've been very interested in your house, Sarah. The paint hasn't faded or peeled, not even in the salt air. I was hoping you would tell me what preservative you used."

Sarah leaned back in her chair, brought the teacup to her mouth. She had a beautiful mouth. Wide and full and curved as if she laughed all the time. Or invited kisses. The thought came unbidden as he stared at her mouth. Sheer temptation. Damon felt the weight of her gaze. Color began to creep up the back of his neck.

"I see. You came out late in the evening even though you were hurting because you were anxious to know what kind of preservative I use on my house. That certainly makes perfect sense."

There was no amusement in her voice, not even a hint of sarcasm, but the dull red color spread to his face. Her eyes saw too much, saw into him where he didn't want to be seen, where he couldn't afford to be seen. He wanted to look away but he couldn't seem to pull his gaze from hers.

"Tell me why you're really here." Her voice was soft, inviting confidence.

He raked both hands through his hair in frustration. "I honestly don't know. I'm sorry for invading your privacy." But he wasn't. It was a lie and they both knew it.

She took another sip of tea and gestured toward his mug. "Drink it. It's a special blend I make myself. I think you'll like it and I know it will make you feel better." She grinned at him. "I can promise you there aren't any toads or eye of newt in it."

Sarah's smile robbed him of breath immediately. It was a strange thing to feel a punch in the gut so hard it drove the air out of one's lungs just with a simple smile. He waited several heartbeats until he recovered enough to speak. "Why do you think I need to feel better?" he asked, striving for nonchalance.

"I don't have to be a seer for that, Damon. You're limping. There are white lines around your mouth and your leg is trembling."

Damon raised the cup to his mouth, took a cautious sip of the brew. The taste was unique. "I was attacked a while back." The words emerged before he could stop them. Horrified, he stared into the tea mug, afraid her brew was a truth serum.

Sarah put her teacup carefully on the table. "A person attacked you?"

"Well, he wasn't an alien." He swallowed a gulp of tea. The heat warmed him, spreading through his body to reach sore, painful places.

"Why would one man want to kill another?" Sarah mused aloud. "I've never understood that. Money is such a silly reason really."

"Most people don't think so." He rubbed his head as if it hurt, or maybe in memory. "People kill for all sorts of reasons, Sarah."

"How awful for you. I hope he was caught."

Before he could stop himself, Damon shook his head. Her vivid gaze settled on his face, looked inside of him again until he wanted to curse. "I was able to get away, but my assistant"—he stopped, corrected himself—"my friend wasn't so lucky."

"Oh, Damon, I'm so sorry."

"I don't want to think about it." He couldn't. It was too close, too raw. Still in his nightmares, still in his heart and soul. He could hear the echoes of screams. He could see the pleading in Dan Treadway's eyes. He would carry that sight to his death, forever etched in his brain. At once the pain was almost too much to bear. He wept inside, his chest burning, his throat clogging with grief.

Sarah reached across the table to place her fingertips on his head. The gesture seemed natural, casual even, and her touch was so light he barely felt it. Yet he felt the results like shooting stars bursting through his brain. Tiny electrical impulses that blasted away the terrible throbbing in his temples and the back of his neck.

He caught her wrists, pulled her hands away from him. He was shaking and she could feel it. "Don't. Don't do that." He released her immediately.

"I'm sorry, I should have asked first," Sarah said. "I was only trying to help you. Would you like me to take you home? It's already dark outside and it wouldn't be safe for you to try to go down the hill without adequate light."

"So I take it the paint preservative is a deep dark family secret," Damon said, attempting to lighten the situation. He drained the tea mug and stood up. "Yes, thanks, I wouldn't mind a ride." It was hard on the ego to have to accept it but he wasn't a complete fool. Could he have behaved any more like an idiot?

Sarah's soft laughter startled him. "I actually don't know whether the preservative is a family secret or not. I'll have to do a little research on the subject and get back to you."

Damon couldn't help smiling just because she was. There was something contagious about Sarah's laughter, something addictive about her personality. "Did you know that when you came home, the wind actually whispered, 'Sarah's back. Sarah's home.' I heard it myself." The words slipped out, almost a tribute.

She didn't laugh at him as he expected. She looked pleased. "What a beautiful thing to say. Thank you, Damon," she said sincerely. "Was the gate really open? The front gate with all the artwork? Not the side gate?"

"Yes, it was standing wide open welcoming me. At least that's how it felt."

Her sea blue eyes drifted over his face, taking in every detail, every line. He knew he wasn't much to look at. A man in his forties, battered and scarred by life. The scars didn't show physically but they went deep and she could clearly see the tormented man. "How very interesting. I think we're destined to be friends, Damon." Her voice wrapped him up in silk and heat.

Damon could see why the townspeople said her name with awe. With respect. Mysterious Sarah. She seemed so open, yet her eyes held a thousand secrets. There was music in her voice and healing in her hands. "I'm glad you've come home, Sarah," he said, hoping he wasn't making more of a fool of himself.

"So am I," she answered.

3

"SARAH!" Hannah Drake threw herself into her sister's arms. "It's so good to see you. I missed you so much." She drew back, stretching her arms to full length, the better to examine Sarah. "Why, Sarah, you look like a cat burglar, ready to rob the local museum. I had no idea Frank Warner's paintings had become valuable." She laughed merrily at her own joke.

Sarah's soft laughter merged with Hannah's. "I should have known you'd come creeping in at two A.M. That's so you, Hannah. Where were you this time?"

"Egypt. What an absolutely beautiful country it is." Hannah sat on the porch swing wearily. "But I'm wiped out. I've been traveling forever to get back home." She regarded Sarah's sleek black outfit with a slight frown. "Interesting set of tools you're sporting there, sister mine. I'm not going to have to bail you out of jail, am I? I'm really tired and if the police have to call, I might not wake up."

Sarah adjusted the belt of small tools slung low on her waist without a hint of embarrassment. "If I can't charm a police officer out of booking me for a little break-in, I don't deserve the name Drake. Go on in, Hannah, and go to bed. I'm worried about our neighbor and think I'll just go scout around and make certain nothing happens to him."

Hannah's eyebrow shot up. "Good heavens, Sarah. A man? There's an honest-to-God man in your life? Where is he? I want to go with you." She clasped her hands together, her face radiant. "Wait until I tell the others. The mighty Sarah has fallen!"

"I have *not* fallen—don't start, Hannah. I just have one of my hunches and I'm going to check it out. It has nothing to do with Damon at all."

"Ooh, this is really getting interesting. Damon. You remember his name. How did you meet him? Spill it, Sarah, every last detail!"

"There's nothing to spill. He just waltzed in asking about paint and wood preservatives." Sarah's tone was cool and aloof.

"You want me to believe he walked in on his own without an invitation? You had to have asked him to the house."

"No, I didn't," Sarah denied. "As a matter of fact the gate was open and the dogs allowed him in."

"The gate was open on its own?" Hannah was incredulous. She jumped to her feet. "I'm going with you for certain!"

"No, you're not, you're exhausted, remember?"

"Wait until I tell the others the gate opened for him." Hannah raised her arms to the heavens and stars. "The gate opens for the right man, doesn't it? Isn't that how it works? The gate will swing open in welcome for the man who is destined to become the love of the eldest child's life."

"I don't believe in that nonsense and you know it." Sarah tried to glare but found herself laughing. "I can't believe you'd even think of that old prophecy."

"Like you didn't think of it yourself," Hannah teased. "You're just going off to do the neighborly thing in the middle of the night and just sort of scout around his house. If you say so, of course I'll believe it. Is that telescope up on the battlement directed toward his bedroom?"

"Don't you dare look," Sarah ordered.

Hannah studied her face. "You're laughing but your eyes aren't. What's wrong, Sarah?" She put her hand on her sister's shoulder. "Tell me."

Sarah frowned. "He carries Death on him. I've seen it. And he read it in the mosaic. I don't know whose death, but I'm drawn to him. His heart is broken and pierced through, and the weight of carrying Death is slowly crushing him. He saw a red ring around the moon."

"Violence and death surround him," Hannah said softly, almost to herself. "Why are you going alone?"

"I have to. I feel . . ." Sarah searched for the right word. "Drawn. It's more than a job, Hannah. It's him."

"He could be dangerous."

"He's surrounded by danger, but if he's dangerous to me, it isn't in the way you're thinking."

"Oh my gosh, you really do like this guy. You think he's hot. I'm telling the others and I'm going up to the battlement to check him out!" Hannah turned and raced into the house, banging the screen door so Sarah couldn't follow her.

Sarah laughed as she blew a kiss to her sister and started down the stairs. Hannah looked wonderful as always. Tall and tanned and beautiful even after traveling across the sea. If her wavy hair was tousled, she just looked in vogue. Other women paid fortunes to try to achieve her natural wind-blown style. Sarah had always been uncommonly proud of Hannah's genuine elegance. She had a bright spirit that shone like the stars overhead. Hannah had a free spirit that longed for wide-open spaces and the wonders of the world. She spoke several languages and traveled extensively. One month she might be found in the pages of a magazine with the jet-setters, the next she was on a dig in Cairo. Her tall slender carriage and incredibly beautiful face made her sought after by every magazine and fashion designer. It was her gentle personality that always drew people to her. Sarah was happy she was home.

Sarah made little sound as she made her way down the small deer path that cut through her property to Damon Wilder's. She knew every inch of her property. And she knew every inch of his. Her hair was tightly braided to keep it from being snagged on low branches or brambles. Her soft-soled shoes were light, allowing her to feel her way over twigs and dried leaves. She wasn't thinking about Damon's broad shoulders or his dark, tormented eyes. And she didn't believe in romance. Not for Sarah. That was for elegant Hannah or beautiful

Joley. Well, maybe not the beautiful, *wild* Joley, but definitely for most of her other sisters. Just not Sarah.

Damon Wilder was in trouble in more ways than he knew. Sarah didn't like complications. Ancient prophecies and broad shoulders and black auras were definite complications. Moonlight spilled over the sea as she made her way along the cliffs, following the narrow deer path that eventually wound down the back side of Damon's property. The powerful waves boomed as they rushed and ebbed and collapsed in a froth of white. Sarah found the sound of the sea soothing, even when it raged in a storm. She belonged there, had always belonged, as had her family before her. She didn't fear the sea or the wilds of the countryside, yet her heart was pounding in sudden alarm. Pounding with absolute knowledge.

She was not alone in the night. Instinctively she lowered her body so she wouldn't be silhouetted against the horizon. She used more care, blending into the shadows, using the foliage for cover. She moved with stealth. She was used to secrecy, a highly trained professional. There was no sound as the branches slid away from her tightly knit jumpsuit and her crepe-soled shoes eased over the ground.

Sarah made her way to the outskirts of the house. She knew all about Damon Wilder. One of the smartest men on the planet. A government's treasure. The one-man think tank that had come up with one of the most innovative defense systems ever conceived. His ideas were pure genius, far ahead of their time. He was a steady, focused man. A perfectionist who never overlooked the smallest detail.

When she read about him, before accepting her watchdog assignment, Sarah had been impressed with the sheer tenacity of his character. Now that she had met him, she ached for the man, for the horror of what he had been through. She never allowed her work to be personal, yet she couldn't stop thinking about his eyes and the torment she could see in their dark depths. And she couldn't help but wonder why Death had attached itself to him and was clinging with greedy claws.

Sarah rarely accepted such an assignment, but she knew her cover couldn't have been more perfect. Meant to be. That gave her a slight flutter of apprehension. Destiny, fate, whatever one wanted to call it, was a force to be reckoned with in her family and she had managed to avoid it carefully for years. Damon Wilder had chosen her hometown to settle in. What did that mean? Sarah didn't believe in such close coincidence.

She had no time to circle the house or check the coastal road. As she approached the side of the house facing her home, she heard a muffled curse coming from her left. Sarah inched that way, dropped to her belly, lying flat out in the darker shadows of the trees. She lifted her head cautiously, only her eyes moving restlessly, continually, examining the landscape. It took a few moments to locate her adversaries. She could make out two men not more than forty feet from her, on the downhill, right in the middle of the densest brush. Sarah had the urge to smile. She hoped for their sakes they were wearing their dogs' tick collars.

Lying in the shrubs, she began a slow, complicated pattern with her hands, a flowing dance of fingers while the leaves rustled and twigs began to move as if coming alive. Tiny, silent creatures dropped from branches overhead, fell from leaves, and pushed up from the ground to migrate downhill toward the thickest brush.

Sarah knew that the one window lit up in Damon's house was a bedroom. If the telescope set up on the battlements of her house happened to be pointed in that direction, it was only because it was the last room she had investigated. It just so happened that it was Damon's bedroom, a complete coincidence. Sarah glanced back at her house overlooking the pounding waves, suddenly worried that Hannah might have her eye glued to the lens.

She hissed softly, melodiously, an almost silent note of command the wind caught and carried skyward toward the sea, toward the house on the cliff. The brush of material against wood and leaves attracted her immediate attention. She watched one of the men scuttle like a crab down the hill toward Damon's house. He crouched just below the lit window, then cautiously raised his head to look inside.

The window was raised a few inches to allow the ocean air inside. The breeze blew the kettle cloth drapes inward so that they performed a strange ghoulish dance. With the fluttering curtains it was nearly impossible to get a clear glimpse of the interior. The man half stood, flattening his body against the wall, tilting his head to peer inside.

Sarah could make out the second man lying prone, his rifle directed at the window. She inched her way across the low grasses, moving with the wind as it blew over the land. The man with his rifle trained on the window never took his gaze from his target. Never flinched, the gun rock steady. A pro, then; she had expected it but had hoped otherwise. She could see the tiny insects crawling into his clothing.

Above her head the clouds were drifting away from the moon, threatening to expose her completely. She wormed her way through the grass and brambles, gaining a few more feet. Sarah pulled her gun from her shoulder holster.

Hearing a slight noise from inside the room, the assailant at the window put up his hand in warning. He peered in the window in an attempt to locate Damon. A solid thunk sounded loud as Damon's cane landed solidly on his jaw. At once the man screamed, the high-pitched cry reverberating through the night. He fell backward onto the ground, holding his face, rolling and writhing in pain.

Sarah kept her gaze fixed on the partner with the rifle. He was waiting for Damon to expose himself at the window. Damon was too smart to do such an idiotic thing. The curtains continued their macabre dancing but nothing else stirred in the night. The moans continued from beneath the window but the assailant didn't get to his feet.

The rifleman crawled forward on his belly, slipping in the wet grass so that he rolled, protecting his rifle. It was the slip Sarah was waiting for. She was on him immediately, pressing her gun into the back of his neck.

"I suggest you remain very still," she said softly. "You're trespassing on private property and we just don't like that sort of thing around here." As she spoke, she kept a wary eye on the man by the window. She raised her voice. "Damon, have you called the sheriff? You've got a couple of night visitors out here that may need a place to stay for a few days and I heard the jail was empty tonight."

"Is that you, Sarah?"

"I was taking a little stroll and saw a high-powered rifle kind of lying around in the dirt." She kicked the rifle out of the captured man's hands. "It's truly a thing of beauty; I just couldn't pass up the opportunity to get a good look at it." There was a hint of laughter in her voice, but the muzzle of her gun remained very firmly pressed against her captive's neck. "You should stay right there, Damon. There's two of them out here and they look a bit aggravated." She leaned close to the man on the ground, but kept her eyes on his partner by the window. "You might want to check yourself the minute you're in jail. You're probably crawling with ticks. Nasty little bugs, they burrow in, drink your blood, and pass on all sorts of interesting things, from staph to Lyme disease. That bush you were hiding in is lousy with them."

Her heart was still pounding out a rhythm of warning. Then she knew. Sarah flung herself to her right, rolling away, even as she heard the whine of bullets zinging past her and thudding into the ground. Of course there had to be a third man, a driver waiting in the darkness up on the road. She had been unable to scout out the land properly. It made perfect sense they would have a driver, a backup should there be need.

The man next to her scrambled up and dove on top of her, making a grab for her gun. Sarah managed to get one bent leg into his stomach to launch him over her head. She felt the sting of her earlobe as her earring, tangled in his shirt, was jerked from her ear. He swore viciously as he picked himself up and raced away from her toward the road. The one closest to the house was already in motion, staggering up the hill, still holding his jaw in his hands. The driver provided cover, pinning her down with a spray of bullets. The silencer indicated the men had no desire to announce their presence to the townspeople.

"Sarah? You all right out there?" Damon called anxiously. Even with the silencer, he couldn't fail to hear the telltale whine of bullets.

"Yes." She was disgusted with herself. She could hear the motor of the car roar to life, the wheels spinning in dirt for a moment before they caught and the vehicle raced away down the coastal highway. "I'm sorry, Damon, I let them get away."

"*You're* sorry! You could have been killed, Sarah. And no, I didn't call the sheriff. I was hoping they were neighborhood kids looking to do a prank."

"And I took you for such a brilliant man, too," she teased, sitting up and pulling twigs out of her hair. She touched her stinging ear, came away with blood on her fingers. It was her favorite earring, too.

The drapes rustled and Damon poked his head out the window. "Are we going to call back and forth or are you going to come in here and talk with me." There was more demand than question in his voice.

Sarah laughed softly. "Do you think that's such a good idea? Can you imagine what Inez would say if she knew I was visiting you in the middle of the night?" She reached for the rifle, taking care to pick it up using a handkerchief. "She'd ask you your intentions. You'd have to deny you had any. The word would spread that you'd ruined me and I'd be pitied. I couldn't take that. It's better if I just slink home quietly."

Damon leaned farther out the window. "Damn it, Sarah, I'm not amused. You could have been killed. Do you even understand that? These men were dangerous and you're out taking a little stroll in the moonlight and playing neighborhood cop." His voice was harsher than he intended, but she'd scared the hell out of him. He rubbed a hand over his face, feeling sick at the thought of her in danger.

"I wasn't in any danger, Damon," Sarah assured him. "This rifle, in case you're interested, has tranqs in it, not bullets. At least they weren't trying to kill you, they wanted you alive."

He sighed. She was just sitting there on the ground with the sliver of moonlight spilling over her. The rifle was lying across her knees and she was smiling at him. Sarah's smile was enough to stop a man's heart. Damon took a good look at her clothes, at the gun still in her hand. He stiffened, swore softly. "Damn you anyway, Drake. I should have known you were too good to be true!"

"Were you believing all the stories about me, after all, Damon?" she asked. But dread was beginning even though it shouldn't matter what he thought of her. Or what he knew. She had a job. It shouldn't matter, yet she felt the weight in her chest, heavy like a stone. She felt a sudden fear crawling in her stomach of losing something special before it even started.

"Who sent you, Sarah? And don't lie to me. Whom do you work for?"

"Did you really think they were going to let you walk away without any kind of protection after what happened, Damon?" Sarah kept the sympathy from her voice, knowing it would only anger him further.

He swore bitterly. "I told them I wasn't going to be responsible for another death. Get the hell off my property, Sarah, and don't you come back." Something deep inside of him unexpectedly hurt like hell. He had just met her. The hope hadn't even fully developed, only in his heart, not his mind, but he still felt it. It was a betrayal and his Sarah, mysterious Sarah with her beautiful smile and her lying eyes, had broken him before he'd even managed to find himself.

"I can assure you, Mr. Wilder, despite the fact that I'm a woman, I'm very capable of doing my job." Deliberately she tried to refocus the argument, putting stiff outrage in her tone.

"I don't care how good you are at your damned job or anything else. Get off my property before I call the sheriff and have you arrested for trespassing." Damon slammed the window closed with a terrible finality. The light went off as if somehow that would cut all communication between them.

Sarah sat on the ground and stared at the darkened window with a heavy heart. The sea rolled and boomed with a steadiness that never ceased. The wind tugged at her hair and the clouds drifted above her head. She drew up her knees and contemplated the fact that old prophecies should never be passed from generation to generation. That way, one could never be disappointed.

4

SARAH didn't bother to knock politely on the locked door. Damon Wilder was hurt and angry and she didn't really blame him. She was nearly as confused as he was. Curses on old prophecies that insisted on messing up lives. If they'd been two people meeting casually everything would have been all right. But no, the gate had to stand open in welcome. It was neither of their faults, but how was she going to explain a two-hundred-year-old foretelling? How was she going to tell him her family came from a long line of powerful women who drew power from the universe around them and that prophecies several hundreds of years old *always* came true?

Sarah did the only thing any self-respecting woman would do in the middle of the night. She pulled out her small set of tools and picked the front door lock. She made a mental note to install a decent security system in his house and lecture him about at least buying a dead bolt in the interim.

As a child she had often played in the house and she knew its layout almost as well as she knew her own. Sarah moved swiftly through the living room. She saw very little furniture although Damon had moved in well over a month earlier. No pictures were on the wall, nothing to indicate it was a home, not just a temporary place to dwell.

Damon lay on his bed staring up at the ceiling. He had started out seething, but there was too much fear to sustain it. Sarah had nearly walked into an ambush. It didn't matter that she had been sent to be his watchdog, she could have been killed. It didn't bear thinking about. Sarah. Shrouded in mystery. How could he fixate on a woman so quickly when he rarely noticed anyone? If he closed his eyes he could see her. There was a softness about her, a femininity that appealed to him on every level. She would probably laugh if she knew he had an unreasonable and totally mad desire to protect her.

Damon bit out another quiet oath, not certain he could force himself to pick up and leave again. Where could he go? This was the end of the earth and yet somehow they had found him after all these months. No one would be safe around him.

"Do you always lie in the dark on your bed and swear at the ceiling?" Sarah asked quietly. "Because that could become a real issue later on in our relationship."

Damon opened his eyes to stare up at her. Sarah. Real. In his bedroom dressed in a skintight black suit that clung to every curve. His mouth watered and every cell in his body leapt to life in reaction. "It happens at those times I've been betrayed. I don't know, really, a knee-jerk reaction I can't seem to stop."

Sarah looked around for a chair, couldn't find one, and shoved his legs over to make room on the bed. "Betrayal can be painful. In all honesty I haven't had the experience. My sisters guard my back, so to speak." She turned the full power of huge blue eyes on him. "Do you believe that having friends insist on your protection is a betrayal?"

He could hear the sincerity in her voice. "You don't understand." How could she? How could anyone? "They had no right to hire you, Sarah. I quit my job, retired, if you want it neat and tidy. I have no intention of ever going back again. I cut all ties with that job and every branch of the military and the private sector."

"You tried to keep everyone around you safe by leaving." It was a statement of fact. He would think she was crazy if she told him he carried Death with him. "What happened, Damon?"

"Didn't they give you a three-inch-thick file to read on me before they sent you here?" he demanded, trying to sustain his anger with her.

Sarah simply waited, allowing the silence to lengthen and stretch between them. Sometimes silence was more eloquent than words. Damon was tense, his body rigid next to hers. His fingers were curled into a tight fist around the comforter. Sarah laid her hand gently over his.

He could have resisted most anything, but not that silent gesture of camaraderie. He twisted his hand around until his fingers laced through hers. "They hit us about five blocks from work. Dan Treadway was with me. We planned to have dinner and go back to work. We both wanted to see if we could work out a glitch with a minor problem we were having with the project." He chose his words carefully. He no longer worked for the government but his work had been classified.

"They beat us both nearly unconscious before they threw us in the trunk. They didn't even pretend to want our money. They drove to a warehouse, an old paint factory, and demanded information on a project we just couldn't safely give them."

Sarah felt his hand tremble in hers. She had read the hospital report. Both men had been tortured. She knew Damon carried the scars from numerous burns on his torso. "I couldn't give them what they wanted and poor Dan had no idea what they were even talking about." He pressed his fingertips to his eyes as if the pressure would stop the pain. Stop the memory that never left him. "He never even worked on the project they wanted information about."

Sarah knew Dan Treadway had been shot in the knee and then again in the head, killing him. Damon had refused to turn over classified information that could have resulted in the deaths of several field agents. And he had steadfastly refused to give up the newest defense system. Damon started a fire with paint thinners, nearly blowing up the building. In his escape attempt he was crushed between the wall of the warehouse and the grille of a car, severely damaging his hip and leg.

"I don't want friends, Sarah. No one can afford to be my friend."

Sarah knew he spoke the truth. Death clung and searched for victims. She wouldn't tell him, but often Death felt cheated. If that were the case, it would demand a sacrifice before it would be appeased. "Does the company know who these people are?" Sarah prompted.

His dark gaze was haunted. "You would know that better than I would. Enemies of our country. Mercenaries. Hell, who cares? They wanted something my brain conceived, bad enough to kill an innocent man for it. I don't want to think up anything worth killing over again. So here I am."

"Did you talk to anyone, a doctor?"

He laughed. "Of course I did. The company made certain I talked to one, especially after I announced my retirement. There were a few loose ends and they didn't want me leaving. I didn't much care what they wanted." He turned his head. Edgy. Brooding. "Is it part of your job to try to get me to go back?"

Sarah shook her head. "I don't tell people what to do, Damon. I don't believe in that." Her mouth curved. "Well," she hedged, "I guess that's not altogether true. There is the exception of my sisters. They expect me to boss them around, though, because I'm the oldest and I'm very good at bossing."

"Did you want to come back here, Sarah?" The sound of the sea was soothing. It did sound like home.

"More than anything. I've felt the pull of the ocean for a while now. I've always known I'd come back home and settle here. I just don't know when I'm going to manage it. Damon, your house has no security whatsoever. Did it occur to you they could waltz in here and grab you again?"

Damon tried not to read too much into that worried note in her voice. Tried not to think that it was personal. "It's been months. I thought they would leave me alone."

Sarah whistled softly. "You even lie with that straight face and those angelic eyes. I'm taking notes. That one is right up there with swearing at the ceiling. You wanted them to come after you, didn't you?" It was a shrewd guess. She hadn't known him long enough to judge his character yet, but she'd read the files thoroughly and every word portrayed a relentless, tenacious man, focused on his goals at all times.

"Wouldn't you? They forced me to make a choice between information that is vital to our nation and my friend's life. He was looking at me when they shot him, Sarah. I'll never forget the way he looked at me." He rubbed his throbbing temple. The vision haunted his dreams and brought him out of a sound sleep so that he sat up, heart pounding, screaming a denial to the uncaring night.

"What kind of a plan do you have?"

Damon felt his stomach knot up. Her tone was very interested. She expected a plan. He had the reputation of being a brain. He should have a plan. His plan had been to draw his enemies to him and dispose of them, first with his cane and then he'd call the sheriff. He doubted if Sarah would be impressed.

She sighed. "Damon, tell me you did have a plan."

"Just because you walk on water doesn't mean everyone else does," he muttered.

"Who told you I walked on water?" Sarah demanded, annoyed. "For heaven's sake, I only did it once and it was just showing off. All my sisters can do the same thing."

He gaped at her, his eyes wide with shock. She kept a straight face, but the laughter in her eyes gave her away. Damon did the noble thing and shoved her off the bed. Sarah landed on the floor, her soft laughter inviting him to join in.

"You so deserved that," she said. "You really did. Walk on water. That's a new one. Where did you hear that? And you believed it, too."

Damon turned on his side, propped up on one elbow to look down at her. "I started the rumor myself at Inez's store. For a minute there I thought I was psychic."

"Oh, thank you so much; now all the kids will be asking me to show them. The next time you come calling I'm going to sic the dogs on you."

"What makes you think I'm going to come calling?" he asked curiously.

"I never told you about the paint preservative. You're a persistent man." She leaned her head against the bed. "Do you have a family anywhere, Damon?"

"I was an only child. My parents died years ago, first my father, then six months later my mother. They were wild about each other."

"How strange that would be, to grow up alone. I've had my sisters always and can't imagine life without them."

His fingers crept of their own accord to find the thick mass of her hair. She was wearing it in a tight braid, but he managed to rub the silky strands between his thumb and finger. How the hell did she manage to get her hair so soft? Mysterious Sarah. He was fast beginning to think of her as *his* Sarah. "Do you like them all?"

Sarah smiled there in the darkness. She loved her sisters. There was no question about that, but no one had ever thought to ask if she liked them. "Very much, Damon. You would, too. Each of them is unique and gifted in her own way. All of them have a great sense of humor. We laugh a lot at our house." He was tugging at her hair. It didn't hurt, in fact it was a pleasant sensation, but it was causing little butterfly wings to flutter in the pit of her stomach. "What are you doing?"

"I snagged my watch in your braid and thought I'd just take it out," he answered casually. He was lying and he didn't even care that it was a lie and that she knew it was a lie. Any excuse to see her hair tumbling down in a cloud around her face.

Sarah laughed softly. "My braid? Or your watch?" He was definitely tugging her hair out of its tight arrangement. "It took me twenty minutes to get my hair like that. I've never been good at hair things."

"A wasted twenty minutes. You have beautiful hair. There's no need to be good at hair things."

Sarah was absurdly pleased that he'd noticed. It was her one call to glory. "Thank you." She tapped her fingers on her knee, trying to find a way to get him to agree with her on his protection. "Damon, it's important to protect your house. I could set up a good security system for you. I'll let the sheriff know we have a problem and they'll help us out."

"Us? Sarah, you need to be as far away from me as possible." Even as he said it, his hands were tunneling in the rich wealth of her hair, a hopeless compulsion he couldn't prevent. He wanted to feel that silky softness sliding over his skin.

"I thought you were supposed to be brilliant, Damon. Didn't I read in your file that you were one of the smartest men on the face of the earth? Along with your swearing issues and your hair issues, please tell me you don't have idiot macho tendencies, too. If that's the case, I'm going to have to seriously study this gate prophecy. I can live with the other things but idiocy might be stretching my patience."

He tugged on her hair to make certain she was paying attention. "*One* of the smartest men? Is that what that report said? I should read the file over for you and weed out the blatant lies. I'm certain I'm *the* smartest, not *one* of the smartest. You don't have to insult me by pretending the report said otherwise. And what is the gate prophecy?"

She waved away his inquiry. "I'll have to tell you about the Drake history sometime, but right now, I think you might clear up the idiot macho issue for me," she insisted. "Brainy men tend to be arrogant but they shouldn't be stupid. I'm a security expert, Damon."

He sighed loudly. "So I'm supposed to tell all my friends that my lady friend is the muscle in our relationship."

"Do we have a relationship?" She tilted her head to look back at him. "And surely the smartest man on earth would have a strong enough ego to be fine with his lady friend being the muscle. Relationship or no."

"Oh, if there's no relationship, I doubt if any man could take that big a blow to his ego, Sarah. We need to call in an expert on this subject, consult a counselor before we make a decision. And it never hurts to get a second opinion if we don't like the first one."

Damon couldn't help the grin that spread across his face. It felt good to smile. She had thrown his life into complete confusion, but she made him smile. Made him want to laugh. Intrigued him. Turned him inside out. Gave him a reason to live. And the heavy weight that seemed to be pressing down on his shoulders and chest was lifted for just a few moments.

"You won't have to worry on that score, Damon. We'll have six very loud and long-winded second opinions. My sisters will have more to say than you'll ever want to hear on the subject. For that matter, on every subject. You won't need a counselor for anything; they'll all be happy to oblige, absolutely free of charge."

Sarah glanced toward the cliff house. Through the bedroom window that should have had the drapes closed. The curtains were parted in the middle, pushed to either side by an unseen hand.

"Sarah." There was an ache in Damon's voice.

Her heart did a funny little jump in her chest and she turned her head to look at him. Her gaze collided with his. Stark hunger was in his eyes. Raw need. Desire. He reached for her, caught the nape of her neck, and slowly lowered his head to hers. His mouth fastened onto hers. They simply melted together. Merged.

Fireworks might have burst in the air around them. Or maybe it was the stars scattering across the sky, glittering like gems. Fire raced up her skin, heat spread through her body. He claimed her. Branded her. And he did a thorough job of it. They fed on one another. Were lost in smoky desire. His mouth was perfect, hot and hungry and demanding and possessive.

No one had ever kissed her like that. She had never thought it would be like that. She wanted to just stay there all night and kiss.

Damon shifted his weight on the bed, deepening the kiss. He tumbled over the edge, sprawling on the floor, pulling her over so that she collapsed on top of him. Instantly his arms circled her and held her to his chest.

Sarah could feel the laughter start deep inside him, where it started in her. They lay in a tangle of arms and legs, laughing happily. She lifted her head to look at him, to trace his wonderful mouth with her fingertip. "Sheer magic, Damon. That's what you are. Does this happen every time you kiss a woman?"

"I don't kiss women," he admitted, shaken to his very core. His fingers were tunneling in her wealth of hair, her thick silky hair that he wanted to bury his face in.

"Well, men then. Does it happen all the time? Because quite frankly it's amazing. You're truly amazing."

The laughter welled up all over again. Damon helped her to sit up, her back against the bed. He sat next to her. Both of them stared out the window toward the cliff house.

"I could have sworn I closed those drapes," he commented.

"You probably did," Sarah admitted with a small sigh. "It's the sisters. My sisters. They're probably watching us right this minute. Hannah came home right before I left and Kate and Abigail arrived about the time the driver was shooting at me. You could wave at them if you felt up to it."

"How are they watching us?" Damon asked, interested.

"The telescope. I use it to watch the sky." She used her most pious voice. "And sometimes the ocean, but my sisters are notoriously and pathetically interested in *my* business. I shall have to teach them some manners." She waved her hand casually, murmuring something he couldn't quite catch, but it sounded light and airy and melodious.

Shadows entered the room. Moved. The drapes swayed gently, blocked the sliver of moon, the faint light reflected by the pounding sea. Damon blinked; in that split second the curtains were drawn firmly across the window.

5

"YOU were kissing that man," Hannah accused gleefully. "Sarah Drake, you hussy. You were kissing a perfect stranger."

Sarah looked as cool as possible under fire. "I don't know what you thought you saw with your eye glued to the telescope lens, but certainly not that! You ought to be ashamed of yourself spying that way. And using . . ." She trailed off to motion in the air with her fingers, glaring at all three of her sisters as she did so. "To open the curtains in a private bedroom is an absolute no-no, which we all agreed on when we set down the rules."

"There are exceptions to the rules," Kate pointed out demurely. She was curled up in a straight-backed wooden chair at the table, her knees drawn up, with a wide, engaging grin on her face as she painted her toenails.

"What exceptions?" Sarah demanded, her hands on her hips.

Kate shrugged and blew on her toenails before answering. "When our sister is hanging out with a man with a black aura around him." She raised her head to look at Sarah, her gaze steady. "That's very dangerous and you know it. You can't play around with Death. Not even you, Sarah."

Sarah turned to glare at Hannah. She didn't want to talk about it, or even name Death, afraid if she gave it substance she would increase its power, so she remained silent.

Hannah shook her head. "It wasn't me ratting you out. You left the tea leaves in the cup and it was there for everyone to read."

"You still had no right to go against the rules without a vote." Sarah was fairly certain she'd lost the argument, but she wasn't going down without a fight. They were right about Death. Just the idea of facing it made her shiver inside. If she wasn't so drawn to Damon, she would have backed away and allowed nature to take its course. For some unexplained reason, she couldn't bear the thought of Damon suffering.

Kate smirked. "Don't worry, we made certain to convene a hasty meeting and vote on whether or not the situation called for the use of power. It was fully agreed upon that it was wholly warranted."

"You convened a meeting?" Sarah glared at them all with righteous indignation. "Without me? Without the others? The three of you don't make up the majority. Oh, you are in so much trouble!" she said triumphantly.

Hannah blew her a kiss, sweetly reasonable. "Of course we didn't do that, Sarah. We contacted everyone on the spot. It was perfectly legit. We told them about the gate and how it opened on its own for him. And how the dogs greeted him. Elle sent hugs and kisses and says she misses you. Joley wanted to come home right away and get in on the fun but she's tied up." She frowned. "I hope not literally, I didn't think to ask and you never know with Joley. And Libby is working in Guatemala or some other place she's discovered with no bathroom and probably leeches, healing the sick children as usual."

"I thought she was in Africa investigating that crawlie thing that was killing everyone when they tried to harvest their crops," Kate said. "She was sending me some research material for my next book."

"Wherever she is, Libby agreed totally we needed to make certain Sarah was safe." Hannah looked innocent. "That's all we were doing, Sarah. Everyone agreed that for your safety we needed to see into that bedroom immediately."

Kate and Abbey burst into laughter again. "I was a bit worried when he got so exuberant he fell on the floor," Abbey said. "But clearly you weren't in a life-threatening situation so we left you to it."

"And boy, did you go to it," Kate added. "Really, Sarah, a little less enthusiasm on your part might have gone a long way toward giving some credence to our chasing-men theory." The three sisters exchanged nods as if research were very important.

Struggling not to laugh, Sarah tapped her foot, hands on hips, looking at their unrepentant faces. "You knew I wasn't in any danger, you peeping Thomasinas. Shame on the lot of you! I'll have you know I was *working* last night."

That brought another round of laughter that nearly tipped Kate right out of the chair. "A *working* girl!"

"Is that what you call it? You were working at *something*, Sarah," Hannah agreed.

"She's a *fast* worker," Abbey added.

Sarah's mouth twitched with the effort to remain straight-faced. "I do security work, you horrible hags. I'm his bodyguard!"

Kate did fall off the chair laughing. Hannah slumped over the table, her elegant body gracefully posed. "You were guarding his body all right, Sarah," Abbey said, just managing to get the words out through the shrieks of laughter.

"*Closely* guarding his body," Kate contributed.

"Locked up those lips nice and safe," Hannah agreed. "Ooh, Sarah, baby, you are *great* at that job."

Sarah's only recourse was to fall back on dignity. They weren't listening to their big sister's voice of *total authority* at their antics. She drew herself up, looked as haughty as she could with the three of them rolling around together, laughing like hyenas. "Go ahead and howl, but the three of you just might want to read that old prophecy. Read the *entire* thing, not just the first line or two."

The smile faded from Hannah's face. "Sarah's looking awfully smug. Where is that old book anyway?"

Abbey sat up straight. "Sarah Drake, you didn't dare cast on us, did you?"

"I don't cast," Sarah said, "that's Hannah's department. Damon is coming over. I wanted him to meet you." She looked suddenly vulnerable. "I really like him. We talked all night about everything. You know those uncomfortable silences with strangers who can't possibly understand us? We didn't have one of them. He's so worn out from carrying Death. Of course, he doesn't know that's what he's doing and if he did, he would have sent me away immediately."

"Oh, Sarah." Hannah's voice was filled with compassion.

"I have to find a way to help him. He couldn't bear another death on his hands. His friend was killed, but he managed to save himself." She swept a hand through her hair and looked at her sisters with desperation in her eyes. "I liked everything about him. There wasn't a subject we skipped. And we laughed together over everything." She lifted her gaze to her sisters. "I really, really liked him."

"Then we'll like him, too," Kate reassured her. "And we'll find a way to help him." She opened the refrigerator and peered in, pulling at drawers. "Did you get fresh veggies?"

"Of course, and plenty of fruit. By the way, congratulations on your latest release. I read it cover to cover and it was wonderful. As always, Katie, your stories are fantastic," Sarah praised sincerely. "And thanks, Kate."

Abbey hugged Kate. "My favorite memories are when we were little and we used to lie on the balcony looking up at the stars, with you telling us your stories. You deserve all those bestseller lists."

Kate kissed her sister. "And you aren't prejudiced at all."

"Even if we were," Hannah said, "you're still the best storyteller ever born and deserve every award and list you get on."

Kate blushed, turning nearly as red as the highlights in her chestnut hair. She looked pleased. "How did the spotlight get turned on me? Sarah's the one who spent the night with a perfect stranger."

"I had to spend the night with him," Sarah insisted. "There's no security at his house. And I've asked Jonas Harrington to drop by this morning to meet Damon."

All three women groaned in unison. "How could you invite that Neanderthal to our home, Sarah?" Hannah demanded.

"He's the local sheriff," Sarah pointed out. "Come on, all that was a long time ago—we were kids."

"He was a total jerk to me and he still is," Hannah said.

The mug, filled with coffee, on the table in front of her began to steam. Hannah looked down and saw the liquid was beginning to boil. Hastily she blew on the surface.

There was a small silence. "Fine!" Hannah exploded. "I'll admit he still makes me mad if I just think about him. And if he calls me Baby Doll or Barbie Doll, I'm turning him into a big fat toad. He already is one, he may as well look like it."

"You can't turn the sheriff into a toad, Hannah. It's against the rules," Abbey reminded her. "Give him a doughnut gut or a nervous twitch."

"That's not good enough," Kate chimed in. "You need imagination to pay that man back. Something much more subtle—like every time he goes to lie to a woman to get her in bed, he blurts out the truth or tells them what a hound dog he is."

"I'll do worse than that," Hannah threatened, "I'll make it so he's lousy in bed! Mister Macho Man, the bad boy who couldn't do anything but make fun of me in school. He thinks he's such a lady's man."

"Hannah." Sarah heard the pain in her sister's voice and spoke gently. "You were then, and still are now, so incredibly beautiful and brainy. No one could ever conceive of you being so painfully shy. You hid it well. No one knew you threw up before school every day or that we had to work combined spells to keep you functioning in public situations. They wouldn't know you still have problems. You've faced those fears by doing the things that terrify you and you're always successful. Outsiders see your beauty and brains and success. They don't see what you're hiding in private."

"Someone's coming up the path," Kate said without looking away from Hannah. She held out her hand to her sister. "We're all so proud of you, Hannah. Who cares what Jonas Harrington thinks?"

"It's not Harrington, although he's close by somewhere," Abbey said. "I think it's Sarah's gate crasher. You know, the one she spent the night with. I still can't get over that, and Elle says she wants every intimate detail the minute you get a chance."

"There are no intimate details," Sarah objected, exasperated. "I'm going to install a security system for him. Kate, don't let them read your books anymore, you're giving them wild imaginations."

"It wasn't our imaginations that he was kissing you," Hannah pointed out gleefully. "We *saw* you!"

"And you were kissing him back," Abbey added.

"Well, that part wasn't altogether my fault!" Sarah defended. "He's a *great* kisser. What could I do but kiss the man back?"

The sisters looked at one another solemnly and burst out laughing simultaneously. The dog curled up in the corner lifted his head and whined softly to get their attention.

"He's here, Sarah, and the gate must have opened for him a second time," Kate said, intrigued. "I really have to take a long look at the Drake history book. I want to see *exactly* what that prophecy says. How strange that something written hundreds of years ago applies to us even in this modern day and age."

"Kate, sweetie," Abbey said, "every age thinks it's progressive and modern but in reality we're going to be considered backward someday."

"He's on the verandah," Kate announced and hurried to the front door.

Her sisters trailed after her. Sarah's heart began to race. Damon was not the kind of man she had ever considered she'd be attracted to, yet she couldn't stop thinking about him. She thought a lot about his smile, the way two small dents appeared near the corners of his mouth. Intriguing, tempting little dents. He had the kind of smile that invited long drugging kisses, hot, melting together. . . .

"Sarah!" Hannah hissed her name. "The temperature just went up a hundred degrees in here. You know you can't think like that around us. Sheesh! One day with this man and your entire moral code has collapsed."

Sarah considered arguing, but she didn't have much of a defense. If Damon hadn't been such a gentleman and stopped at just kissing, she might have made love to him. All right, she *would* have made love to him. She *should* have made love to him. She lay awake all night, hot and bothered and edgy with need. Darn the man for having chivalrous manners anyway. She smiled and touched her mouth with a feeling of awe. He had kissed her most of the night. Delicious, wonderful, sinfully rich kisses . . .

"Sarah!" All three of her sisters reprimanded her at once.

Sarah grinned at them unrepentantly. "I can't help it, he just affects me that way."

"Well, try not to throw yourself at him," Abbey urged. "It's so unbecoming in a Drake. Dignity at all times when it comes to men."

Hannah was looking out the window. She wrinkled her nose. "Kate, when you open the door for Damon, do let the dogs out for their morning romp. They've been cooped up all night, the poor things."

Kate nodded and obediently waved the dogs through as she greeted Damon. "How nice to see you, Mr. Wilder. Sarah has told us so much about you."

The dogs rushed past Damon. He leaned heavily on his cane, watching the large animals charge the sheriff, who was making his way up the path. Just as the man reached the gate, it swung closed with a loud bang. The dogs hit it hard, growling, baring their teeth, and digging frantically in an effort to get at their prey.

"This isn't funny, Hannah!" Jonas Harrington yelled. "I was *invited* by your sister and I showed up as a favor. Stop being so childish and call off your hounds."

Hannah smiled sweetly at Damon and held out her hand. "Pay no attention to the toad, Mr. Wilder, he comes around every now and then playing with his little gun, thinking he's going to impress the natives." She yawned, covering her mouth delicately. "It's so boring and childish but we have to humor him."

Sarah whistled sharply and the dogs instantly ceased growling, backing away from the fence to return to the house. When the animals were safely by her side, the gate swung open invitingly and the sheriff stalked through, his face a grim mask, his slashing gaze fixed on Hannah.

"What happens if you don't humor him?" Damon asked.

"Why, he throws his power around harassing us with tickets for speeding," Hannah said, holding her ground, her chin up.

"You *were* speeding, Hannah. Did you think I was going to let you off just because you're beautiful?" The sheriff shook hands with Damon. "Jonas Harrington, the only sane one when it comes to Baby Doll's true character."

Hannah flashed him a brilliant smile. Her sisters moved closer to her, protectively, Damon thought. "Why not, Sheriff? All the other cops *always* let me off." She turned on her heel and walked away.

Kate and Abbey let out a collective soft sigh.

"You gave my sister a ticket?" Sarah asked, outraged. "Jonas, you really are a self-centered toad. Why can't you just leave her alone? It's so high school to keep up grudges. Get over it."

"She was the one speeding like a teenager," Jonas pointed out. "Aside from feeding me to your dogs, did you have a real reason for inviting me up here?"

Taunting laughter floated back to them. "Don't flatter yourself, Harrington; nobody *wants* you here."

As Jonas Harrington stepped into the house, the ivy hanging from the ceiling swayed precariously and a thick ropy vine slapped him in the back of his head. Jonas spun around, his hands up as if to fight. He shoved the plant away from him and stormed into the living room, muttering foul curses beneath his breath.

Damon was behind him and stopped immediately, looking warily around the room, then back to the ivy. "Do your plants eat your visitors often?" he asked with grave curiosity as he pushed the vine away from him with his cane. Gingerly he walked around the masses of greenery.

"Only the ones who are mean to my sisters," Sarah replied.

Without warning, startling both of them, Damon suddenly reached out, caught Sarah by the nape of her neck, and dragged her to him. His mouth fastened on hers hungrily. Sarah melted into him. Merged. Became liquid fire. Went up in flames. Her arms crept around his neck. The cane dropped on the floor and they were devouring each other. The world fell away until there was only Damon and Sarah and raging need.

"*Sarah!*" The name shimmered in the air, breaking them apart so that they just stood, clinging, staring into each other's eyes, drowning. Shocked.

Sarah blinked, trying to focus, then looked around and blushed when she saw Jonas Harrington gaping. "Close your mouth, Jonas," she commanded, her tone daring him to make a comment. She'd known Jonas all of her life. Of course he couldn't pass up the opportunity. She waited, cringing.

"Holy smoke." Jonas held out his hand to Damon. "You're a god. Kissing a Drake woman is dangerous, kind of like taking a chance on kissing a viper. You just dove right in and went for it." He pumped Damon's hand with great enthusiasm.

"Ha ha." Sarah glared at the sheriff. "Don't you start, and don't you spread any rumors either, Jonas. I'm already annoyed with you for giving Hannah a ticket."

The smile faded from the sheriff's face. "I don't think because a woman is drop-dead gorgeous she should be treated any differently. She has everything too easy, Sarah. You all treat her like a little baby doll."

"You don't know Hannah at all, Jonas, and you don't deserve to know her. She wouldn't expect you to let her slide because of her looks, you idiot." Sarah threw her hands into the air. "Forget it, I'm finished trying to explain anything to you. If you don't understand friendship by now you never will. Let's get on with this. Damon and I have a busy schedule today." She gestured toward a chair.

Harrington was looking toward the stairs.

"Sit!" Sarah demanded. "This is business. Murder. Right up your alley, Jonas."

6

JONAS Harrington listened calmly while Sarah told him the events that had taken place the night before. His dark features hardened perceptibly while she talked. He flicked a smoldering glare toward Kate and Abbey. "Why wasn't I called last night? I might have been able to do something last night. Damn it, Sarah, where's your head? You could have been killed!"

"Well, I wasn't. I saved the rifle for you, hoping you might get prints off of it, but I doubt it." Sarah smiled at him.

Jonas shook his head. "Don't do that; you've been giving me that same smile since kindergarten and it always gets you out of trouble." He gestured toward her face. "Take a long look at her, Damon, because that's going to be her answer every time she does something you don't like." He leaned forward in his chair, his eyes slashing at her. "What about your sisters? Did it even occur to you that you might bring these people down on your own house?"

Furious, he rose, a big man, moving like a jungle cat, pacing restlessly through the long living room. "These men are professionals. You both know that. Whatever you did to bring this on . . ."

"He worked in a high-security job, Jonas, nothing illegal. It isn't drug related so get that right out of your head."

Damon leaned back in his chair, torn between worry that he'd placed the Drake family in danger and feeling pleased that Sarah had turned protective. She immediately had become a fierce tigress ready to spring if the sheriff continued to cast aspersions on his character.

"I want to know what we're up against. And don't start throwing words around like security clearance to me. If we have a couple of men willing to break into a house with a high-powered rifle—"

"They had a tranq dart in it," Sarah interrupted hastily.

"I was kidnapped, along with my assistant, nearly a year ago. My assistant was killed and I barely escaped with my life." As Damon spoke, a dark shadow fell across the room. Outside, the ocean waves thundered and sprayed into the air. "They wanted information that could have affected the security of our nation and I refused to give it to them." Damon passed a hand over his face as if wiping away a nightmare. "I know that sounds melodramatic, but . . ." He slowly unbuttoned his shirt to expose his chest and the whorls and scars left behind. "I want you to know what these people are like."

The shadow lengthened and grew along the wall behind Damon. The shadow began to take shape, gray, translucent, but there all the same, growing in form until a faceless ghoul emerged with outstretched arms and a long thin body. The mouth yawned open wide, a gesture of greed and craving for the addiction Death had developed. The arms could have been reaching for either Jonas or Damon.

Damon hunched away from Jonas, pain flickering across his face, his shoulders stiffening as if under a great load.

Alarmed, Hannah reached out and jerked Jonas halfway across the room out of harm's way. Jonas swore under his breath and planted his feet firmly, thinking she was attempting to throw him out of the house.

Sarah adjusted the blinds at the window, filtering out the light, and returned to Damon's side, touching him gently. That was all. The lightest of touches. She simply laid her hand over his, yet peace stole into him as he buttoned his shirt. The terrible weight that always seemed to be pressing him into the ground lightened.

Kate's eyes filled with tears and she pressed her fingers to her mouth.

Abbey left the room to return with a cup of tea. "Drink this, Damon," she said. "You'll enjoy the taste."

The aroma alone added to the soothing touch Sarah had provided. He didn't think to ask how she had managed to make hot tea in a matter of seconds.

"I could use a cup of tea," Jonas said, "if anyone's asking. And a touch of sanity in the house would be nice, too. Baby Doll was going to huck me right out the door and you all just stood there watching."

"I'll make it for you." Hannah leaned against the door frame and looked up at the sheriff. Her fingers twisted together, the only sign of her agitation. "Do you like it sweet? I'm certain I can come up with an appropriate concoction."

"I think I'll pass altogether. One of these days I'm going to retaliate, Hannah."

She made a face at him as he crossed to the sliding-glass door to stare outside at the pounding waves. "I have a bad feeling about this, Sarah. I know you're used to doing things differently and people have no idea how you do it. Maybe you don't know either, I certainly don't, but I believe in you. I sometimes just feel things. It's one of the things that makes me good at my job." He turned to look at her. "I have a *very* bad feeling about this. Frankly, I'm afraid for all of you."

There was a small silence. "I believe you, Jonas," Sarah said. "I've always known you had a gift."

His gaze moved around the room, restlessly touching on each woman. "I've known this family since I was a boy. Feuds"—his smoldering gaze went to Hannah—"are petty when it comes to your safety. I'm not losing any of you over this. I want to be called if one of you stubs your toe. If you see a stranger or you hear a funny noise. I'm not kidding around with you over this issue. I want your word that you'll call me. You have my private number as well as the number to the office and 911."

"Jonas, don't worry, we'll be fine. I'm very good at what I do," Sarah said with complete confidence.

Jonas took a step toward her, very reminiscent of a stalking panther. Damon was grateful he was too old to be intimidated. "I want your word. Every one of you."

Damon nodded. "I have to agree with Harrington. These men tortured us. They don't play around. I'll admit when I'm around you, I feel magic in the air, but these men are evil and capable of torture and murder. I have to know you're all safe or I'll have to leave this town."

"Damon!" Sarah looked stricken. "They'll just follow you." Worse, he would carry Death with him wherever he chose to go.

"Then cooperate with the sheriff. Give him whatever he needs to stop these men." As ridiculous as it seemed when he'd just met her, Damon couldn't bear the thought of leaving Sarah, but he wasn't about to risk her life.

"I don't mind calling you, Jonas," Kate said readily.

Abbey held up her hand. "I'm in."

Sarah nodded. "I'm always grateful for help from the local law."

All eyes turned to Hannah. She shrugged indifferently. "Whatever helps Damon, I'm willing to do."

Jonas ignored the grudge in her voice and nodded. "I want all of you to watch your step. Be aware of your surroundings and any strangers. Keep those dogs close and lock up the house!"

"We're all over it," Sarah agreed. "Really, Jonas, we don't want any part of men with guns. We'll call you even if the cat meows."

He looked a little mollified. "I'll want extra patrols around here as well as around Damon's house, Sarah."

"Well, of course, Jonas," Sarah agreed.

"It will give me every opportunity to make friends with them," Hannah said. "I don't know many of the new people in town."

Jonas glared at her. "You and your slinky body can just stay away from my deputies."

Hannah made a face at him, raised her hand to push at the hair spilling across her face. An icy wind rushed through the room, giving life to the curtains, so that they danced in a macabre fashion, fluttering, reaching toward Jonas as if to bind him in the thick folds.

Sarah glimpsed a dark shadow moving within the drapes. Her hands went up in a casual, graceful wave. Kate and Abbey followed the gentle movements with their own. The wind died abruptly and the curtains dropped into place.

Damon cleared his throat. "Does someone want to tell me what happened?"

Jonas shook his head. "Never be dumb enough to ask for an explanation from any of them, Damon. You might get it and your hair will turn gray." His gaze swung to Hannah. "Don't even think about it. Ladies, I can find my own way out."

Damon didn't take his eyes from Sarah. She was looking at Hannah and there was accusation in her gaze. Out of the corner of his eye, he could see Abbey and Kate doing the same thing.

Hannah threw her hands into the air. "I wasn't thinking, okay? I'm sorry."

The silence lengthened, disapproval thick in the room.

Hannah sighed. "I really am sorry. I forgot for just a moment about Dea—" She broke off abruptly, her gaze shifting to Damon. "About the other thing we're dealing with. It won't happen again."

"It better not," Sarah said. "You can't afford to forget for one moment. This is too dangerous, Hannah."

"Wait a minute," Damon interrupted. "If you're talking about me and those men the other night, I don't want your family involved in any way."

"The men?" Kate raised her eyebrow. "Not in the least, Damon, didn't give them a thought. There are things far more dangerous than human beings."

He watched the four women exchange long knowing looks and was exasperated. They knew something he didn't. Something regarding him. "I can understand why poor Harrington gets so frustrated with you."

Sarah rose and blew him a kiss. "He loves all seven of us. He just likes to puff out his chest."

"He was genuinely worried," Damon said. "And I am, too. The things he said make sense. It's bad enough to think of you in danger, let alone all your sisters." He raked a hand through his hair in agitation. "I can't be responsible for that."

To his shock they all laughed. "Damon." Sarah's voice was a mixture of amusement and tenderness. "We accepted responsibility for our own decisions a very long time ago. We're grown women. When we choose to involve ourselves in problems, we accept the consequences." She leaned toward him.

Abbey groaned dramatically. "She's going to do it. She's going to kiss him right in front of us."

"That is so not fair, Sarah," Hannah protested.

"Go ahead," Kate encouraged. "I need to write a good love scene."

When Sarah hesitated, her gaze lost in his, Damon took advantage and did the job thoroughly, not wanting to let Kate down.

7

DAMON heard laughter drifting up from the beach as he limped around the corner of his deck to set his teacup on the small table beside his rocking chair. His hip was bothering him more than usual and Sarah wasn't there to make it better. She'd spent the last several days dragging more and more equipment into his house, setting up a security system that might rival Fort Knox.

Jonas Harrington followed him, but instead of taking the chair Damon waved him toward, he stepped to the corner of the deck to watch the figures running barefoot in the sand on the beach far below. "They're up to something."

Damon sank into his chair where he had a great view of that small, private beach. The Drake sisters often were on it, day or night, their laughter drifting on the wind, the sound as soothing as the sea itself.

He missed Sarah. It was silly to miss someone when he saw her every single day. He'd always been a loner and it didn't make sense to him to need to see her quick, flashing smile. He especially loved to watch her eyes light up each time she saw him. He'd take the memory of that expression on her face to his grave.

"I'm beginning to think there really is something magical about the Drake family. I've never needed to be around anyone, but I can't imagine never seeing Sarah Drake again. I thought my life was my work. My brain runs a hundred miles an hour, always sorting through ideas, but she calms me. Don't ask me how." Damon could pick her out easily, her long dark hair blowing free in the wind. She often swept it up in a ponytail, her natural beauty so real to him when she thought nothing of her looks. "She doesn't think she's beautiful. Isn't that strange?"

Jonas shrugged. "I don't think any of them think about their looks all that much, other than Baby Doll. They spoil her and treat her like a little princess." He raked a hand through his hair, frowning. "Well, I shouldn't say that." His gaze remained on the tall, thin blonde with the waves of platinum hair streaming down her back. "Sometimes I think they cater to her—and other times I think they take advantage of her. Don't ask me how, it's just a feeling."

"You like them." Damon took a sip of the hot tea. He never drank tea as a rule, but Sarah had brought him a special blend from Hannah and he found it made him feel better when the weight of guilt and memories seemed to crouch heaviest on his shoulder.

"I love them," Jonas corrected. "They're family. *My* family. I take that very seriously, even if they don't. They spend all of their time getting into trouble, and I don't mean something casual, I mean something dangerous."

"Like me." Damon returned the cup to the saucer and sighed. "Sarah won't back off. She took the job of guarding me and nothing I say will stop her. I've thought a hundred times about leaving so she'd be safe, but . . ." He trailed off, wishing he were a bigger man. He'd never had anyone look at him the way Sarah did and he just couldn't quite make himself give that up.

"She'd just follow you, Damon," Jonas said. "The Drakes are tenacious. Once they sink their teeth into a problem, it gets resolved, because they don't know the meaning of the word quit. Sarah won't quit you, so don't quit her."

Damon didn't flinch away from the steel in Jonas's eyes. "Don't worry, Harrington, I hear your warning. I doubt very much I can hurt Sarah, other than if my past does, but she's in danger of ripping out my heart and handing it to me on a silver platter."

"You've got it that bad?"

"Hell yes, I do. I never thought it would happen to me and in such a short time, too. I can't stop thinking about her." His mouth was dry and his heart pounding just talking about Sarah. He couldn't imagine why a woman so full of life and laughter and love would choose to be with someone so melancholy and dark. He didn't have the least bit of social skills and tended to run roughshod over people with his intellect. He rarely engaged in small, polite conversation and, in fact, knew he was rarely polite. It had never mattered before, but it mattered to Sarah.

"If it helps, I've never seen Sarah really interested in a man before. She dated some, but kept it away from the family and Sea Haven. All the girls probably have dated, but we don't see it here." Jonas frowned and turned back toward the sounds drifting on the wind, his gaze finding the tallest of the Drake sisters.

"What is up with that locked gate they all talk about?" Damon asked.

"The infamous gate." Jonas smirked. "They keep that gate padlocked at all times, like that's going to save them from something."

"Save them from what?"

Jonas shrugged. "I think love. I hear them talk sometimes, but they don't tell me much and in all honesty, I don't want to know. Their house holds generations of power. Real power. I hate talking about this stuff because it sounds too *heebie-jeebie* for me. I like to deal in facts, not magic, but you can feel the power in the house. A few years back they decided to padlock that gate and it's been kept that way ever since."

"It wasn't locked a week after Sarah came home. When I came up the path leading to the house, it was standing open. I felt like the house was welcoming me. The inscriptions on the bottom of the gate, one in Italian and one in Latin say the same thing."

"You can read Italian and Latin?" Jonas grinned at him. "No wonder Sarah's attracted to you. What does it say? I always wanted to know but wasn't about to ask them."

"'The seven become one when united.' All the symbols have meanings as well. Several are symbols of protection. Do they practice ancient religion?"

"Who the hell knows what they practice. They're magic and they have very real powers. Libby is a doctor and I've seen her work miracles. Abigail is a loose cannon sometimes. She utters the word 'truth' and everyone around her starts telling every secret they have. Hannah's just plain scary. Elle's very quiet and she doesn't talk much about what she can or can't do, but if she loses her temper, she could probably flatten Sea Haven. It drains them, though, to use their gifts. I've seen them to the point they can't walk or even talk. They drop in their tracks and it takes time for them to recover."

Damon looked up at the worry in the sheriff's voice. "What are you not saying to me? Why do you have that look on your face?"

Jonas nodded toward the beach. "They know something. Sarah has precog. At least I think she does. Every single morning I see her drive to your house."

"She's been working on a security system."

"I noticed. It's state of the art. But she didn't come this morning and she wasn't here this afternoon. And now it's evening and they're on the beach."

"Believe me, I know Sarah hasn't come to see me. It's all I can do not to pick up the phone and call her or go on down to that beach to see what she's up to."

"I think you should."

"Go down to the beach? I looked at the trail, Jonas. I don't think my hip will hold up."

"I'll be happy to help you."

"Why do I have the feeling you're trying to get me into big trouble with those women?"

Jonas flashed another grin. "Better you than me. The sun's going to be setting soon and they're preparing for that. The moon rising to meet the setting sun. We can make it to the small dunes and sit there and watch them up close and personal. If you want to be part of Sarah's family, you're going to have to just accept that they can do extraordinary things."

"Like walk on water?"

"I wouldn't rule it out."

"You really are a believer. I don't know that I can believe in anything I can't back up with scientific fact."

Jonas's grin grew wider. "You're in for a few shocks, Wilder. Come on, you may as well learn what the Drake family is all about."

Damon wanted to see Sarah. And he was curious about the magic they supposedly wielded. He didn't believe in voodoo and other religions that called on something he couldn't see or feel. Hell, he didn't even know if he believed in God anymore. He had the sneaking suspicion he was beginning to believe there really was something different about the Drakes. And if that were true, where did that leave him? A man of science, grounded firmly in fact.

He stood up, leaning heavily on his cane. "Hell. It would be just my luck to fall in love with a woman who can do some kind of magic. I don't even go to magic shows. I can't enjoy them until I figure out how they do what they do and then it isn't all that impressive anymore."

"Prepare to be impressed and you're not going to find a scientific answer for anything these women do. I wouldn't even bother to try, Damon, you'll just drive yourself crazy. Let's take the car as far as we can and save your leg."

"You're off duty tonight?"

Jonas nodded. "The sisters are home so I figured I might con them out of a home-cooked meal. I like to spend time with them when they're home. They rejuvenate me. Sometimes my job is disturbing. Too many accidents on the highway. The crime in Sea Haven is about nil, but the outlying areas get a bit more. For all their nonsense, the Drakes soothe me."

Damon followed him out to the car, aware, as they walked, Jonas's restless gaze was quartering the area back and forth all around them, looking for danger. Damon ducked his head. He hated that small feeling, so helpless with his damaged hip and damaged soul. He couldn't stop the nightmares and he couldn't prevent others from being in danger just because they were around him.

Jonas started the car and pulled onto the highway. "There's a small dirt road leading to the back of the Drake property. We can reach the very top of the path down to the beach from there. Steps have been dug out and most of the way down there's actually a handrail. I think you'll be safe. In any case, you'd better be or Sarah will have my hide."

"She'll probably have it anyway," Damon said.

Jonas's grin was very much in evidence. "You do know that woman, even on such short acquaintance. She can keep the others in line as well. If you're really serious about her . . ." He glanced sideways at Damon for confirmation.

"Very serious."

"Sarah doesn't put up with nonsense. She likes straight answers. She's very tolerant of people, don't get me wrong, but she's loyal and has integrity and she expects the same from the people she lets into her life."

"Thanks, Harrington," Damon said gruffly.

"For what?"

"For thinking I have a chance with her. I never expected to fall in love. Certainly not this fast. I can't tell if she's just feeling sorry for me because my life's gone down the drain, or if she's genuinely interested."

"She kissed you, Wilder. Sarah doesn't go around kissing just anyone and certainly not in front of her family."

Damon couldn't help the little spurt of happiness that seemed to ease the weight bearing down so hard on his shoulders and chest. There were some mornings when he woke up feeling as if someone was crouched on top of him. On those days, he could hardly get out of bed and only Sarah's smile brought him a semblance of peace.

This morning he had awakened with sweat pouring from his body and the dark specter of death echoing through his dreams. His shower hadn't helped lift the weight and the rest of the day had been long and difficult. He'd been grateful to see Jonas when the sheriff had stopped by to check on him. Part of Damon was afraid he was getting too used to Sarah's presence and already relying on the joy and light that always surrounded her. He brooded over the fact that she hadn't come to see him, hadn't even called him. That scared the hell out of him. He didn't look at Jonas as they drove the small distance to the driveway leading to the Drake's private beach entrance.

Jonas parked the car just above the path leading to the beach below. He stepped out and went around to help Damon. The wind touched his face gently, almost as if fingertips were caressing him, seeking his attention. The sound of the surf pounded below him and the sound of women's voices drifted up with it. He couldn't tell if they were chanting, the voices sounded rhythmic, but for some reason, he felt a chill go through his body.

As Damon stepped out of the car, a dark shadow passed over-head. Jonas glanced up, but there were no clouds, only the setting sun and the rising moon, crossing paths over the wild waves of the sea. He glanced back at Damon and his breath caught in his throat. There was a black shadow on the rising wall behind them. The dark shape appeared to be hovering over Damon, actually crouching on his shoulders. Damon bent over with the weight of the apparition, lean-ing heavily on his cane.

Ice cold fingers of fear frissoned down Jonas's back. The black shape took on a face, a grinning skull with skin stretched back and bony arms stretching toward Damon. Jonas stepped in front of the other man instinctively. He heard the chant swell in volume, the voices much more clear, carried on the breeze. The sky turned blood red and the boom of the sea was louder as the wind rose to a shriek, ripping and tugging at the black shape in an effort to dislodge it from Damon's shoulders.

Weight settled on Jonas and he watched the black shadow on the rock as it stretched in an effort to encompass his frame as well as Damon's.

"I can't move," Damon said. "And I'm cold all the way through my body." He hunched his shoulders against a terrible weight, his hand absently rubbing his chest, right over his heart. "What's wrong with me?"

"I don't know," Jonas said grimly. But he feared he did know. The Drake sisters were fighting for Damon's life and because he had dared to step between Damon and that shadow, they were fighting for his life as well. He felt helpless standing there with the wind blowing on his face, afraid to move, afraid the shadow would take Damon. The claws seemed stretched with greed, the head of the thing leaning to-ward Damon as if trying to draw the breath from his body.

The voices swelled in volume—feminine, strong, united. Not just the four on the beach, but the three other sisters reaching from distant places to join so the seven had become united as one. Jonas felt the strength and power pouring through them into him. Small glittering colors sparkled and leapt with life. Small fireworks crackled as they formed a wall between the two men and the apparition.

The shadow drew back sharply, careful to avoid the sizzling lights.

Jonas felt the weight on his shoulders lessen. Damon stood a little straighter. The gray lines etched so deep in his face faded.

Jonas drew in a breath as he felt a hand brush his. He looked down, expecting to see someone beside him, gripping his fingers tightly. The sensation was there. Soft. Firm. In control. Yet no one was there. He stood alone with the wind on his face, ruffling his hair and the feel of someone holding him tightly, a feminine body pressed close to his. Everything male in him roared with protest. One of the Drakes—it felt like Hannah—shielded him, and that was just unacceptable.

He made out the shapes of several women with long flowing hair, arms raised to the sky in the midst of the crackling fireworks, insubstantial figures wavering in the air as if they were spirit rather than flesh and blood. Behind him, Damon swore softly under his breath, the actual words unintelligible, but Jonas had the same strong sense of real danger. Damon didn't want to hide behind the women any more than Jonas did.

Jonas tried to move, to step forward, to push his way through that wall of glittering lights and transparent figures to get at the crouching dark shape that was retreating slowly, driven back by the women as they pushed him away from the cliff and out toward the ocean. The soft chant was clear now, the voices strong, blending with the wind and pounding sea, filling Jonas's head with a strange kind of music.

He turned his head to follow the movement of the shadow as it took to the air, the retreat painfully slow as it moved over the sea. A whale breached and three dolphins spun in the air, spraying droplets of water in an arc over the crashing waves, all four silhouetted against the bloodred sky. The shadow's mouth yawned wide as it looked back toward the beach where the four women danced, arms raised, bare feet following a complicated pattern in the sand, arms lifted toward the heavens.

The wind howled, rose to a shriek, and gusted toward the apparition, driving it so far away it was merely a spec on the horizon. Jonas stared at it, blinking. When he looked around, the glittering fireworks were gone and the wind had died down to nothing. He glanced at the beach below and saw Sarah, Kate, Abigail, and Hannah lying unmoving on the sand.

"Get in the car, Damon." Jonas yanked the door open. "Hurry."

Damon did as directed, the echoes of the strange terror still gripping him. "What the hell is going on? I didn't see anything but fireworks, but I was . . ."

"Afraid," Jonas finished for him. "I don't know what the hell went on here tonight and I'm not sure if I want to know. Just get in the car. I need to take you home."

"Where's Sarah?"

"She's with her sisters on beach. I'll go down to them, but the things I have to say are better said alone." Grimly the sheriff slammed the door and drove faster than he should have to return Damon to the safety of his home. "Stay inside and use that security system Sarah's always fussing over. I'll call later to make certain everything's all right. My deputy, Jackson Deveau, will drive by several times tonight."

Jonas would have used the siren to return to the beach if it would have gotten him there faster. He was so angry he was certain he shouldn't go, he should stay away from the Drakes until his temper cooled and the fear left his body, but he couldn't just leave them lying exhausted on the beach.

He strode across the wet sand, fury building with every step he took. "What the hell did you all think you were doing?" The sight of their pale faces, worn with fatigue only stepped up his anger. "You were playing with something you sure as hell shouldn't have been playing with."

Sarah lifted a weak hand and waved him away. Hannah didn't look up and Kate and Abbey stared at him, their eyes enormous in their pale faces. He dropped onto his knees in the middle of them, reaching out to run his hand up and down over their arms to rub warmth back into them.

"What was it, Sarah?" he asked.

"Do you really want to know?"

She sounded so utterly weary he nearly kept his mouth shut. For once, Hannah wasn't sassing him and all of the Drakes looked frightened.

"Hell yes, I want to know."

"Death. You saw death, Jonas. It's how you're connected to us, why you are." Sarah glanced at her sisters and then back at his face. "You have a gift, just as we do. You deny yours and we embrace ours. Death showed you his face and he'll be back. We weakened him, but he'll be back and soon. He has too tight a grip on Damon." She said the last with a small hiccup in her voice.

At once her three sisters put their hands on her in an obvious attempt to comfort her. Jonas moved closer to Hannah and lifted her slightly so she could rest her head in his lap. He dragged Abigail closer as well until she had her head on his thigh. Sarah and Kate followed suit. He listened to the sound of the ocean, allowing the familiar melody to calm his mind and think more rationally.

"Why is death after Damon?" He felt like a fool asking the question. When the Drakes did their magic he preferred to be somewhere distant. He knew what they did and he even accepted it, but he always rationalized anything too spooky. Tonight didn't fit into a neat box and he sure as hell was never going to admit to seeing anything or having gifts or curses or anything else he couldn't find a scientific explanation for.

Sarah shrugged. "I don't think it much matters who death takes as long as he has someone. I don't want that someone to be Damon—or you."

"Me?"

"You stood in front of it. You confronted Death. Why did you do that?"

"Damn it, Sarah. It was a shadow. A shape on the wall and it looked as if it wanted to consume Wilder. I was afraid for him. I just did what seemed right."

"You brought yourself to his attention. You never want to do that," Sarah said. "Some things are better left alone."

"Well, you sure as hell must have his attention. And don't ever protect me like that again. I don't want any of you hurt trying to keep something like that off of me. I don't even know if I believe in all this mumbo jumbo. And if I don't, it can't hurt me." He wanted to shake some sense into them and at the same time he wanted to hold them close where he could protect them. Give him a flesh-and-blood criminal any day of the week, one he could see and fight. He forced calm into his voice when his heart was still pounding in fear for them. "Just don't ever do that again. I protect you. That's the way it's always been with us and that's the way it always will be. I'm taking you all up to the house and making you tea. Unless I decide to drop one or two of you in the ocean. I never want to talk about this again and if you bring it up, I swear I'm denying everything."

He wasn't making much sense but he didn't care. He just wanted them back inside their home where he knew they would be safe. And then he was going to think long and hard about getting drunk.

8

"So, Sarah," Damon said, putting down his glass of iced tea as they sat on his porch. Damon and Sarah spent every minute they could find together. Taking walks on the beach. Working on a security system for his house. Lazy days of laughter and whispered confidences. Damon enjoyed every moment spent in her home, getting to know her sisters. He never ran out of things to say to Sarah and he loved her stories and open personality. There was sunshine in his life and its name was Sarah.

She took a handful of his chips and smiled at him. Overhead the seagulls circled, looking down with hopeful eyes. Damon had had no more unwelcome nighttime visitors and appreciated the regularity of the sheriff driving by to check the neighborhood.

Damon shook his head, dazzled by her smile. She could take every thought out of his head with that smile. "Sarah, are you afraid for me or for everyone else? It's occurred to me that there's always this buffer between everyone we run across and me. I didn't really notice at first, but last night I was thinking about it. I'm getting to know you and I think you prefer that your friends don't see you with me."

Sarah's breath caught in her throat at the hint of pain in his voice. The more time she spent with him, the more she wanted to be with him. And the dark shadow surrounding him gripped him all the harder. "I don't mind anyone seeing us together. You're the one worried about gossip. I'm used to it and it doesn't bother me."

"Then we'll go into town together." It was a challenge.

Sarah let out her breath. The early morning fog had burned off, leaving the sky an amazing shade of blue. She could see clouds gathering far out over the sea. She looked carefully at Damon, inspecting every inch of him. There was no dark shadow around him and his shoulders weren't hunched as if carrying a great weight. "Sounds great, if you're really certain you want to brave it."

He stood up and held out his hand to her. "Come on."

"Right now?" She hadn't expected he would really want to go, but she obediently took his hand and allowed him to help her up.

"Yes, while I have my courage up. Walking with you through town should set a match to the gossips. The story will spread like wildfire."

Sarah laughed softly, knowing it was true. Once they had walked the short distance to the town, she started in the direction of the grocery store, determined to get it over with.

"I feel a little sorry for Harrington," Damon said as he walked with Sarah along the main street of town. "He drops by the house sometimes and he's very nice." He reached out and tangled his fingers with Sarah's.

"Are you certain you want to do this?" Sarah's voice was skeptical. "Holding my hand in public is going to bring the spotlight shining very brightly on you. Rumors are going to race through town faster than a seagull flies. I know how much your privacy means to you."

"That was before I retired. When I worked from morning until night and had no life." Damon laughed softly. He was happy. Looking at her made him happy. Walking with her, talking with her. It was ridiculous how happy he was when he was in her company. It made no sense but he wasn't going to question a gift from the heavens. "We may as well give them something real to gossip about."

Sarah's laugh floated on the breeze, a melodious sound that turned heads. "Not 'gossip,' Damon, it's 'news.' No one gossips here. You have to get it straight."

Damon listened to the sound of their shoes on the wooden walkway. Everything was so different with Sarah. He felt as if he'd finally come home. He looked around him to the picturesque homes, so quaint and unique. It no longer felt alien or hostile to him; the people were eccentric, but endearing. How had Sarah done that? Mysterious Sarah. Even the wind welcomed her back home. His fingers tightened around hers, holding her to him. He wasn't altogether certain Sarah was human and he feared she might fly away from him without warning, joining the birds out over the sea.

She waved to a young woman on a porch. "They're good people, Damon. You won't find more accepting people in your life than the ones living here."

"Even Harrington?" he teased.

"I feel a little sorry for him, too," Sarah answered seriously. "Most of the time, Jonas is a caring, compassionate man and very good with everyone, but he just refuses to see the truth about Hannah. He looks at her and only sees what's on the outside. She's always been beautiful. He was very popular with the girls in school, an incredible athlete, tons of scholarships, the resident dreamboat. He thought Hannah was stuck up because she never spoke to him. He made her life a living hell, teasing her unmercifully all through school. She's never forgiven him and he'll never understand why. He's a good man and he wasn't being malicious in school. From his perspective, he was just teasing. He has no idea Hannah is painfully shy and he never will."

Damon made a dissenting noise in his throat. "She's a supermodel, Sarah—on the cover of every magazine there is. She travels all over the world. And, I have to say, she appears very confident on every television and news interview and talk show I've seen her on. I would never associate her with the word 'shy.'"

"She hyperventilates before speaking in public; in fact, she carries a paper bag with her. Most of the talk show hosts and interviewers are careful with her. Because she's painfully shy doesn't mean she allows it to affect her life."

"Why wouldn't you just clue Harrington in?"

"Why should he judge Hannah so harshly, just because she looks the way she does? My sister Joley is striking as well, although not in exactly the same way. Jonas would never dare torment her. All of my sisters are good-looking and he doesn't use that sarcastic tone on them. He only does it to Hannah and in front of everyone."

Damon heard the fierce protective note in her voice and smiled. He drew her closer beneath his broad shoulder. His Sarah. Without warning, fear struck, deep, haunting, sharp like a knife. His breath left his lungs. "Sarah? Are we thinking the same thing? I've never wanted someone in my life before. Not once. I've only just met you and can't imagine the rest of my life without you." He raked his fingers through his hair, his cane nearly hitting his head. "Do you know what I sound like? An obsessed stalker. I'm not like this with women, Sarah."

Her eyes danced. "That leaves wide-open territory, Damon. You're talking about a family with six sisters and a billion cousins. I have a million aunts and uncles. You can't leave yourself open like that or they're going to tease you unmercifully."

They halted in front of the grocery store. Damon faced her, catching her chin in his hand to tilt her face up to his. "I'm serious, Sarah. I know I want a future with you in it. I have to know we're on the same page."

Sarah went up on her toes to press a kiss to his mouth. "Here's a little news flash for you, Damon. I don't compromise my jobs by getting involved with my clients. I don't, as a rule, kiss strange men and spend the night wishing they'd make the big move."

"You want me to make a move on you?"

Sarah laughed, tugged at his hand, dragging him into the store. "Of course I do."

"Well, this is a hell of a time to tell me."

Inez was at the store window with three of her customers, staring at Sarah and Damon with their mouths open. Damon scowled at them. "Is it fly-catching season?"

Sarah squeezed his hand tightly in warning. All the while she was smiling serenely. "Inez! We just dropped in for a quick minute. Kate and Hannah and Abigail are in town for a few days and they can't wait to see you! Joley and Elle and Libby send their love and told me to tell you they hope to get back soon." Her voice was bright and cheerful, dispelling an air of gloom in the store. "You do know Damon, of course."

Inez nodded, her hawklike gaze narrowing in shock on their linked hands. Her throat worked convulsively. "Yes, of course I do. I didn't know you two were *intimate* friends."

Damon glared at her, daring the woman to imply anything else. Sarah simply laughed. "I snagged him the minute I saw him, Inez.

You always told me to settle down with a good man and, well . . . here he is."

"I never guessed, and Mr. Wilder didn't say a single word," Inez said.

Damon forced a smile under the subtle pressure of Sarah's grip. Her nails were biting into his hand. "Call me Damon, Inez. I never managed to catch you alone." It was the best excuse he could come up with and sound plausible. It must have worked because Inez beamed at him, bestowing on him a smile she reserved for her closest friends. In spite of himself, Damon could feel a tiny glow of pleasure at the acceptance.

"How is everything lately?" Sarah asked before Damon could warn her it was a bad idea to get Inez started.

"Honestly, Sarah, Donna over at the gift shop is a lovely woman but she just doesn't understand the importance of recycling. Just this morning I saw her dump her papers right in with plastic. I've sorted for her many times and showed her the easiest way to go about it but she just can't get the hang of it. Be a dear and do something about it, won't you?"

Damon's mouth nearly fell open at the request. What did Inez want Sarah to do? Separate the woman's garbage for her?

"No problem, Inez. I'll go over there now. Damon and I are hoping some of our friends will help us with a small problem. There are some strangers who have been in town, probably for a week or two—three men. We'd like to know their whereabouts, their movements, that sort of thing. Unfortunately we don't have a clear description but one of them has a facial injury, most likely around his jaw. I'm hoping another might have gotten bitten by a tick." She paused, a wicked little grin playing around the corners of her mouth. "Maybe a lot of ticks."

"What have they done?" Inez asked, lowering her voice as if she'd joined a conspiracy.

"They tried to break into Damon's house. Jonas has all the information we could give him. He was going to check the hospital and clinic." She'd turned over the tranquilizer gun to him, too. "If someone spots them, or mentions them to you, would you mind giving me a call? And maybe it would be good to call Jonas, too."

"Now, dear, you know I don't believe in sticking my nose into anyone's business, but if you really need me to help you, I'll be more than happy to oblige," Inez said. "There are always so many tourists but we should be able to spot a man with something wrong with his jaw."

Sarah leaned over to kiss Inez affectionately. "You're such a good friend, Inez. I don't know what we'd all do without you." She turned to look at the three customers. "Irene, I hope you don't mind me bringing Damon when I call on you and Drew this afternoon." She wanted to assess Drew's condition before she brought her sisters over and raised Irene's hopes further. "We just want to visit with him a few minutes," she added hastily. "We won't tire him."

Irene's expression brightened considerably. "Thank you, Sarah; of course you can bring anyone you want with you. I told Drew you might be dropping by and he was so excited. He'll love the company. He rarely sees even his friends anymore."

"Good, I can't wait to see him again. Now don't go to any trouble, Irene. Last time I came to visit, you had an entire luncheon waiting." Sarah rubbed Damon's arm. "Irene is such a wonderful cook."

"Oh, she is," Inez agreed readily. "Her baked goods are always the first to go at every fund-raiser."

Irene broke into a smile, looking pleased.

The warmth in Damon's heart rushed to his belly, heated his blood. Sarah spread sunshine. That had to be her secret. Wherever she went, she just spread goodwill to others because she genuinely cared about them. It wasn't that she was being merely tolerant; she liked her neighbors with all their idiosyncrasies. He couldn't help the strange feeling of pride sweeping through him. How had he gotten so lucky?

Damon pushed his sunglasses onto his nose as they meandered across the street. He saw they were heading toward the colorful gift shop. "Are you really going to sort some woman's garbage, Sarah?"

"Of course not, I'm just popping in to say hello. Maybe our intruders will buy a memento of their stay or possibly a gift for someone. You never know, we may as well cover all the bases," Sarah replied blithely.

Damon laughed. "Sarah, honey, I hardly think kidnappers are going to take the time to buy a memento of their stay. I could be wrong, but it seems rather unlikely."

Sarah simply grinned at him. She took his breath away with her smile. She should have always been in his life. By his side. All those years working, never thinking about anything else, and Sarah had been somewhere in the world. If he had met her earlier, he might have retired sooner and . . .

"Do you have any idea how perfectly tempting your mouth is, Damon?" Sarah interrupted his thoughts, her voice matter-of-fact, intensely interested.

"Sarah! Sarah Drake! Yoo-hoo!" A tall woman of Amazonian proportions and extraordinary skin waved wildly, intercepting them. An older man, obviously her father, and a teenage boy followed her at a much more sedate pace.

The clouds, gathering ominously over the sea, so far away only minutes earlier, moved inward at a rapid rate. The wind howled, blowing in from the sea, carrying something dark and dangerous with it. Icy fingers touched Sarah's face, almost a caress of delight . . . or challenge. She watched Damon's face, his body, as he accepted the weight, a settling of his shoulders, small lines appearing near his mouth. He didn't appear to notice, already far too familiar with his grim companion.

She moved closer to Damon, a purely protective gesture as the two men approached them in the wake of the woman. The welcoming smile faded from Sarah's face. A shadow moved on the walkway, slithering along the ground, a wide dark net casting for prey. "Patsy, it's been a long time." But she was looking at the older man. "Mr. Granger. How nice to see you again. And Pete, I'm so glad we ran into you. I'm visiting Drew soon. I'll be able to tell him I saw you. I'll bet he'll be happy to hear from you."

Pete Granger scuffed the toe of his boot on the sidewalk. "I should go see him. It's been awhile. I didn't know what to say."

Sarah placed her hand on his shoulder. Damon could see she was worried. "You'll find the right thing to say to him. That's what friendship is, Pete, to be there in good and bad times. The good is easy, the bad, well"—she shrugged— "that's a bit more difficult. But you've always been incredibly tough and Drew's best friend. I know you'll be there for him."

Pete nodded his head. "Tell him I'll be over this evening."

Sarah smiled her approval. "I think that's a great idea, Pete." She touched the elder Granger with gentle fingers. "How did your visit to the cardiologist go?"

"Why, Sarah," Patsy answered, "Dad doesn't have a cardiologist. There's nothing wrong with his heart."

"Really? It never hurts to be safe, Mr. Granger. Checkups are always so annoying but ultimately necessary. Patsy, do you remember that cardiologist my mother went to when we were in our first year of college? In San Francisco?"

Patsy exchanged a long look with her father. "I do remember, Sarah. Maybe we could get him in next month when things settle down at the shop."

"These things are always better if you insist on taking care of them immediately," Sarah prompted. "This is Damon Wilder, a friend of mine. Have you three met yet?"

Damon was simply astonished. Pete was going to go visit his very ill friend and Mr. Granger was going to see a cardiologist, all at Sarah's suggestion. He looked closer at the older man. He couldn't see that Granger looked sick. What had Sarah seen that he hadn't? There was no doubt in his mind that the cardiologist was going to find something wrong with Mr. Granger's heart.

Sarah asked the three of them to keep an eye out for strangers with bruises on their face or jaw and the trio agreed before hurrying away.

"How do you do that?" Damon asked, intrigued. She was doing something, knew things she shouldn't know.

"Do what?" Sarah asked. "I have no idea what you're talking about."

Damon studied her face there on the street with the sunlight shining down on them. He couldn't stop looking at her, couldn't stop wanting her. Couldn't believe she was real. "You see something beyond the human eye, Sarah, something science can't explain. I believe in science, yet I can't find an explanation for what you do."

Damon was looking at her with so much hunger, so much stark desire in his expression, Sarah's heart melted on the spot and her body went up in flames. "It's a Drake legacy. A gift." Wherever she had been going was gone out of her head. She couldn't think of anything but Damon and the need on his face, the hunger in his eyes. Her fingers tangled in the front of his shirt, right outside the gift shop in plain sight of the interested townspeople.

"The Drake gate prophecy forgot to mention the intensity of the physical attraction," she murmured.

A man could drown in her eyes, be lost forever. His hands tightened possessively, brought her closer to him, right up against his body. Every cell reacted instantly. Whips of lightning danced in his bloodstream while tongues of fire licked his skin, at the simple touch of her fully clothed body. What was going to happen when she was naked, completely bare beneath him? "I might not survive," he whispered.

"Would we care?" Sarah asked. She couldn't look away from him, couldn't stop staring into his eyes. She wanted him. Ached for him. Wanted to be alone with him. It didn't matter where, just that they were alone.

"You can't look at me like that," Damon said. "I'm going up in flames and I'm too damned old to be acting like a teenager."

"No, you're not," Sarah denied. "By all means, I don't mind at all." She half-turned toward the street, still in his arms. "I think Inez is falling out of her window. Poor thing, she's bound to lose her eyesight if she keeps this up. I should have suggested she get a new pair of glasses. I'll let Abigail suggest it. You have to be careful with Inez because she's so sensitive."

It was the way Sarah said it, so absolutely sincere, that tugged at his heartstrings. "I never could get along with people. Ever. Not even in college. Everyone always annoyed me. I preferred books and my lab to talking with a human being," he admitted, wanting her to understand the difference she'd made. He was actually beginning to care about Inez and that was plain damned scary. He was finding the townspeople interesting after seeing them through her eyes.

"Let's go back to my house," he suggested. "Didn't you say there could be bugs in that security system you installed?"

"I'm certain I need to check it over," Sarah agreed, "but I do have to make this one stop first. I promised Inez."

9

THE small gift shop was cheerful and bright. Celtic music played softly. New Age books and crystals of all colors occupied one side of the store while fairies and dragons and mythical creatures reigned supreme on the other. Damon had been prepared for clutter after the comments on the shop owner's lack of recycling education, but the store was spotless.

"I think Donna knows her recycling stuff," Damon whispered against Sarah's ear. "She probably brushed up after she saw Inez peering at her through the store window with her lips pursed and her hands on her hips." His teeth nibbled for just a moment, sending a tremor through her. "Let's get out of here while we have the chance."

Sarah shook her head. "I have an especially strong feeling we should talk with Donna today." She was frowning slightly, a puzzled expression on her face.

Damon felt something twist and settle around his heart. Knowledge blossomed. Belief. He was a man of logic and books, yet he knew Sarah was different. He knew she was magic. Mysterious Sarah was back home and with her, some undefined power that couldn't be ignored. He felt it now for himself, after having been in her presence.

It was very real, something he couldn't explain but knew was there, deep inside of her.

His knowledge made it much easier to accept the amazing intensity of the chemistry between them. More than that, it helped him to believe in the powerful emotions already surfacing for her. How did one fall in love at first sight? He'd always scoffed at the idea, yet Sarah was wrapped securely around his heart and he had known her for only a few days.

"If you feel we should talk to Donna, then by all means, let's find the woman," he agreed readily. She had changed him for all time. *He* was different inside and he preferred the man he was becoming to the man he had been. If he spent too much time thinking about it, his feelings made no sense, but he didn't want to think about it. He simply accepted it, embraced the opportunity destiny had given him.

Sarah called out, moving through the store with the natural grace Damon had come to associate with her. "Donna's daughter went to school with Joley. Donna is a sweetheart, Damon— have you met her?" She peeked around the bead-curtained doorway leading to the back of the store.

"I've seen her," Damon said, "in Inez's store. She and Inez like to exchange sarcasm."

"They've been friends for years. When Inez was sick a few years ago, Donna moved into Inez's house and cared for her, ran her own gift shop and the grocery store. They just like to grouse at one another, but it's all in fun. The back screen is open. That's strange. Donna has a phobia about insects. She never leaves doors open." There was concern in her voice.

Damon followed Sarah through the beaded curtain, noting the neatly stacked paper tied with cord and the barrel of plastic labeled with inch-high letters. "I'd have to say Donna knows more about recycling than most people."

"Of course she does." Sarah's tone was vague, as if she wasn't paying much attention. "She just likes to give Inez something to say."

"You mean she does it on purpose?" Damon wanted to laugh but Sarah's behavior was making him uneasy. They stepped out of the shop onto a back porch.

The wind rushed them, coming at them from the sea. Coming

from the direction of the cliff house. Sarah raised her face to the wind, closed her eyes for a moment. Damon watched her face, watched her body. There was a complete stillness about her. She was there with him physically, but he had the impression her spirit was riding on the wind. That mentally she was with her sisters in the cliff house.

The wind chilled him, raised goose bumps on his arms, sent a shiver of alarm down his back. Something was wrong. Sarah knew something was wrong and he knew it now as well.

Sarah opened her eyes and looked at him with apprehension. "Donna." She whispered the name.

The wind whipped leaves from the trees and whirled them in small eddies of chaos and confusion. Sarah watched the whirling mass of leaves intently. Her fingers closed around his wrist. "I don't think she's far but we have to hurry. Call the sheriff's office. Tell them to send an ambulance and to send a car over. I think one of your kidnappers did decide to shop at Donna's."

She started away from him, toward the small house that sat behind the gift shop. It was overgrown with masses of flowers and bushes, a virtual refuge in the middle of town. "Wait a minute!" Damon hesitated, torn between making the phone call and following Sarah. "What if someone's still there, and what if the sheriff thinks I'm a nut?"

"Someone is still there and just say I said hurry." Sarah flung the words back over her shoulder. She was moving fast, yet silently, lithely, so graceful she reminded him of a stalking animal.

Damon swore under his breath and hurried back inside the store. Inez was standing just inside the beaded curtain. Her face was very pale. "What is it?" she demanded, her hand fluttering to her heart.

"Sarah said to call the sheriff and tell them to hurry. She also said to call an ambulance. Would you do that so I can make certain nothing happens to Sarah?" Damon spoke gently, afraid the older woman might collapse.

Inez lifted her chin. "You go, I'll have a dozen cops here immediately."

Damon breathed a sigh of relief and hurried after Sarah. She was already out of his sight, lost behind the rioting explosion of flowers. He silently cursed his bum leg. He could go anywhere if he went slowly enough but he couldn't run and even walking fast was dangerous. His leg would simply give out.

His heart was pounding so hard in his chest he feared it would explode. Sarah in danger was terrifying. He had thought there was nothing left for him, yet she had come into his life at his darkest hour and brought hope and light. Laughter and compassion. She was even teaching him to appreciate Inez. Damon swore again, pressing his luck, using his cane to hold back the bushes while he tried to rush over the cobblestones Donna had so painstakingly used to build the pathway between her house and her shop.

A soft hiss to his left gave Sarah's position away. She was inching her way toward the door of Donna's house, using several large rhododendrons as cover. Her hand signal was clear: she wanted him to crouch low and stay where he was. A humiliating thought. Sarah racing to the rescue while he hid in the bushes. The worst of it was, he could see that she was a professional. She moved like one, and she had produced a gun from somewhere. It fit into her hand as if she were so familiar with it, the gun was a part of her.

Damon realized, for all their long talks together, he didn't know Sarah very well at all. His heart and mind and soul wanted and needed her, but he didn't know her. Enthralled, he watched as she gained the porch. Even the wind seemed to have stilled, holding its breath.

Sarah turned back to look up at the sky, to lift her arms toward the clouds. Her face was toward the cliff house. Damon had a sudden vision of her sisters standing on the battlements in front of the rolling sea, raising their arms in unison with Sarah. Calling on the wind, calling on the elements to bind their wills together.

The wind moaned softly, carrying the sound of a melodious song, so faint he couldn't catch the words but he knew the voices were female. Dark threads spun into thick clouds overhead and the wind rushed at the house, rattling the windows and shaking the doors. The sky darkened ominously, fat drops of rain splattered the roof and yard. Damon tasted salt in the air. The rain seemed to come from the ocean itself, as if the wind, in answer to some power, had driven the salt water from the sea and spread it over the land.

The wind pulled back, reminiscent of a wave, then rushed again, this time with a roar of rage, aiming at the entry. Under the assault, the door burst inward, allowing the chilling wind into the house. Sarah rolled in behind it, as papers and magazines flew in all directions, providing a small distraction. She was already up on one knee in a smooth motion, tracking with her gun.

"I don't want to have to shoot you, but I will," she said. The words carried clearly to Damon although her voice was very low. "Put the gun down and kick it away from you." Damon hurried up the porch steps. He could see that Sarah's hand was rock steady. "Donna, don't try to move, an ambulance is on the way." Her gaze hadn't shifted from the man standing over Donna's body.

Damon could see the lump on Donna's head, the blood spilling onto the thick carpet. His fingers tightened around his cane until his knuckles turned white. He transferred his hold to a two-handed grip. Fury shook him at the sight of the woman on the floor and the man he recognized standing over her.

"Damon." Sarah's voice was gentle but commanding. "Don't."

He hadn't realized he had taken an aggressive step forward. Sarah hadn't turned her head, hadn't taken her alert gaze from Donna's attacker, but she somehow knew his intention. He forced himself back under control.

"Why would you attack a helpless woman?" Damon asked. He was shaking with anger, with the need to retaliate.

"Don't engage with him," Sarah counseled. "I hear a siren. Will you please see if it's the sheriff?"

Damon turned and nearly ran over Inez. He caught her as she tried to rush to Donna's side. "You can't get between Sarah and the man who attacked Donna," he said. Inez felt light and fragile in his hands. She never seemed old, yet now he could see age lined her face. She looked so anxious he was afraid for her. Very gently he drew her away from the entrance, pulling her to one side.

The wind whipped through the room, sent loose papers once more into the air. Inez shivered and reached to close the door on the chilling sea breeze.

"No!" Sarah's voice was sharp this time, unlike her.

It was enough to stimulate Damon into action. He held the door open to the elements. It was only then that he felt the subtle flow of power entering with the wind. Faintly he could hear, or imagined that he heard, the chanting carried from the direction of the ocean . . . or the cliff house.

He studied Donna's assailant, one of the men who had tortured him. The man who had pressed a gun to Dan's head and pulled the trigger. Why was he simply standing there motionless? Was it really the threat of Sarah's gun?

Damon had no doubt that she would shoot, but would that be enough to intimidate a man like this one? He doubted it. There was something else in the room, something holding the killer.

A sense of rightness stole into his heart, carried with it a sense of peace. Sarah was a woman of silk and steel. She was magnificent.

"Jonas is coming," Inez whispered to Damon. "Sarah's going to have a problem. She'll be weak and sick after this. She won't want anyone to see her like that."

Damon could see the acceptance of his relationship with Sarah in Inez's expression. It made him feel as if he truly belonged. Inez's approval meant more to him than it should have, made him feel a part of the close-knit community instead of the outsider he always seemed to be wherever he went.

He nodded his head, pretending to understand, determined to be there for Sarah the way she seemed to be for everyone else.

Jonas Harrington came through the door first, his eyes hard and unflinching. He had Donna's assailant in handcuffs immediately. Sarah sank back on her haunches, her head bowed. She wiped sweat from her brow with the back of a trembling hand. Damon went to her immediately, helping her up, forcing her to lean on him when she didn't want to, when she was worried about his hip and leg.

Sarah went down the hall with Damon's help, found a chair in the kitchen where she could sit. She looked up at him and smiled her appreciation. That was all. And it was everything. He got her a glass of water, helped her steady her hands enough to drink it. She recovered fairly quickly, but she remained pale.

"Are your sisters feeling the same effects?" he asked.

Sarah nodded. "It isn't the same as casting. It takes a tremendous amount of our energy to hold someone against his or her will. It wasn't in his nature to be passive." She held out her hand. "I'm doing better. I need to eat something and sleep for a little while." She sighed. "I promised Irene I'd go visit Drew tonight but I don't have any strength left after this, not the kind I'd need to help them." She pressed her fingertips to her temples. "I can't really do anything for Drew and Irene knows that. Extending his life might not be the best thing. If only Libby were here."

"Sarah." He spoke in his most gentle tone. "Leave it alone for now. Let me take you home; I'll fix you a good meal and you can sleep. I'll talk to Irene myself. She'll understand."

"How did you know my sisters were helping me?"

"I felt them," he replied. "Are you steady enough to talk with the sheriff?"

She nodded. "And I want to make certain Donna's all right."

When they returned to the living room, Harrington already had Donna's assailant in the squad car. Donna burst into tears, clinging to Sarah and Inez, making Damon feel helpless and useless but filled with a deep sense of pride in Sarah and her sisters.

"Why did he attack you, Donna?" Sarah asked.

"I noticed he had your earring, Sarah. The one Joley made for you. He was wearing it. It's one of a kind and I thought you must have lost it. So I asked him about it. He hit me hard and dragged me out of the store back into my house. He kept asking me questions about you and about Mr. Wilder."

Sarah pressed her hand against Donna's wound, just for a moment. Damon watched her face carefully, watched her skin grow paler until she swayed slightly with weariness. Sarah leaned down and kissed Donna's cheek. "You'll be fine. Don't worry about the store, we'll lock up for you."

"I'm going to the hospital with her," Inez said, glaring at the paramedics as if daring them to deny her. She held Donna's hand as they took her out.

"Sarah?" Jonas Harrington stood waiting against the wall. "You have a permit to carry that gun?"

"You know I do, Jonas," she replied. "You've seen it more than once. Yes, it's up-to-date. And I didn't shoot the man, although I was inclined to with Donna lying on the floor bleeding. And he is wearing my earring. I want it back."

"I'll get it back for you," Jonas was patient. "I know you're tired, but I need you to answer a few questions."

"That's one of the men who kidnapped me. He's the one who killed my assistant," Damon explained. "The other two must be staying somewhere in town. It shouldn't be that hard to find them now that we have him."

"I'll find them." Jonas's voice was grim. "Sarah, will you come by the office later and give me a full statement? I've sent the perp in the squad car down to the office. There's already an outstanding warrant for his arrest and the feds are going to be swarming all over this place as soon as we notify them. They're going to want to talk to the two of you, so you'd better go rest while you can."

Damon circled Sarah's shoulders with his arm. "Can you give us a ride to my place, Sheriff?"

"Sure. Let's lock up and get out of here before Sarah keels over and her sisters haul us both over the coals. You've never seen them en masse, coming after you." He shuddered. "It's a scary sight, Wilder."

"You're the only one it's ever happened to so far," Sarah pointed out.

10

DAMON stared down into Sarah's sleeping face. She was beautiful lying there in the middle of his bed. He had been standing there, leaning against the wall, for some time just watching over her. Guarding her. It seemed rather silly and melodramatic when she was the one with the gun and the training, but it felt as necessary to him as breathing.

Where had such a wealth of feeling come from nearly overnight? Could a man fall deeply in love with a woman so quickly? She was everything and more than he'd ever thought of or dreamed about. How could anyone not love Sarah with her compassion and tolerance and understanding? She genuinely cared about the people in her town. Somehow that deep emotion was rubbing off on him.

She could have been killed. The thought hit him hard. A physical blow in the pit of his stomach. How was it possible to feel so much for one person when he'd just met her? His entire life he'd barely noticed people, let alone cared about their lives. From the moment he'd heard her name whispered on the wind, he knew, deep down where it counted, that she would change his life for all time.

Their walks together, all the times on the beach, whispering in his house, or hers, even spending time with her family had only strengthened his feelings for her.

Sarah opened her eyes and the first thing she saw was Damon's face. He was leaning against the far wall, simply watching her. She could see his expression clearly, naked desire, mixed with knowledge of their future. His emotions were stark and raw and so real it brought tears to her eyes. Damon hadn't expected to like her, let alone feel anything else for her.

She held out her hand to him. "Don't stand over there all alone. You aren't alone anymore and neither am I."

He heard the invitation in her voice and his body began to stir in anticipation. But he stood there drinking her in. Wanting her in so many ways that weren't just physical.

"You weren't, you know, Sarah. You've never been alone. You don't need me in the same way I need you. You have a family and they wrap you up in love and warmth and support. I never considered the value of family and love. Sharing a day with someone you care about is worth all the gold in the world. I didn't know that before I met you."

She sat up, studying him with her cool gaze. Assessing. Liking what she saw. Damon didn't know why but he could see it on her face. "I'm glad then, Damon, if I gave you such a gift. My family is my treasure."

He nodded. What would it be like to wake up every morning and hear her voice? There was always a caress in her voice, a stroking quality that he felt on his skin. Deep in his body. "And you're my treasure, Sarah. I had no idea I was even capable of feeling this way about anyone."

Sarah smiled. The smile she seemed to reserve for him. It lit up her face and made her eyes shine, but more, it lit up his insides so that he burned with something indefinable. "You brought me life, Sarah. You handed me my life. I existed before I met you, but I wasn't living."

"Yes, you were, Damon. You're a brilliant man. The things you created made our world safer. I watch your face light up when you tell me about other ideas you have and what the possibilities are. That's living."

"I had nothing else but my ideas." He straightened suddenly, coming away from the wall, walking toward her, confidence on his face. "That was how I escaped, into my brain and the endless ideas I could find there." He traced the classic lines of her face, her cheekbones. Her generous mouth. "Take off your blouse, Sarah. I want to see you."

A faint blush stole into her cheeks but her hands went to the tiny pearl buttons on her blouse and slowly began to slide the edges apart. His breath caught in his throat as he watched her. Sarah didn't try to be sexy, there was never anything affected about her, yet it was the sexiest thing he'd ever seen. The edges of her blouse slowly gaped open, to reveal her lush creamy flesh beneath it. She had a woman's body, shaped to please a man with soft curves and lines.

Her breasts were covered with fine white lace. Sarah stood up, her body very close to his. Damon felt a rush of heat take him, a whip of lightning dance through his body. His blood thickened and pooled. His body hardened almost to the point of pain. He embraced it, reveled in the intensity of his need for her.

"You're so beautiful, Sarah. Inside and out. I still can't believe I could go from living in hell straight to paradise."

She reached for him. "I'm not like that at all, Damon. I'm not truly beautiful, not by any stretch of the imagination. I'm not even close. And living with me would not be paradise. I'm outspoken and like my way."

With exquisite tenderness, he bent his head to find her mouth with his. For a moment they were lost together, transported out of time by the magic flowing between them. When Damon lifted his head to look down at her, his gaze was hungry. Needy. Possessive. "You're beautiful to me, Sarah. I will never see you any other way. And lucky for you, I'm stubborn and very outspoken myself. I think those are admirable traits."

"That is lucky," she murmured, allowing her eyelashes to drift down and her head to fall back as he pulled her closer, his mouth breathing warm, moist air over her nipple right through the white lace. Her arms cradled his head as she arched her body, offering temptation, offering heaven.

His mouth was hot and damp as it closed over her breast. Fire raced through her, through him. Sarah gave herself up to sensual pleasure as his tongue danced and teased and his mouth suckled strongly right through the lace. He took his time, a lazy, leisurely exploration, his hands shaping her body, using the pads of his fingers as a blind man would to trace every curve and hollow. Memorizing her. Worshipping her.

Sarah was lost in sensation. Drowning in it. She couldn't remember him unsnapping her jeans, or even unzipping them. But her lacy bra had long ago floated to the floor and somehow he managed to push denim from her hips. In a haze of need and heat she stepped out of the last of her clothes.

He was never hurried, even as his mouth fused once more with hers and she was trying to drag his shirt from his broad shoulders so she could be skin to skin with him. He was patient and thorough, determined to know her body, to find every hidden trigger point that had her gasping in need. His hands moved over her, finding the shadows and hollows, tracing her ribs lovingly. He allowed Sarah to drag his clothes from his body, not appearing to notice or care, so completely ensnared by the wonders of giving her pleasure. He loved the little gasps and soft cries that came from deep in her throat.

Sarah. So responsive and giving. He should have known she would be a generous lover, merging with him so completely, giving of herself endlessly. Her selfless gift only made him want to be equally generous. For the first time his scars weren't shameful and something he hid. When her fingertips traced them, there was no reluctance, no shrinking away from the ugly memories of torture and murder. She soothed his body, caressing his skin, arousing him further, eager to touch him, wanting him with the same urgency he wanted her.

He lowered her slowly to the sheets, following her down, settling his body over hers. Her face was beautiful as she stared up at him. He kissed her eyes, the tip of her nose, the corners of her mouth.

Everywhere he touched her he left flames behind. Sarah was astonished at the sheer intensity of the fire. He was so unhurried, taking his time, but she was going up in flames, burning inside and out, needing his body in hers. She heard her own voice, a soft plea for mercy as his lips nipped over her navel, went lower. His hands moved with assurance, finding the insides of her thighs, the damp heat waiting for him at the junction of her legs.

"Damon." She could barely breathe his name. Her breath seemed to have permanently left her body. There wasn't enough air in the room.

His finger pushed deep inside her, a stroke of sensuality that drove her out of her mind. Every sane thought she'd ever had was gone. There was a roaring in her head when his mouth found her, claimed her, branded her his. She couldn't keep her hips still, writhing until his arms pinned her there, while his hot mouth ravaged her and wave after wave of pleasure rippled through her body with the force of the booming ocean. Her fingers tangled in his hair, her only anchor to hold her to earth while she soared free, gasping out his name.

Damon moved then, blanketing her completely, his hips settling into the cradle of hers. He was thick and hard and throbbing with his own need. He pushed deep inside of her, his voice hoarse as he cried out as the sweeping pleasure engulfed him. She was hot and slick and tight, a velvet fist closing around him, gripping with a fire he'd never known. Sarah. Magical Sarah.

He began to move. Never hurried. Why would he hurry his first time with Sarah? He wanted the moment to last forever. To be forever for both of them. He loved watching her face as he moved with her. As his body surged deep and her body took him in, her secret sanctuary of heat and joy. Her hips rose to join him, matching his rhythm, tilting to take him deeper and deeper with every stroke, wanting every inch of him. Wanting his possession as much as he wanted her.

The fire just kept building. He was in complete control one moment, certain of it, reveling in it, and then the pleasure was almost too much to bear, hitting him with the force of a freight train, starting in his toes and blowing out the top of his head. His voice was lifted with hers, merged and in perfect unison.

He could feel the aftershocks shaking her, tightening around him, drawing them ever closer. They lay together, not daring to move, unable to move, their hearts wild and lungs starving for air, their arms wrapped tightly around one another. The ocean breeze was gentle on the window, whispering soothing sounds while the sea sang to them with rolling waves.

Damon found peace. She lay in his arms, occasionally rousing herself enough to kiss his chest, her tongue tracing a scar. Each time she did so, his body tightened in answer and hers responded with another aftershock. They were merged so completely, so tightly bound together he couldn't tell where he started or left off.

"Stay with me the rest of the day, Sarah. All night. We can do anything you like. Just be with me." He propped himself up on his elbows to take most of his weight off of her. He wanted to be locked together, one body, sharing the same skin, absorbing her.

She reached up to trace the lines of his face. "I can't think of anywhere I'd rather be or who I'd rather be spending time with."

"Do you wonder why you chose me? I stopped asking myself that question and just accept it. I'm grateful, Sarah."

"I look at you and I just know. Who can say why one heart belongs to another? I don't ask myself that question either, Damon. I'm just grateful the gate opened for you." She laughed with sudden amusement. "It has occurred to me you might be seducing me to try to get the secret of paint preservation."

He tangled his fingers with hers, stretched her arms above her head. "It did seem a good idea. Maybe one of these days I'll be able to speak when I'm making love to you and I'll be able to pry the secret out of you."

"Good plan; it might work, too, if I could manage to speak when you're making love to me." She gasped as he lowered his head to her breast. "Damon." Her body was hypersensitive, but she arched into the heat of his mouth.

"I'm sorry, you looked so tempting, I couldn't help myself. How do you feel about just lying here without a stitch on while I build a fire and cook something for you to eat? I'm not certain I can bear for you to put your clothes back on." His teeth scraped back and forth over her breast. His tongue laved her nipple.

Sarah's entire body tightened, every muscle going taut. "You just want me to be lying here waiting for you?"

"Waiting *eagerly* for me," he corrected. "Needing me would be good. I wouldn't mind if you just lay here on my bed thinking of my body buried inside you."

"I see. I thought it might be better if I just followed you around, looking at you, touching you while you worked. Inspiring you. I have my ways, you know, of inspiring you."

There was a wicked note in her voice that made his entire body aware of how receptive and pliant she was. He was all at once as hard as a rock, thick with need. Damon watched her eyes widen in pleased surprise. Desire spread through both of them, sheer bliss. "I've never felt this way with any other woman, Sarah. I know it isn't possible. I think you really could walk on water."

"For a man who spent a lot of time in a laboratory, you know your way around women," she pointed out. He was moving with that exquisite slowness he used to drive her straight up the wall. The friction on her already sensitive body was turning her inside out. It didn't matter how many times she went over the edge, Damon moved with almost perfect insight, perfect knowledge of what she needed. What she wanted.

"I can read your face and your body," he said. "I love that, Sarah. You don't hold anything back from me."

"Why should I?" Why would she want to when the rewards were so great? If Damon was the man destiny insisted would be the love of her life, her best friend and partner, she was willing to accept whatever he had to give.

Sarah loved the sound of his voice, the thoughtful intelligent way he approached every subject. And she loved his complete honesty. There was that same raw honesty in his lovemaking. He gave himself to her, even as he took her for his own. She *felt* his possession deep in her soul, branded into her very bones.

There was that patient thoroughness and then, when he was fully aroused, his body was a driving force, each stroke hard and fast and insistent, taking them both soaring out over the sea, free-falling through time and space until neither could move again.

Damon held her in his arms, curled next to her, not wanting to end the closeness between them. They were completely sated for the moment, exhausted, breathing with effort, yet there was the same sense of absolute peace. "Sarah." He whispered her name, a tribute more than anything else.

"All those things you feel about me," she said, snuggling closer to him, "I feel about you. I didn't want anyone in my life any more than you did. I sometimes tire of giving pieces of myself to other people, yet I can't help myself. I find places I'm safe, places where I'm alone and can crawl into a hole and disappear for a while."

"Now you have me. I'll be your sanctuary, Sarah. I don't mind running interference in the times you need to regroup." His smile was against her temple. "I've never had a problem bossing people. I've always had a difficult time communicating with people. They never understood what I was talking about and it drove me crazy. Sometimes when you have an idea and it's so clear and you know it's right, you just have to share it with someone. But no one has ever been there."

Sarah kissed his fingertips. "You can tell me any idea that comes into your head, Damon. I admire you." Her smile was in her voice. "And I'm *very* good at communicating so you'll never have to worry about that."

"I noticed," he said. "Speaking of communication, I made certain the curtains couldn't creep open. I safety-pinned them together just in case any of your sisters decided to go up on the battlements to look through the telescope."

Sarah laughed just as he knew she would. "They know I'm with you. They wouldn't invade our privacy when we're really making love. They simply love to tease me. You'll have a lot of that come morning."

Damon didn't mind at all. He tightened his arms around her and found he was looking forward to anything her sisters might want to dish out.

11

"OKAY, have any of you really read this prophecy?" Kate demanded as they walked along the sidewalk toward Irene's house. The fog was thick and heavy, lying over the sea and most of the town like a blanket. "Because I have and it isn't good news for the rest of us."

"I don't like the sound of that," Hannah said. "Maybe we shouldn't ask. Can ignorance keep us safe?"

"What prophecy?" Damon asked curiously. They had spent the morning together over breakfast, teasing him unmercifully, making Sarah blush and hide her face against his chest. He had felt just as he anticipated—part of a family—and the feeling was priceless.

Sarah laughed in wicked delight. "You all thought it was so funny when it was happening to me, but *I* had read the entire thing. I know what's in store for the rest of you. One by one you'll fall like dominoes."

Abbey made a face at Sarah. "Not all of us, Sarah. I don't believe in fate."

The other girls roared with laughter. Sarah slipped her hand into Damon's. "The prophecy is this horrible curse put on the seven sisters. Well, we thought it was a curse. I'm not so certain now that I've met you."

His eyebrow shot up. "Now I'm really curious. I'm involved with this prophecy in some way?"

The four women laughed again. The sound turned heads up and down the street. "You are the prophecy, Damon," Kate said. "The gate opened for you."

Sarah gave a short synopsis of the quote. "Seven sisters intertwined, controlling elements of land, sea, and air, cannot control the fate they flee. One by one, oldest to last, destiny will find them. When the locked gate swings open in welcome, the first shall find true love. There's a lot more, but basically it goes on to say, one by one all the other sisters shall be wed."

Sarah's three sisters muttered and grumbled and shook their heads. Damon burst out laughing. "You have to marry me, don't you? I've been wondering how I was going to manage to keep you, but you don't have a choice. I like that prophecy. Does it say anything about waiting on me hand and foot?"

"Absolutely not," Sarah replied and glared at her laughing sisters. "Keep it up—the rest of you, even you, Abbey, are going to see me laughing at you." She tightened her fingers around Damon's hand. "We all made a pact when we were kids to keep the gate padlocked and never really date so we could be independent and free. We've always liked our life together . . . and poor Elle—the thought of seven daughters is rather daunting."

"Thank heavens Elle gets all the kids," Abbey said. "I am going to have one, and only because if I don't the rest of you will drive me crazy."

"Why does Elle have to have the seven daughters?" Damon asked.

"The seventh daughter always has seven daughters," Kate explained. "It's been that way for generations. I've been reading the history of the Drake family and I've found over the years, from all the entries made, we at least have a legacy of happy marriages." She smiled at Damon. "So far I haven't seen anything that indicated waiting on the man hand and foot but I'll keep looking."

"While you're at it, will you also keep an eye out for the traditional obey-the-husband rule?" Damon asked. "I've always thought that word was crucial in the marriage ceremony. Without it, a man doesn't stand a chance."

"Dream on," Sarah said. "That will never happen. The problem with being locked up in a stuffy lab all of your life is becoming evident. Delusions start early."

They were passing a small, neat home with a large front yard surrounded by the proverbial white picket fence. An older couple was working on a fountain in the middle of a bed of flowers. Sarah suddenly stopped, turned back to look at the house and the couple. A shadow slithered across the roof. A hint of something seen, then lost in the fog. "I'll just be a minute." She waved to the older couple and both stood up immediately and came over to the fence.

Sarah's sisters looked at one another uneasily. Damon followed Sarah. "It isn't necessary to speak to every citizen in town," he advised Sarah's back. She ignored his good judgment and struck up a conversation with the older couple anyway. Damon sighed. He had a feeling he was going to be following Sarah and talking to everyone they met for the rest of his life.

"Why, Sarah, I'd heard you were back. Is everything all right? I haven't seen you for what is it now? Two years?" The older woman spoke as she waved to the sisters.

"Mrs. Darden, I was admiring your yard. Did you remodel your house recently?"

The Dardens looked at one another then back to Sarah. Mr. Darden cleared his throat. "Yes, Sarah, the living room and kitchen. We came into a little money and we always wanted to fix up the house. It's exactly the way we want it now."

"That's wonderful." She rubbed the back of her neck and looked up at the roof. "I see you've got ladders out. Are you re-roofing?"

"It was leaking this winter, Sarah," Mr. Darden said. "We lost a tree some months ago and a branch hit the house. We've had trouble ever since."

"It looks as if you're doing the work yourself," Sarah observed and rubbed the back of her neck a second time.

Damon reached out to massage her neck with gentle fingers. The tremendous tension he felt in her neck and shoulders kept him silent. Wondering.

"I hear Lance does wonderful roofing, Mr. Darden. He's fast and guarantees his work. Rather than you climbing around on the roof, wasting your time when you could be gardening." She turned her head slightly to look at Damon. "Mr. Darden is renowned for his garden and flowers. He wins every year at the fair for his hybrids."

Damon could see shadows in her eyes. He smiled at her, leaned forward to brush a gentle kiss on the top of her head when she turned back to the Dardens. "Lance probably needs the work and you'd be doing him such a favor."

Mrs. Darden tugged at her husband's hand. "Thank you, Sarah, it's good advice and we'll do that. I've been worrying about Clyde up there on that roof but . . ." She trailed off.

"I think you're right, Sarah," Mr. Darden suddenly agreed. "I think I'll call Lance straightaway."

Sarah shrugged with studied casualness but Damon felt her shoulders sag in relief. "I can't wait for the fair this year to see your beautiful entries. I really wanted you to meet Damon Wilder, a friend of mine. He bought the old Hanover place." She smiled sweetly at Damon to include him. "I know you're often in the garden and working on your lovely yard—have you noticed any strangers around that were asking questions or making you feel uncomfortable?"

The Dardens looked at one another. "No, Sarah, I can't say that we have," Mrs. Darden answered, "but then we strictly mind our own business. You know I've always believed in staying out of my neighbors' affairs."

"It's just that with you working outdoors so much I thought you might be able to keep an eye out for me and give me a call if anything should look suspicious," Sarah said.

"You can count on us, Sarah," Mr. Darden said. "I just bought myself a new pair of binoculars and sitting on my front porch I have a good view of the entire street!"

"Thank you, Mr. Darden," Sarah said. "That would be wonderful. We're just on our way to visit Irene and Drew."

The smile faded from Mrs. Darden's face. "Oh, that's so sad, Sarah, I hope you can help them. When is Libby going to come home? She would be such a help. How's she doing these days?"

"Libby's overseas right now, Mrs. Darden," Sarah said. "She's doing fine. Hopefully she'll be able to get home soon. I'll tell her you were inquiring about her."

"I heard the awful news on Donna," Mrs. Darden continued. "Are these strangers involved in her attack? I heard you shot one of them. I don't believe in violence as a rule, Sarah, now, you know that, but I hope you did enough damage that he'll think twice before he attacks another woman."

"Donna's going to be fine," Sarah assured her, "and I didn't shoot him."

Mrs. Darden patted Sarah's shoulder. "It's all right dear, I understand."

Sarah turned away with a cheery wave. The sisters erupted into wild laughter. Damon shook his head incredulously. "She thinks you shot that man. Even now, with you denying it, she thinks you shot him."

"True." Sarah pinned him with a steely gaze. "She also believes someone saw me walk on water. Now who could have started that rumor?"

Hannah tugged at Damon's sleeve in a teasing way, a gesture of affection for her. "That was a good one, Damon, I wish I'd thought of it."

Kate threw back her head and laughed, her wild mane of hair blowing around her in the light breeze. "That was priceless. And you should hear what they're saying about you. The whisper is, you're some famous wizard Sarah's been studying under."

"Now really," Sarah objected, "at least they could have said *he's* been studying under *me*. I swear chauvinism is still rearing its ugly head in this century."

Damon could feel a glow spreading. He felt a part of their family. He belonged with them, in the midst of their laughter and camaraderie. He didn't feel on the outside looking in, as he had most of his life. Sarah's sisters seemed to accept him readily into their lives and even their hearts. Tolerance and acceptance seemed a big part of Sarah's family. It suddenly occurred to him, even with a threat hanging over his head, that he'd spent less time thinking of past trauma and more about the present and future than he had in months.

"I think I like being thought of as a wizard," Damon mused.

"Sarah says you're a brain." Kate waved at Jonas Harrington as he cruised by them in his patrol car.

"What are you doing?" Hannah hissed, smacking Kate's hand down. "Don't be nice to that idiot. We should make him drive into a ditch or something."

"Don't you dare," Sarah told her sister sternly. "I mean it, Hannah, you can't use our gifts for revenge. Only for good. Especially now."

"It would be for good," Hannah pointed out. "It would teach that horrible man some manners. Don't look at him. And Damon, stop smiling at him. We don't want him stopping to talk." She made a growling noise of disgust in the back of her throat as the patrol car pulled to the sidewalk ahead of them. "Now see what you've done?" She threw her hands into the air as Harrington got out of his car. A sudden rush of wind took his hat from his head and sent it skittering along the gutter.

"Very funny, Baby Doll," Harrington said. "You just have to show off, don't you? I guess that pretty face of yours just doesn't get you enough attention."

Kate and Sarah both put a restraining hand on Hannah's arm. Sarah stepped slightly between the sheriff and her sister. "Did you get anything out of your prisoner, Jonas?" Her voice was carefully pleasant.

Jonas continued to pin Hannah with his ice cold gaze. "Not much, Sarah, and we still haven't located the other two men you say were at Wilder's house the other night. You might have called me instead of charging in on your own."

Hannah stirred as if she might protest. Damon could see the fine tremor that ran through her body but her sisters edged protectively closer to Hannah and she stilled.

"Yes, next time, Jonas, I'll do that: leave the three men with guns trained on the window, sneaking up on the house, while I go find a phone and call you. Darn, those cell phones just don't seem to work on the coast most of the time, do they?" Sarah smiled right through her sarcasm. "Next time I'll drive out to the bluff and give you a call before I charge in on my own."

Jonas's gaze didn't leave Hannah's face. "You do that, Sarah." He knotted his fists on his hips. "Did any of you consider Sarah might have been killed? Or how I might feel if I found her dead body? Or if I had to go up to your house and tell you she was dead? Because I thought a lot about that last night."

"I thought about it," Damon said. "At least about Sarah being killed on my account." He reached out to settle his fingers possessively around the nape of her neck. "It scared the hell out of me."

Kate and Abbey exchanged looks with Hannah. "I didn't think of that," Kate admitted. "Not once."

"Thanks a lot, Jonas," Sarah said. "Now they're all going to be making me crazy, wanting me to change my profession. I'm a security expert."

"It may beat being a Barbie doll, but I think you went overboard, Sarah," Jonas replied. "A librarian sounds nice to me."

Hannah clenched her teeth but remained silent. The wind rushed through the street, sweeping the sheriff's hat toward a storm drain. It landed in a dark puddle of water and disappeared from sight.

Harrington swore under his breath and stalked back to his car, his shoulders stiff with outrage.

"Hannah," Kate scolded gently, "that wasn't nice."

"I didn't do it," Hannah protested. "*I* would have had the oak tree come down and drive him underground feet first."

Abbey and Kate looked at Sarah. She merely raised her eyebrow. "I believe Irene and Drew are waiting."

Damon burst out laughing. "I can see I'm going to have to watch you all the time." Why did it seem perfectly normal that the Drake sisters could command the wind? Even Harrington treated it as a normal phenomenon.

They stopped in front of Irene's house. Damon could see all the women squaring their shoulders as if going into battle. "Sarah, what do you think you can do for Drew? Surely you can't cure what's wrong with him."

Sadness crept into her eyes. "No, I wish I had that gift. Libby is the only one with a real gift for healing. I've seen her work miracles. But it drains her and we don't like her doing it. There's always a cost, Damon, when you use a gift."

"So you aren't conjuring up spells with toads and dragon livers?" He was half-serious. He could easily picture them on broomsticks, flying across the night sky.

"Well . . ." Abbey drew the word out, looking mischievously from one sister to the other. "We can and do if the situation calls for it. Drakes have been leaving each other recipes and spells for hundreds of years. We prefer to use the power within us, but conjuring is within the rules."

"You never let me," Hannah groused.

"No, and we're not going to either," Sarah said firmly. "Actually, Damon, to answer your question, we hope to assess the situation and maybe buy Drew a little more time. If the quality of his life is really bad, we prefer not to interfere. What would be the point of his lingering in pain? In that case, we'll ease his suffering as best we can and leave everything to nature."

"Does Irene think you can cure him?" Damon asked, suddenly worried. He realized what a terrible responsibility the Drakes had. The townspeople were used to their eccentricities and believed they were miracle workers.

"She wants to believe it. If Libby and my other sisters were here, all of us together might really be of some help, but the most we can do is slow things down to buy him time. We'll find out from Drew what he wants. You'll have to distract Irene for us. Have her go into the kitchen and make us lemonade and her famous cookies. She'll be anxious, Damon, so you'll really have to work at it. We'll need time with Drew."

His gaze narrowed as he studied Sarah's serious face. "What about you and your sisters? Are you going to be ill like you were last time?"

"Only if we work on him," Sarah said. "Then I don't know how you'll get us all home. You'll have to ask Irene to drive us back."

"We should have thought to bring the car," Kate agreed. "Do you think that's a bad omen? Maybe there's nothing we can do."

"Don't go thinking that way, Kate," Abbey reprimanded. "We all love to walk and it's fun to be together. We can do this. If we're lucky we can buy Drew enough time to allow Libby to come home."

"Is Libby coming back?" Damon asked.

"I don't know, Damon," Hannah said, her eyebrow raising, "that's rather up to you, now, isn't it?"

"Why would it be up to me?"

"I thought you said he was one of the smartest men on the planet," Kate teased. "Didn't you design some top-secret defense system?"

Damon glared at the women, at Sarah. "If I did and it was top secret, no one would know, now would they?"

Hannah laughed. "Don't be angry, Damon, Sarah didn't tell us. We share knowledge, sort of like a collective pool. I can't tell you how it works, only that we all have it. She would never give out that kind of information, even to us. It just happens. None of us would say anything, well," she hedged, "except to tease you."

"So why is it up to me whether or not Libby comes home?"

"She'll come home if there's a wedding," Kate pointed out with a grin.

12

DAMON looked around him at the four pale faces. Each of the Drake sisters was lying on a couch or draped over a chair, exhaustion written into the lines of her face. For a moment he felt helpless in the midst of their weariness, not knowing what to do for them. They had sat in Irene's car, not speaking, with their white faces and trembling bodies. He had barely managed to help them into the cliff house.

The phone rang, the sound shrill in the complete stillness of the house. The women didn't move or turn toward the sound so Damon picked up the receiver. "Yes?"

There was a long pause. "You must be Damon." The voice was like a caress of velvet. "What's wrong with them? I can feel them all the way here." The voice didn't say where "here" was.

"You're a sister?"

"Of course." Impatience now. "Elle. What's wrong with them?"

"They went to Irene's to see Drew." Damon could hear the sheer relief in the small sigh on the other end.

"Make them sweet tea. There's a canister in the cupboard right above the stove, marked MAGIC." Damon carried the phone with him into the kitchen. "Drop a couple of teaspoons of the powder into the teapot and let the tea steep. That will help. Is the house warm? If not, get it warm: build a fire and use the furnace, whatever it takes. When's the wedding?"

"How soon can you and your sisters get back home?" Damon asked.

"You know I should be angry with you. Not that burner, use the back burner. That's the right canister."

"I don't see what difference a burner makes, but okay and why should you be upset with me?" He didn't even wonder how she knew what he was doing or what burner he was using. He took it as a matter of course.

"Because I'm concentrating on it, the burner I mean. As for being upset, I think you started something we have no control over. I have no intention of finding a man for a long while. I have things to do with my life and a man doesn't come into it, thank you very much. The infuser is in the very bottom drawer to the left of the sink." She spoke as if she could see him going through the drawers looking for the little infuser to put the tea in.

The house shuddered. Stilled. A ripple of alarm went through Damon.

"What was that?" Elle sounded anxious again.

"An earthquake maybe. A minor one. I've got the kettle on, the teapot is ready with the powder, two teaspoons of this stuff? Have you smelled it lately?" Damon was tempted to taste it. "It isn't a dragon's liver, is it?"

Elle laughed. "We save those for Harrington. When he drops by we put it in his coffee."

"I really feel sorry for that man." To his astonishment the teakettle shrilled loudly almost immediately. He poured the water into the little teapot and tossed a tea towel over it for added warmth. "Are you really going to have seven daughters?" he asked curiously, amazed that anyone would even consider it. Amazed that he was talking comfortably to a virtual stranger.

The house shuddered a second time. A branch scraped along an outside wall with an eerie sound. The wind moaned and rattled the windows.

"So the prophecy says," Elle replied with a small sigh of resignation. "Damon, is something else wrong there?"

"No, they're just very tired." Damon poured the tea into four cups and set the cups on a tray. "And the house keeps shaking."

"Hang up and call the sheriff's office," Elle said urgently. "Do it now."

He caught the sudden alarm in her voice and a chill went down his spine. Damn them all for their psychic nonsense. There wasn't really anything wrong, was there?

The dogs roared a vicious challenge. The animals were in the front yard, inside the fence, yet they were hurling their bodies against the front door so hard the wood threatened to splinter. Damon did as Elle commanded and phoned the sheriff's office for help.

No one screamed. Most women might have screamed under the circumstances but none of them did. When he carried the tray into the living room, all four of the Drake sisters were sitting quietly in their chairs. He ignored the two men standing in the middle of the room with guns drawn. Where before, when confronted with guns and violence, he had panicked, this time he remained quite calm.

He knew they were killers. He knew what to expect. And this time, he knew he wouldn't allow them to hurt the Drake sisters. It was very simple to him. It didn't matter to him if he died, he needed the women to survive and live in the world. They were the ones who mattered, all that mattered. The women *would* remain alive.

Damon set the tray on the coffee table and handed each of the sisters a cup of tea before turning to face the two men. He remembered them in vivid detail. The man with the swollen jaw had taken pleasure in torturing him. Damon was glad he had swung his cane hard enough to fracture the jaw.

Damon straightened slowly. These men had murdered for the knowledge Damon carried in his brain. They had crippled him permanently and changed his entire life. Now they stood in Sarah's home, sheer blasphemy on their part. They had entered through the sliding-glass door and had left it open behind them.

Outside, the sea appeared calm, but he could see, in the distance, small frothy waves gathering and rolling with a building boom on the open water. He felt power moving him, a connection with the women through Sarah. Beloved, mysterious Sarah. He waited while the women sipped their tea. Stalling for time, knowing exactly what he would do.

"You two seem to keep turning up," Damon finally greeted. He took two steps to his right, closer to Sarah, turning slightly sideways so she could see the small gun he had taken from the hidden drawer where Elle had said he would find it. "Do you not have homes and families to go to?"

"Shut up, Wilder. You know what we want. This time we have someone you care about. When I put a gun to her head I think you're going to tell me what I want to know."

Damon looked past the man to the rolling sea. The wind was gusting, chopping the surface into white foam. The waves crested higher. The dogs continued roaring with fury and shaking the foundations of the living room door. Damon calmly raked his fingers through his hair, his gaze on a distant point beyond the men. The sisters drank the hot sweet revitalizing tea. And the power moved through Damon stronger than ever. Around each man a strange shadow flitted back and forth. A black circle that seemed to surround first one, then the other. At times the shadow appeared to have a human form. Most of the time it was insubstantial.

"Would you care for a cup of tea?" Sarah asked politely. "We have plenty."

"Do sit down," Kate invited. She shifted position, a subtle movement hardly noticeable, but it put her body slightly between the guns and Hannah.

"This gun is real," the man with the swollen jaw snapped. "This isn't a party." He grinned evilly at his partner. "Although when it's over we might take one or two of the women with us for the road."

Sarah looked bored. "It's very obvious neither of you is the brains in this venture. I can't imagine that the man in jail is, either. Who in the world would hire such comedians to go looking for national secrets? It's almost ludicrous. Are you in trouble with your boss and he's looking to get rid of you?"

"You have a smart mouth, lady; it won't be so hard to shoot you."

"Do have some tea, at least we can be civil," Abbey said sweetly. There was a strange cadence to her voice, a singsong quality that pulled at the listeners, drew them into her suggestions. "If you're going to be with us for some time, we may as well enjoy ourselves with a fine cup of tea first and get to know one another."

The air in the room was fresh, almost perfumed, yet smelled of the sea, crisp and clean and salty. The two men looked confused, blinking rapidly, and exchanged a long bewildered frown. The man with the swollen jaw actually lowered his gun and took a step toward the tray with the little teapot.

Kate stared intently at the locks on the front door, and the knob itself. Sarah never took her eyes from the two men. Waiting. Watching. The huntress. Damon thought of her that way. Listening, he thought he heard music, far out over the sea. Music in the wind. A soft melodious song calling to the elements. All the while the dark shadow edged around the two intruders.

Hannah lifted her arms to the back of the couch, a graceful, elegant motion. The wind rose to a shriek, burst into the room with the force of a freight train. The men staggered under the assault, the wind ripping at their clothing. The bolt on the door turned and the door burst open under the heavy weight of the dogs. The animals leapt inside, teeth bared. Damon blinked as the crouching shadow leapt onto the back of one of the men and remained there.

Sarah was already in motion, diving at the two men, going in low to catch the first man in a scissor kick, rolling to bring him down. He toppled into his partner, knocking him down so that his head slammed against the base of a chair. Sarah caught the gun Damon threw to her.

The man with the swollen jaw rose up, throwing the chair as he drew a second gun. Damon attempted a kick with his one good leg. Sarah fired off three rounds, the bullets driving the man backward and away from Damon. She calmly pressed the hot barrel against the temple of the intruder on the floor. "I suggest you don't move." But she was looking at the man she shot, watching Hannah and Abbey trying to revive him. Watching the dark shadow steal away, dragging with it something heavy. Knowing her sisters could not undo what she had done. Sarah wiped her forehead with her palm and blinked back tears.

Kate collected the guns. Abbey held back the dogs by simply placing her hand in warning on their heads.

"I'm sorry, Sarah," Damon said.

"It was necessary." She felt sick. It didn't matter that he'd intended to kill them all, or that Death had been satisfied. She had taken a life.

The wind moved through the room again, a soft breeze this time, bringing music with it. Touching Sarah. She looked at her sisters and smiled tiredly. "Hannah, the cavalry is coming up the drive. Do let them in and don't do anything you'll regret later."

Hannah rolled her eyes, stomped across the room, landing a frustrated kick to the shins on the man Sarah was holding. "Thanks a lot, I have to see that giant skunk two times in one day. That's more than any lady should have to deal with."

Abigail leaned down, her face level with Sarah's prisoner. "You'd really like to tell me who you're working for, wouldn't you?" Her tone was sweet, hypnotic, compelling. She looked directly into his eyes, holding him captive there. Waiting for the name. Waiting for the truth.

At the doorway, Hannah called out a greeting to Jonas Harrington. "As usual, you're just a bit on the late side. Still haven't quite gotten over that bad habit of being late you set in school. You always did like to make your entrance at least ten minutes after the bell." She had her hand on her hip and she tossed the silky mass of wavy hair tumbling around her shoulders. "It was juvenile then and it's criminal now."

Deliberately he stepped in close to her, crowding her with his much larger body. "Someone should have turned you over their knee a long time ago." The words were too low for anyone else to hear and he was sweeping past her to enter the room. Just for a moment his glittering eyes slashed at her, burned her.

Every woman in the room reacted, eyes glaring at Jonas. Hannah held up her hand in silent admission she'd provoked him. She allowed the rest of the officers into the room before she took the dogs into the bedroom. Damon noticed she didn't return.

All the women were exhausted. Damon wanted everyone else gone. It seemed more important to push more tea into the Drake sisters' hands, to tuck blankets around them, to shield them from prying eyes when they were obviously so vulnerable. He stayed close to Sarah while she was questioned repeatedly. The medical examiner removed the body and the crime scene team went over the room.

Each of the sisters gave a separate report so it seemed an eternity until Damon had the house back in his control. "Thanks, Abbey, I don't know how you managed to get that name, but hopefully they'll be able to stop anyone else from coming after me."

Abbey closed her eyes and laid her head against the backrest of the chair. "It was my pleasure. Will you answer the phone? Tell Elle we're too tired to talk but have her tell the others we're all right."

"The phone isn't ringing." But he was already walking into the kitchen to answer it. Of course it wasn't ringing. Yet. But it would. And it did. And he reassured Elle he wouldn't leave her sisters and all was well in their world.

It seemed hours before he was alone with Sarah. His Sarah. Before he could frame her face in his hands and lower his head to kiss her with every bit of tenderness he had in him. "There was something I saw, a shadow, dark and grim. I felt it had been on me, with me, and now it's gone. That sounds ridiculous, Sarah, but I feel lighter, as if a great burden is off of me. You know what I'm talking about, don't you?"

"Yes." She said it simply.

His gaze moved possessively over her face. "You look so tired. I'd carry you to bed, but we wouldn't make it if I tried."

She managed a small smile. "It would be okay if you dropped me on the floor. I'd just go to sleep."

He helped her through the hall to the stairs. "Hannah has the turret leading to the battlement, doesn't she?"

Sarah was pleased that he knew. "The sea draws her. The wind and rain. It helps her to be there, up high, where she can see it all. I'm glad you understand."

He went up the stairs behind her, ready to break her fall should there be need. Ready to do whatever it took to protect her. "It surprises me that I feel the power in this house, but I do. I'm a scientist. None of this makes sense, what you and your sisters are. Hell, I don't even know how I'd describe you, but I know it's real."

"Stay with me tonight, Damon," Sarah said. "I feel very weary, like I'm stretched thin. When you're with me, I'm not so lost."

"You'd have to throw me out, Sarah," he replied truthfully. "I know I love you and I want you for my wife. I don't ever want us to be apart."

"I feel the same, Damon." Sarah pushed open the door to her

bedroom and collapsed on the large four-poster bed. She looked beautiful to him, lying there, waiting for him to stretch out beside her.

Her window faced the sea. Damon could see the water, a deep blue, waves swelling high, collapsing, rushing the shores and receding as it had for so many years. Peace was in his heart and mind. Soft laughter came from various parts of the house. It swept through the air, and filled the house with joy. Sarah was back. Sarah was home. And Damon had come home with her.

OCEANS OF FIRE

This book was written with love for

Carol Anne Carter,
who inspired me so many times;

Kathi Firzlaff,
who loves Creative Memories;

and Sheila Clover,
who knows what magic is all about.

ACKNOWLEDGMENTS

So much research was done for this book, but one person in particular aided me tremendously: Mike Higgins, one of the Bad Boys of BASK (Bay Area Sea Kayakers), a title earned by getting into trouble on the water too many times. Mike was kind enough to answer all my questions, open his journals to me, and share his photographs of the rocks and caves along the coast. He took the particular journey Abigail and Aleksandr did, and even found me the perfect cove! I greatly appreciate his help.

Thanks to the owner and manager of Caspar Inn, who so graciously allowed me to use their wonderful bar in my novel. I love the music and the atmosphere!

And thanks to my son, Brian, who spent many hours talking over action scenes, even in the middle of the night when he wanted to sleep!

These things say she
Who holds the gifts of the seven
Who walks at twilight
Holding the seven golden lamps

Seven sisters intertwined
Controlling elements of air, land and sea
Cannot control the fate they flee
One by one, oldest to last, destiny shall claim them

When the locked gate swings open in welcome
The first shall find true love
As the sisters stand in wonder
At what destiny has done

Within each sister's heart now beats passion
While love turns as a key
By the time the year is ended
Each will follow thee

Remember therefore from whence you came
Knowing that in the end it is the seventh
That will renew the line again
Seven daughters of a seventh daughter

Each gifted each giving each tied to one another
For those who have ears let them hear
For those who have eyes let them see
For all that I have said shall come to be

To the eldest is gifted agility, grace
And the knowledge to see what future we face
Second in line speaks peace with a word
While the third calls truth from the unspoken word

Next comes the healer with hands that can find
That which is deadly and make it unbind
The fifth harnesses elements of air, wind and sea
As the sixth sister sings a spell over thee

Last of the seven youngest of all
Possesses the greatest gift of them all
To her falls the bearing of children to be
So that the line will continue and forever more be

Each gift has a challenge which must be overcome
The seven free sisters must act now as one
With grace and agility comes great bodily fatigue
While speaking peace raises ire and continual need

The calling for truth from the unspoken word
Gives way to illusion for naught has been heard
She whose hands can undo death for another
Will take on the illness and hope to recover

The harnessing of wind tides and sea
Gives way for the unknown to be
As the spell singer sings casting her spell
One misspoken word and all's to no avail

For the seventh child of the seventh daughter
New corridors open holding illusion, power
But which path to take and where does it lead
Choices to make while each plants a seed

These things I have spoken so harken ye well
For lives you are changing with each casting of spell
But know in your heart when you must turn away
For some will be lost as it is destiny's way

Yours is a legacy not easily borne
So beware of the pitfalls and careful of thorns
The gifts they are many
Born from the past

Surviving the years for the future to last
From mother to daughters
And back through the line
The gifts that you carry always will bind

Prophecy written by Anita Toste,
eleventh daughter in the infamous
and magical King family,
in the year before the great wars
between Magick and Science

1

BRIGHT colors; orange, pink, and red streaked across the sky, turning the ocean into a living flame as the sun set low over the sea. Twenty feet below the surface of the water, Abigail Drake stilled, mesmerized by the sudden, rare beauty of fire pouring into the sea like molten lava.

The dolphins swimming in lazy circles around her took on a completely different appearance as the bands of orange shimmered through the water, casting shadows everywhere. She was suddenly, acutely aware of night falling and that just a few feet away, murky darkness could so easily hide danger. She knew better than to dive alone. It was one of the stupidest things she'd ever done, but she hadn't been able to resist when the day had been so perfect and she'd spotted the wild dolphins and knew they'd come looking for her.

Sea Haven on the northern California coast was her hometown. Abigail was one of seven sisters born to the seventh daughter of the magical Drake family, each gifted with unique talents. The Drake sisters were well known in Sea Haven, protected, cherished even, and it was the one place they could relax and be themselves. Except Abigail. Only here, in the sea, was she truly at peace.

The northern California coast was also home to several species of dolphin and she knew most of them, not only by sight, but also by their signature whistles. A signature whistle was as good as a name, and most researchers agreed that dolphins used each other's name when communicating. This particular group of dolphins had a signature whistle for Abigail and she'd heard them calling to her as she stood on the captain's walk of her family home. She'd been away for months researching in other oceans far away, yet when she returned, the dolphins welcomed her home just like always.

A few years earlier she'd worked with this particular group of dolphins while earning her Ph.D., cataloging them, each contact, every sighting, paying special attention to communication. She was intrigued by their language and wanted to be able to understand them. She'd worked with two of the males on understanding some sign language. Over the years, each time she came home, she visited with them, maintaining a relationship. Although none of her sisters had been available to dive with her, the call of "her" dolphins had been irresistible and she'd taken out her boat to join them.

Federal law required a special permit to swim with wild dolphins in the United States and Abigail had been fortunate enough to be granted permission for her research off the California coast a second time, but she was careful to keep a low profile, not wanting to draw attention to the presence of the dolphins. They could travel fifty miles easily and were difficult to track on a daily basis, but this group, as well as many others, often called to her using the same whistle. It was very unusual to have the dolphins identify her and give her a name and she was particularly pleased that they knew she was back after her long absence.

Abigail rolled over and swam belly to belly with Kiwi, a large adult male who had formed a tight bond with Boscoe, another male. The two males normally swam in synchronization, their movements an astonishing underwater ballet. Boscoe curved his body in the exact motion at precisely the same time as Kiwi and swam close to Abigail as the three of them made a lazy loop together while several other dolphins danced in a long curving circle as if they had choreographed every move ahead of time.

Dancing with dolphins was exhilarating. Abigail studied, photographed, and recorded dolphins, but tonight she was simply enjoying them. Her equipment, always with her, was nearly forgotten as they performed the strange, intriguing ballet for the next forty minutes. At first the red of the sinking sun spotlighted them in a fiery gold, but as dusk fell and the night darkened, it was much too difficult to continue, much as she wanted to stay.

Reluctantly, Abigail pointed to the surface and shifted position to begin her ascent. The dolphins swam around her in loose circles, their bodies flexible, unimpeded by their heavy muscles and enormous strength. It was surprising how the dolphins could rocket through the water, diving as deep as they did and using so little oxygen. Abigail found them fascinating.

She surfaced, pushing her mask on top of her head and lying back to float as she stared up at the big round ball in the sky. Her soft laughter echoed across the water. Waves lapped at her body and splashed over her face. She allowed her legs to gently sink so she could tread water as she stared in awe at the whitecaps, turned into sparkling jewels by the brilliance of the full moon.

Beside her, a bottlenose dolphin surfaced, circling her in a graceful loop. The dolphin shook its head from side to side, emitting a series of squeaks and clicks. She struck out for her boat, a lazy crawl, whistling to the dolphins in the short, chirpy good-bye she always used.

It took only a few minutes to stow her camera and recorder before climbing in. Shivering, she again glanced at her watch. Her sisters would be very worried and she was in for a lecture she knew she deserved. The dolphins poked their heads out of the water, grinning at her, round black eyes shining with intelligence.

"I'm going to get in big trouble thanks to you two," she told the males.

They shook their heads at her in perfect synchronization and dove together, disappearing beneath the surface only to come up on the other side of her boat, whistling and squawking at her. Abigail shook her head just as firmly. "No! It's dark—or it would be if the moon weren't so full. You two are really trying to get me one of Sarah's lectures. When she starts, the rest of us cringe."

While she had everything fresh in her mind, she sank down onto the cushioned seat and hastily scribbled notes on her observations. She recorded everything to look at later, but she always dictated while she was driving the boat after first jotting down details of sightings and any identifying marks of new dolphins in the area. It was important to her study to get DNA samples to test for pesticides and any other man-made toxins in the dolphins' systems as well as for communicable diseases and, of course, family ties.

Boscoe whistled, a distinct note that made her smile. Abigail leaned over the side of the boat. "Thanks for giving me a name, boys, but it isn't enough to make me risk a Sarah lecture. I'll see you tomorrow if you haven't taken off."

She'd let the time get away from her so that darkness had really fallen as she wrote out her notes. She was still a good distance from home and she heaved a sigh, knowing she wouldn't get away un-scathed this time. Sarah, her oldest sister, was certain to be waiting, tapping her foot, hands on hips. The image made her smile.

The moon spilled brightly onto the water, forming mystical fan-tasy pools of liquid silver on the surface. Small whitecaps glistened across the sea as far as she could see, adding to the beauty. She turned her face up to feel the slight breeze as she started the engine and began to make her way back to the small harbor where she kept her boat. She'd gone several miles out to sea to join the dolphins and she was grateful for the moon as she picked up speed to reach the coastline. Boscoe and Kiwi raced along beside her, zooming through the water like rockets and leaping playfully.

"Show-offs," she called, laughing. Their acrobatics delighted her and they followed her right through the narrows beneath the bridge into the harbor.

Without warning, the two male dolphins raced directly in front of her boat, crisscrossing so close she throttled down, shocked by their behavior and terrified for them. They continued to repeat the maneuver, over and over until she had no choice but to halt her boat just inside the harbor, the wharf in sight.

"Kiwi! Boscoe! What are you doing? You're going to get hurt!" Abigail's heart leapt to her throat. The dolphins often rode the bow of the boat, leaping and performing in the current, but they'd never repeatedly crossed so close in front of the boat. The large males kept surfacing, side by side, standing on their tails and chattering at her. She had no recourse but to stop the engine completely and drift in the sea to keep them from injury. Here, the swells were larger, so the boat was tossed a bit by the heavier waves at the mouth of the harbor.

The moment the engine was quiet, Kiwi and Boscoe returned

to the side of the boat, spitting water at her from the sides of their mouths and shaking their heads vigorously as if to tell her something. Several other dolphins poked their heads out of the water, spy-hopping as they looked toward the wharf. She knew spy-hopping was a common practice dolphins and whales used to view the world outside of their water environment by simply sticking their heads high in the air above the surface. They seemed to be looking for something outside the water.

Abigail sat still for a moment, baffled by their unusual behavior. She'd never seen either male dolphin act in such a way. They were highly agitated. Dolphins were enormously strong and fast and could be dangerous, and bottlenose males sometimes formed coalitions with other males and herded a lone female until they captured her. Surely they weren't doing such a thing with her? Had they formed a coalition with the rest of the male groups to keep her from the harbor?

She glanced from them to shore. The moon spilled light across the dark waters and the wooden boards that ran out over the water. Buildings rose up, two restaurants with glass facing the sea, illuminated by the moonlight, but the businesses were closed and the harbor was devoid of the bustle of activity that took place during the day.

Her boat rose with the waves and slid deeper into the calmer waters of the harbor itself. Sounds drifted across the bay, voices, muted at first then rising as if in anger. Abigail immediately scooped up her binoculars and focused her attention on the wharf. A party fishing boat was tied up as usual beside the restaurant. Just beyond the wharf was a second pier in front of a metal business building. A fishing boat was moored there, which was highly unusual. The fishing boats used the other side of the harbor and she'd never seen one tied up close to the businesses.

A small speedboat, a Zodiac, engine humming softly, was moored beside the fishing boat. She could make out at least three men in the speedboat. One, wearing a plaid shirt, had his arm extended and, looking closely, Abigail suddenly feared he held a gun. A second man stood up. The action put him directly in the moonlight. It spilled across him, revealing his salt-and-pepper hair, navy shirt, and the gun in his hand. Both guns were pointed at a third man, who was sitting.

White tendrils of fog had begun to float from the sea toward shore, forming ghostly fingers, obscuring her vision even as her boat drifted closer to the wharf. She blew softly into the air, raised her arms slightly to bring the wind. It rushed past her, taking the streamers of gray mist with it, clearing the way across the expanse of water.

Someone spoke harshly in what sounded to her like Russian. The man sitting replied in English, but the ocean boomed against the pier as her boat drifted even closer and she couldn't hear the words. Abigail held her breath as the seated man launched himself at the one in the plaid shirt. The man in the navy shirt picked up a life jacket, held it over the muzzle of the gun, and pressed it against the back of the victim's head as he struggled desperately for possession of the other gun.

"Shoot him now, Chernyshev! Shoot him now!" The voice carried clearly, thick with a Russian accent.

She heard the muffled explosion, a pop, pop, pop that Abigail knew would forever haunt her. The victim's body slowly crumpled and fell to the bottom of the boat. The fishing boat next to the pier moved slightly and both men turned their heads, one shouting an order.

Gasping, she realized the distinctively marked fishing boat was one she recognized. Gene Dockins and three of his sons ran a fishing business out of Noyo Harbor. The family lived in Sea Haven and was well liked. To her horror she saw Gene slowly rise from where he'd been crouching in the bottom of his boat. His hands were raised in surrender. He was a large bear of a man with wide, stooped shoulders and a shock of gray hair that fell to his ears in a shaggy bowl, wild and untamed like the seagoing man he was.

Her breath caught in her throat and her heart began to pound. The man gestured with his gun for Gene to climb out of his boat. The fisherman went to the ladder, paused, then dove into the sea just as the guns went off. Abigail knew, by the way his body jerked as he fell, that Gene was hit, but she could see his arms move as he hit the water and went under. He was definitely still alive. The two gunmen cursed and began shooting into the darkened waters, spitting the bullets through life jackets in an attempt to muffle the sound.

Abigail gave Boscoe's signature whistle, throwing her arm forward in a command, hoping the dolphin would obey. Though she only had a small ability for telepathy with her sisters, she had a much stronger connection to the dolphins and they often either understood or anticipated what she wanted. Boscoe took off like a rocket, heading for the pier instantly and erupting with several squeaks and whistles that were clearly signals to the other dolphins in the pod.

As she reached for her radio to call for help, the two men in the speedboat spotted her. At once the man with the salt-and-pepper hair turned and brought up his arms in a two-handed stance. Abigail's blood froze with sudden fear. Other than the sharp diver's knife attached to her belt and a long punch stick, a device of her own making she carried to ward off sharks in the event they attacked her during a dive, she had no weapons. No real way to protect herself. Bullets hissed into the water and thunked into the side of her boat. Snatching up the punch stick, she dove. Something hot sliced across her back and shoulder just as she hit the water. Salt stung, adding to the burning pain, but then she went numb with the combination of adrenaline and the icy blast of the ocean.

She came up gasping, worried about more than just the pair of gun-wielding murderers. Ordinarily only sand and a few leopard sharks inhabited the harbor. The fishermen were meticulous about keeping any fish remains from the harbor waters, but several more dangerous species of shark inhabited the waters along the coastline, preferring the shallow channels. The area was known to have great whites as there was a seal rookery close by. With both her and Gene bleeding in the harbor's water she knew she had to get to safety as soon as possible. She faced away from the harbor, toward the cliffs of Sea Haven, lifting both arms up and out of the water, still clutching the punch stick in her hand as she called the wind and sent it across the ocean in a message to her sisters.

The speedboat was bearing down on her fast, both men firing at her. Bullets zipped through the water; one cut through the air so close to her ear she heard it as it whistled past and penetrated the water behind her. She dove again, kicking her legs up to get a faster push toward the deeper water, her heart pounding as the boat came up on her, the propeller cutting dangerously close.

She had to hurry, had to get to Gene. Boscoe, if he was holding Gene at the surface, would be vulnerable to attack from sharks, should any be drawn into the harbor. The dolphin couldn't hold the bleeding fisherman up for long if sharks became aggressive. Looking up through the motion of the water, she could see the two men peering over the edge of their now stationary boat, trying to get a shot at her. She moved carefully, knowing she had to come up for air and attack all at once. Kiwi brushed close to her in reassurance, and took off to the opposite side, drawing the attention of the two men by suddenly leaping out of the water almost in the face of the man in the plaid shirt.

Kiwi signaled with a series of clicks as he leapt and Abigail lunged out of the water on the opposite side of the boat. Chernyshev's gun was tracking the dolphin as his partner fell back in alarm. Chernyshev fired off a round just as Abigail slammed the end of the punch stick against his calf and triggered it. He screamed as the blow was delivered with tremendous force, the sound muting as she disappeared back beneath the water.

The water closed over her head and Abigail kicked away strongly, swimming down a few feet for cover in the murkier depths and heading out to sea, away from where they would expect her to come up. Almost at once she felt the water tugging at her, grasping her body and rolling it. She was coming up on a shallow channel and the back wave was dragging her down.

Kiwi bumped her, sliding his fin almost under her hand in invitation, and she grabbed with more instinct than thought. He took her through the stinging sand with a burst of speed and rocketed into the calmer waters of the harbor straight toward the pier. When she couldn't hold her breath any longer, she let go and kicked strongly for the surface, coming up choking, spinning wildly around to keep the speedboat in sight.

The speedboat was beside her own vessel and the man with the plaid shirt leaned in to grab something, before shoving off out toward open sea. Kiwi nudged her again, presenting his fin. He was clicking and squawking, pushing at her in urgency. She caught his fin and went under, allowing him to pull her through the water at a pace she'd never be able to go herself.

Kiwi halted abruptly just as Abigail was certain her lungs were deprived forever of air. She kicked strongly, anxious to rise to the surface. Something brushed against her back. Eerily, it felt like fingertips skimming across her shoulder blades and she spun around to find she was face-to-face with a dead man. His eyes were open and he stared at her in a kind of macabre horror, his dark hair floating like strands of seaweed and his face pale beneath the water. His arms were outstretched as if on a cross, yet swaying with the movement of the water, and he rolled with the incoming wave, his body bumping against hers.

Her stomach lurched, and she gasped, losing her last bit of air and swallowing seawater. She kicked, desperate to reach the surface, her head breaking through as she coughed and gagged. Her eyes burned from the salt, or maybe from tears, but she dragged air into her lungs and caught at Kiwi a third time. Something scraped down the back of her leg as the dolphin pulled her through the water. A gray shadow slid noiselessly by.

Abigail fought the urge to try for the surface. She knew the skin of a shark was covered with hard toothlike scales, called dermal denticles, and when rubbed from tail to head felt like sandpaper, the exact sensation she had had down the back of her leg. Whatever had scraped her was following, trying to circle, but Kiwi was taking her through the water at a dizzying speed. Kiwi's echolocation was so precise they nearly hit Boscoe, who was still valiantly keeping Gene's face above the water.

Astounded, Abigail watched as several dolphins began to ram sharks, driving them to the bottom with such force that debris rose from the floor of the ocean and churned in a dark mass. The normally docile sand and leopard sharks were aroused by the scent of blood. If a great white was in the vicinity, she was certain it would be rocketing through the water to join in the frenzy. She added to the melee, shoving her punch stick against a small shark and triggering the pressure block to deliver a forceful, powerful punch to the shark's nose in an effort to deter it. She reset the stick as quickly as she was able and swam to the pier.

Tossing the punch stick onto the wooden planks, Abigail attempted to pull herself out of the water. Her back burned and her arms protested. She fell back into the sea almost on top of a small shark. Kiwi rammed it, hitting it hard, driving it down toward the bottom as she made another try. Using one of the dolphins as a stepping-stone, she was able to drag herself out of the water far enough to gain a crosspiece of wood to use as a ladder.

Immediately she reached down and snagged Gene's shirt, pulling him around and freeing Boscoe so the dolphins could swim away from the sharks. She hooked him under his shoulders and dragged him, wincing as she scraped his back against the wood. He was a big man and his waterlogged clothing added to his weight. She struggled to hold him, whistling to the dolphins, begging for further aid. Boscoe returned, using his enormous strength to shove the unconscious man up and out of the water. She was able to pull Gene nearly all the way onto the pier, although his legs dangled over the edge. She saw Kiwi come up from a dive, blowing water from his airhole and dragging the dead man by the arm. As she reached down to get the stranger, she was horrified to see blood on the dolphin. The bullet must have skimmed him just as one had sliced across her. She dragged the dead man onto the pier, pulling him back behind her and away from Gene.

Abigail signed for Kiwi to go out to sea, to head for Sea Lion Cove. More than anything she wanted him safe after all he'd done for her, but she had to try to save Gene. She knew her sisters were out on the captain's walk. Worried. Waiting. Ready to help.

"Come on, Mr. Dockins, you can't die on me," she whispered. She had no idea how he'd gotten mixed up in this, but she didn't believe for one moment that he could have done anything illegal. She'd known him most of her life. His wife, Marsha, had often comforted her when other children were afraid to play with her. Gene had taken her out in his boat often and told her his tales of the sea.

She could see where three bullets had torn into his body, one in the shoulder, one in the chest, and one that had shaved skin from his skull. He was bleeding profusely now so she clamped down hard on the two worst wounds.

The back of her neck prickled in alarm. Somewhere, out at sea, a dolphin squawked a warning. She swung around, reaching for the punch stick, a pitiful weapon against a gun.

"Don't you move." The voice was low and shook with rage and the accent was not as distinct, but it was definitely Russian.

Abigail froze, her stomach clenching. The dolphins couldn't help her now. She could only hope that her sisters had sent aid and it was on the way. She sensed movement behind her, but she didn't hear footsteps. Her entire body tensed. She shifted slowly, enough so when she turned her head, she could see shoes and trousers. He was standing over the dead man.

A stream of Russian curses burst from his mouth. He stepped forward and grabbed her braid, yanking her head back to press the muzzle of his gun between her eyes hard. Her heart stopped. Her gaze collided with a pair of midnight blue eyes, black with ice cold rage. There was a moment of absolute terror and then recognition fought its way into her brain. Her heart resumed its frantic pounding. She kicked out at him, suddenly furious herself, slapping the gun away from her face. "Get the hell away from me!"

"Calm down. I'm not going to hurt you." He tried to fend off the kicks to his shins. "Damn it, Abbey, what the hell are you doing here? Look at me! You know me. You know I would never hurt you. It's over. You're safe. I'm not going to let anything happen to you."

She choked back a sob and turned away from him, trying to regain control of herself. She hadn't seen those eyes in four years. Aleksandr Volstov, Interpol agent and heartbreaker extraordinaire. He was the last person she expected to see here. The last person she wanted to confront when she was on the verge of hysteria. Damn him anyway. She had the right to be hysterical after he shoved a gun in her face. Avoiding looking at him, she crawled over to Gene again and pressed her hands to the wounds to try to stop the flow of blood. He was deathly pale, and his lungs were laboring for air.

"Who did this, Abbey?"

She didn't look up. "Two men in a Zodiac. They took off out of the harbor and if you call the sheriff and coast guard, they may be able to catch them."

"Did you get a look at them?"

"I'm trying to keep Gene alive and it takes concentration. I can't answer your questions right now."

"That man lying there dead is my partner, Abbey. Who did this?" There was ice in the voice, a warning.

She felt a shiver go down her spine but she kept her attention focused on the fisherman. "Call the coast guard, and an ambulance. I doubt if they were stupid enough to take the speedboat out to open sea where they could be caught, but you might get lucky. There are a few caves along the coastline large enough to hide that small of a boat and it's calm tonight, so if they know what they're doing that's where they'll be."

Aleksandr crouched beside her and caught sight of the blood on her back and down the back of her leg. "You're hurt!"

"I've got to work on Gene," she protested when he tried to tug her to him.

"I'm sorry, *lyubof maya,* but this man cannot possibly live."

His gentle tone, a caress of black velvet, was almost her undoing and she turned on him, furious, fighting back tears. "Don't you tell me he won't live! The dolphins risked their lives for him and I'm not giving up. Just keep your enemies off my back while I do this."

It wasn't fair that she was angry with him. And maybe she wasn't. Her body was shaking with shock and overload of adrenaline. And she could feel her own wounds burning and throbbing. Mostly she felt fear for Gene and his family. She wasn't Libby or Elle or even Hannah with their tremendous powers. Even Sarah would be better than Abigail, but she was all Gene had. "And don't call me your love, either. I'm not *your* anything."

She raised her arms up over her head to bring the wind, to whisper a chant, a plea, a need for a joining, and she sent the wind out over the ocean to the cliff house where she knew her sisters waited. Where she knew, would always know, she was accepted, flawed or not, and they would *always* come to her aid when needed.

She heard the sirens fast approaching. She heard the boom of the sea and the song of the whales and her own heartbeat. There was a rhythm of life there, an ebb and flow that was continuous and strong. And she found Gene's heartbeat. Slow. Stuttering. Out of sync with the universal flow. "I've got you," she whispered softly. "I won't let you go."

Abigail didn't have a first aid kit, but she had the Drake magic. It welled up like a fountain, a power from deep within her, fed by the wind and sea. She could feel herself connecting with Hannah and Sarah, feel strength pouring into her as she placed one palm over Gene's head wound and the other over the small hole in his chest.

Wind rushed up from the surface of the sea. Dolphins leapt and somersaulted. At a distance, several whales breached. Power crackled in the air all around her. Through her. She felt Elle, her youngest sister, join in, the rush of power welling up from somewhere inside Abigail to burn down her arms and into her palms. Kate's strength added to the steady stream. Joley joined in, her voice strong on the wind, her power pouring into Abigail. And then, from a distance, Libby joined them, aiding Abigail with her tremendous gift of healing. The surge was so strong she shook with the force of it, the burning in her palms so pronounced it was difficult to keep her hands steady over the wounds.

The wind blasted her face and brought with it the fog, obscuring all vision on the water so that she was wrapped in a silvery cocoon, kneeling there on the pier with Gene lying so still and Aleksandr's body heat warming her. The relief nearly overwhelmed her. Hannah and Joley and Elle were often conduits for power, but never Abigail. It was both frightening and exhilarating to feel the strength and heat pour from her into the mortally wounded fisherman. It wasn't the same as her gift, but much stronger and more focused. She felt his skin burn beneath her palm as if absorbing healing properties. She felt his chest rise as if Gene struggled for breath and she knew he lived, although his injuries were grave.

As the power faded, her legs gave out and she sank back onto the pier shaking, arms and legs like lead. The terrible price for having and using power was a debilitating weakness afterward. She lay helpless, listening to the waves lapping at the pier and the wailing of the sirens as vehicles filled the parking lots along the harbor.

"Abbey." Aleksandr's voice was gentle. He took off his jacket and spread it over her violently shaking body. "The paramedics are here. How bad are you hurt?"

She looked up at him. The lines and planes of his face so achingly familiar to her. Tears blurred her vision. Fog swirled above her head. She knew her sisters lay on the captain's walk, or wherever they had been when they had completed the joining, just as drained of strength. The wind fluttered softly without the power of the Drake sisters carrying it and she heard the last notes of Joley's incredible voice fade away.

Footsteps thundered toward her. The wooden planks of the pier creaked and groaned in protest, shaking beneath the weight of people running. She wondered if the boards would give out and she'd be dropped back in the ocean for sharks to feast on. She was definitely hysterical. It wasn't a good time to be staring into Aleksandr's eyes and wondering why his lashes were so long. Or wondering why she could never get his face out of her dreams. Why she heard his voice calling to her across oceans. Abigail closed her eyes and turned away from him.

"You. Stand up slowly with your hands where I can see them. Back away from her." She recognized Jonas Harrington, the sheriff. He was using his voice of total authority, which he did often, but this time it carried a hint of something deadly in it.

Abbey's heart contracted. Her eyes locked with Aleksandr's. His expression was hard, his eyes as cold as the arctic sea. She knew he could kill a man swiftly and efficiently, going from stillness to action in the single beat of a heart.

"Don't hurt him." The words escaped, so low they were barely discernible, but Aleksandr could read the fear so apparent on her face. And it wasn't for him.

"This is the sheriff and I'm ordering you to get your hands where I can see them and back away from the woman."

"Please." She whispered the plea to the Russian.

Beside her, Aleksandr rose with unhurried ease. Calm. Cool. Never ruffled. He turned to face Jonas, his hands up, palms out.

"You." Jonas nearly spat the word. Jonas holstered his gun and reached down to check the pulse of the man lying so still. "Volstov. I should have known you'd be involved in this somehow. This man is dead. Who is he?"

"My partner. The ones who murdered him are out there somewhere." Aleksandr indicated the expanse of sea beyond the harbor.

Jonas examined Gene next. His eyes met the Russian's and he heaved a sigh as he went to Abigail. Jonas crouched down beside her, taking her hand. Jackson, one of the deputies, stood at his back, facing out toward sea, but his body posture was clearly protective. "Let's get the medics in here, Jackson."

It occurred to Abigail that Jackson was being drawn into the Drake family circle whether he wanted to be or not. Jonas always had been there. Tough. Uncompromising. Someone to count on when things got bad. Her fingers wrapped around his wrist and held him there.

He glanced from her to Aleksandr and his face hardened perceptibly. "What's the damage, Abbey?"

She made an effort to tell him Gene needed immediate help. Jonas shook his head. "We'll get life flight en route, hon, we'll get him to San Francisco. The paramedics are with him. I want to take a look at you."

"Home." She managed the word, lying back to stare up at the wisps of drifting fog. She wanted to get home where she was safe, surrounded by her sisters and protected by the walls of her house.

"I want them to examine you, Abbey, and don't give me any grief over it, either," Jonas said, moving back to give the paramedics room, but retaining possession of her hand.

"Libby," she said, trying to pull her hand away so she could push at the paramedics.

"Not Libby. She's going to be as weak as you are. Maybe weaker. Good old-fashioned medicine will have to do," Jonas replied firmly as he stroked back her hair.

Aleksandr leaned over her. "What did they look like?" His fingertips brushed droplets of seawater from her face with exquisite gentleness. The pads of his fingers slipped over her cheekbone and then her lower lip.

She wanted to tell him, but the moment his face was in front of hers, tears burned and she hurt, inside and out. His touch sent butterflies winging in her stomach. As hard as she tried to form the words to describe what she had witnessed, nothing would come out. She turned her face away, closing her eyes in desperation.

Jonas immediately shifted position so that Aleksandr was forced to move back and break contact with Abigail. "Can you talk, Abbey?" he asked.

His voice was so gentle she wanted to tell him to stop being nice. She really had to fight the tears. She shook her head.

"You'll have to question her later, Volstov," Jonas said abruptly.

Aleksandr lifted his gaze to the other man's face, a cold raking that would have given a lesser man pause, but Jonas didn't even flinch.

"We're going to shift you, Abbey," the paramedic said.

She opened her eyes and blinked several times to clear her vision. She'd gone to school with Bob Thornton. She nodded and helped roll so they could look at the back of her legs and shoulder. It hurt more when she moved. She was suddenly acutely aware of the wounds, when before it was mostly the terrible lethargy that distressed her.

"The bullet sliced through her skin, Jonas, but it doesn't look too bad," Bob reported. "See here, it's a bit deeper through the muscle on her shoulder, but relatively shallow along her back."

"Thank God," Jonas said, relief clear in his voice. "What happened to her leg?"

"I'd guess a shark raked her while making a pass."

"Damn it, Abbey." Jonas rubbed his thumb over her hand. "She looks pale, Bob. Are you sure she's going to be all right?"

Aleksandr made a small sound, a growling in his throat that might have been a protest of her injuries. He moved around Jonas to Abbey's other side. She kept her eyes firmly closed and he didn't make much noise when he moved, but she felt him brush her arm just before he circled her wrist and brought her palm against his thigh. She was shivering and couldn't stop no matter how hard she tried. His body felt warm against hers and unfortunately, tipped on her side the way she was, he was pressed close to the front of her. As soaked as she was, she was getting his immaculate suit wet as well.

"She's in shock, Jonas," Bob said. "Wouldn't you be? Someone shot her. A shark nearly got her. She pulled Gene out of the water, at least it looks that way. And there's a dead body here. I'd say she has reason to be pale. This is going to hurt, Abbey," he warned.

Whatever he used on her leg and back robbed her of every bit of air from her lungs. She almost lunged out from under the paramedic and Jonas, desperate to get away from the fire racing over her skin, but she ended up practically in Aleksandr's lap. He caught her in a firm grip and held her still while the paramedic worked on the wounds.

"I can do that, Volstov," Jonas offered. "I'm sure you have more important things to do." He paused for a moment as the other paramedics lifted the unconscious fisherman onto a gurney and raced him toward the helicopter. "Gene's safe now, Abbey," he added. "They're taking him to San Francisco."

"I wouldn't want to mess up your crime scene," Aleksandr replied before Jonas could shift him. "My partner is dead. There is not much I can do until Abbey tells me what she knows. You go on ahead and get what you have to get done, and I'll take care of Abbey."

"My crime scene people are the ones entering the crime scene. My officers know what they're doing."

Aleksandr ignored the edge to Jonas's voice, refusing to relinquish his place holding Abigail. "You'll have to go to the hospital," he said to her.

"Home, to Libby." She was adamant. "Jonas. Take me home."

"Don't worry, Abbey," Jonas reassured her. "As soon as you're cleared, I'll have Jackson take you, but I'm going to need answers as soon as you're feeling stronger."

"I can't clear her to go home," Bob protested. "Abbey, you know I can't do that. You need to be checked out by a doctor. You have serious wounds."

"Libby is a doctor," Jonas said. "Bob, you know she has to go home."

"I'll take her," Aleksandr said decisively. "If her sister is a doctor and she isn't in danger of bleeding to death, I'll take her to her house."

"No, you won't," Jonas said firmly. "You're going to stay here and tell me what the hell you're involved in that I have one dead body, another nearly dead, and Abigail Drake injured."

"And in danger," Aleksandr said.

2

ALEKSANDR ignored Jonas and carried Abigail off the pier. "I'm already wet. There's no need for the both of us to be soaked. In any case I have to ask her a few questions when she's feeling better." He kept walking, not giving Jonas a chance to protest as he carried her to the sheriff's vehicle and slid into the backseat with her in his arms. He needed answers and getting into the inner sanctum of the Drake home was the only way he was going to get them. He refused to notice Jonas's glare and simply tightened his arms around Abigail.

Aleksandr rarely showed emotion on the outside. He was a master at hiding his feelings from others, but Abigail knew him. She knew he was enraged over his partner's death, although he seemed to take it quite calmly. She also knew Jonas was suspicious because Aleksandr hadn't given his partner's body more than a cursory inspection. But Jonas hadn't been there a few minutes earlier when Aleksandr had shoved the muzzle of his gun against her forehead and she had stared into death. He was hanging on to his control by his sheer discipline, but she felt his rage roiling just below the surface. She remained very still as he cradled her close to his chest.

"I notice you didn't ask any questions about Abbey and why she can barely move," Jonas said, slamming his door closed. "How much have you heard about the Drake sisters?"

Abigail winced. Aleksandr had firsthand knowledge of the strange gifts and talents she possessed. More than once he'd seen her use them and become drained of all energy. He knew her capabilities and weaknesses all too well. Tears burned and a small sound of despair slipped out.

Aleksandr nuzzled the top of Abigail's head. It seemed a miracle to be holding her in his arms again. He wasn't a man to believe in miracles, until he'd met her. Even with his partner lying dead on the pier, and rage and the need for vengeance consuming him, the moment he'd had a clear enough head to recognize her, some small measure of hope had entered his heart.

He was used to concealing his feelings. In Russia, everything was political and the wrong expression, the whisper of scandal, anything at all could be the end of his career, and now, with the stakes so high, he was grateful for that training. He and Danilov had stumbled onto something bigger than they had anticipated and it had gotten Danilov killed. The last thing he needed was the distraction of Abigail Drake, but if Jonas thought to be rid of Aleksandr, either in the investigation or with Abigail, he was wrong. Jonas might be dating Abbey now—he certainly acted proprietary around her—but Aleksandr had the prior claim. He wasn't going to hand her over without a fight any more than he would back off of his investigation.

"Abigail is engaged to me." He announced it without hesitation, staring down into her face, at the twin crescents of red-gold lashes, willing her to look at him.

Her eyes snapped open and she blinked up at him. Aleksandr could see the flames building in her eyes. Abigail had always reminded him of the sea, calm and peaceful and soothing, or turbulent and wild. She walked away from most arguments and simply disappeared rather than fight, but she had red hair for a reason. She was quite capable of rising up like a silent shark out of the depths and taking a big bite unexpectedly. At that moment he was eternally grateful for the Drake curse of weakness after using their powers.

"That's impossible," Jonas said.

Aleksandr held Abbey's blazing stare with one of his own. He wasn't about to back down, wanting her to know there was more than one reason for his being in Sea Haven and he wasn't going to go away. "I assure you, it is not."

Abigail shook her head and closed her eyes again, groaning softly.

Aleksandr looked down at her face. He remembered every curve, the feel of her skin, the laughter in her eyes. The love. He wasn't going to let her get away from him a second time. He didn't want to fight with, or frighten her, but he *was* angry with her. Angry that she hadn't given him a second chance, angry that she'd nearly gotten herself killed. Angry that her American boyfriend would be sitting in the front seat telling him what he could or couldn't do. That she would even have an American boyfriend. *Any* boyfriend at all. Her heart should have been locked up, devastated without him, the way his had been without her. He had the sudden urge to shake her and he knew that wasn't a good sign. His control was slipping and that was a dangerous thing.

"How strange that she wouldn't have said a word to me about an engagement," Jonas said. "Or to any of her sisters." He didn't bother to keep the note of disbelief out of his voice.

"Very strange," Aleksandr agreed. Abigail tensed in his arms, but the effort to fight him was apparently too exhausting and she relaxed again, her expression stubborn. If she kept that look on her face he might be tempted to take advantage of her weakness and kiss her right in front of her new lover. He shoved the thought away, feeling murderous. It was enough to have lost Danilov without discovering that another man had taken his woman from him.

"What happened tonight, Volstov?" Jonas made a point of staring at him in the rearview mirror. "Is Abbey a part of this?"

"No." Aleksandr was grateful for the interruption of his thoughts. "I was as shocked to find Abbey on the scene as you were." He bent over her, rubbing at what he hoped was a smudge and not a bruise forming between her eyes.

She managed to bring up her hand to slap at his arm. He waited until she settled down and went right back to rubbing with the pad of his finger. Small, round caresses. Gentle. Stroking. Telling her with his touch that he wasn't going anywhere. The faint mark wouldn't go away. She had pale, almost alabaster skin and he remembered she bruised easily. It was a hell of a way to announce his return, but like the mark, he was back in her life to stay and she was going to have to deal with their past whether she liked it or not.

"So what are you and your partner doing in my county?" Jonas asked. "You introduced yourself to me, but you neglected to say you were going to leave dead bodies in our harbor."

"We've been working this case for some time and we've traced three shipments in the past two and a half years to this coast. There's been a steady stream of stolen antiquities, including an impressive collection of jewelry, going out of Russia. My partner, Andre Danilov, managed to get a job on a fishing boat out of the harbor and was keeping an eye out for any suspicious activity. We've known for some time that artifacts have been smuggled through a route here, but this was the first time we knew the actual freighter and when it would arrive."

Jonas was silent for a moment and then he sighed. "Gene Dockins came to me a few months ago and said he was concerned something was happening out at sea with one of the boats—the *Treasure Chest*. The captain is a man named John Fergus and I've known him several years. He's never given us any trouble. Several local businessmen own the boat and all of them have lived in the area most of their lives. Most own other businesses. I did a little discreet inquiry down around the harbor and turned the matter over to the coast guard, but, to my knowledge, they didn't turn up anything unusual. Gene didn't say anything further to me and I presumed the matter was taken care of. Obviously, I was wrong."

"Gene Dockins actually contacted Interpol, saying he thought there was smuggling going on. He thought drugs, or with the terrorist scare he was afraid a bomb might be smuggled into the United States via this coastline. He and his son Jeremy had been doing a little undercover work and managed to take pictures of something being offloaded onto the *Treasure Chest*. As we knew this area was hot, we followed up on his inquiries and took him up on his offer to continue helping."

Jonas swore aloud. "Why the hell didn't they come to me? For that matter, *you* should have come to me instead of using a local for your undercover work. Jeremy's only a kid. Damn it!" He slammed his open palm against the steering wheel. "I should have been more on top of it. I knew Gene was concerned, but I thought once I'd turned it over for investigation he'd dropped it." He sighed. "I sent Jackson to their home to break the news to Gene's wife but I'd better warn him to keep on eye on Jeremy. That boy doesn't have the sense to be afraid and I'll be damned if I'll let anything happen to him. If he comes around wanting to help by taking his father's place, you tell him no."

Aleksandr waited before responding until Jonas finished his call outlining the dangers to Jeremy Dockins to his deputy. "Your report to the coast guard filtered through Interpol just about the same time Gene Dockins sent us the photographs and his concerns. We contacted Mr. Dockins and he agreed to help us by placing an undercover agent in his boat and on the docks working with him. It was the perfect cover for Danilov." Aleksandr was damned if he was going to give Jonas the satisfaction of feeling his regret. Of course he was upset his partner was dead and the civilian fisherman was near death, but Aleksandr was doing his job and in his high-risk position danger went with the territory. Losing Danilov was a tremendous blow, both professionally and personally. He had been Danilov's backup and he had arrived too late to protect him. It mattered little that Danilov hadn't told him he was going out with Dockins that night; Aleksandr felt responsible.

"I did a little research on you, Volstov, after you introduced yourself. There were a lot of gaps in your earlier years. Big ones. But I did find that you've spent several years working to bring down the Russian mafia. They're a particularly violent organization. Are you trailing them? I'd like to know if they have a foothold in my jurisdiction."

"They're in San Francisco," Aleksandr admitted. "But you probably know that. We were hoping they weren't involved in this, but little happens in Russia along the smugglers' routes without the mafia being involved."

"Is your name on a hit list?" Jonas asked bluntly.

Aleksandr felt Abigail tense in his arms. Her eyes opened and he held her gaze as he admitted in a low voice, "Yes. Very near the top."

Abigail blinked and turned her head away from him.

Jonas turned the car onto the long, winding drive that led to a sprawling house on the cliffs. The house was an imposing sight, three stories high with a tower, balconies off of nearly every room, and a captain's walk out over the sea. Wind-swept cypresses and groves of evergreen and redwood trees clung to the hillside and color exploded among the brilliant green plants as wildflowers fought for space among the brush. A heavy iron gate wrought with symbols of the earth and stars swung open as the vehicle approached.

"What happened tonight, Volstov?" Jonas asked.

Aleksandr studied the grounds carefully, noting every path and every locked gate. "I received a call tonight from Danilov saying he had some evidence that a shipment of stolen artifacts we were tracking had been spilled into the sea as it was being transferred from a freighter to a fishing boat. He'd taken pictures and had a witness. He must have gone out with Dockins on his boat without informing me before he went." His gaze swept over the house and he mentally recorded the position of all the windows and doors that he could see. Exits. Escape routes. His way of life.

Jonas parked the car and turned to study the Interpol agent. Aleksandr Volstov looked calm, almost expressionless, mild even, until you looked into his eyes. Jonas had met men like Volstov before, had fought alongside of them. They made relentless, bitter, merciless enemies and the most loyal of friends. They were the type of men you wanted in your corner when push came to shove because they would never desert you and would go into the fire to pull you out. Volstov wasn't calm about losing his partner and he wasn't going to stop until he found every last man involved in Danilov's death. And that could mean a bloodbath in Sea Haven and the surrounding towns if the Russian mafia was involved.

"This isn't Russia," Jonas felt compelled to point out.

Aleksandr merely looked at him with Siberian-cold eyes, then slid out of the car still cradling Abigail in his arms. "So this is the Drake house."

"You're obviously aware they become weak after using their gifts. All of Abbey's sisters are going to be in the same state. They won't like feeling vulnerable in front of you," Jonas warned.

"You've obviously witnessed this aftereffect on more than one occasion," Aleksandr pointed out as Jonas led the way along a winding path to the front door.

"I'm family," Jonas said.

"Seeing as how Abbey is engaged to be married to me, I would have to claim the same thing," Aleksandr replied quietly. Abigail stirred in his arms, opening her eyes with another stormy glare, which he ignored.

The door was opened by an attractive middle-aged woman, with shrewd, assessing blue eyes and a wealth of gray-blonde hair clipped at the nape of her neck.

"Aunt Carol!" Jonas enveloped her in his arms and kissed her cheek. "I had no idea you'd be here." He stepped aside, holding the door to allow Aleksandr to bring Abbey inside.

"The girls didn't know," Carol assured him. "I arrived a few hours ago, thinking I'd help plan the weddings, and found them all in such a state. Here," she directed Aleksandr, "put her on the couch." She trailed after him. "I've made tea, Abbey. You'll be fine in half an hour."

"She's soaking wet from the sea," Aleksandr protested. "Is there somewhere I can get her out of her wet clothes?" He felt Abbey's body stir again in protest and tightened his arms to prevent anyone from seeing her shaking head.

"Where are the others?" Jonas asked, stepping around Libby, who was sprawled out on the floor, a pillow under her head. Elle lay slumped in a chair. Both had a cup of tea beside them. Keeping Gene Dockins alive had obviously cost them all a great deal. Jonas had seen the Drake sisters very vulnerable after the use of their powers, but never to such an extent. Gene must have been close to death to drain them this deeply. He cast a concerned glance up the stairs. "Aunt Carol, are they all right?"

"Yes, dear. I couldn't very well carry them down the stairs. They're stuck out on the captain's walk."

"I'll get them." Jonas was already moving, taking the stairs two at a time, leaving Aleksandr to face Abbey's aunt.

Carol regarded him with her hands on her hips. "I'll get a blanket to wrap her in. I can't very well have you taking her clothes off."

"I'm her fiancé," Aleksandr stated without the least compunction. "Please just show me to her room and I'll do the rest."

At his declaration, both Libby and Elle tried to push themselves up, although neither succeeded.

Carol didn't ask for more of an explanation, but guided him up the stairs to Abbey's room. Her bedroom was spacious with French doors that led out onto a wide balcony overlooking the sea. "You'd better be telling the truth, young man. I'm not without my own gifts and that lovely accent will not save you from my wrath should you be lying." She closed the door before he could reply.

"I know you're angry, Abbey," Aleksandr said as he laid her on a blanket on the floor, "but you brought this on yourself. I gave you plenty of time." He began to peel off her wet suit, an incredibly difficult task when it was as snug as a second skin. "I've only got so much patience." He wrapped a robe around her the moment he stripped her and tried not to notice her body.

Not that it mattered. Even with his eyes closed he remembered the feel of her body, her lush, generous curves, warm and soft, skin pressed tightly against him. Abbey in his arms. Fitting so perfectly. He cinched the robe around her waist, careful of her wounds, and squeezed a towel around her thick red braid to soak up the excess water.

She pushed at him with feeble hands. "Angry is an understatement. Go away."

"No. Not this time. It's taken me four years to catch up with you. There's no way I'm going to walk away. Especially when you get yourself mixed up with this mess. If the Russian mafia is involved, Abbey, it's going to get messy. And Jonas Harrington can go to hell if he thinks he's got a claim on you. We're engaged and I'm not letting you out of it."

"You don't really think I'm going to let you walk back into my life!" She pressed her fingers to her temple. "I need to be downstairs with my sisters."

She was getting her voice back and that wasn't good. "Where are your sweats? I'm not taking you down there if Jonas is going to know you aren't wearing anything under that robe."

Her eyebrow shot up but she indicated her second drawer, not wasting energy on an argument with him. The truth was, she was shocked to see him. She could barely stand to look at him, to see him, so solid and real instead of the man haunting her dreams.

Aleksandr scooped her up once she had wiggled into her sweatpants. "I'm taking you down there, but don't make the mistake of making eyes at him."

"Do shut up, Sasha." The nickname slipped out without conscious thought. He'd always had a jealous streak and it annoyed her no end. *Everything* about Aleksandr annoyed her, especially his complete confidence. And his attitude. As if *he* had the right to be angry with *her*.

"Do you want to tell me what you were doing in the sea by yourself?" He gave her a little shake in his arms. "And you should have more sense than to be caught in the open when bullets are flying." The angrier he got, the thicker his accent became. All the while his arms were gentle.

She didn't want to remember that about him. "I don't have to tell you anything."

"Yes, you do. You have to answer for taking ten years off my life, not to mention the four lost between us." He strode down the stairs and into the living room as if he owned her house, as if she weighed no more than a child. As if he were in charge.

"Put her on the floor, over there," Carol directed, pointing to a spot where she'd spread a few cushions.

Aleksandr propped Abigail against the sofa and sat beside her. Close. His thigh touching hers. "She has a bullet wound across her back and a shark scraped down the back of her leg."

"Oh, dear." Carol put her hand over her mouth. "I've brought her tea, but that won't help her injuries."

"The paramedics disinfected them but she refused to go to the hospital."

Libby moved then, dragging herself across the few feet that separated her from Abigail, and reached out to touch her sister's leg.

Abigail shook her head violently and tried to pull her leg out of reach. "No, Libby. You're too weak." She gasped the words, fighting for energy just to speak.

"Just rest, Libby," Carol admonished. "You can't heal another person after what you've been through. Drink your tea." She made it an order. "All of you." She looked at Aleksandr. "I'm gone a few years, and they all grow up and forget everything we taught them. It's a good thing I've come home."

Libby reached for Abbey's hand. "I'm sorry," she whispered.

Abbey shook her head. Libby was the healing force of the Drake sisters. Through her, unbelievable results could be achieved, but she paid for it dearly, often taking on the pain and illness of the injured or sick person she was aiding. "We're fine. We're all fine," she assured her sister.

Aleksandr pressed the cup of tea into Abigail's other hand and helped her bring it to her mouth. She didn't fight him, but watched instead as Jonas returned from the captain's walk carrying her sister Hannah.

Hannah stared at Aleksandr with curious eyes. "Who?" she mouthed.

"None of your concern," Jonas snapped. "Did you pay the slightest bit of attention to how close you were to the edge when you were casting? You nearly fell over the railing, Hannah. Another inch and we might have lost you."

"There, there, dear." Carol patted Jonas as if he were a boy. "There's no way of knowing when the weakness is going to hit. Hannah commands the winds. She has to reach out to the sea. Don't give her a lecture when she can't even defend herself."

"That's the best time," Jonas muttered. "In fact now would be a good time to give them all a lecture on safety. Do you realize Abbey was diving in the sea alone?"

"Go get Sarah and Kate and Joley, Jonas," Carol said. "We'll make certain Abbey never does such a foolish thing again." She gave him a little push toward the stairs.

Aleksandr wanted to laugh at the sheriff's expression. Aunt Carol had reduced Jonas's dangerous image to that of a "bad boy" with a few well-chosen words and her tone. The Drake women were truly perilous to the opposite sex, but then he had firsthand knowledge of that. His hand slid over Abbey's until he could intertwine his fingers with hers.

She looked at him. Tears swam in her eyes and his heart jerked hard in his chest. He'd never been able to stand her tears. That day, the day neither of them would ever forget, he hadn't gone to her because her tears would have changed the course of his life and he hadn't been able to afford what would have resulted. He leaned over her, blocking her from the sight of the others. "Don't cry, *lyubof maya*. You are my heart, my world." He murmured the words in his own language because it was the only way he could tell her. He'd never stopped loving her. He had nothing without her. He'd learned that in the emptiness of his violent world. In the endless travels and the bleak hotel rooms. There was no home without her, not even his beloved Russia.

Abigail shook her head. "Go away, Sasha, don't come back here again."

He brought her hand to his mouth, his lips sliding over her knuckles, his tongue tasting her. Salt and sea. That was Abigail. "I go only because there is no talking to you when you are like this. And you've had a bad fright, but I will return, and we will sort this out."

Aleksandr pushed himself up as Jonas returned carrying another Drake sister. "I will go, but you know where I'm staying. Please do me the courtesy of informing me of any information you might procure."

"Oh, don't worry, Volstov. I'll be seeing you the minute I leave here," Jonas assured him. "You want me to call for a ride?"

Aleksandr shook his head and deliberately looked at Abbey. "I'm staying close by so I can keep an eye on things." He had done what he could to stake his claim, but he knew Abbey well enough to know she was going to be upset that she was so vulnerable and he had taken advantage. Damn Jonas Harrington for having the inside track.

Carol showed him to the door. "I'll take good care of her," she assured him, "no need to worry about Abbey. As soon as Libby is feeling better, she'll attend to her sister."

Carol closed the door and immediately hurried over to Abigail. "Are you all right, dear? Shall I call your mother?" Her expression betrayed her anxiety. "How bad are your injuries?" She glanced toward the door. "And that fiancé of yours has the sexiest accent. When he was speaking in Russian I nearly fell on the floor."

Abigail didn't want to agree with her aunt, but she was grateful she was already on the floor. No matter how many nightmares, no matter how often she relived Aleksandr's behavior, the moment she saw him, heard his voice, touched him, she knew she would have to be very careful. "I'll be fine, Aunt Carol," Abbey assured her. "I just want to go to sleep."

"Not before you talk to me," Jonas decreed, depositing Joley in a chair beside Kate. He suddenly crouched down beside Abigail and took the hand Aleksandr had held. He took a breath. It seemed the first he'd taken in several long hours. "I was really scared for you, Abbey. I saw him standing over you. I saw the gun and the two men down. There was blood everywhere and I thought for a moment we lost you." He sighed and rubbed his chin, his eyes avoiding hers. "I came close to killing him with no warning. I was that scared." He hung his head for a moment. "I nearly pulled the trigger just to get him the hell off of you."

"Jonas." Abigail let her breath out. "It was horrible, of course you would have thought he was trying to hurt me."

"I almost killed a man in cold blood, Abbey. I never want to feel like that again." He rubbed his hand over his face. "I've done a lot of things in my life, but I've never killed an innocent man."

She tightened her fingers around his. Without warning her skin prickled and she looked up to see Aleksandr watching them from outside the window. His expression hardened and his eyes grew even colder, if that were possible. Her heart jumped and began a wild beat she couldn't control. He held her stare for a moment then turned and disappeared from sight. Abbey cleared her throat and tore her gaze away from the window. "It's not going to happen again, Jonas. I'll be careful."

"You'd better be." He took the cup of tea Carol handed to him and immediately sipped the hot, rejuvenating drink. "Thanks, Aunt Carol. It's been a hell of a night." He sank back, resting his head against the sofa, and looked around him at the Drake sisters. "Abigail witnessed a murder tonight and I'm afraid the Russian mafia may be involved. They're a very violent and messy bunch. I don't want *any* of you involved in this, and Abbey, you stay the hell away from Volstov. I don't know why he's claiming to be engaged to you and I don't have a clue if you knew him somewhere before this, but he's a very dangerous man and he's up to his neck in the mess."

Sarah roused herself to wave her hand. "He's claiming he's engaged to Abbey?"

Abigail could feel color sweeping into her neck and face as all of her sisters, her aunt Carol, and Jonas stared at her. She drank more tea to give herself time to think up an answer.

"Abbey?" Kate prompted.

"Well," Abbey hedged. "Yes. I mean no. Not really. Maybe." She drew up her legs. "I'm confused."

"Just how long have you known that man?" Jonas demanded.

Abigail clenched her teeth. She detested being the center of attention. "I don't want to talk about it, Jonas."

He was silent for a moment as he drained the rest of the tea from the mug Carol had given him. "Tell me what happened tonight, Abbey. And don't leave out anything, even a small detail you think may be insignificant."

Abbey set the teacup on the floor between them as she related the evening's events. She could feel the tension rising between her sisters but none of them pressed her for details or for explanations and she knew they wouldn't until Jonas left. Once he was gone she would really have to explain things and already she was getting the classic headache from magic overload.

"Oh, my." Carol broke the silence after Abbey finished. "This could be an international spy case, or something equally intriguing. All of you stay right there. I'll need to get the camera. We should record this for your children's children." She hurried into the kitchen.

"Murder isn't very intriguing, Aunt Carol," Sarah called after her. "It's just plain nasty. And we look awful. You can't take our pictures like this."

"Darling"—Carol bustled back into the room with a small camera in her hand—"these are the best photos of all. Unrehearsed and yet significant. The moment you all embarked on an international crime-fighting case involving foreign spies and handsome agents." She smiled happily at Abbey. "I know a dozen good love potions and even more spells, dear." She clicked away with the camera, taking pictures from several angles. "You just let me know if you need them with your young man."

"I don't have a young man," Abbey protested.

"He seems to think so," Carol said. "You have to learn to make yourself clear in matters of the heart. Believe me, I know. Hannah, dear, quit making faces at me. You should be used to having your picture taken."

"Not without fifteen makeup men to help her out," Jonas said.

"Go away," Hannah directed him, waving her arm. "I'm too tired to fight with you." She ignored Carol snapping more shots ferociously.

"You even manage to look elegant when you're sending me away, Hannah," Jonas said, standing up. "I've got to go, but I'll be back later to check on everyone. Anyone want help up to their room before I take off?"

"Are you sick? You never call me Hannah." Hannah pushed herself upright and regarded Jonas with a troubled gaze. "Are you all right?"

Her thick mass of platinum hair fell over her shoulder and pooled in spirals over the back of the couch. He looked away from her, refusing to meet her eyes.

"Jonas," Hannah insisted, "we can help you feel better. Just give us a minute."

His smile was tired. "Thanks, but I'm not allowing you to expend more energy in my direction. I just have a bad taste in my mouth right now. It isn't pleasant to find out that, under the right circumstances, you might be willing to kill someone in cold blood."

"You're human, Jonas," Sarah said gently. "We're your family. Of course you'd feel protective of us. And magic ties us all together with a much stronger bond. We don't know how it works in extreme circumstances. You didn't kill him. You did the right thing and you brought Abbey home to us. That's all that matters."

"I was never so glad to see someone in my entire life," Abbey added. "I feel so bad for Gene's family. They must be so frightened right now. He looked bad."

"He would have been dead without you, Abbey," Jonas confirmed. "If he makes it, he owes it to all of you. I've got a lot of work to do tonight, but call me if you remember anything else, Abbey. I'll check on you later and I'll step up patrols in this area as well."

"Thanks, Jonas," Sarah said. "We'll make certain Abbey's careful."

"All of you be careful," he insisted. "If it is the Russian mafia, they won't hesitate to kill all of you."

"Oh, dear," Carol said and fanned herself with her hand. "I've come at just the right time."

"Aunt Carol," Kate protested, "aren't you afraid?"

"I came home hoping to put excitement back in my life," Carol explained. "I'm still a young enough woman to find a good man. I loved my darling Jefferson, but he's been gone five years and I'm tired of sitting in that huge southern house all alone, surrounded by my photograph albums and nothing else. I love my job as a Creative Memories consultant, but I want to *make* my memories, not just advocate to others to preserve theirs."

"We're glad you've come, Aunt Carol," Kate said. "We especially need help planning the weddings." She looked at Sarah. "Or should we say wedding? Sarah and I want to have a double wedding."

"What about Abbey?" Joley said mischievously, nudging Abigail with her bare foot. "Maybe we'll have three brides."

"Very funny, Joley. Aunt Carol, take a picture of Joley. You'll make a fortune on the Internet. Rock star lounging at home in her favorite superstar PJs. You could sell it to the tabloids," Abigail suggested.

Joley merely rolled her ankle in small lazy circles. "You'd better spill the beans, Abbey. I've got the mother of all headaches and the least you can do is tell us how you sort of are, but maybe not, engaged to a Russian stranger who just happens to be a spy."

"He's not a spy," Abbey said.

"How do you know, dear?" Carol asked as she tipped the camera to get a better angle on Joley. "Joley, move your head just a little. I'm picking up a glare."

"You can't be picking up a glare," Joley protested, turning her head to look behind her. "It's dark outside."

"I'm certainly picking up a light at the window. Oh, it's gone. It must have been the moon."

There was a sudden silence. The seven Drake sisters looked at each other uneasily. Hannah raised her arms and a wind rushed through the house, setting the drapes dancing closed across the windows. Joley sketched a complicated pattern in the air. At once silver symbols leapt to life, sparkling and fading away just as fast.

"What did you see, Sarah?" Carol asked, her voice losing the teasing notes and becoming serious. "Because I didn't like what I saw."

Carol had the gift of "sight" just as Sarah did. She was the eldest of her seven sisters. Sarah and Carol exchanged a long look and then both turned to Abigail.

Abbey felt a chill sweep down her spine.

"What happened in Russia, Abbey?" Sarah asked. "There is death between you and this man. I see blood and death and violence."

There was no accusation in Sarah's voice, none in her expression, but Abbey wanted the floor to open up and swallow her. She was different. Flawed. Her crime an unspeakable one. She shook her head. "I can't. Please don't ask me. Everything will change and you're the only refuge I have left to me besides the sea. If you love me, don't ask me to explain."

"It's because we *do* love you," Sarah said gently.

Abigail dragged herself up, tears in her eyes. "I'm sorry. I can't talk about it." She couldn't talk about it, couldn't think about it, slamming the door in her mind closed to prevent throwing herself off a cliff. She would never be free of what she'd done, the harm she'd caused. And she'd never be free of Aleksandr Volstov.

3

CONCEALED in the shrubbery at the bottom of the hill, Aleksandr stood staring up at the house on the cliff. Abigail Drake. She'd haunted him for years. He knew which room was hers. It faced out over the hillside, with an ocean view from her balcony. The sliding glass doors were wide open and white lace drapes danced with the breeze coming in off the ocean. He had been most careful to observe every entry point, every weakness of the house, when he was inside. He'd even tested the stairs for creaks.

The house was enormous and seemed shrouded in secrets. Fog lay heavy around the sprawling building and in the trees, as if guarding the structure and its occupants. The misty tendrils were eerie in the silvery moonbeams, wrapping the balconies and windows in ghostly gray.

She was up in that house. In that room. Only a few yards away from him, no longer halfway around the world. She couldn't escape him this time. She'd returned every letter he'd painstakingly written. He'd put his heart and soul into those letters and she'd rejected them without even opening them. Some of the letters had traveled to several countries to reach her. He still had every one of them, smudged with half a dozen postmarks. He'd told himself he was a fool, but he couldn't let it go. Couldn't forget about her. Couldn't stop the way she crept into his mind a hundred times a day and remained in his dreams night after night.

He took a cautious step onto the property. Clouds spun across the moon, casting an eerie mix of shadows and flickering moonlight over the landscape. Trees and shrubs swayed as if something guarded the hillside hidden beneath the dense thicket of leaves and branches. Some branches were raised toward the sky while others bent in twisted, sweeping shapes toward the ground, long arms bent on deterring intruders. It was as if the property itself wanted to keep out intruders.

Once again he went still, getting a feel for the rhythm of the night, uneasiness creeping into his mind and body so that he felt the hair on his neck rise. He shrank down instinctively, his body aware there was more than fog and moonlight in the trees almost before his brain registered the information. He was tuned to every night sound, every cricket and frog. The tendrils of fog shrouding the house reached out like macabre snakes, twisting through the dense foliage, further obscuring vision, but he was relying on instincts, not sight.

Aleksandr slid deeper into the shadows and went motionless again, his senses heightened and on full alert. He heard nothing, saw nothing, yet he knew he was not alone. He waited patiently, shifting position only when he had full cover. Finally he caught glimpses of a dark shape moving stealthily through the trees. The fog and shrubbery obscured his vision, but he heard the scuff of shoes on rocks and dropped to the ground. Aleksandr was a big man and needed stealth to move in close to the hunter. He drew his gun and slithered through the brush. A man stood in the shadow of the trees staring up at the house through a pair of binoculars. Aleksandr's heart jumped when he realized the binoculars appeared to be trained on Abigail's room.

The drapes on the French doors swayed and Aleksandr tensed when he saw Abigail walk out onto the balcony and face the sea. She was wearing a pair of drawstring pajama bottoms and a thin spaghetti-strap tank that didn't quite cover her flat belly. She leaned her elbows on the railing and stared out over the ocean. The wind tugged at her long mass of bright red hair and pushed her thin top across her breasts. Her hair fell below her waist in a long bright red cascade, the wind sweeping it across her pale skin. He remembered the feel of the silky strands, soft and sensual, sliding over him.

It took all of his self-control not to call out a warning to her. He inched his way toward the man in the shadows. The man turned his head slightly and Aleksandr's gut clenched and rolled. *Prakenskii.* He was considered a violent killer and a termination order had been out on him for years. What was he doing in the small town of Sea Haven? Aleksandr crept within striking distance. He could not afford to leave Prakenskii any room to maneuver. His entire world narrowed to his task. Kill Prakenskii and keep Abigail safe. Nothing else mattered at that moment, or could matter.

"Just keep your hands right where they are, Ilya Prakenskii," Aleksandr ordered, his voice low. "Stay where you are."

Prakenskii stiffened, raised his hands slightly. "Aleksandr. I had no idea you were in the vicinity. We meet in the strangest of places." A small smile touched his mouth. "Have you recovered from our last little 'talk'?"

"Completely," Aleksandr said pleasantly. "A few weeks of recuperation." He shrugged. "Such is life. And you?"

"A little reminder when it grows cold, but thank you for asking."

"What brings you to this part of the world?"

"I was about to ask you the same thing," Prakenskii said. "Although, now that I've seen the woman, I don't need an explanation. It was rumored you'd lost interest in her."

"The rumors were wrong."

"She's the one the scandal was about, isn't she? You nearly lost your career and you made a very bitter enemy."

"I've made my share of enemies," Aleksandr agreed with a small shrug. "So have you. It is our way of life."

"True. I was hoping your superiors would let you go, but they appear more intelligent than I gave them credit for and they kept you." He tilted his head. "Or you have far more power than I believed."

"Turn around, Ilya." Aleksandr refused to be drawn into a discussion of politics. They both had firsthand knowledge that the red tape of the various government organizations, splinter groups, and jealous coworkers could be a minefield.

"One never likes to hear that you are anywhere near, Aleksandr,"

Prakenskii remarked as he turned, his hands still in plain sight, the binoculars conspicuously in his left fist. "She's a beautiful woman. It's always a shame when a beautiful woman dies, don't you think?"

"Fortunately my enemies know me, Ilya, so she is in no danger. I would hunt down and kill anyone who harmed her. And I would kill their families and their friends and their every associate until I was caught." Aleksandr spoke matter-of-factly. He shrugged, but the gun remained rock steady. "It would take even Interpol a long time to catch me and there would be a bloodbath before it happened. Drop the binoculars, and I don't want to see your shoulder move. Open your hand and let them fall to the ground."

"Come now, Aleksandr, these are very expensive. You just can't expect me . . ." Ilya threw the binoculars, snapping them hard into Aleksandr's chest and rushing forward to chop viciously at his gun hand.

Almost too late, Aleksandr saw the thin razor blade in Ilya's hand as he sliced toward Aleksandr's stomach. Killers like Prakenskii used poison, coating the blade with a lethal dose so all it took was the lightest of nicks and their victim was dead within minutes. He leapt back so that the blade narrowly missed him and slammed the butt of his gun on the back of Ilya's hand so that the knife fell to the ground. His foot lashed out, smashing hard into the side of Ilya's knee, collapsing the leg, forcing him to stagger.

It gave Aleksandr enough time to bring his gun into position as Ilya drew his secondary weapon and aimed between Aleksandr's eyes. They stood face-to-face, both ready to die in a single heartbeat.

Aleksandr thought of Prakenskii stalking Abbey, plunging the knife into her or shooting her until her lifeless body lay bloody and broken. One move was all it took to prevent her dying, a slow squeezing of the trigger.

"I am merely the agent, not the sender," Prakenskii pointed out, reading death in the other man's eyes. "If you want her to live, you need me to return to the others and give them your message. They will not want you coming after them. It is that, or we both die here."

"I think we both die."

Prakenskii shook his head. "It is foolish of you to waste your life. I believe you will do as you say and come after anyone who harms her. I have no wish to be looking over my shoulder for you for the rest of my life. I will not touch your woman and I will deliver the message that she is to be left alone."

Aleksandr studied Ilya's expressionless face. He had known the killer to be many things, but a liar wasn't one of them. "Did you kill Danilov?"

There was a small silence. "I don't know Danilov."

"He was my partner."

Ilya shook his head. "Not me. I've never heard of him."

Aleksandr believed him and that made Prakenskii's presence even more of a mystery. "If you get in the way of my investigation, Ilya, or if you're involved in any way, I'll have to bring you in. You know that."

"You can try, Aleksandr, but we both will end up with more scars and my arthritis will be bad in my old age."

"If you don't stop working for Sergei, you won't live to be an old man."

"I'm walking away, Aleksandr." Prakenskii took a cautious step back. "There's no reason to do this. I wasn't here to kill the woman."

"Why were you here?"

Prakenskii hesitated, a small smile touching his cold mouth briefly. "Curiosity. I wanted to see what kind of woman could have so many men tied up in knots."

"Who?" The last thing Aleksandr wanted was for Sergei Nikitin to be interested in Abigail Drake. His mouth went dry at the thought. Prakenskii wasn't the only killer working for Nikitin. And some of the others didn't have Prakenskii's discipline or respect. They hadn't trained with Aleksandr and didn't know his reputation or capabilities the way Prakenskii did. "Why would Nikitin be interested in Abigail?"

"I'm going, Aleksandr. Stay out of my way."

Aleksandr matched him step for step, the gun never wavering as they moved like dancers down the rough slope. "I heard my name was at the very top of a hit list, Ilya; is that why you've come?"

"I would kill you to defend my life, Aleksandr, but even I have a code. I'm not here for you." The hit man shrugged.

His reply told Aleksandr that Prakenskii felt much the same way as Aleksandr did. They'd grown up together and had few people they were loyal to. It still mattered. It was one of the reasons Aleksandr never tried too hard to bring Prakenskii in. One never knew if he really was the killer he was reputed to be, or if he'd merely made powerful enemies in the wrong place. Just as Aleksandr had done.

"You work for Nikitin, and I've heard he is in bed with Ignatev." Aleksandr threw the name out to see what came back.

"Women are trouble, Aleksandr, you should have remembered that." Prakenskii risked a glance toward the cliff house. "Ignatev is a vengeful man and his hatred runs deep. He is a man who craves power and will get it any way that he can."

Aleksandr kept his gun trained on Prakenskii and continued to move with him step for step, careful to keep him in sight. He was a dangerous man, but he had a strange set of ethics. Aleksandr couldn't quite figure him out. They both had grown up in and been trained in the same school, both perfecting the art of killing. Aleksandr had grown weary of the politics of espionage and chose police work. Prakenskii had grown impossible to control and the government put out a termination order on him. Everyone sent against him had been returned in a body bag. Aleksandr and Prakenskii had known each other too many years and they avoided one another unless Prakenskii was on the wrong side of one of Aleksandr's cases. Their meetings usually ended up in a bloody battle neither won.

Would she be safer with Prakenskii dead or alive? Killing Ilya would cost Aleksandr his own life. He had no doubt about that and his death would leave Abbey without protection against Sergei Nikitin. Aleksandr risked a glance up at the balcony. Abbey had gone inside, unaware of the two men facing off on the hillside leading to her home.

He let his breath out in a sigh of relief and continued to follow Prakenskii, hoping for a mistake on the hit man's part. Ilya didn't lose his footing on the steep slope, nor did he take his gaze from Aleksandr, as he made his way to the car hidden partially by a wild bramble of bushes.

"Watch your back, Aleksandr," Prakenskii advised as he slid behind the wheel of the black Acura. His gun remained pointed at Aleksandr's head. "There are things here best left alone."

"Abigail Drake is best left alone," Aleksandr replied.

"She is a weakness that can be exploited."

"She is death for any who seeks to harm her."

Prakenskii started up his car. "You have many enemies here, my friend. And they will not all look like enemies."

Aleksandr slid his gun back into his shoulder harness as he watched Prakenskii drive away. Only when he was certain the other man was gone did he turn his attention to Abbey's balcony and the open French doors. What was she thinking to leave an invitation to everyone? Especially after witnessing a murder and nearly being murdered herself.

He hurried up the slope through the trees to the house on the cliff. It was the replica of a villa he'd seen in the south of France, also with many windows, balconies, and a tower. The one in France was used as a hotel and was certainly large enough for it.

He looked straight up from the foundation of the building. The structure rose three stories high and, of course, Abigail's balcony was at the highest point. He stood beneath the balcony and studied the vine-covered walls for the best way up. It wasn't easy and it wasn't fast, but he made it with a steady crawl, more annoyed than ever that anyone could have gotten into the house. Worse, he found finger- and footholds where there shouldn't have been, almost as if an invisible ladder was stretching up the wall of the house for him, *or anyone else*.

Gaining the balcony, he went over the railing and sat for a moment on the floor, listening for sounds of movement. He took a few minutes to check the grounds below before going into Abigail's room, in case Prakenskii returned. As he walked boldly through the open doors, he felt a curious electrical charge running through his body and the air seemed to light up with tiny sparks much like fireflies. He blinked and the peculiar sensation was gone, as if it had never been.

Abigail lay on the bed beneath a thick quilt, her fist clenching the soft folds. Her bright red hair spilled across her pillow and pooled on the sheets. He made no sound as he crossed the room and sank down onto the full-sized four-poster bed. Her lashes were spiky wet as if she'd been crying, but when she opened her eyes, there were no tears, only blazing hot anger mixed with panic as she launched herself at him.

He caught her and slammed her back down to the mattress, hissing at her. "You don't want to wake your sisters." Until that moment, he hadn't realized the rage that seethed just below the surface. Maybe the night's events fed it, maybe her careless actions and even the danger to her contributed, but more than that, it was her steadfast implacable resolve not to give him a chance. She had tossed him aside so easily, without a confrontation, without a single word spoken, without allowing for any explanations.

Aleksandr took a breath and let it out slowly, careful that his grip on her couldn't possibly hurt.

Abigail stared up at his broad shoulders and familiar face. She loved his face. Loved the angles and planes and lines etched deep that spoke of hardship. Right now his eyes were ice cold and she knew he meant business, but she didn't care. "You mean you don't want me to wake them. They'll call Jonas and you'll be the one hauled to jail. It won't be as bad as what happened to me, but you won't like it."

Aleksandr let her go. "Go ahead and scream, Abbey. Let your sisters call your annoying friend. Just know that I'm not in the mood to be generous tonight." He leaned down to remove his shoes. "It's on you if anything happens. I'm just too damned tired to care."

"What are you doing?" Abigail sat up, her eyes smoldering with temper.

"I just told you. I'm tired. It's been a hell of a day. I'm going to lie down while we talk."

"In my bed?" Her voice was strangled with outrage. "I don't think so." She looked wildly around for her robe. "You're such a pompous ass, thinking you can come into my bedroom and crawl into my bed like nothing happened. Get out before I lose my temper. You have no idea what could happen if I lost my temper, Aleksandr." Neither did she, but for a moment she wished she were Hannah and could turn him into a reasonable facsimile of a toad.

Before she could get her hands on her robe, he bunched it in his fist and tossed it across the room. "You were parading around on your balcony for the entire world to see—including a Russian hit man, a particularly efficient one." He glared at her. "I don't think you need a robe to talk to me."

That stopped her. She stared up at him, horrified. "What do you mean, a Russian hit man? Here? After me? Are my sisters and my aunt in danger?" She slipped off the bed to pace across the floor. Aleksandr wouldn't lie to her about something like that. "Because of what I saw? What I heard?"

"What did you hear?"

"A name, that's all. One was called Chernyshev. I told you what I saw. Why would they send a hit man after me?"

"I don't know that he was after you. I only know he's a very dangerous man. Chernyshev is a fairly popular surname in my country." He sighed heavily. "If he belongs to the mafia, they are very violent."

"He was very violent. He was shooting everybody and everything, including the dolphins." She swept her hand through her hair as she paced. "I've got to leave, get away from my family. I won't put them in danger."

"Slow down, Abbey. We don't even know what's happening yet."

"What's going on? You have to know or you wouldn't be in Sea Haven. All of a sudden we have Russians killing each other and hit men are hanging around outside my family home? Why are you here, Sasha? Why would you come here?" She came back to him, knelt on the floor beside the bed, and stared at him with her incredible eyes.

He had forgotten how her eyes looked up close. They could be as clear and beautiful or as turbulent and wild as the sea she loved so much. Kneeling there with her abundance of rich red hair cascading to the curve of her bottom, she looked the witch some people called her. The witch his people had thrown out after first putting her through hell.

He had called in every favor owed to him, had even used old contacts and routes he had long ago given up for police work, to get her safely out of the country. She didn't know the risks he'd taken or the consequences of his actions. She didn't know about the bloodbath left in her wake. But she knew he was responsible for the government picking her up in the first place. He was responsible for a lot of things. Mostly for putting the wariness into her eyes. The fear. She had never really been afraid until she met him.

"You returned every single one of my letters unopened." He lay back, his fingers linked behind his head.

"Why are you here?" she repeated.

"Because you're here."

Abigail closed her eyes, briefly allowing pain to wash over her. She'd lived with heartache for so long it was a part of her. She detested pathetic, weeping women who couldn't live without the man who broke their heart. She was always strong. She never had a problem walking away. And no one pushed her around. Until Aleksandr. She was weak-willed with him. Was it just because she wanted the chance to lie beside him, feel his raw strength, his warmth, just one more time?

Aleksandr turned her well-ordered world upside down. He could make her body come alive with one smoldering look. With a touch. Just by walking toward her. She'd actually become that pathetic. Fury swept through her, temper rising to give aid to her instincts of self-preservation. She wasn't going through hell again. She had some small measure of self-respect. Well . . . maybe not. Maybe it was self-preservation, because he'd almost destroyed her. He'd ruined her joy of life, and he'd shattered her trust in herself. He'd damaged a lot of the qualities that defined Abigail Drake and he'd left her an empty shell.

"Damn you, Sasha. Go away. My home is the only refuge left to me."

"All you had to do was read my letters, Abbey. You didn't even do me that courtesy."

She turned her head to look at him, suddenly furious. It welled up, a hot fountain of rage, and she allowed it to boil over. She leapt up, detesting the image of a woman kneeling at his feet. "*Courtesy*? Do you think I owe you courtesy? You let them drag me off and treat me like an *animal*. You knew what they were doing to me. Do you want to know how many times they hit me? How many hours I was interrogated? Slapped? Spit on? Do you want the ugly little details? Or do you already have them?" She stared down into his face. His handsome, chiseled face that never gave anything away. She wanted to slap him so she twisted her fingers together and fought for control. "You *betrayed* me. You betrayed everything we were together. Damn you for that."

At the sound of footsteps running down the hall, Abigail turned toward the door and waved her hand. Locks clicked in place.

"Abbey!" Hannah's voice cried out. "Are you all right?"

"Stay out," Abigail ordered. "I'm perfectly fine."

"You're not all right," Joley insisted. "We can all feel you."

"I'm handling it," Abigail said. "Please, just go back to bed. I need to do this."

There was a small silence. "If that's what you want, Abbey," Hannah said.

"It's what I need," she said and turned to look down at Aleksandr.

He lifted his hand to touch her. He knew it was a mistake when he did it, but he couldn't resist. Her eyes held too much sorrow, too many shadows, and it tugged on his heartstrings. The moonlight spilled across her face, bathing her face and hair in silver and she looked a temptation, a red-haired vision he couldn't get out of his mind. His hand slid into the mass of silky hair; his thumb caressed her soft skin as he framed her face. "I dream about you every night."

"I have nightmares about you." Why couldn't she pull away? Any other man would be writhing on the floor. Why did he make her so weak? Why did she crave him like some terrible drug? She hadn't been a weak woman until he came into her life. "You nearly destroyed me. Do you really think I want anything to do with you?"

"Did it occur to you it nearly destroyed me as well? I love you, Abbey. You're my heart and soul. Did you ever, even *once,* wonder why, wonder what was happening?"

"Of course I did. I loved you." She deliberately used the past tense. That got his attention. His eyes glittered at her, a warning, but she was beyond caring. "I didn't want to believe you would betray me and leave me when I needed you the most, but you did. I didn't want to hear an explanation. Either I was important to you or I wasn't. Obviously I wasn't, so I moved on. That's life, Aleksandr."

"What is going on between you and your policeman friend, Harrington?" Aleksandr kept his voice mild, but his gut was churning. Abigail was a stubborn woman. If she made up her mind not to give him a chance, it would be nearly impossible to change her decision. His one hope was that she was at last arguing with him. Abigai walked away from confrontations. She once had confided that her temper terrified her and she refused to allow herself to be placed in any position where she would want to retaliate.

She was also very loyal. He had learned that the hard way. In the days of interrogation, she'd refused to betray him, remaining stubbornly silent no matter what was threatened or done to her. He rubbed his hand over his face, chasing away the nightmares of watching the tapes. She had been so alone. So frightened. And she hadn't known he was working frantically behind the scenes to get her free, to have her deported. She hadn't known that things had gone so drastically wrong.

"You stay away from Jonas Harrington."

There was fierce protection in her voice. And affection. He flinched from that realization. "What is he to you?"

"None of your business."

"I've lost my partner, Abbey. I nearly killed you. I just had an encounter with a very dangerous man who tried to kill me outside your house. More than anything I'm worried about you because when he goes hunting, he doesn't miss." And it didn't make sense to him. If Prakenskii had been ordered to kill Abigail Drake he would have done so with no hesitation. What other reason could he have for being there? Aleksandr squashed the urge to go after the man. He had learned a hard lesson about acting without all the facts and he wasn't about to make another, perhaps fatal mistake.

"Tell me more about him," Abigail urged.

"His name is Ilya Prakenskii. We were raised in a state-run home together and we watched each other's back. It had to be that way. Even there, when we were young and they were training us for our work, there were always power plays going on. It's a way of life where I come from."

"You know him?"

"Probably better than anyone else," he confirmed. "If there's one man I respect and even like, it's Ilya, but our handlers didn't encourage friendship. He went one way and I went another. But Ilya doesn't miss. I don't know why he's here, but he said he didn't know Danilov and I believe him. He's reputed to work for Sergei Nikitin and Nikitin is mafia, a very violent man who likes to solve his problems in extreme ways."

Abigail's heart jumped into her throat. "You said there was a hit out on you. Is he here for you?"

"He says not."

"But he was here, and he knows you would come here. Why else would he be watching this house and me unless it had something to do with me witnessing your partner's death or to get at you? It's the only logical explanation."

Aleksandr nodded. "That's true, but I don't think I'm his target. He warned me I had powerful enemies."

"Do you?"

"Of course. I wouldn't be where I am without having made enemies. You have to understand the dynamics going on in my country. There've been so many changes over the last twenty years, so many shifts in power, and no one ever wants to give up power."

"What did you do that's so bad someone would put out a hit on you?"

There was a small silence. Abigail's heart sank. She sat on the edge of the bed. "It was something to do with my leaving Russia, wasn't it?"

"Yes." He wasn't going to lie to her. "I had enemies I didn't know about and they took their opportunity when they had it after what happened."

She sucked in her breath sharply, holding up her hand to stop him. "Shut up. Just shut up. Don't talk about it."

"If we don't talk about it, we'll never get past it," he said gently.

"There is no getting past it. Not now. Not ever. Do you have *any* idea what you put me through? You tore out my heart and you just let them beat me. Damn you, Sasha, don't even pretend you didn't know what they were doing to me. You knew everything going on. You had too many contacts not to know. You *let* them." She was sick again. Her stomach was protesting, a sickness that never seemed to go away no matter how many antacids she took.

"I didn't know until it was too late and then I moved heaven and earth to get you out fast. And damn it, you know why."

She covered her face with her hands. "I don't want to think about it. I don't want to *ever* think about it. I may as well have pulled the trigger myself. That poor man and his poor wife. I have to live with the responsibility of his death. I know that, but I didn't deserve what you did to me. If that's your idea of punishment . . ."

"Stop!" For the first time he raised his voice in a string of Russian curses. "It wasn't a punishment. You were never responsible for the death of that man. There were all kinds of things leading up to it, none of which you had a hand in. His death was a terrible tragedy, and one I regret, but it had nothing to do with you." He forced his body to relax, forced air through his lungs. "Is that what you really think? That I was punishing you?"

"You left me completely alone. I know you deserted me when I needed you most. You turned me over to the authorities and you let them interrogate me. You knew what that meant and you did nothing about it."

"How do you think you got out of the country? You aren't rotting in prison. You were deported and out of the country within days of your arrest. Do you think that really happens in Russia? If you believed I deserted you, why didn't you accuse me? Why didn't you name me when they were asking for information?"

Abigail sank down onto the edge of the bed. "I don't know. I didn't know what would happen to you." She shook her head again. "I thought I deserved how they treated me after what happened. I should have known he felt guilty because of his daughter's death, not that he *was* guilty. I shouldn't have had any preconceived notions when I went into that room. Everyone sounded so certain he'd murdered her, that he was the one who was killing those children, but I shouldn't have let that influence me. You were asking him so many questions, firing them at him over and over, and the other cops were doing the same. He acted guilty. He wanted to confess something. Anything. When I asked if he was guilty and he said yes, I *felt* it was wrong, but I was so busy listening to the officers, to you." She broke off and covered her face again. "I betrayed my own gift. I asked the wrong questions and he confessed his guilt, just as I led him to do. And then he reached for the gun that stupid officer had sitting there so conspicuously."

"If we drove him to commit suicide we were all to blame, not you," he said.

"*If? If?* There is no if. He was made to believe he was guilty for the loss of his child. No one comforted him. No one counseled him. He felt guilty because he was watching her while his wife was away and he fell asleep. He took a nap."

"He was drinking. He drank too much and he went to sleep in the afternoon."

"Does that absolve what we did to him? He wasn't the killer, but you suspected he wasn't. You suspected it even when you brought him in for questioning, didn't you?"

"We always look at the parents first."

"But you didn't tell me your suspicions. You already had a suspect."

"I had no evidence, Abbey. I had to follow procedure. I brought the parents in and questioned him just as I would any other suspect."

"But you didn't believe he was guilty. Everyone was hammering away at him and I just joined in." Abbey bit at her knuckles in agitation. Night after night she saw the man's face and her own hands covered in his blood. "I helped kill him."

"Damn it, Abbey. He shot himself. We question suspects all the time. They don't kill themselves."

"You can absolve yourself of all responsibility, Aleksandr, but I can't. And what you did to me afterward is inexcusable, and it isn't the actions of a man in love. You may want to sleep with me, but I'm not willing to settle for that."

"Far more was going on in that room than either of us knew." He pushed a hand through the dark waves of his hair. "I had risen through the ranks fast and solved cases and had come to the attention of my superiors quickly. I had a background in . . ." He hesitated. "I was a very successful operative before I was a police officer. I became a detective when others had worked many years to get there. I also had people in high places owing me favors. I knew how to get through red tape and move around power struggles. When that happens, you step on toes and make enemies you aren't always aware of."

Abigail struggled to breathe, to think beyond that traumatic moment when the young father had reached for the gun. She hadn't been able to stop time or slow it down or relive the minutes before he had pulled the trigger.

"That officer, the one who let him near his gun, was waiting for his opportunity. He worked for a man named Leonid Ignatev. My career had surpassed Ignatev's and he took advantage of every mistake I made and every vulnerability I had to sabotage my career. I knew he was dirty. I suppose we all are to some extent, we have to work deals all the time to get anywhere, but Ignatev was in bed with the mafia. He had his plant on my team and when things were chaotic, as they often are in an interrogation, his man allowed the suspect to take his gun. I should have known what was going on when he wasn't arrested immediately too, but I was focused on you. I was certain my name would keep you safe, but Ignatev had his men working on you."

Abigail took a deep breath and looked at him. "And then it stopped, very abruptly after two days, and the new men were very subdued and I could smell their fear. That was even more frightening. You did that, didn't you?" Her heart was pounding now, so hard her chest hurt. She didn't want the truth because she couldn't face that part of him. She knew he was ruthless, but she didn't know if she could look at how deep that trait ran in him. The men interrogating her had whispered among themselves, casting glances her way, obviously very frightened of even talking with her. She had been afraid, at first, that she was going to be shot "accidentally," but then she heard Aleksandr's name whispered and the things they said had terrified her.

"I did what I had to do to protect you and get you safely out of the country. In doing so, I made a bitter, relentless enemy and he retaliated by putting out a hit on me."

Abigail shook her head. She didn't want to know what he'd done to get her out of the country. She'd been glad to go and was grateful she had gotten out, but she was very much afraid it had cost lives and she already had enough blood on her hands.

"Aleksandr, how can you be so calm about it? How can you sit there calmly and tell me someone is going to try to kill you?"

"It's a way of life, Abbey. It's the only way I know."

"Well, it sucks."

"Quite possibly."

He was looking at her with his heart in his eyes. Not pleading. Aleksandr never pleaded, but all the same, he looked at her as if she belonged to him. She shook her head fiercely. "It isn't my world. I can't live like that and you can't take back everything that happened. You just can't."

"I'm not trying to take it back. There were mistakes, I'll admit that, but we have to find our way back to one another. I know you don't love Jonas Harrington. And I can't look at other women. What are we doing apart?"

Abigail shook her head, her hand going defensively to her heart. "There is no way back. I'm not willing to risk who and what I am again. I don't trust you enough to hand either my life or my magic over to you again."

"Damn it, Abbey. You had to have understood I couldn't be implicated in any way. In my country there is always a scapegoat. I was so close to catching the killer. If I were removed from the case, he would have had months, maybe years to continue. It took me so long to even get close to him."

"Whatever you did afterward to get me out of the country, I'm grateful for, but you *gave* me to them. You sacrificed me."

"There was no other choice. You would be detained and interrogated, but I knew with my contacts I could get you free and out of the country immediately. It never occurred to me that Ignatev would choose that opportunity to strike at me. It should have, but it didn't." Aleksandr could see the hurt on her face. It ran deep and he hated that he'd been the one to put it there. "I was so close, Abbey, to catching that child killer. I could reach out and touch him, I was that close. If I had come forward everything would have been lost and I would have been responsible for any children he killed after that. My every instinct was to protect you first, to protect *you,* my heart and soul, but it would have been selfish."

"How was it selfish to tell the truth? You saved your career and you obviously got a promotion. You're working with Interpol so you're still in good standing. You weren't the one being slapped and kicked in that interrogation room. You weren't the one with that poor man's blood all over your clothes. They didn't even let me change. It doesn't really matter that you thought I'd be all right. You let them take me. It was a betrayal whether you want to see that or not. *You let them take me.*"

"Damn it, Abbey." Aleksandr rubbed his face hard to rid himself of the image of her, crying, covered in bloodstains, two men towering over her to intimidate her, shouting at her, accusing her. "If it hadn't been for those children, don't you think I would have stepped forward right away?"

"I don't know, Aleksandr. How could I know? I lived through hell and I couldn't even come home and get comfort from my sisters. How could I tell them what I'd done, what I'd been responsible for? A man died because of me. I used my gifts for something I should never have been involved with because of you. Because I loved you and I would have done anything for you. Because I believed in you.

You took everything away from me. Even this." She spread her arms wide to encompass her home. "You left me nothing."

He touched her because he had to, even though he knew she would flinch away from him. "I never meant to hurt you."

"Well, you did. You destroyed me. I don't know why you're here, Aleksandr, the real reason, and I'm not going to ask you. I don't use that part of me *ever*. For any reason. My gift is flawed, or perhaps it's me, but it's more harmful than good." Abbey leapt up before he could stop her and paced across the room again. "I don't understand how the house let you in."

"The door was wide open. I'm telling you, Abbey, it's dangerous. You have to have tight security around here until we figure out what Prakenskii is doing here."

"The house would never allow an enemy in. We were careless once and nearly were killed. Even Aunt Carol helped us tonight and she's very powerful." She was talking more to herself than to him.

"I am not your enemy. Even your damned house knows that, Abbey. Will you pay attention to what's important? Put aside your anger toward me for long enough to understand that you're in danger. Your sisters could be in danger. Prakenskii wouldn't be here scouting out your home if someone weren't interested in you, even if it is because of your relationship to me. And his friends are not nice."

"I don't suppose they are. I'll be careful, Aleksandr." She had to remember to call him by his more formal name rather than the more intimate Russian form. She could so easily be swept away by him. He was a strong man, tough and hard inside and out, even lethal, yet with her he had always been so loving and gentle and protective. He said things to her that sounded like sheer poetry . . . until she needed him. And then, when it mattered the most, he had denied everything between them and left her alone to be terrified and humiliated. "Now please go. Whatever you really came here for, I want no part of it."

Aleksandr sighed. Her soft mouth was set in a stubborn line and no matter what he said, she wouldn't hear him. She wouldn't let herself hear him. "I'll go, Abbey, but this isn't over between us."

He put his shoes on again, taking his time while she watched him in silence. "I'm not going to just quietly go away. This isn't over between us." He stood up, towering over her. "Take some precautions. All of you. Make the others understand these people play for keeps."

"I said I would. Go out the door. I'll walk you down." The thought of him climbing down the side of the house was frightening.

"I'll go out the same way I came in." He walked right up to her. Abbey didn't back up, but then he knew she wouldn't. Abbey was a strong woman and she didn't let too many things threaten her. "Stay away from Harrington until we work this out."

Abigail could hardly breathe with him so close to her. "I'm not going to dignify that with a response."

He bent his head toward her upturned face until their lips were a breath apart. "You know me better than any person alive. You know the truth about who and what I am. I gave you the truth when you asked for it. I said I loved you with everything in me. I don't love easily, but I love completely. I want you back, Abbey, and I'm going to do whatever it takes."

For a moment she thought he was going to kiss her. She could see it in his eyes. The need. The longing. But he turned and left her bedroom.

4

"JOLEY, come on. Wake up!" Abbey shook her sister.

Joley groaned and pulled the covers over her head. "Are you crazy? It's still dark. I *never* get up this early. It isn't sane."

"Get up. You have to come with me."

"Abbey, you're freakin' crazy. Go back to bed. I'm definitely *not* getting up before the sun is up. Noon. Wake me at noon."

"Not noon . . . now! I think one of my dolphins is hurt. I want to go take a look at him."

Joley pulled down the cover so she could glare at her sister. "You *think* he's hurt? It's freezing cold in the ocean. And there are sharks. It isn't happening. Haven't you heard? I'm an honest-to-God celebrity. I don't do mornings."

"Get your butt out of bed." Abbey ripped off the blanket and hit Joley over the head with a pillow. "You aren't the star of anything in this house. I need someone with me and you're elected."

"Why me?" Joley wailed, sitting up.

"Because, aside from Hannah, you have the skills I need. And if something goes wrong, Hannah's not a strong swimmer."

"Great, that sounds ominous. Well the least you could have done was get me a cup of tea. *And* you could tell me about your mysterious visitor last night. Sheesh, it was hell trying to get to sleep wondering."

"I don't want to talk about him. Not now. Maybe never."

"Great. That's great, Abbey, wake me up and don't even give me any good gossip. I don't do mornings."

"I hear the dolphins calling me, Joley," Abbey said. "Something's wrong."

"Oh, all right. But you owe me big-time. And so do the dolphins. You can tell them you're going to bring me swimming with you when you go out next and they have to be nice and accept me." Joley trudged across the floor to the bathroom. "Do I need a wet suit?"

"No, but you might want to bring a gun."

Joley stuck her head around the door, her toothbrush in her mouth. "A gun?" Her face brightened considerably. "Why do I need a gun? Who do I get to shoot?"

"You don't *get* to shoot anyone, you nut. It's only just in case. That, and you're a good shot."

"Better than Hannah," Joley acknowledged. "She closes her eyes when she squeezes the trigger. It drives Jonas up the wall."

"That's probably why she does it, although she can hit a target dead center nine times out of ten. You just happen to hit dead center every time. And Hannah wouldn't actually kill anyone and you would."

"It might be you if you ever drag me out of bed this early again," Joley warned. "But I would forgive you if you'd give me gossip about your midnight caller. . . ." She looked hopeful. When Abbey shook her head and frowned at her, Joley sighed and capitulated. "Where are we going? I thought your boat was floating out at sea somewhere, or did Jonas have it towed in?"

"Of course Jonas had the boat towed; he always takes care of every little detail. But the dolphins are in Sea Lion Cove so you won't have to go out in a boat if we're lucky."

"That's good. Do I really need a gun?"

"Yes. And you might have to use it. Some hotshot hit man was skulking around last night."

"Good God, Abbey, we need to call Jonas." Joley dragged on a pair of sweatpants and a heavy shirt. "What in the world have you gotten yourself involved with? I'm the one usually in trouble. You're the good girl."

Abbey studied her sister. "How do you manage to look like you do first thing in the morning? No makeup, you haven't even combed your hair, and you're in sweats, yet you manage to look like a million bucks. I swear, you and Hannah did something right in another life. I wouldn't mind waking up and looking like you."

Joley blew her a kiss. "That's a nice thing to say, especially after you didn't have the decency to bring me a cup of tea. If you aren't taking out a boat, how are we going to get down to the cove? Are we climbing down the cliffs? My rock-climbing skills leave something to be desired."

"I thought we'd use the old smugglers' route. I have a key to the old mill. Kate's renovating it with Matt's help, although they're so busy with their wedding plans they haven't done much work on it yet. There's an old stairway leading through the tunnel to the cove. Kate told me it was an old smugglers' route a hundred years ago or something like that. I didn't want to take the time to drive to the harbor, so the stairs will be the quickest way."

"Why is it I feel like we're about to get into big trouble?" Joley asked as she pulled a gun from her top drawer, loaded it, and slipped it into her purse.

"Why do you have your own gun?" Abbey asked. "I thought we'd use the one Jonas left here for protection, or maybe one of Sarah's."

"Because I get weird letters from crazed fans that scare the hell out of me sometimes," Joley answered. "I told you, now confess everything." She tiptoed down the stairs, following close on Abigail's heels. "Start with the hot Russian you may or may not be engaged to. From there, go to the hotshot hit man."

Abbey paused on the stairs. "What do you mean you get weird letters from crazed fans? You said something at Christmas about that. What's going on?"

Joley shrugged. "It comes with the territory. Hannah's a well-known model and she gets them. Kate writes books and she's had a few. I sell a few million albums and get out on a stage and sing to forty or fifty thousand people at a time and I receive them as well. It isn't a big deal, but sometimes it gets to me."

"Good grief. I had no idea. Have you told Sarah? She has tons of experience. She worked in security forever. And what about Jonas? He'd have an idea or two."

Joley laughed. "He'd make us all quit and hide in a closet. The point is, we're in the public eye where disturbed people can fixate on us and then threaten us for who knows what reason. A perceived slight maybe. But you work out in the ocean with dolphins. Hotshot hit men shouldn't be interested in you."

"No, they shouldn't. Maybe it was one of you he was interested in." Abigail frowned. "I didn't think of that because the man who was killed yesterday was Russian and the men who killed him were obviously Russian. Aleksandr is Russian and works for Interpol and something big is obviously happening around here. I was going to call Jonas, but have to see if I can help the dolphins first. They saved my life. And if Gene lives, they saved his life too."

Joley followed Abbey out of the house. "Why would the Russians even be remotely interested in you—or me, for that matter? I can't imagine our little Hannah or Kate getting them riled up. And how in the world did you meet that incredibly good-looking Aleksandr?"

"Remember when I was diving in Patagonia, studying dusky dolphins?" Abigail replied. She opened the front door with stealth, not wanting to wake her other sisters. "Joley, do you think the binding spells we use on the house work? Remember the time Sarah was guarding Damon, before they were engaged, and those men broke in and were going to shoot us?"

"We certainly got off the subject quick," Joley groused. "Every time I want an answer to something you just slide right onto another subject. What does that have to do with the hot Russian?"

"Don't call him hot. I don't want to think about him being hot or cold or anything else. I wish he'd go back to Russia." Abigail toed one of the two bags she had packed and had waiting on the steps. "Here, you take this one. It's not that heavy."

Joley picked it up and glared at her sister. "Are you out of your mind? This thing weighs a ton. And it doesn't exactly leave my gun hand free. If we get shot dead, don't you go blaming me. And for your information, Patagonia is *not* part of Russia." She carried the bag to the car, muttering every inch of the way.

"Are you always like this?"

"Like what?" Joley stuffed the bag in the backseat and frowned at Abigail.

"Whine, whine, whine."

"Yes. At three o'clock in the morning with no tea or coffee, yes absolutely I whine. Humans aren't meant to wake up before noon and if you want me to be pleasant, come talk to me then." Joley slid into the passenger seat and crossed her arms.

"You are such a baby. Put your seat belt on. And for your information, it isn't three in the morning, it happens to be six-thirty."

Joley shrugged. "Same difference. And if you want cooperation, get back to the hot Russian. It's the only subject worth discussing."

"Believe me, he isn't worth discussing. Don't go falling for him, either."

Joley snorted. "I don't fall for men. I run as fast and as far as I can. I am *not* about to get all gooey-eyed like Kate and Sarah." She shuddered. "The idea is downright scary." The teasing glint faded from her eyes. "Why are you worried about the house?"

"It let him in. Last night. All of us lit the candles and performed the ritual to bind the house, but he was able to get in. Even Aunt Carol helped and she's very powerful. Elle and you and Hannah all can cast and yet the house let him in."

Joley glanced sideways at Abigail and then away. She cleared her throat. "Him? The Russian?" Joley kept her tone casual.

"Yes, of course the Russian." Abbey bit the admission out through clenched teeth. The fog had drifted in as it often did in the early morning and lay heavy over the twisting highway. She drove slowly, not taking any chances, when she felt like racing to get away from the implications of her home's acceptance of the Interpol agent. "The house allowed him entry after *all* of us linked together to put a binding spell on it. Our magic isn't working."

"That would be one explanation," Joley ventured cautiously.

Abigail's fingers tightened around the steering wheel until her knuckles grew white. "It's the *only* explanation. I'll have to let the others know the house isn't safe."

"The house doesn't keep all people out, Abbey. Sarah and Kate's fiancés can come and go with the doors locked. Don't you remember how the padlocked gate swung open for Damon the first time he came to meet Sarah?"

"I met Aleksandr *before* the prophecy began unfolding and in any case, Matt and Damon are *engaged* to Sarah and Kate. That's *completely* different." Abigail glared at Joley, daring her to continue the conversation.

"Hmmm." Joley studied her fingernails. "I do believe I heard a rumor you were engaged to this man."

"Do shut up. I can't drive with you annoying me."

Joley laughed as they turned onto the long drive leading up to the old mill. "You seem to have managed just fine, if you ask me."

"Which I didn't." Abigail parked the car as close to the old building as she could. The mill had been for sale for years, until their sister had recently decided to purchase it. The sprawling building overlooked Sea Lion Cove and had once been a small but thriving lumber mill hiding the much more lucrative business of smuggling. The mill had tremendous history behind it. Kate Drake wanted to preserve as much of the old building as possible when she renovated it into her bookstore and coffee shop. Once the renovations were complete, a large deck and a floor-to-ceiling wall of glass facing the ocean would offer a breathtaking view of California's rugged coast.

"Do you ever wish you were normal, Joley?" Abigail asked as she pulled a heavy case from the car.

Joley shrugged, watching Abigail's face carefully. "What's normal, Abbey? We have each other and that's what really matters in the long run. We have our aunts and our parents and cousins. Our family is different, yes, and maybe we pay a price for our gifts, but the good outweighs the bad." She reached into the backseat and lifted out the other case. "You've been carrying a burden for some time. Don't you think it's time to share it with us?"

Abigail looked away from her, her body going stiff with rejection. "I'm not ready yet, Joley."

"That's all right, Abbey," Joley said. "Just remember we love you and no matter what's wrong, we'll find a way to help."

Abigail blinked back tears. "I took my magic for granted for so long, Joley. Don't do that. Don't think you can just get comfortable with it and just use it without thought." She turned her face away from her sister toward the sea. "Do you hear them?"

Joley had a million questions but she pressed her lips together and nodded. Abigail seemed fragile to her. Way too fragile. She was going to have to talk to Libby and see if she could help ease whatever trouble Abigail was carrying. Joley was suddenly very afraid for her sister. She swallowed every question and sought for something to say that would lift the sudden tension. "I think I do hear them, Abbey. I remember all your work, listening for hours with headphones and scanning your video footage all the time, but I never paid that much attention. They sound like clicks and whistles, don't they?"

Abigail unlocked the door to the mill. "Each sound is used for a variety of reasons. All of them seem to have a signature whistle, rather like their name. I think it identifies the individual and they call to one another using that specific whistle. Many of the researchers believe, like me, that they do communicate on a much greater scale than we first thought."

"They have their own language?" Joley had hit on the right thing to say. Abigail was so devoted to the dolphins and her research that her tone had brightened considerably.

"I think they do, but it certainly isn't anything like our language."

"They always seem so intelligent and happy. Whenever I see them I have this crazy urge to dive into the ocean and join them. And you know me and the ocean."

"Just keep in mind that they are wild, Joley. Dolphins can be aggressive and they certainly could hurt someone given the right circumstances. All too often people misinterpret what a dolphin is doing simply because they seem to be smiling."

"Well, I'm not really planning to dive into the sea with them," Joley admitted. "I just meant the impulse is there. I know you do it, but I like to keep my distance from anything weighing more than I do."

Abbey grinned at her sister. "That includes men?"

"Damn straight. Ever since that gate opened and the prophecy started unfolding I'm not even dating. I'm not even looking! Not me. No way. No how," Joley declared. She watched as Abigail unlocked a second door leading down into the basement. "Isn't that where the earthquake cracked the seal and allowed that spirit to escape?" She shivered. "I really need a cup of tea."

"All this time I thought you were the adventurous one."

"I'm *very* adventurous after twelve in the afternoon," Joley pointed out. "And I really rock after midnight."

Abigail laughed. "Be careful on these stairs; they're old and crumbling. Kate told me there's a place where the tunnel caved in but we can get through the rubble."

"How exciting," Joley said, rolling her eyes. "You owe me so big-time for this." She made her way down the basement stairs and waited while Abigail searched for the entry to the tunnel that led to the cove.

"Have you ever met a man you considered marrying?" Abbey asked.

Joley tossed her head. "Not likely. No one could stand me. I'm too mean."

Abbey laughed. "You really are a nut. You don't let anyone push you around, but you're one of the nicest people I know."

Joley blew her a kiss. "Thanks, Abbey, but since I happen to know you don't know very many people—in fact, you shun people—that isn't much of a testimonial."

"I don't shun people. They shun me." Abigail found the entrance and stepped through, wrinkling her nose. "It smells musty and fishy in here. And we'll need a flashlight."

"I brought a gun, not a flashlight." Joley bumped into her sister as Abbey stopped to drag a flashlight from her bag. "I should have known you'd be prepared."

"Naturally."

"People don't shun you, Abbey," Joley said. She glanced nervously into the tunnel, then took a deep breath and followed Abigail.

"Yes, they do. Wouldn't you if you weren't my sister? Do you remember all those years in school when I couldn't quite control my gift? All I had to do was accidently use the word *truth* and everyone within hearing distance would give the truth to me. Kids blurted out all kinds of things around me that they didn't want known. Would you want to risk your deepest darkest secret? Look what happened when Inez roped me into joining the Christmas pageant committee last year. I caused a huge scandal."

"That wasn't your fault. That spirit had escaped and was wreaking havoc on all our gifts. You used the word *truth* in a room and Sylvia Fredrickson's lover confessed they were having an affair."

"It was so horrible. Two marriages broke up over that. And Sylvia slapped me in front of everyone."

"You should have decked her." Joley picked her way through the rubble of debris on the narrow stone stairs. "It's wet and moldy down here. Ew."

"I did cause it to happen. She went to school with us and she knew very well I did it," Abigail said with a small sigh. "I didn't really blame her for being angry."

"She's the one who was having the affair with a man whose wife was about to give birth. Sylvia's always after somebody else's husband," Joley replied with a little sniff. "And if she's the one shunning you, count yourself lucky."

"It's wet down here." Abbey played the light over the wall of the tunnel. Most of it was rock, but there was one section where water seeped out and dripped onto the stairs, making them slick. "Watch your step right here. It looks as if someone fell."

Joley stiffened. "What do you mean, someone fell? Katie and Matt haven't been down here yet. Matt was going to close it off. He thought it was dangerous to keep the stairs. Did he come down here?"

"Either that, or the Russians are using this route to smuggle something into the country," Abbey said.

"That's not funny. Maybe I ought to get the gun out of my purse."

"Actually, I'm not joking," Abigail said, halting to study the skid marks in the slimy mud. "This happened fairly recently. We'll have to ask Matt if he's been down here, which is entirely possible, so let's not panic."

"I wasn't going to panic," Joley protested. "I was going to get out the gun. I really didn't like the sound of a hotshot hit man. No one's been in this tunnel for years, Abbey. And no one has access to the cove. You don't really think they're smuggling something through here, do you?"

"It's a possibility we have to consider."

"Great, Jonas is going to turn into the mad, tyrannical dictator. He'll lose his mind over you going to the cove, Abbey."

"What do you mean, *me* going to the cove? *You're* with me."

Joley laughed. "Jonas doesn't expect me to exhibit any sense. I was smart enough to carefully cultivate the appearance of being a complete ditz. You, however, have all those impressive letters after your name and write papers published in journals and generally are expected to have tremendous sense at all times." She peered closely at the scuff marks. "Matt's a big man. Does it look like it could have been him?"

"It's impossible to tell." Abbey met her sister's gaze. "Look, Joley. I didn't expect this. I think one of the dolphins was shot last night. They risked their lives to save me and I have to go to the cove and try to help, but you don't. Why don't you go back to the house and call Jonas and let him know what's going on? I don't think anyone's here, but it's better to play it safe."

"You're out of your mind if you think I'm leaving you here, Abbey. Just get moving. I'm too bullheaded to be afraid. I get mad when people threaten me or someone I love, you know that. I mean it, get moving."

Abbey touched Joley's arm. "Thanks, Joley. I can't leave the dolphin if he's in need of medical help. They've come into the cove—they like the shallow water—and I'll be able to treat him. Another few steps and we should be nearly to the beach. Let me go first just in case. When I know everything's all right, I'll call you."

"I'm coming with you."

Abbey shone the light along the bottom stairs. It was useless to argue with Joley once she made up her mind to do something. And truthfully, Abigail was grateful for her presence. She followed the stairway all the way down to a narrow entryway that opened into a natural cave. The ceiling had been painstakingly carved out until one could walk stooped over to gain entrance to the cave. Early morning sunlight filtering through the cave's mouth provided enough illumination for them to see where they were going without the flashlight. The sound of the sea mixed with the whistles and chirps of the dolphins. The wind blew steadily and salt spray dashed against the rocks along the caves.

"It's a beautiful morning," Abbey said.

Joley rubbed her nose and grinned at her sister. "I haven't seen one in a while. Yes, it is." The sun had risen over the water, scattering rays of gold and silver along the surface to form gleaming pools in the cove, shimmering with invitation. "No wonder you spend so much time in the sea."

Abbey caught her arm before she could step out of the cave. "Let's be careful. Do you see those tracks in the mud? Several people have been here recently."

"Could be kids."

"Maybe. Maybe not." Abbey looked carefully around the cove. The beach appeared deserted. Out in the water, several dolphins spy-hopped. One called to her, using her signature whistle. "Stay here, Joley, and cover me."

Joley put down the case she was carrying and fished her gun out of her purse, all business. "Be careful, Abbey. And if I yell, you hit the ground."

"Will do." Abbey picked up both cases and strode out over the coarse sand. She examined every nook and cranny, every hiding hole she could see as she walked to the water's edge. Once there, she allowed her gaze to travel upward to examine the cliff above the cove.

When Abigail was positive she was alone in the cove, she signaled the all-clear to Joley and waited for her sister to join her.

Joley stared in awe at the sleek heads bobbing in the ocean. "I've never seen so many dolphins."

"They're beautiful, aren't they?" Abbey waded out into the shallow water, whistling softly. "Keep a watch on the cave and the cliffs, Joley. I'm going to call Kiwi in." She took a last look around the cliffs and out to sea, searching for a boat that might be concealed in the rocks and ensuring there were no spectators. She lifted her arm and made a small circling motion and then brought her hand back toward her as she repeated a strange high-pitched whistle. "Kiwi is coming in."

The large male dolphin swam into the shallows, until he was in about a foot of water. Abigail waded the rest of the way out to him. Joley held her breath. The dolphin was enormous up close and very powerful looking. Abigail talked soothingly and ran her hands over the dolphin while she examined the wound.

"How bad, Abbey?" Joley called. She had a clear view of the dolphin's eye. It was definitely intelligent and seemed to be nervous as it watched Joley. "It doesn't like me here, does it?"

Abbey rolled the animal gently in the surf to get a better angle on the wound. "It's not that. He feels very vulnerable. They seem to be able to know when we all join together so I doubt he's upset that you're here. I've been trying to figure out how the dolphins know when we reach out to one another."

"Energy? We can feel the energy, maybe they can."

"Maybe," Abigail mused. "Kiwi's wounds aren't too bad, but he'll need the antibiotics I brought. The bullet shaved the skin off my back and shoulders, and Kiwi's wound seems much like mine. We were both lucky."

"Libby will want to take a look at you this morning, Abbey. She isn't going to leave your treatment to a paramedic."

"I don't want her to waste her strength on me. It hurts a bit, but nothing I can't handle. My leg is worse."

"Did a shark really bite you?"

"No! Of course not, and it wasn't an attack." Abbey quickly opened her bag and dragged out a thick salve and a bottle of pills. "A shark has rough skin and I think he just raked me as he made a pass."

Joley made a face. "Don't talk about it. I'm always afraid when you go swimming with the dolphins. I used to have nightmares about some sea creature dragging you down into a watery grave."

"Really?" Abbey laughed. "I've always loved the sea and found it a wonderful fantasy land. It's interesting and different every single day. I like that there's an aspect of danger and I have to be alert all the time."

"Abbey, what are you doing?" Joley watched as her sister smeared a thick paste over the wound and then crouched down in the water near the dolphin's head.

"I'll have to treat him several times to make certain this doesn't get infected. Joley, it's important you don't repeat the hand signals I used to call him to me, or the whistles and chirps. He trusts me, but if that trust were broken, I wouldn't be able to have any kind of a working relationship with him or a friendship."

"I'm not about to break the code of silence," Joley said, "but I have to object to you putting your hand in that dolphin's mouth. It has more teeth than a shark." Alarm spread fast as she watched Abigail's hand disappear into the open mouth. "What are you doing?"

"Giving him antibiotics orally. He needs a combination. Don't worry."

"Please take your hand out of there before I flip out and scream or something equally sissy lala. You're really scaring me, Abbey. I'd rather have the Russian hit man try something."

"He's being so trusting and good," Abigail said. "Aren't you, Kiwi?" She signaled to him that she was finished. "He's such a steady dolphin. They're all different. Some of them are much more nervous and high-strung. I'm sending him back out to sea, but most likely they'll stay in the shallows. I just don't want anyone noticing and bothering them. Kids can be silly and sometimes cruel. I'd be really upset if someone threw sticks in their blowholes. It's happened in some of the places I've been and I can't seem to control my temper."

Joley laughed softly. "You wouldn't have to worry. If you told Hannah, they'd only do it the one time and she'd do something spectacular to teach them a lesson. Word is, Sylvia has this recurring rash on the left side of her face. It shows up in the form of a handprint every time she flirts."

Abigail rolled her eyes. "Didn't Hannah remove that?"

"She says only Sylvia can by doing the 'right' thing."

"What is that? She can't help flirting. Flirting defines who she is."

"I think Hannah expects her to apologize to you."

"The world will come to an end first. Sylvia has never apologized to anyone for as long as I can remember, and we went to kindergarten together." Abigail watched the other dolphins as they moved around Kiwi. "I want to get a couple of shots of them with him. They know I've put something on his wounds." She pulled her camera out of her bag. "Do you mind staying a little longer, Joley?"

Joley shook her head, a small grin on her face. Abigail was already shooting away with the camera, snapping pictures like a madwoman, doing their aunt Carol proud, wading out into the water to her waist to get better shots, oblivious of the cold water soaking her jeans.

The wind came in off the sea and the gulls took flight, circling above them as the dolphins began to form small groups and go off in different directions to hunt for food. "Look what they're doing," Abigail said, obviously excited. "See how they leap and spy-hop? They're communicating where the hunt is on. See how they're herding the fish into a smaller and tighter ball? They're calling in the others."

"What the hell are you doing, Abigail?" The voice broke the early morning silence, thick with ire and Russian accent.

Abigail nearly dropped her camera in the water, juggling it to keep it from falling. She spun around to face Aleksandr Volstov. He looked handsome. Clean. Immaculate in a suit. Not in the least rumpled or wet. Even his hair was combed. "Great. How did you get down here? You're on private property."

"I ought to shake you. You have about as much sense as a crab."

Joley coughed delicately, earning her a glare from her sister.

"Don't you ever sleep, Aleksandr?" Abigail demanded. "Sheesh, Joley. What good are you with that gun? Why didn't you just shoot him? I brought you along for a reason and it wasn't to be staring at the scenery. You were supposed to be on guard. I thought you were going to shoot anyone who came near us."

"You have a gun?" Aleksandr demanded, his accent so thick they could barely understand him. "I would be asleep if I didn't have to worry about you ignoring every warning I give you. Damn it, Abbey, what the hell is wrong with you? Do you have a death wish?"

"No, I have a gun," she replied calmly. "We were very careful. What did you expect me to do? Crawl into a hole because you claim some hit man might be gunning for me? I have important work to be done. I have a life here. I have two sisters who are about to get married and we're planning a double wedding. I'm not slinking around my own backyard because someone may want me dead. You're an Interpol agent. Go arrest him and stop bugging me."

"Go, Abbey!" Joley cheered. She stepped forward and stuck out her hand. "I'm Joley Drake, by the way, one of Abbey's many sisters. I saw you last night but we weren't properly introduced."

"The singer," Aleksandr said. "I have heard you on the radio. Your voice is beautiful."

"Thank you."

Abbey made a growling noise. "Why are you being nice to him? You're *my* sister. Don't let his charm fool you."

"I was admiring his shoulders and chest more than his charm," Joley admitted, winking at the Russian. "Besides, didn't I hear that you're engaged to him?"

"I am *not* engaged to him."

"Yes, you are," Aleksandr said. "You said yes when I asked you and you took my ring. I believe you still have it."

Joley stared at her sister with wide eyes. "Is that so?"

Aleksandr nodded. "It was a family heirloom. And in Russia we honor our word. She agreed to marry me and so we are engaged. We have only to get married."

"It was most definitely *not* a family heirloom, you liar. We bought it at that little shop. And we aren't getting married," Abigail corrected.

"Why not?" Joley asked.

"Because I absolutely *detest* him, that's why," Abigail said. "And if you keep coming on Drake property, Sasha, I'll have you arrested."

"By your boyfriend?" There was a distinct drop in the temperature of Aleksandr's voice. It went from warm to ice cold.

Joley shivered. "I thought you were her boyfriend."

"I'm her fiancé. Harrington is her boyfriend."

Joley stared at him with a mixture of shock and horror. She burst out laughing. "Boy, are you misguided. Seeing as how you're going to be family and all, I'll be happy to set you straight."

"I'm not in the least bit amused, Joley," Abigail said. "Do not say another word to him unless you're escorting him off the property. In fact, you're useless as a bodyguard. Give me the gun."

"Abbey, honey," Joley said, "as I recall you didn't hit the target one single time in all the practice sessions we had. You were too busy looking at the clouds or some strange little bug crawling across the ground."

"Well, I'm paying attention now."

"Harrington isn't her boyfriend?" Aleksandr asked, ignoring Abbey.

"Jonas? He's practically our brother," Joley said. "Abigail and Jonas aren't dating. He'd probably faint if you told him you thought they were. He loves us all dearly, and we love him, but we're not exactly the type of woman he dates."

"Does he date?" Abigail asked, distracted by the idea. "Who does he date?"

"Not you," Joley said. She eyed Aleksandr. "What did you do to my sister that made her detest you so much?" She glanced at Abbey. "Is he the one the house let in?"

Aleksandr sighed in exasperation. "Houses don't let people in them. Her balcony door was wide open in invitation to anyone at all."

Joley shook her head. "Our house is protected, Aleksandr. May I call you that? And it is a *big* thing if the house allowed you in the other night."

"Joley." Abigail's voice was very much a warning.

Every time she was near Aleksandr, she remembered how gentle he could be in spite of his size, how his smile could warm up his eyes. She didn't want to remember a single good thing about him. He had made her believe she could fit in, that her talent was as useful as all of her sisters' talents. He had made her believe she was lovable, that in spite of all her flaws, he would always be there. She knew what love was and refused to settle for less.

She turned away from them and withdrew into her own private world. She wanted to be in her beloved ocean swimming in a world of color and sound far away from where she was now. She heard the lapping of the waves as they rolled gently through the cove in invitation. She heard the cry of the gulls and chatter of the dolphins. The wind kissed her face as she stared up at the drifting clouds.

Cold water hit her in the face. Startled, she looked down at the dolphin only feet from where she stood. It spit water a second time. She became aware of the frantic clicks, of the bodies thrashing in the water instead of hunting food as they should have been. She slammed her shoulder hard into Aleksandr, calling out to Joley as she did so. Aleksandr was the biggest target and she needed to take him down.

He must have recognized the warning as well because at the exact same moment his arm curved out to sweep Joley into the water too. As the sea closed over them, Aleksandr rolled to cover the women with his larger body.

5

ALEKSANDR felt the impact of a bullet slamming into his back. He was wearing a vest, but the punch was hard enough to drive him against the churning sand. He'd had no time to take a breath before going under and he doubted if either of the Drake sisters had either. Abigail was tugging on his jacket sleeve so he followed her lead. She knew the cove better than anyone else and he had to rely on her judgment.

Just ahead of him, Abigail swam with strong, steady strokes out toward deeper water, moving among the dolphins to gain the rocks. His lungs burned and deep inside him, rage was a living, breathing entity. He had made many enemies, but to have someone shoot so close to Abigail was intolerable.

Abigail pointed to the dark shapes in front of her and tried to get past him to reach Joley. Aleksandr dragged Joley to the rocks and kept an arm firmly around Abigail. She wasn't going to get away from him and try anything as heroic and stupid as drawing fire while he hid.

Dragging air into his lungs, he kept his head down. "Are either of you hit?"

"No," Joley said, "and I managed to hang on to the gun."

The waves were stronger, pushing them against the rocks, so Aleksandr braced himself and held the two women away from the water-worn boulders. "We can't stay here. The force of the waves is going to crush us." They were all in heavy clothing. The only thing they had going for them was the fact that the channel was relatively shallow.

Abigail nodded her head in agreement. "There's a series of caves just over there." She pointed to the north side of the cove. "The entrance is underwater and it takes a bit to get to them. You'll feel claustrophobic and want to try to reach the surface, but you're swimming through a tube of rock and there's no way to get air. You'll both have to take a deep breath right before we try to enter the caves."

"Won't we be stuck there?" Joley asked. A frothy wave poured over her head, rolling her under. Aleksandr yanked her up before she crashed against the rocks. Joley spit water and coughed, but she was glaring toward the cliffs, more mad than afraid. "I don't want someone to wait for us in a boat or up on the cliffs. I'd rather take my chances in the sea."

"Joley. . . ." Abbey wiped sea spray from her face, feeling her sister's rebellion and reluctance. Joley was stubborn when she wanted to be and this wasn't the time.

"I'm *terrified* of closed-in places," Joley confessed. "I panic, Abbey. I'll never be able to do it. It was bad enough making myself use the stairs at the mill. And if we're trapped in the cave . . ."

"I'm sorry, hon, I should have remembered, but the caves are safer than trying for the cove. There's supposed to be an old tunnel that connects with Kate's smugglers' stairs. We'll try to find it and use that route to get back to the main road," Abigail explained. "It's our only chance if they're on the cliffs. We're targets in the sea, Joley." She didn't want to mention the fact that great white sharks frequented the area, drawn by the abundance of seals. The ocean was just too rough and cold and this particular section contained riptides. With the sharks, the rocks, and the vicious undertows, heading for open ocean would be serious trouble. They had to get to shelter.

A wave slammed Abigail against the rock before Aleksandr could reel her in. The air left her lungs in a rush and she threw her arms up, trying to find a purchase with her fingers on the slippery surface.

At once a barrage of bullets knocked chunks off the rock. Aleksandr pulled her to him, locking his arm around her to bind her to his chest. "Are you hit?"

She shook her head, plunging her arm into the cold water. The back of her hand stung where pieces of the rock had flown up and struck her. "We can't stay here. The waves are too strong. You're going to be exhausted trying to hold us, Sasha." Another wave was building and she slipped beneath the water, not taking chances on being crushed coming up after the wave had passed. They had to move. It was madness to stay trapped the way they were. She was furious with herself for getting Joley into such a mess. If anything happened to her . . . Abigail couldn't think about it. She had to get them to the caves.

Aleksandr struggled out of his jacket. His clothes were weighing him down and he had to reserve all of his strength to keep the two women from being slammed into the dangerous rocks. He signaled to Abigail to lead the way.

"Stay close," she cautioned Joley.

"I'm right behind you," Joley assured her, but there were tears in her eyes. The idea of swimming into a small cave and being unable to surface was beyond terrifying to her, but she wasn't about to hold Abigail back from safety.

Without warning, the wind rushed past them, heading from the sea to the cliffs, a fierce, howling gust of anger. Water spouted into the air, several whirling geysers. White foam capped the waves and debris from the sea was hurtled through the air onto land. The waves crashed high against the cliffs and splashed upward as if seeking prey. Seagulls screamed, gathering in the sky from every direction, and began to dive-bomb the cliff, plunging fast, straight downward, long wicked beaks stabbing at something moving fast along the top.

Joley and Abigail exchanged a long look. Both began to smile.

"Let me in on it," Aleksandr said, trying not to gasp as another wave nearly slammed all three into the rocks.

"Hannah woke up and she's royally pissed," Joley said. "Let's go while our hit man is otherwise occupied."

"That's definitely got a touch of Elle in it," Abbey said with satisfaction. "The seagulls are Elle's work. Hannah likes drama, but Elle goes for the throat." She dove under, kicking strongly to take her along the bottom toward the northern side of the cove.

Joely followed her, Aleksandr close behind. They stayed in communication through touch. The water was cold and Aleksandr feared hypothermia would set in before any of them realized it. Both Joley and Abigail were shivering continually although neither appeared to notice. He knew the adrenaline pumping through them would be giving them a false feeling of warmth.

He felt the brush of a larger body and was aware the dolphins were close as they swam along a shallow channel. Just as he was certain his lungs would burst, Abigail rose to the surface and drew a deep breath of air. Her anxiety was plain as she regarded her sister.

Joley's eyes were wide with horror. Aleksandr caught her to him. "Listen to me." He kept his voice gentle. "You can do this. When you feel panic because of the smallness of the space, concentrate on something else. Use lyrics of songs or poetry. Make up a song, and remember you are not alone. I'll be close enough to touch."

"I'll be in front of you, Joley," Abigail reassured her, "and I'd never leave you."

Joley regarded them both for a moment, then nodded. "I'm ready."

"A big breath," Abigail cautioned and once more went under.

Aleksandr shoved Joley ahead of him, propelling her through the cold waters into the underwater cave. His shoulders scraped as he went through the entrance. Abigail had been right when she said they might feel claustrophobic. Every instinct told him to get to the surface. He could feel rock above his head and on both sides. Worse, he couldn't turn around. If he felt that way, he knew Joley must be going through hell. He brushed his hand along her leg several times to reassure her. He concentrated on ensuring she made it through the watery darkness.

Abigail was aware time was running out on them. They'd been in the water too long and her body was becoming sluggish. Joley rarely went swimming in the ocean and she would tire easily. Abigail pushed herself, stroking through the disorienting tunnel to emerge in the small interior cave at the end. Her head broke the surface and she gasped for air even as she reached back to pull Joley up. Joley coughed and clung to Abigail as Aleksandr joined them.

Aleksandr helped both women out of the water. It was so dark that they had to feel their way to the water's edge to pull themselves onto the dry rocks. Fortunately, without the steady wind, it was a little warmer in the cave but Aleksandr was worried about both women. They were shaking uncontrollably. "We have to get you somewhere warmer," he said. "We need light to see what we're doing."

"There used to be a torch on the north wall," Abigail said, her teeth chattering. "A lighter was kept right under it, on the ground for any divers using the cave. It might still be there."

Aleksandr felt around until his hands encountered the torch. At the base lay the lighter. "Does everyone know about this cave?" He lit the torch to illuminate the small grotto the ocean had carved out of the rocks.

"Only a few divers and history buffs. I haven't been here in about five years, not since I did my research on the dolphins in this area." She rubbed her hands up and down Joley's arms to try to provide her with some warmth. "I've never used the stairs out of here, but I know the tunnel was intact five years ago."

"How come I'm the only one who doesn't know these things?" Joley asked. "I grew up here—you'd think I'd know about things like hidden caves."

"You were too busy singing, which is a good thing since you have a beautiful voice," Abbey pointed out, kicking at the small rocks she was worried Joley might stumble over. "Over here, Sasha. Can you bring the light?"

"And you spent all of your time in the sea," Joley said. "Aleksandr, thank you for helping me in the water. I didn't like not being able to see. For a moment I thought I'd have a heart attack and then you touched my leg and it was all right again."

"I was happy to help."

Abigail fell silent, staring down at something Joley couldn't see. "Aleksandr. You'd better take a look at this, because I think it's real and I don't want to touch it."

He came up beside her, real and solid, his body brushing hers. "What is it, Abbey?" His arm slid around her and he drew her beneath his shoulder. "You're freezing."

"You're wearing a vest."

"Which was a good thing, otherwise I'd be dead."

She turned her head sharply. "You were hit? Where? Let me see."

The anxiety in her voice turned his heart over. "It's nothing, *baushki-bau*, a bruise, no more. What have you found?"

"I don't know. Take a look."

Aleksandr crouched down to examine the necklace that had apparently been unknowingly dropped and was now half buried in rubble. Abigail took the opportunity to look at his back. There was definite evidence of a bullet hole in the vest he wore. Her heart nearly leapt out of her chest. She pressed a hand over the small hole and glanced at Joley. "I'm sorry, hon, I should never have asked you to come with me."

"Are you kidding? Aunt Carol is right. This is the adventure of a lifetime. We need pictures to put in our albums!" Joley tossed her wet hair and managed a smile through her chattering teeth. "How often do hotshot hit men from Russia try to kill you?"

"It couldn't have been Prakenskii," Aleksandr said as he carefully dug the necklace out of the rubble and lifted it reverently.

Joley put her hand on her hip. "Don't kill the fun here, Aleksandr. I'm trying to look on the bright side."

"You're turning blue, Joley. Let's get moving," Abigail said. "Why couldn't it have been Prakenskii? How many people are running around trying to shoot at us?"

"Evidently more than one." Aleksandr sounded vague. Distracted. "It wasn't Prakenskii or we'd all be dead."

"Good to know," Joley said. "I want to go now. I've had enough drama for the day. I haven't even had a cup of tea yet and people are shooting at me. I'm calling it quits. Find the stairs because I don't want to swim back through that black hole."

"The entrance is right over there." Abigail gestured, but her attention was on Aleksandr. "Just beyond Sasha. What is it? That thing is real, isn't it?"

"Yes." Aleksandr let his breath out slowly, staring down at the piece of history in his hands. "At least I think it is. I think it is a necklace that has been missing for years. In March 1917 Czar Nicolas II abdicated the throne of the Russian empire and a provisional government was set in place." The reverence spread to his voice. "The czar, his beloved wife, Empress Alexandra Feodrovna, and their five children were deported to Siberia. It was said that they had a small collection of jewels the czar kept for his wife. In 1918 the entire family and four of their faithful retainers were secretly executed."

"Well, of course I've heard the story," Abigail said, the back of her neck beginning to prickle. She and Joley exchanged a long look. "What does that story have to do with this necklace?"

Aleksandr straightened up, the heavy jewels in his hands. "It's rumored Nicolas commissioned a very special necklace for Alexandra before they were wed. In fact, she had refused him at some point because she had been made to feel less than welcome in Russia. The necklace was made of only the rarest and most perfect stones and was intended to show Alexandra how much the czar loved and admired her."

"Is that true?"

He shrugged. "Until now, the only proof I've ever seen that the necklace existed was a small painting. And that painting was stolen from a collection about four years ago. There were so many rumors that the necklace surfaced here or there, but no one actually could ever find the piece. You have no idea how many national treasures have been taken from our country. Pieces of our history that belong to our people." He shook his head and turned to look at them. "We were on the trail of artwork. If this is authentic, it is a find beyond anything I ever dreamed. This is a priceless treasure."

"But how would it have gotten in this cave?" Abigail asked.

"I think that's a very good question." The two shivering women caught Aleksandr's attention. "Forgive me, we must get you somewhere warm."

"We'll have to take the torch because we don't have a flashlight," Abigail said. "Come on, Joley, just a little bit more and we'll be warm."

Joley followed her sister to the entrance to the stairs. "You want me to go up that?" The steps were cut into the cliff itself, very narrow and steep, winding upward into the rock. It was dark and the overhead ceiling dripped in places and hung ominously low in others. She stepped back, shaking her head. "I'll face the hotshot hit man."

Abigail put her arm around Joley. "I know you don't like closed-in places, but the stairs should connect at some point with Kate's underground stair system and lead us to the basement of the old mill."

"Abbey can lead the way and I'll be right behind you," Aleksandr reassured Joley. "I will sing you a Russian song." He laughed softly. "A lullaby, it's all I know how to sing."

Joley took a deep breath and nodded. "I'm really not a chicken most of the time. I just have this problem with confined spaces."

"No one thinks you're a chicken, Joley," Abigail said. "Let's just get it over with. Hannah and Elle would have called Jonas and he'll be losing his mind out over the cliffs thinking we're dead or drowned." She started up the steep stone stairs, holding the torch with Joley's fist clenched in the hem of her wet shirt.

"If he calls search and rescue I'll be mortified," Joley said. "Can you imagine the tabloids? They'd have a field day."

"He won't call them until Hannah or Elle gives the word. They know we're alive," Abigail told her. "Sasha, are you going to sing or not?"

He cleared his throat. "I was only encouraging your sister. I'm not really going to sing in front of her."

"Now would be a good time, Aleksandr," Joley said.

He sighed. "I'll do it, but you must never tell anyone."

Abigail steeled herself for the sound of his voice when he sang. Years earlier, when she lay in his arms late at night, he had sung to her in his rich, wonderful voice. He always sang in his own language and she had never been able to resist him when he sang to her. The song was a traditional Cossack lullaby and she knew he was singing it deliberately to remind her. His voice seemed to vibrate through her body and touch every nerve ending until tears burned behind her eyelids and she had to blink rapidly to clear her vision.

"I understand a few of the words," Joley said. "Something about 'sleep my baby, my beautiful baby,' but then you use that word, the one you called Abbey. *Baushki-bau*. What does that mean?"

"There is no translation. It is an endearment. I often call her my beautiful baby as well, but she objects."

Abigail shook her head, not wanting to hear him. Not wanting to feel or remember what it had been like to be with him. To be held by him. He had always been so protective. . . . And that had been the biggest illusion of all.

"You have a beautiful voice. You should have been a singer," Joley said, astonished. "I'd love to sing something with you."

"It is enough that I will be able to sing our children to sleep."

Abigail clenched her fist around the torch. There would be no children with her. How many times had they talked about having children together? He wanted a big family because he'd never had one of his own. No siblings, no relatives. He would say he wanted five children of each sex and she would laugh and shake her head, trying to get him to settle for a much more reasonable number.

She had to change the subject, get him talking about something that didn't have any underlying personal meaning. He needed to go away where she couldn't breathe him in, feel him skin to skin against her body so vividly. "Tell us more about what happened to the necklace."

Joley tightened her fist in Abbey's shirt, a silent communication of understanding. She might tease Abigail, but right now, she could feel her sister's pain and she wanted to take it away. Whatever had happened between Aleksandr and Abigail had been terrible and Joley's heart went out to both of them. For a moment, she wished that she had Libby's gift of healing so she could cure whatever wounds lay between the couple.

"After their execution, the bodies of the Romanovs were driven to the chosen burial site. It was a spot just north of Ekaterinburg. That particular area was mostly swamp, peat bogs and abandoned mine shafts. The guards stripped the bodies and all valuables were taken. Through accounts from those present we know that several pounds of diamonds were found on the bodies. Several versions of the story related that the empress was wearing or had the necklace on her person and it was removed by one of the guards, but the necklace was never turned over to the government. If it was found on the family, it was taken and kept in hiding."

"Where has it been all this time?" Abigail asked. Her voice was tight, her throat constricted and raw. She kept her gaze forward, not wanting to look at him and see knowledge in his eyes. He knew her too well, knew there was nothing casual about her reaction to him.

"Good question. Before I get too excited, I want to have it authenticated."

Abigail stopped so abruptly Joley nearly ran into her. "I can't tell whether this is a cave-in or whether I've hit a wall and the entrance to Kate's set of stairs is somewhere close." She shone the light across the rock wall.

Joley shivered. "Find it fast, Abbey."

Aleksandr rested his hand briefly on Joley's shoulder. "It's here, no doubt about it," he said with absolute conviction.

"How do you know?" Joley asked.

It was Abigail who answered. "Because someone is using the caves below and these stairs to smuggle something into the country. Probably whatever Aleksandr and his partner were trailing. That means there has to be a way to the surface."

"She's right, Joley," Aleksandr agreed. "Just a few more minutes and we'll be out of here."

"Do you think whoever shot at us is still there?"

Abigail laughed. "You've got a hopeful note in your voice. You're not going to get the chance to shoot anybody. I'm sure Jonas is already on the scene and the gunman is long gone. Hannah and Elle probably drove him away with the seagulls."

"Well, that just sucks. I haven't had my morning tea and I was driven into the icy cold sea and crammed underground with tons of rocks over my head. Vengeance is the only solution that is going to make me feel any better."

"Why hasn't anyone recruited you yet?" Aleksandr asked. "There, Abbey. The break is right there. See how the rock has that enormous crack? It isn't natural. Step back in case it has some sort of trap."

"I'd make a great Interpol agent," Joley said. "I'm so anonymous." She managed a quick grin at her sister.

"Actually Joley would make an excellent agent," Abbey said with pride. "She's cool under fire and she's very good at martial arts. She thinks on her feet and even when something is difficult for her, like this, she still does it." She stepped back, crowding close to her sister as she ran her fingers along the top and bottom of the crack. "There's a catch here."

"Let me get it," Aleksandr ordered.

"There's no room," Abigail pointed out. "We can't switch positions in here." Her fingers found a pin holding the weighted slab in place. The moment she pulled it, the door began to swing open, creaking and groaning as it did so. She heard Joley catch her breath and reached back to take her hand. "Almost to Kate's mill, Joley," she promised.

"More rock over my head. It's kind of like a tomb." Joley shuddered. "Let's just hurry fast."

"Wait, Abbey, don't go in," Aleksandr warned. "I'll go first."

"We came in through the stairs leading down to the sea from the mill," Abigail said. "Don't you think if someone was going to set a trap they'd have done it by now?"

"The optimum place is right where you're about to step." His voice had turned from a rich mellow tone to steel. "They can't rig the staircase in the mill because your sister or someone working there legitimately might get hurt and there would be an investigation. A diver might discover the cave and try to go up the stairs to see how far they lead up the cliff. It's only this area they need to protect. This is their escape route and the route to the main highway where they can easily transport whatever they've brought into the country."

Abigail immediately flattened herself against the wall. "Joley, can you make yourself really small and press tight against the wall so Aleksandr can try to get by?"

"Great," Joley groused. "You just had to be a big man with shoulders as wide as the Mississippi." She tried to squish herself against the rock.

Aleksandr managed to squeeze past Joley muttering his apologies. He caught Abigail by the shoulders and tried to slide past. The moment his body was pressed against hers, the moment he felt her soft skin, as wet as she was, smelling of the ocean, his body recognized hers. She fit. She belonged. Every part of him, body and soul, wanted her. Even needed her. He swore softly, his fingers tightening on her shoulders as reaction slammed into him hard and wrenching and far more powerful than he expected.

Abigail looked up at him, compelled by the heat and hardness of his body, even though it was the last thing she wanted to do. The torch she held illuminated his face, the lines etched so deeply, the eyes that had seen too many horrors in life. She had thought she knew him, the things he was capable of to keep others from harm. She had always thought herself one of the protected yet he had sacrificed her in just the same way he did the others he used for information. For his career. To reach his ultimate goal. She understood that now and she had learned the hard way.

Abigail shook her head, denying the way something deep inside of her reached out to him. She would not be drawn in by the lingering melancholy in his eyes. She wouldn't let him touch her with his sadness, or his need, or even his terrible solitude. She wouldn't let the greatness she saw in him persuade her. Yes, he dedicated his life to catching monsters, to tracking criminals. She knew he had a sense of honor and loyalty to his homeland, but she also knew that he was as merciless and as ruthless as any of the criminals he was after.

She let him see it in her eyes. She would not risk herself again. Not her life and not her magic. She turned her face away.

Joley tightened her fingers around Abigail's, drawing her attention. Magic bound them together along with their blood. What one felt, so did the other, and Joley blinked back tears, understanding something traumatic had happened to Abigail. Abbey squeezed her fingers in reassurance. She couldn't protect her younger sister from the strong emotions they shared. It was the last thing she wanted to happen. She dreaded telling her sisters the truth of what she'd done, but she knew she had no choice.

Aleksandr leaned down, his lips pressed against Abigail's ear. "You used to have an open mind."

Her heart jumped in her chest. "That was a long time ago."

"Not to me, *baushki-bau,* never to me."

"You're hurting me." The words slipped out before she could stop them. Four years was a long time and she should have been over it, but it was all there, every vivid detail, cutting into her when it should have been long buried.

He slid past her without another word, taking the torch from her hand. "Stay here until I give you the okay."

He was all business again as if the small exchange had never happened. Abigail clung to Joley, not realizing she was doing so. He could turn his emotions on and off at will. Why hadn't she seen that when she'd been so in love with him? It was a glaring flaw she should never have overlooked.

Joley made a single sound of distress as the light from the torch moved away from them, leaving them in darkness. "I can't do this anymore. I'm sorry, Abbey. I have to go back. I can't breathe. My heart's going to explode."

"All right, honey. I'm so sorry. I completely forgot about your claustrophobia."

"I'm nearly to the other stairway," Akesandr called back. "I'll need a little help, ladies. Joley, why don't you sing for me so I know how far away you are."

"Aleksandr"—Abigail was suddenly afraid—"don't mess with anything lethal. We'll just go back. The shooter has to be gone by now. We can swim for it."

"I've almost gotten to the other side, *malutka*." There was a distinct drawling caress to his voice.

Abigail didn't trust him. He said all the right things. He was distracting Joley, his voice sexy and filled with reassurance and concern, but in the end, what mattered was that he wanted to follow the smugglers' route. He wanted to go up the stairs and see where the smugglers went. She always had to remember there was a purpose behind everything he did.

"I know you hate to sing, Abbey," Joley whispered, "but just this one time."

Abigail closed her eyes. She had to help Joley out when she'd placed Joley in such an uncomfortable and dangerous situation. Abigail was afraid of using her voice. Joley had control of her spell singing. Abigail didn't. She could wreak havoc with her voice. She sang to the dolphins and whales, to all the sea creatures out in her boat when she was alone, but not in front of people.

She began one of Joley's original songs, a soft melody of heartache, because her heart wasn't only aching, it was shattering all over again. She could feel the intensity of Joley's shocked stare in the darkness, but Joley still joined in, her normally strong voice a little hesitant, but picking up strength as they harmonized.

Aleksandr stopped moving as the two voices joined together singing. The Drake sisters had incredible power. There was something compelling, almost hypnotic about the voices. One could get lost in the sound, be drawn into another time and place, into either seduction and paradise or such loss one wanted to weep. He shook his head, trying to break the spell and find the small, hidden trap he knew had to be in the narrow tunnel.

"Oh, yes, here it is, ladies. A very simple but effective device. It's more of a warning system for them, to let them know if someone has used the stairs and discovered their route. I doubt if they use it more than once a month, maybe even less than that."

The singing stopped abruptly. "How dangerous, Aleksandr?" He preferred Abigail to call him by the more intimate version of his name, because he knew when she did, it was because she wasn't holding him at arm's length. Like she was now.

Aleksandr studied the trip wire. "Not at all. It's a small trip wire attached to a very small stick. If we kick it over, they know someone has used the stairs and their route is blown. With the light, you'll both be able to clear it, no problem. It's dry in here and the stairs are completely of rock. I'm coming back for you."

"Won't they know anyway?" Joley asked. "Your hit man friend must have known we'd come in here."

"It wasn't the same man who was at your house last night. I know his work. This is someone else." The light from the torch spilled over them and Joley took a visible breath of relief. "How many enemies do you Drakes have?"

"You were the one he shot," Abigail pointed out. Her stomach rebelled against the idea, lurching and rolling; she pressed a hand hard against it in protest.

Aleksandr didn't reply but turned back to lead the way. It was slow going as they followed. The tunnel had less seepage and was sheer rock, but it was extremely narrow and the ceiling overhead was uneven and jagged in places.

"Careful here," he instructed. "Step over this little wire." He held the torch as high as possible in the confined space. "Do you see it?"

Once pointed out it wasn't that hard to get over the obstacle and they hurried across the short distance.

"You've never admitted to having a great voice, Abbey," Joley said as they moved into the small section of stairs that intersected with the mill's staircase. "You have such perfect pitch. How could I not know that?"

Abigail didn't answer. She stared at a spot between Aleksandr's shoulder blades and kept walking.

"Both of you have an element not found in other voices," Aleksandr said without turning around. "I'm guessing that would be magic."

"Yes," Joley confirmed. "I can weave certain spells, help Libby heal, make people happier, that sort of thing. It's a wonderful gift and I try very hard to use it wisely. There have been times when it's tempting to use it when someone really annoys me, but Abbey has never sung a single note in front of me. And my sisters can't have known about her voice either or they would have told me." She nudged Abigail in the back. "Why are you hiding your ability?"

"I'm not discussing it," Abbey said, her voice tight.

Aleksandr glanced over his shoulder at her. "There seem to be a lot of topics you don't want discussed lately. Your voice is beautiful and should not be hidden from the world. We often talked about our children and singing them lullabies but never once did you offer to sing to them."

Abigail's breath came out in a rush. Anger swirled to the surface even though she tried hard to contain it. "Yes, well, we both know things go wrong with my magic. Unlike Joley, mine is flawed. Or perhaps the wielder is flawed. I would never take a chance on harming one of my children."

6

ABIGAIL knew there was no hope of lingering any longer in her bathroom. Her sisters were waiting downstairs for an explanation. Worse, Jonas was wearing a path in the living room floor with his pacing. Leaving her hair to dry on its own after the warmth of a shower, she met her aunt Carol in the hall. Family members weren't supposed to have favorites, but Carol held a special place in Abbey's heart. She'd always made each of the girls feel incredibly special. Throughout their childhood she had always called, sent gifts and cards, and listened to them. Abigail put her arms around her aunt and held her. "I'm so glad you've come."

"I know you're having a hard time, Abbey," Carol said. "We'll get through it the way we always do, as a family. I don't know what I would have done without you girls when Jefferson died. I leaned on you tremendously. I hope you know you can do the same. And your parents will come home if you need them. I can call them for you."

"No, no, don't do that. Mom and Dad will come home before the weddings. They're having such a wonderful time together and I don't want anything to mar that." Abigail smiled. "All those years of raising us, they never really had time for each other, to just be alone. I know they both were looking forward to living in Europe for a couple of years. We're adults and we don't need them to come rushing home when we stumble a little."

Carol hugged her a little tighter. "Is this a stumble or a fall? You feel . . . sad to me. Hurt. I can't just kiss you better as much as I'd like to."

Abigail smiled. "When I saw you back in the house, the world was a little brighter and the load lifted. I'll be fine, Aunt Carol. I'm a Drake. We're made of strong stuff." She kissed her aunt on the cheek and started down the hall toward the stairs. "You would have been so proud of Joley. You know her one big fear is tight places and she handled it like a trouper."

"Of course she did," Carol said. "Hannah and Elle both woke at the same time and rushed out onto the captain's walk. The rest of us took a bit longer, I'm sorry to say, but the girls had it all under control by the time we arrived to help." She patted Abigail's shoulder, reminding Abbey vividly of her youth. Carol had so often comforted her when she was a young girl struggling to contain her magic. "It will work out, honey, you'll see."

Abigail took a minute to study her aunt. Her hair was the color of rich champagne. There was laughter and warmth in her blue eyes. As always, she carried a camera around her neck. She loved her job as a Creative Memories consultant and believed wholeheartedly in her work. She had encouraged her sisters and then her nieces and nephews to take pictures at every event, to write journals and prepare beautiful scrapbooks for their descendants. Abigail was rather proud of her albums on dolphins and the places she'd gone to do research. She'd found it was a way to remember funny, touching, and dangerous moments. She couldn't imagine Carol without her camera or her smile and somehow having her there with her familiar warmth gave Abbey a sense of peace as she went down the stairs to face her sisters.

Jonas halted his pacing as she entered the room. Her sisters fell silent. Joley lifted a hand and gave her a faint, encouraging smile. Carol shifted closer, pressing her arm with gentle fingers. "I'll get you a cup of tea, dear. And you haven't had a thing to eat."

"Are you all right, Abbey?" Sarah asked. The eldest of the Drake sisters, she was the acknowledged leader.

Abigail nodded. "I can't believe I've been shot at two days in a row. I'm beginning to think someone has a grudge."

"Maybe someone does," Jonas said.

"Only Sylvia Fredrickson, and I can't imagine her hiring a hit man." Abigail sank into a chair beside Hannah and leaned over to kiss her sister on the cheek. "Thanks. You and Elle saved us."

"Elle lost her temper," Hannah reported with a grin. "That ought to make your shooter easy to identify, Jonas," she added happily. "And just in case you're looking into Sylvia, she'd more likely go after me."

"This is serious, Hannah," Jonas said. "I want all of you to listen up, especially you, Abbey. You had no business going out to Sea Lion Cove after what happened last night and you know it."

"Actually, I have business that can't be put off," Abbey corrected. "The dolphin was injured while risking his life to save not only mine, but Gene's as well. He needs treatment and he trusts me to give it to him. I can't very well hide in my room because some nutcase is running around with a gun."

"I have to go with Abbey on this one, Jonas," Sarah said. "She can't let the dolphin develop an infection and possibly die from neglect."

"Abbey," Jonas said, "you witnessed the murder of an Interpol agent."

"I didn't see them all that clearly. Even with the full moon, I was a good distance away, Jonas," Abigail pointed out. "If they think I can identify them, I can't, so they're being utterly ridiculous to risk exposing themselves in order to silence me. Well, unless I happened to run into one of them, face-to-face, on the street. I did hear the name Chernyshev and I wrote it all down and dated it to give you the report."

"Then you did see them." Jonas pounced on that.

Abigail shrugged. "They don't have to know that."

"What about the man Aleksandr was talking about?" Joley asked. "He was so certain the man wasn't involved but—" She broke off when Abigail shook her head.

"What man?" Jonas asked. When neither Joley nor Abbey answered he glared at Abigail. "I'm not one to tell you what to do . . ."

A chorus of laughter drowned out the rest of his warning. "Jonas," Kate said, "you always tell us what to do."

"You're so bossy it's unbelievable," Hannah contributed. "You're a dictator."

"You can't open your mouth without giving us the manly decree," Joley said. "Give it up, Jonas. Even you can't say it with a straight face."

"I only give advice when you clearly need it," he defended with a faint grin. "I can't help it if that means all the time. If you weren't always in some kind of trouble, I wouldn't have to give you lectures."

"Actually you could have stopped several years ago," Joley said. "We have them memorized. Just give us an indication of which one it's going to be and we'll recite them for you. My particular fave is the one where you tell us we have no common sense."

"Ha ha ha, you're all so funny!"

"Jonas, dear, do sit down," Carol said. "You're making me nervous with all that posturing. You started bossing the girls when you were about ten and you haven't stopped since. They don't mind—do you, girls?" She beamed at her nieces as she set a tray laden with sandwiches on the small table in front of them. "Eat up. There's plenty for you too, Jonas."

"Aleksandr Volstov is a very dangerous man. I can't even begin to tell you how dangerous he is, Abbey." All the teasing had gone from Jonas's voice, leaving him deadly serious. "I know he's calling himself an Interpol agent and I've checked his credentials, but I can tell you, he didn't start out that way." Jonas pulled a chair close to Abigail, trying to read her expression. "You know me, hon. You know the places I've been. I was a Ranger in the army. I'm telling you, I can see it in him. I've met very few men in my life that have ever scared me, but this man is one of them."

Abigail twisted her fingers together as she glanced around the room at her sisters. They looked alarmed, just as she knew they would be. Jonas might be bossy, but he told the truth and he could be dangerous when called upon. If he said Aleksandr was a danger to Abbey, her sisters would fight with everything they had, including magic, to keep her safe.

It was Sarah who asked, "Why do you say that, Jonas?"

"It's in his eyes. The way he carries himself." Jonas kept his gaze on Abigail. "The other night when I came up on you, with him standing over you and I had a gun on him, you were afraid he'd kill me, weren't you?"

"Yes," she answered, very low. "He's had extensive training."

"I'll just bet he has. What's he really doing here, Abbey?"

"I didn't know he was here until I saw him at the harbor. I have no idea how long he's been here either. I know less than you." She worked at keeping her voice expressionless.

Jonas caught her chin in his hand, tilting up her face, studying the smooth curves. "He put that neat little circle right between your eyes, didn't he? He slammed that gun into you hard enough to give you a bruise and he would have pulled the trigger if it had been anyone else."

"I can't say what he would have done," Abbey protested, pulling her face out of his hands, "and it's a smudge. He thought I'd killed his partner. You were pretty upset that night as well. All of us were."

"You should have seen him examining the cliff," Jonas said. "He knew exactly what to look for. He saw something I didn't. I've gone back three times to try to figure out what he saw that we missed. He was like a damned bloodhound." There was self-disgust mixed with reluctant admiration in his voice.

"He's a good detective. Why can't you work together?"

"Because he isn't working with me. He 'did me the courtesy' of telling me he was in the area. He neglected to say he had a man under-cover and he only gave me the bare outline of what he was after."

Abigail shook her head. "I don't know any more than you do."

"I know there's something between you, Abbey. I really, really don't want to stick my nose in where it isn't wanted, but I can't, in good conscience, let this go. He's from Russia. The world over there is very different from ours. I'm guessing, from the way he moves and the way he acts, that he was trained in something a little more lethal than police work. His background, if one tries to look into it, is a huge mystery. I'm betting he's an intelligence operative and I don't like that idea at all."

"You're being melodramatic and you're making him sound like a spy. He's a police officer, no different from you, and if you checked up on him then you know he's legitimate." Abigail had no idea why she couldn't stop defending Aleksandr, but the words kept tumbling out of her mouth in spite of every intention to remain silent. "I know you, Jonas. If you didn't think he was Interpol, he'd be in jail or thrown out of the country. You have too many friends."

"He has more than I do. Whatever he is, he's got a lot of heavy people behind him. Things work differently in other countries. Before you get upset"—he held up his hand—"I know you've traveled extensively, but there are places where the police just shoot the suspect rather than try to bring them before a judge. And there are worse things going on. I've seen men like Volstov and he's not just a cop."

"It happens here as well," Abigail pointed out. "But I understand what you're saying to me and I promise I'll be careful."

"Abbey, I don't think you are understanding what I'm saying to you." Jonas sat back as he pushed a hand through his hair, betraying his agitation. "Men like Aleksandr Volstov can be in the same room with you and you don't even know they're there. They can move fast and if you blink you miss them. They walk down a street as casual as can be and someone passing by falls to the sidewalk dead before their body ever hits the ground. They're already gone and no one can quite remember how to describe them. That's his world and he lives in it and he's comfortable in it and make no mistake, he'll kill to protect it. You could get hurt."

Abigail avoided looking him in the eye. "I know that, Jonas."

"What is he to you? How far into this relationship are you and can you back out of it?" Jonas leaned closer. "It isn't just you we have to worry about. These people play rough. His partner has been killed. Somehow I don't think he's going to take that lying down. That mark between your eyes tells me that. Tell me what you know about him."

Abigail wanted to deny any relationship. They didn't have one anymore. They were never going to have one again. "Only that he was a policeman in Russia and that he says he works for Interpol. That's it. That's all I know."

"Damn it, Abbey!"

"Jonas Harrington! You watch your mouth in this house," Carol admonished. "I won't have you browbeating Abigail. I won't have it even if you are the sheriff."

"Watch it, Aunt Carol, he'll threaten to arrest you," Hannah said. "He's always threatening me."

"With good reason," Jonas said. He leaned over to kiss Carol's cheek. "You, I would never arrest."

"Are you going to tell us what's going on here in Sea Haven?" Kate asked. "Does it have something to do with the old mill?"

"Yes, tell us what's going on, Jonas," Joley said. "If we're all going to be looking over our shoulders, we may as well know what it's all about."

Jonas sighed. "I wish I knew what to tell you. Several months ago, Gene Dockins and his youngest son, Jeremy, thought they saw one of the local fishing boats rendezvousing with a freighter out at sea. They became suspicious and talked to me about it and I notified the coast guard. Gene never said another word to me about the incident and, to be honest, with everything else going on up and down the coast I didn't give it another thought. Then about a month or so ago, Jeff Dockins—"

"He owns the local gas station, Aunt Carol," Sarah supplied. "He's Gene's oldest son, remember?"

"Of course I remember him, dear," Carol said. "He's very handsome."

"Aunt Carol!" All seven sisters made the protest.

Carol burst out laughing and her hand fluttered to her hair. "I'm not as young as I used to be, girls. You're flattering me. I hardly think at my age I'm going to cause another scandal in Sea Haven."

"You never cause scandals, Aunt Carol" —Hannah blew her a kiss—"just stir things up a bit, which is good every now and then."

"I'm certainly not going to win any beauty contests," Carol said, "but I do intend to renew my acquaintance with a few old friends."

"Jeff is happily married," Jonas felt compelled to point out. He wiped his brow, not in the least surprised he was sweating. The Drake women could do that to a man. All he needed was the additional trouble of Carol and her love potions. The rumor was, there had been more than one scandal and quite a few fights over her. In fact, Inez, owner of the grocery store, loved to tell how two of the local men broke out the door and three windows at a dance in a brawl over Carol. There were many such tales and Jonas had heard, and believed, them all.

"I never go near married men," Carol said. "It can be fatal. It would have been to any woman who came after my Jefferson."

"Then you haven't met Sylvia Fredrickson," Joley said. "She was in Abbey's class and even as a teen, she was after married teachers. It seems to be her goal to break up every marriage in Sea Haven."

"Not anymore," Hannah said smugly.

Jonas shot her a quelling glance. "Did you have something to do with that rash that keeps appearing on her face?"

"You mean the one in the shape of an open-handed slap that comes out whenever she flirts with a married man? Why ever would you think I had anything to do with it?" Hannah examined her fingernails.

"I can't wait to meet Frank Warner again," Carol said. "He's such a sweetheart and he sent me an invitation to his fund-raiser at the gallery next Tuesday. I'm really looking forward to seeing him. We had dinner right after my husband died and he was very interested, but I just wasn't up to a new relationship. I do love artists. They're so inventive."

Jonas buried his face in his hands. "Where the hell are Matt and Damon? I need some men in this household. I'm drowning here."

"Matt's at work and Damon had some wonderful idea that he had to share with his former bosses. Something to do with a satellite security system." Sarah shrugged. "He left last night in the middle of the night for San Francisco. A helicopter was picking him up and taking him to some undisclosed location for a meeting."

"I thought he was completely out of that work," Kate said, leaning forward, concerned. "He was so scarred when he came here, both physically and emotionally. Are they pressuring him to come back to work?"

Sarah shook her head. "His brain just works on things. He can't help it. He knows the defense systems inside and out and when he figures out things that make them better, he can't help perfecting the ideas and wanting to share them."

"So basically, Damon is back as the think tank for the Defense Department," Kate said.

"How long will he be gone?" Libby asked. "We're in the middle of planning your wedding."

Sarah laughed. "He can design a defense system, but if you ask him about wedding cakes he looks blank."

"Matt's just the opposite," Kate said. "He wants to take over the entire event. I think it's the architect in him."

"It's because he's a Granite and bossy," Hannah said and glared at Jonas.

He put both hands up in protest. "I'm not a Granite."

"You could be," she said.

Jonas ate two of the sandwiches and washed them down with tea. "Before you set your cap on Frank Warner, Aunt Carol, Aleksandr Volstov is investigating the theft of artifacts stolen from Russia. Warner owns a flourishing gallery and is a collector of artifacts. I've seen part of his collection and it's amazing. He also ships to the Bay Area all the time and he is a part owner of the fishing boat that Gene saw rendezvousing with the freighter. And I know you'll keep this information confidential." While he spoke, his gaze was on Abigail.

"Oh, bosh," Carol said. "Frank Warner has absolutely no need to deal in stolen goods and he's been a part of this community for years." She drummed her fingernails on the coffee table and heaved an exaggerated sigh. "All right then, I'll go undercover for you. It's obvious you need me to do it, although I don't like spying on my friends. But you're family, Jonas, and if you need me to get information out of him, I have my little ways and because of my looks, men tend to underestimate my intelligence."

"Which you encourage," Jonas accused. "Absolutely not, Aunt Carol. I forbid it. Sarah, you talk to her and make her understand this is dangerous and an ongoing investigation. She could ruin things or get hurt, neither of which is acceptable. I'm trusting you with this information so you avoid him, not vamp him."

"But I'm a natural for the job," Carol protested. "Everyone is used to me taking pictures and I can offer to help with his scrapbook album. He started one the last time I was here. I'll just naturally bring him more product. Wouldn't it be a good thing to have pictures of his artifacts to compare with the stolen ones?" Her smiled widened. "A Creative Memories consultant turned spy. I'll be able to journal my experiences. I'm very excited about helping you, Jonas."

"I said *no!* And I mean it," Jonas said. He glanced around the room at the Drake women. "All of you can quit grinning. If something happened to Carol you wouldn't be laughing. Abigail, you stay away from Aleksandr Volstov. And if you remember anything else not in your report call me immediately and give me the information. And Aunt Carol, you stay away from Frank Warner." He stood up and shoved a hand through his hair. There was sweat on his forehead. "The entire bunch of you is giving me gray hair."

Hannah's mouth twitched behind her hand and her eyes danced

as Jonas stalked out of the house, closing the door with a resounding bang. "I'm so glad you've come, Aunt Carol. That's the first time I've ever seen him flustered."

Carol grinned at her. "I suppose it wasn't very nice of me, but I couldn't resist." She patted Abigail's knee. "He didn't upset you, did he?"

Abigail shook her head. "Jonas is always looking out for us. I know he means well. It isn't his fault there are so many of us and we're always getting into some kind of a scrape."

Hannah gave a derisive and very inelegant snort. She tossed her mass of platinum hair and rolled her eyes. "Don't even cut him any slack. You didn't hear him ranting and raving about your Russian before you came down. And speaking of your Russian, Abbey, tell us everything. Are you or aren't you engaged to the man and where did you meet him?"

"How long have you known him?" Kate asked.

"Is anything Jonas said about him true?" Sarah wanted to know.

"Probably everything Jonas said about Aleksandr is the truth, but I honestly don't know. When I met him, four years ago, he was a detective. I was doing the tourist thing and he was standing on a corner. He was . . ." Abigail paused, searching for the right word. "Incredible. Impressive. I looked at his shoulders first and then his eyes. I had to get his picture." She exchanged a small smile with her aunt.

"Of course you did, dear," Carol said, pleased.

Abigail's smile widened at the memory. "I tried to get it without him seeing me, because I felt silly taking a stranger's picture and I was doing it because he was just plain hot. Of course he noticed and he wasn't all that thrilled with having his picture taken." She rubbed at an imagined fleck on her slim pants. "Moscow is so unbelievably old world. The buildings, the streets . . . even with the more modern look, it's just so beautiful and he seemed such a part of that world. Like an old-time fairy tale. He was actually standing right outside the gates of the Kremlin and he looked like a prince in front of a palace."

"You're blushing," Joley observed, leaning forward. "That must have been some first meeting."

"I'd never met anyone like him. He smiled at me as he came up to me and all I could think about was how it should be against the law to have his smile. I didn't even notice when he took the camera out of my hand. He was dazzling."

Sarah exchanged a long look with Kate. "You sound like you fell in love with him, Abbey," she ventured gently.

Abigail blinked and sat back in her chair. "Who wouldn't fall in love with him? He was charming and handsome and everything a man should be."

Joley leaned into her sister, laying her head back on her shoulder. "Why didn't you ever tell us about Aleksandr?" She was very careful of her tone, not wanting to make Abigail feel guilty and not wanting to allow a "push" of magic into her voice.

Abigail swallowed the sudden lump in her throat. "I just couldn't. It hurt too much. I'm sorry about all of this, Joley. I know the one thing that makes you crazy is tight places. I had no idea anything would happen to make you have to go into an underwater cave. I would never, never willingly place you in danger."

Joley shrugged. "Seriously, it's no big deal. I actually was rather proud of myself for conquering my fear enough to go through the rock to get to the mill. I love challenges and this one was very cool. I got to see you with that dolphin. That was so great, Abbey, that it would just come up to you like that and trust you to help it. It was amazing." She smiled at her sister. "But it still doesn't explain Aleksandr."

Abigail spread out her hands in a gesture of confusion. "There's no way to explain Aleksandr. I just can't even tell you what it was like. He offered to show me around and we walked through Red Square and visited the Cathedral of Vasily. All the while he talked about the history of the buildings. His voice, his accent, all of it just added to his attraction. He knew so much about everything and he spoke with such pride. He loved his country every bit as much as I love mine. He made me feel like the most beautiful and important woman in the world. We laughed so much together, and he held my hand. That sounds so juvenile, but you know I didn't really even date before. I was always so focused on my career and here I was, walking around this incredible city with a handsome, attentive man. I wanted to stay in his company forever."

"My Jefferson made me feel that way," Carol said. "Of course you wanted to be with him."

"We spent the day together and then stayed up all night talking. It was like there was always so much more to say. I loved the sound

of his voice. His smile, the way his eyes lit up when he looked at me."
Abigail blinked back tears. "In a million years, I never thought I'd
ever feel that way about someone. He didn't know anything at all
about me. He didn't know I was a Drake. That I had magic, that I
had talented, beautiful sisters who all had made names for themselves
in amazing ways. He saw me. Abigail. And it was enough."

There was a silence in the room. Abigail knew her sisters were
empathic and they could feel the sudden pain knifing through her.
Libby crossed her arms over her stomach and Elle huddled into a
little ball.

"You have to tell us, Abbey," Sarah pressed. "What good does it
do to hold it to yourself? We've all known you've been unhappy. You
can't be near us and not have us feel it."

Abigail shook her head. "I did something so stupid. So wrong. I
don't know how to tell you. I used my gift in a way that I shouldn't
have and a man died. He didn't deserve to die, but he did. I've always
known I couldn't wield what was given to me. It was always more
than I could handle. I blurted things out in school and kids were hurt
by it. Teens got in trouble, and even last Christmas look what happened. I knew better than to use it, but I wanted to please him. I
wanted to be so much more in his eyes." She covered her face with
her hands.

Carol slipped her arm around Abigail. "You aren't the first Drake
to be overwhelmed with the power we wield. It's such a terrible responsibility. Have you read the prophecy? Really read it? I think each
of you girls should. It was written several hundred years ago and
serves as both a warning and a foretelling."

Hannah waved her hands and candles leapt to life throughout the
downstairs, flickering and dancing. Scents wafted through the house,
mingling together to provide a semblance of peace. In the kitchen the
teakettle whistled merrily. Hannah jumped up, her tall, elegant body
encased in pencil thin blue jeans and an oversized white silk shirt.
"I'll make you a cup of tea, Abbey, something soothing."

"Thanks, Hannah," Abigail replied, managing a smile. Next to
Libby, Hannah and Elle were the most empathic of the sisters.

"I think we all avoided reading the prophecy too closely when we
made the pact to stay independent," Sarah explained. "I was fifteen

at the time and we all thought getting married meant being under a man's thumb. We were watching all our friends in school turn silly and giggle and basically act like idiots and none of us wanted to be like that so we swore off relationships."

"Not just being under his thumb," Kate clarified, "but making fools of ourselves. We felt our friends were changing who they were and what they believed in just to have a boy like them. And we grew up with the boys—they just weren't all that attractive as boyfriends to us."

Carol fluffed her hair and winked at Abigail. "I should have taken you girls in hand a long time ago. Being a woman is just plain fun, and flirting is half the fun. And it shouldn't have prevented you from studying the prophecy. I have a few things to say to your mother when I see her."

"We read the part about the gate swinging open in welcome and so we padlocked the gate and put the prophecy in with the journals," Kate admitted. "And we didn't say a single word to Mom about our pact. She was pushing us to learn the language in some of the journals and that was so annoying."

"At the time," Sarah qualified. "Since then, we've learned a few hard lessons about why we should have listened to her."

Hannah returned with the cup of tea. "This will help, Abbey. I worked on the combination of herbs and I think it really relaxes and helps soothe." She pushed the teacup into Abigail's hands.

Abigail forced a faint smile as she looked up at her sister. If there were favorites within a family, Hannah would be everyone's. Abigail felt closest to her and she was fairly certain her other sisters felt the same way. It wasn't that Hannah was saintly, not by any means; Hannah had a definite mischievous streak, but she was so compassionate and caring. And her painful shyness made it necessary for them all to stay connected to her in order to allow Hannah the freedom of a career. No one had thought when she'd first taken a modeling job that she would soar to the top and become such a success, but they were all proud of her, especially knowing what it took for Hannah to appear in public. "Thank you, Hannah, even the aroma is soothing."

Carol glanced at her watch with a small frown. "I'm going to have to cancel my meeting so we can finish this talk."

"What meeting?" Sarah asked curiously. Carol hadn't been back in Sea Haven more than a day.

"I belong to the Red Hat Club, dear, and we're having a bit of fun today. I was so pleased that they had a chapter here in Sea Haven. It will give me a chance to reestablish old friendships. I want to get to know all the ladies in town again. We can wear our red hats and purple shirts and walk barefoot on the beach. Inez Nelson is very involved and hopefully she can pass on news as to how Gene is doing. I haven't heard yet."

Sarah nodded. "Inez is always a wonderful source of information. She cares about Sea Haven and is very active in the business community as well as with all the programs for theater and dance. She was here a few days ago getting consent to have Kate, Joley, and Hannah's names used for the write-up on Frank Warner's big event. If Frank had asked, Inez knew they would have turned down the invitation to attend."

"It turns into a freak show," Hannah said, making a face. "It isn't quite so bad when Kate and Joley are there."

"Especially Joley," Kate added with a quick grin at her sister. "You seem to be a huge draw. I think people want to know if the tabloids have all your exploits right."

Joley laughed. "Aw, if only I had the exciting life the tabloids write about."

"We'd have to disown you," Sarah said.

Abigail pressed a hand to her chest. Sarah didn't mean to hurt her. She couldn't possibly know how those teasing words would cut so deep.

"Abbey." Sarah rose instantly and knelt in front of her sister, putting her arm around her. "No matter what, you are our sister, loved and cherished always."

Abigail shook her head. How had she had failed the gifts handed down to her through centuries of generations? Never once had she been told stories of magic failing. Of one of the sisters so flawed she caused the death of an innocent man.

Sarah was so good at everything she did. Kate was magical, bringing tremendous peace to those in need and showing such courage when elements got out of control. Libby saved lives over and over.

Hannah's gift was powerful and she gave of herself without reservation to her sisters. Joley had the voice of a spell singer and she was able to use her gift for good. Elle was the most powerful, holding all gifts within her, yet she was humble and steady and always ready to help. Only Abigail was flawed, unable to wield the power of the truth. Unable to use the voice given to her. Unable to bring forth pure magic. Because of her weaknesses, her gift was twisted and uncontrolled and wreaked havoc on those around her.

7

"ABIGAIL." Carol's voice was very gentle. "You can't hold something like this in. If you don't trust your family to love you and help you through the worst times in your life, you'll never be able to trust anyone."

"It isn't a matter of trust, Aunt Carol," Abbey explained. "It just makes it all the more real if I talk about it. I always feel so apart from everyone else."

"Abbey," Sarah said, "life is to be lived. If you're living, you're going to stumble along the way."

"All the time?" Abigail leapt to her feet and began to pace. "I have such a bad temper and when I was in my teens, I wasn't above using my gift for revenge. None of you did that."

Joley slowly raised her hand, sliding down in the chair as she did so. Hannah followed suit, although she didn't look in the least remorseful. Sarah shrugged her shoulders and raised her hand and glared at Elle, who just grinned sheepishly and put up a couple of fingers. Carol tossed her head and waved her arm with gusto.

"You did *not!*" Abigail said, shocked.

"We aren't angels," Sarah pointed out. "Especially Hannah and Joley." She gave them both a stern look.

"Like I'd let those girls be mean to me or any of you," Hannah said with a little disdainful sniff. "Once Sylvia Fredrickson said right in front of Anita Monroe that she could have *any* boy in town. Including Jonas Harrington, by the way."

"Jonas?" That got all of their attention instantly.

Hannah nodded, her hands on her hips. "She really made me mad the way she was talking about him. He was in college, but came home as often as possible. Remember when his mother was so ill? Sylvia claimed she was going over to his house that night and sneaking in his bedroom window."

"What did you do, Hannah?" Abigail asked, unable to prevent herself.

"Nothing much. I just stirred up the wildlife in the area a bit. The yard and particularly Jonas's room were overrun with anything reptilian. She has a very loud scream," she added with satisfaction. "Not that it taught her any lessons. And that oaf Jonas suspected I might have done it out of retaliation for his obnoxious comments when we met earlier in the day and he referred to me as a cutesy little Barbie doll."

Kate and Libby exchanged a long look. "I don't think this is very fair," Kate said. "In fact I'm jealous that I couldn't use my talent for anything but good. I had a few people who weren't so nice in school I would have liked to do something to."

"Me too," Libby agreed. "The rest of you have all the fun."

"Don't worry," Hannah said. She, Joley, and Elle exchanged a long, satisfied grin. "We were looking out for you. No one ever suspected your younger sisters."

"And I don't believe for one minute that the two of you never used your gifts inappropriately," Carol said. "Confession time."

Kate's grin widened. "I am not about to lose my halo. Suffice to say, I did experiment a little."

"I just don't believe this." Abigail looked at Libby. Libby was the middle child, gifted with healing. She always managed to look serene, even in the middle of a crisis. She wore her heavy mane of jet black hair short and her eyes were a startling, very intense green that gave her an otherworldly appearance. Of all the Drakes, she was the one the local children called witch when they wanted to be cruel. Abigail had never seen her react, although once in a while she had cried in her room and that sent Hannah, Joley, and Elle whispering up on the captain's walk. "Elizabeth Jane Drake. Not you too? I swear, all my illusions are being shattered."

"I admit to nothing."

Laughter bubbled up in Abigail. At the same time she wanted to weep. At every crisis within the family as far back as she could remember, her sisters had pulled together. Her mother and the aunts had always been the same, as had her uncles and cousins. She was very thankful for the wonderful legacy of family devotion handed down to her.

"Oh, dear," Carol said just as Sarah jumped to her feet and went to the door.

They all heard a knock a minute later. Abigail froze, hand to her throat, her heart suddenly beginning to pound.

"Relax, dear," Carol said, "it's only Inez and a few others from the Red Hat Club. They've come to get me, as I didn't call right away." She patted her niece's shoulder and hurried to find her ornate red hat. "I've been leaving the gate open for my friends during the day."

Several ladies poured into the room, dressed in either flowing skirts or pants, but all with bright purple shirts and red hats on their heads. They laughed as they greeted the girls. "Carol was late so we decided not to let her miss the meeting. We're dragging her off with us and don't expect her back early! It's our girls' day out and we intend to have fun."

"I'm ready." Carol rushed into the room waving her arm, her camera slung haphazardly around her neck. "Unless you girls need me. . . ." She trailed off, looking at Abbey.

Abigail kissed her. "No, we'll be fine. Just don't get into too much trouble."

That sent another round of laughter floating up from the women. "Like the time we had to bail you out of jail," Inez said.

"Or the time you got stuck in that tree with Tommy Lofton and we had to call the fire rescue," Donna added.

"Aunt Carol!" Hannah looked proud.

"I'm certain they're making it all up!" Carol blew kisses at her nieces and followed the women out.

The Drake sisters listened to the laughter as it slowly faded into the distance. "We might have to bail them out," Sarah warned. "I think Carol's going to be a very bad influence on that group, and worse, that they want her to be."

"Most of them went to school together. It's so nice that they've remained such good friends," Kate said.

Hannah slipped off the chair and stretched out on her stomach on the floor, patting the place beside her in invitation as she looked up at Abigail. "I don't know all that much about things, Abbey, but I do know guilt can eat you alive. You can't let it rule your life. Aunt Carol never has. She pretends to be a little on the wacky side, but she lives large and she's happy."

One by one the other Drakes lay on the floor as they did when they were children. Each stretched out a hand and placed it in the middle of their circle, one on top of the other in a gesture of solidarity. Abigail took her place beside Hannah and felt the warmth of her sisters' hands over hers.

"I think I'm too old for the floor," Sarah said. "We need mats."

"I have noticed you aging, Sarah," Joley agreed. "Especially since you became engaged. Too funny, if you ask me. Sarah, turning into a yeswoman."

Sarah threw her wadded-up napkin at Joley. "I am *so* not a yeswoman. You can just take that back before I decide to thump you."

Joley feigned a bored yawn. "It's not going to happen because you're just as anxious as I am to hear all about Aleksandr the Russian hottie with the sexy voice."

Abigail blushed. "Okay," she conceded. "He does have a sexy voice. *Totally* sexy."

"And he sings, too," Joley added. "He has a beautiful voice. He used to sing her to sleep with a lullaby." She grinned wickedly. "Well, *after,* you know."

Abigail's blush deepened. "I didn't tell you that!"

"You didn't have to tell me that."

Hannah raised her hands in the air and made intricate patterns in the air. "I could use some cookies fresh out of the oven. Anyone else?"

Abigail leaned over and nudged her shoulder with her chin. "You always eat cookies when we have a family conference. How do you stay so thin? I make two of you."

"Jonas once said I'm a wire hanger the designers drape their clothes on," Hannah confessed. There was a note of hurt in her voice.

"He's such a jerk sometimes. Then he was mad at me because toads followed him around croaking. He claimed it sounded like they were saying 'liar, liar,' which by the way, could happen to Aleksandr if you needed to let him know you aren't going to take any of his nonsense."

Abigail rubbed Hannah's back gently. "Jonas deserves toads following him around, especially if he hung out with Sylvia. Who is he dating now?"

"Someone with a figure," Hannah said. "Her bones won't jab him every time he holds her." She caught the plate of cookies as it started to float by.

A collective gasp went up. "He didn't say that to you!"

"Oh, he said it all right. He saw the magazine with the designer dresses from Italy. You know the ones without much in the back and very little in the front? He has to make some snide comment every single time I go out on a job. There was one picture of me with an Italian male model in a particularly sexy pose and Jonas was extraordinarily nasty about it. He was lucky it was only toads serenading him all night." Hannah passed the plate of chocolate chip cookies around to her sisters. "Did Aleksandr say mean things to you, Abbey?"

"Aleksandr has never made any personal comment to me to make me feel less than beautiful. Just the opposite." Abigail bit down on the warm chocolate and let it melt in her mouth while she thought about Aleksandr Volstov. "He made me feel beautiful every moment I was with him. He always acted like he couldn't see another woman." She smiled around the mouthful of cookie. "He did tell me I had a bad temper once, though."

"Well, you do," Joley said. When Abigail glared at her she shrugged. "You do. You know you do. Not as bad as mine, but you have one."

"Men are just so bossy," Abigail said. "It's annoying sometimes."

"Sometimes?" Joley's eyebrow shot up. "It's annoying all the time. I don't know how any of you put up with it. Seriously, Kate, Sarah, you both should think long and hard before you commit to this marriage thing. Men just like to take over." She caught up three cookies and placed the plate in the center of the seven sisters. "Aleksandr is absolutely the bossy type."

"You don't have to tell me," Abigail admitted. "He definitely doesn't lack for confidence."

"What does he lack?" Sarah asked, her voice gentle.

Abigail took a deep breath and let it out. "Maybe I'm the one lacking, I don't honestly know, or maybe I expected a knight in shining armor. I told him about everything. Us. All of our gifts, the bad, the good, and everything that came with having talent. I told him how difficult it can be and how exhilarating. And I told him how you all had wonderful gifts that seemed so useful and yet mine only did damage. I think he was skeptical at first, but he has a tremendous sense of intuition. So he would throw out little tests, at least that's how I thought of them, and eventually he asked me to sit in on the interrogation of some of his prisoners. For the first time in my life, I felt like my talent made a difference, actually had a purpose. I knew I was helping him and doing something worthwhile."

There was eagerness in her voice her sisters couldn't fail to notice, but Abigail couldn't hide it. For the first time in her life she had felt part of something and worthy of being a Drake. "It wasn't just the fact that I was working with him, and that he was proud of me, but it meant that I measured up to the rest of you and all the Drake sisters who had gone before us."

"Abigail," Libby said, reaching out to wrap her fingers around her sister's arm, "how could you think that way?"

Immediately, at Libby's touch, Abigail's pain eased. She sent Libby a faint smile. "That's why. You're so extraordinary, all of you, the things you can do for people. All of these years being in Sea Haven, has anyone ever asked me for help? They avoid me. Most don't engage me in conversation. I have a few friends outside this family, but not very many. The townspeople are so proud of the rest of you and you're always being asked to help. I know it isn't easy for you and I'm not trying to belittle the fact that it takes so much out of you, but to *never* be asked made me feel so far from the rest of you." Abigail looked around at her sisters. "Do any of you understand?"

Hannah nodded. "I'm always the bad girl. It's probably from having to stay to myself so much. I spend a lot of time thinking about things I shouldn't. I can't help it and I wonder sometimes how everyone else can be so good." She took a chocolate chip cookie out of Joley's hand and took a bite. "Well, except for Joley, but she never gets lectures because everyone expects it out of her."

"Damn straight," Joley said. "I earned my reputation and it keeps growing even when I don't do anything."

"Stop trying to look pathetic, Joley," Sarah admonished. "You can't pull it off."

"Sheesh. I get no respect in this house. It isn't easy to get the kind of publicity I do. My all-time fave was the time someone sent Mom and Dad the tabloid with the headlines 'Caught in the Act' and 'Confessions of a Sex Addict.' Mom called me and said she and Daddy were leaving the country. She neglected to tell me they'd been planning their trip for years, so I was mortified."

The sisters erupted into gales of laughter. "Well, you shouldn't have confessed to your addiction," Abigail pointed out.

"I wish," Joley said. "Who the hell am I supposed to have sex with? I'm on the road all the time and I flirt like crazy but I think they're all afraid of my reputation."

"Ooo!" Hannah said. "What you need, Joley, is for us to do the red panty ceremony for you. Do you have a pair upstairs? Everyone we've done it for says it works."

"It worked for me," Abigail reported. "Aleksandr loved the red panties and I was very, very lucky the night I wore them."

"No way!" Joley held up her fingers in a cross. "I'm not going to saddle myself with a man as arrogant and bossy as Aleksandr. I'm going for the type I can dominate totally. He'll adore me and do every single thing my little heart desires. If the red panty ceremony nets you a hot bossy man, I am so not there!" She looked curiously at Hannah. "What about you? Have you tried it?"

Hannah shuddered openly. "Sleeping with someone generally requires a date of some kind and dating generally requires talking to someone and as I have never been able to actually talk with a man I like without looking like an idiot, I've passed on the sacred ceremony, thank you very much."

"You talk to Jonas," Sarah pointed out.

"Is he actually a man? I think he's an android." Hannah managed a sniff of disdain. "I doubt seriously if he counts and no one—*no one*—in their right mind would ever go out with him."

They all looked at Elle. She held up both hands. "As no form of birth control is going to work for me, I figure it's in my best interest to stay as far away from that particular ceremony as possible." She grinned at Abigail. "Although I did participate in Abbey's ritual just before she left on vacation. I chanted, lit candles, and had a lot of fun and then hid in the nearest closet just in case there was a backlash. I'm so pleased to hear it worked."

"It definitely worked," Abigail confirmed. "He took one look at me the day I wore them and he was so hot I didn't think we'd make it to his room. He had me up against the wall and . . ." She trailed off, fanning herself. "Suffice it to say, the ritual works."

"Thanks a lot, Abbey," Elle said, "that's just not right. I'm eating the last cookie and I deserve it."

They all watched solemnly as Elle ate the last chocolate chip cookie.

"So he made you feel beautiful, he's great in bed, and he's smart and funny and sings to you," Sarah ventured. "He even had you believing in yourself and sharing your gift. So tell us more about what went wrong, Abbey."

"He was working very hard on a case. He had several, but this one investigation was ongoing and he'd been working on it nearly two years. It was awful. At first he didn't want to talk about it because it involved a series of brutal child murders. He was certain he was getting close to finding the murderer. It's very different there than here and he was frustrated at times with the level of cooperation and the threats from his superiors. I know the deaths haunted him and he felt responsible because the killer eluded him for so long."

"How terrible." Joley sat up, frowning. She put one hand on Libby. Hannah did the same. They were all empathic, but Libby would feel the most, especially with her sister, and Abigail was in pain. "For everyone. The parents, the children, Aleksandr, and you as well. It must have been so awful for you to experience what he and the parents were feeling. Was he aware how empathic you are?"

"How could he be? How can anyone be? Look at how Irene Madison keeps insisting Libby heal her son, Drew, of cancer. She has no idea how dangerous even trying would be. It's the same with everyone. And when we try to explain it, they don't want to hear because whatever they're asking is that important to them. Aleksandr reached a point where he wanted me involved because all that mattered was saving children and I agreed."

Abigail sat up and leaned her head back against the sofa. She looked at her hands. "How many times do you think we start things with the best of intentions and end up hurting other people?"

"Abbey," Kate said, "all of us have done things we're not proud of. Everyone makes mistakes. We all make choices based on the information we have at the time. It's all well and good to look back after the fact and see what we should have done, but we rarely know what path is best when we take that first step."

"When I went to the station to meet Aleksandr, I was told he'd brought in a suspect and that he was in an interrogation room waiting for me to help question the man. All I knew was that Aleksandr had told me he was close to breaking the case. I assumed the suspect in custody was the man he was certain was the killer. When I went in several officers were in the room and everyone was yelling at the suspect. They stood over him and pounded the table and accused him over and over."

"I'm so sorry, Abbey," Sarah whispered. "That wouldn't be easy for any of us."

Abigail shook her head. "Don't feel sorry for me. I wanted to be there. I wanted to help him solve the murders. I wanted to be important to him." She rubbed her forehead with the heel of her hand. "I was so stupid. I wasn't thinking. I didn't go in there thinking of the suspect or even with a clear mind. I went in thinking about myself. My own glory. Of helping Aleksandr and making him happy." She hit the back of her head three times against the sofa cushions in an agony of recrimination. "Stupid. Stupid. Stupid."

"It's human, Abbey, not stupid. You loved this man and you wanted to help him. Using magic takes steps, we all know that, but all of us have skipped those steps in the heat of the moment. I imagine it was very emotional for everyone concerned."

"I asked him if he was guilty. But I didn't ask what his crime was or what he had done to the child, I simply asked if he was guilty. The other officers were shouting questions and Aleksandr was using his cold, very frightening voice and I was just so certain that I could make him confess his guilt. And I did. He said yes and then he calmly reached over and took a gun one of the officers had so conveniently laid on the table and he shot himself in the head."

"Oh, my God!" Kate was horrified. "Honey, I'm so sorry."

"Abigail . . . ," Sarah began.

Abigail shook her head. "You know what his crime was? He fell asleep while he was supposed to be watching his child. He was drinking and he got sleepy and he lay down and she left the house to play with her friends. The real killer snatched her. Of course he felt guilty. What parent wouldn't? He was the child's father—not that I knew that at the time. They didn't tell me and, worse, I didn't think to ask." She looked at her sisters, tears shimmering in her eyes. "Even when he said he was guilty, I knew he wasn't, but I didn't have the time to say it. He just went for the gun." She lifted her hands. "I had his blood all over me. Some nights I wake up and I'm still covered and I can't wash it off no matter how hard I try."

"You have nightmares," Hannah said. "I hear you crying but your door won't open for me."

Abigail held out her hand to her sister. "I'm sorry, Hannah. I know that distressed you, but I just couldn't face anyone. I couldn't tell you what I'd done."

"Is that the reason you won't have anything to do with Aleksandr?" Joley asked.

Abigail let out her breath. "I don't know. I only know that it was one of the most horrifying moments in my life and I expected him to comfort me—to do something—but all of the officers began talking really fast, especially the one whose gun it had been. The next thing I know I was dragged out of the room and Aleksandr just stood there and watched them take me away."

Sarah frowned. "I don't understand. Were they accusing you of something? What did he do?"

"He stood there so still, his eyes as cold as ice, and he watched them drag me out of the interrogation room as if I were a suspect in one of his murders. I was covered in the poor man's blood and they took me right past his wife. I looked at her and she was staring at me so hopelessly. She'd lost her daughter and in a few minutes someone would come and tell her about her husband."

"That rat bastard!" Joley exploded. "And all this time I was harboring a plot to get the two of you back together."

"Toads aren't good enough for him," Hannah declared.

Sarah held up her hand for silence. "Abbey, honey, I know this is hard for you to tell us, but we need to know everything that happened to you in order to help."

Abigail shook her head. "So you and Libby and everyone can make me feel better about what I did? I can't take it back. That small moment in time when I walked into that room so filled with my own importance. So certain I'd catch a killer and Aleksandr would be grateful to me. So sure that my magic was wielded with every bit of power and expertise as all of yours." She leaned back, fighting tears. "We never can just stop time. Or take moments back. Life doesn't work that way, does it?"

"No, it doesn't, Abbey," Kate said. "But we go on. And we learn from our experiences. Tell us the rest. Tell us what happened to you."

"They interrogated me for two days and nights. Apparently the officer who was careless with his gun accused me of upsetting the prisoner with my questions. They were horrible, hitting me and shouting." She broke off, shaking her head. "I thought they were going to kill me. They wanted to blame someone for the poor man's death and I guess I was the perfect scapegoat. I didn't have anyone to stand up for me and they wouldn't allow me to call the embassy."

"How terrifying. That doesn't make any sense," Libby said.

"They didn't even let me change my clothes. I was so frightened and I kept thinking Aleksandr would come and get me out of there, but he didn't." Abigail looked down at her hands. "I was so far away from all of you and too ashamed to reach out. I was so scared, but I was more afraid you'd find out what I'd done and never be able to forgive me. I still can't forgive myself."

"And you can't forgive him," Sarah said quietly.

Abigail shook her head. "Somewhere deep inside me, I know it's selfish to want him to put me first. To want him to comfort me when my world has fallen apart."

"It isn't selfish, Abbey," Joley said. "It's human. Normal. You're not a martyr, you're a woman. Of course you would want your man to put you first and, for God's sake, help you out when you need it." She clenched her fist. "I wish I'd known all this when I was letting him charm me. I would have punched his lights out."

The wind came up from the sea, howling as it battered the house.

The sisters looked at Hannah. She shrugged. "It happens when I'm really angry, a leftover childhood thing. I can't always control it."

"Do we want to know what they did to you while they interrogated you or are Hannah and Joley going to go psycho on us?" Kate asked.

Abigail shook her head. "I'm not going to talk about that. It was horrible and I was more scared than I've ever been in my life, even more frightened than all the times I've been diving and run into sharks."

Elle closed her eyes and turned her face away, tears on her lashes and running down her face. "They hit you over and over. One man slapped your face a lot." Her voice sounded distant and there were lines of strain around her mouth. "They threatened you and made lewd comments. They called you witch and they tried to get other names out of you. The man slapping you wanted you to name Aleksandr, to say he left the gun there on purpose." Elle opened her eyes and looked straight into Abbey's eyes.

Abigail felt her heart jolt painfully. It was always that way when facing Elle. She looked so young with her vivid red hair and her pale skin, but when you looked into her eyes, they were too old and filled with knowledge, filled with things no one else saw.

"You never said his name."

"No, I didn't."

"Why?" Elle asked softly.

Abigail shook her head. "I don't know."

"Yes, you do."

"I loved him."

Elle sighed. "You did love him very much, but that wasn't why you didn't name him. You were angry and frightened and you're as stubborn as hell, Abbey. That wasn't the reason you refused to give him up. And it wasn't because you wanted him to save you. After the first three hours of that man standing over you, spitting and slapping and threatening you, it didn't matter to you if Aleksandr saved you or not."

"I was angry," Abigail whispered.

"At all of them," Elle said. "Somewhere inside you is that answer. When you get past anger and disappointment and you let go of guilt, you'll know why. And then it got worse, didn't it, because you suspected Aleksandr had to do something terrible in order to get you released."

Abigail nodded. "The men interrogating me suddenly were pulled from the room and others took their place, but they didn't talk to me. They whispered back and forth and they acted very different—fearful— and they didn't ask me anything at all, just whispered together, clearly very afraid. They seemed to be constructing some story to tell their superiors. I knew something terrible had happened."

"You . . ."

"No!" Abigail shook her head at Elle. "Don't say it. Don't even think it. I don't want to know what Aleksandr did to get me out of there. If he killed someone to get me free, if someone else died because of me, I couldn't live with it."

"Abbey . . . ," Sarah started.

"No, I mean it. I can hardly breathe sometimes thinking about that poor woman without her husband and daughter. I can't go there. Don't ask me."

"And maybe that's what you run from in Aleksandr," Elle said. "Not his mistakes, but his strength. The very things you relied on and admired in him are the things you fear the most."

Abigail couldn't look away from Elle. "You knew. All this time, you knew."

Elle shrugged. "I know a lot of things. People are entitled to their secrets, Abbey, even my sisters. If you had wanted us all to know, you would have said so. All of us felt your unhappiness and you knew that we did, but you didn't give an explanation, nor should you have to do so." She flashed a wan smile. "It isn't always easy or comfortable catching glimpses of my sisters' lives. We all want privacy, me included. I've learned to keep my mouth shut."

Libby immediately reached out and put her hand on Elle's shoulder. "You bear such a terrible burden, Elle."

"We all do," Sarah said. "We need to have more compassion for one another. I'm ashamed to say I've never given any thought to how Elle must feel knowing things about us we don't want known." She looked at her youngest sister. "It must make you feel different and alone, just as Abigail does with her gift. And Libby. Everyone wants something from Libby everywhere she goes. There's no respite, not even here when our home should be a refuge."

"Each of us has to be careful with our magic," Kate said. "And Abbey, all of us have made mistakes. We can't be perfect, no matter how hard we try." She flashed a brief smile at Hannah and Joley. "Some of us don't even want to try."

Joley gave a small salute. "Way to go, sister!" She held up her palm for Hannah to high-five.

"That would be us," Hannah agreed.

Sarah tapped Hannah's foot. "Keep it up, smart one—Mom and Dad are coming home for the wedding and they might have a few things to say to you."

"No one would dare rat me out," Hannah said complacently.

"Just so you know, Hannah, and everyone else who might have retaliation and vengeance on their mind," Joley said, "the house let Aleksandr in the other night."

A collective gasp went up and the sisters all stared at Abigail. She covered her face. "I know. I know. Something had to have gone wrong. We didn't work the spell right and it failed." She lifted her face. "I had the doors to my balcony wide open, maybe that was the problem."

"Oh, Abbey," Hannah said, "I'm so sorry."

"It just can't be him. I don't care what the prophecy says and I don't care whether the house let him in or not. I don't want to see him or speak to him or have anything whatsoever to do with him," Abigail declared.

"Oh, no," Sarah said. She glanced at the phone and made a face.

As if on cue, the phone rang.

"Don't answer it," Abigail said. She looked at Sarah. "It's him, isn't it? It's Aleksandr."

Sarah nodded.

"Let it ring," Abigail instructed.

"I don't mind telling him to go fry himself," Hannah volunteered. "And I could over the phone."

"Hannah," Sarah warned. "You wouldn't want to do anything you would regret. Abbey, answer the phone."

Abigail would have refused had it been any other than Sarah, or Elle, but both had the gift of "sight" at times. She picked it up. "What do you want?"

"Nice to hear your voice too. Meet me in half an hour at Mc-Kerricher Park."

"I'm not going to meet you anywhere, Sasha."

Aleksandr sighed. "Do we have to do this every time? I don't have time to argue with you. Meet me there in half an hour. We're going kayaking, so dress appropriately. The weatherman is predicting four-foot swells so we might get lucky and be able to investigate along the coast for caves the smugglers may be using. They had to have hidden their boat somewhere and I'm going to find out where."

"I'm not going."

"You know the coastline better than anyone. I can't go alone, Abbey, and you know it. This has to be done."

"Take Jonas or Jackson, his deputy. They both know the coastline. Or better yet, call the coast guard. They'll help you out." Abigail rubbed at her throbbing temple. Why was it every time she heard his voice she lost her resolve?

"Abbey, we've already wasted too much time. If we don't go now, the ocean could be too rough tomorrow. I've got a car already waiting at the harbor so we can kayak along the coastline at least as far as Noyo. You don't want me to go alone. It's dangerous and I could get lost. I've picked up a couple of ocean kayaks and if we leave now the ocean is relatively calm and we can get this done."

"I really detest you, Sasha. You know darn well you aren't going to get lost following the coastline." She glanced at her watch. "I'll be there in forty minutes. And next time don't call me."

"Fine, I'll just pick you up next time and save myself the argument." He hung up before she could reply.

Abigail slammed the phone down and glared at Sarah. "He's impossible."

"You caved, Abbey!" Joley was horrified. "You just agreed to everything he wanted and he wasn't even all that nice about it. What is wrong with women when they fall in love?" She and Hannah and Elle shook their heads.

"I'm not in love," Abigail asserted. "I just want him to finish his business here and go away."

"So why didn't you fill in the gaps for Jonas when Aleksandr told him exactly nothing this morning," Joley asked.

"Don't you need to go back to bed?" Abigail demanded. "I don't know why I didn't tell Jonas anything. Aleksandr does a lot of work that might put his life in jeopardy. I'm not about to make a mistake by talking too much about things I know nothing about. I want him suffering and pining away for me and I want him on his knees begging forgiveness, which I'll *never* give him, but I don't want him hurt."

"That makes perfect sense to me," Hannah declared.

"I think we can all agree on that," Sarah said.

8

"YOU don't need to help me," Abigail lied as she watched Aleksandr maneuver over the rough sand, carrying her kayak. "I'm perfectly capable of doing this myself. In fact, I'm probably far better at it than you."

"I wouldn't think of insulting you that way," Aleksandr said. "Where do you want to put in the water?"

"The best place is over there." She indicated a long sandy beach near where he'd already unloaded his kayak. "The breakers are mild and we'll have less trouble getting to the rocks. We want to paddle between them where it's a bit calmer and we can study the formations along the coastline. I know several caves and inlets capable of hiding a boat, but the driver would have to be an expert and the water fairly calm, which it was that night. We should be able to get to them easily using the kayaks." She knew he enjoyed white-water river kayaking, but she doubted if he'd done much in the ocean. The Pacific coast could be particularly rough.

"You're the boss."

Abigail glared at him. She had the childish desire to kick him in the shins as he walked with the kayak on his shoulder without the least indication that the weight or shape of it was a burden.

The boats slid into the water easily just as she predicted. More often than not, the water along the Mendocino coastline was rough with enormous swells so Abigail felt lucky to be able to paddle between rocks where the water was calm as they set out.

"It's a beautiful day," Aleksandr observed. She was beautiful, but he wasn't about to make the mistake of telling her so. The sun shone on her hair, turning it into a vibrant blaze of color. Her skin looked soft and he tightened his grip on the oar to keep from reaching out to touch her. He ached to touch her. She'd given him insomnia and he paced most nights, staring up at the stars and wondering where in the world she was. Now she was with him and yet there could still be an ocean between them.

She narrowed her gaze against the sun. "Why aren't you talking to Jonas about whatever you're doing? He's very good at his job."

"I agree he's good at his job, and it's obvious he means a great deal to you and to your sisters. He'll have his hands full investigating Danilov's death." He didn't want to talk about Jonas Harrington and he damn well didn't want to talk about Danilov. Cold rage swirled in his gut. He'd been fifteen minutes too late for Andre Danilov. The highway was narrow and winding and a car had pulled out in front of him, slowing him down. By the time he'd gotten around it and reached the marina, Danilov was dead. Sometimes it seemed like he was always running to catch up with killers and stumbling over the victims every time he turned around. Danilov had been a good man, a good agent, and Aleksandr was not going home without knowing he'd provided his own brand of justice.

"Isn't that what you're doing right now?" Abigail dipped her paddle into the water and sent her kayak gliding over the surface.

"The two things are tied together." Aleksandr kept pace effortlessly. "Danilov was undercover looking into the moving of artifacts and he was killed. I'd say there's a direct connection to my investigation as well as the fact that he's my responsibility. I'm going to find the son of a bitch who killed him."

Abbey paused and looked over at his face. There was no inflection in his voice, no anger or rage, but he said it with absolute conviction. "You're not just a policeman, are you, Sasha?"

He glanced at her as he sent his oar into the water with a powerful stroke so that his kayak shot ahead of hers. "Don't ask if you don't want to know something, Abbey," he cautioned. He should have known he would reveal too much to her. She was good at picking up every nuance. A seeker of the truth. Even her voice could make a man want to confess his every sin . . . and, God only knew, he had a lot of them.

After his part in what had happened in Russia, Abigail feared him. He could see it in her eyes, in the shadows that lurked there. He hated that he'd done that, put those shadows there, but he had no way to change who he was or what he was. He couldn't undo the past and he couldn't erase what was a large part of his character.

"This just gets better and better, doesn't it? Why in the world did you ever start up with me in the first place? I don't think you even know who you are."

"I know myself very well, Abbey, and I'll be damned if I apologize for the choices I've made. They were hard decisions, but I had good reasons for making them." He had sworn he wouldn't defend himself, but he had underestimated her reaction to what had happened, and her stubborn refusal to give him a chance to explain had caught him unawares. In Russia she'd always been so gentle and compassionate, her love for him so complete and unwavering. He was at a loss as to how to deal with her. He knew she could be stubborn and he knew she had a temper, but he hadn't counted on catching a tigress by the tail.

"Did you know about me? When I went to Moscow four years ago, did you know about my sisters and me?" It seemed ludicrous that someone in Russia would have knowledge of the Drakes, but her heart was beating overtime and she was certain she was right.

A gull shrieked overhead. Even with her dark glasses, the sunlight on the water dazzled her eyes when she attempted to read his expression. The kayak cut through the small swells as she paddled in silence. The surface resembled green glass and just below she could see occasional strands of kelp. She blinked rapidly as she stroked the oar through the water. "You did, didn't you? It wasn't just a chance meeting."

Aleksandr heard himself swear. Inside his head, in his mind, he was repeating every curse he knew. She was burying their chances as surely as if she took out a gun and shot him through the heart. He couldn't lie to Abigail, her voice always prevented that, but if he told the truth, she would never forgive him. "Don't you think you have enough to condemn me with without going into how it all started? It started. I fell in love with you." All he had in his defense was the truth. And it was only the truth that could seal the rift between them for all time.

They paddled fast in silence, past several sandy beaches, and entered a long stretch where the waves increased in size and strength. There were no rocks to use as protection and Abigail signaled to go out further from shore to avoid the larger breaking waves.

When they fell into a rhythm together in the calmer swells, Abigail glanced at him. It hurt to look at his face. She loved him so much she ached inside. "It mattered to me that you wanted Abigail Drake, just a woman without any magic, or any gift. Me. It mattered more than you know. Am I supposed to believe that the one part that's real and the truth is that you fell in love with me, when everything else has been a lie?"

"Ask it of me then," he challenged. "Your gift is to seek and find the truth. Ask me if I love you."

She turned her face away from him, staring straight ahead as they glided along the stretch of beach that was unfortunately free of rocks. They wanted to run in close to the shore but it was impossible with the rougher swells so they continued paddling, keeping the coastline in sight.

Abigail usually enjoyed kayaking along the coast. She could see the water-cut rocks up close and get into places her outboard could never reach. Powering herself through the water gave her a tremendous feeling of freedom. Right now, she felt threatened in some undefined way. Aleksandr wasn't in a conciliatory mood. In fact, if anything, she had the feeling he was angry with her.

"You aren't going to ask me, are you?" He wanted to drag her to him and shake some sense into her. They were good together. They fit. His life had never been right until he had Abigail. He'd never felt complete. He'd never had a home or a family. He'd never had anyone to come home to. Hell, he'd never wanted to go home. Abigail had changed everything and he couldn't go back to emptiness. She filled his life with laughter and love. She found soft spots in him, tenderness, a gentleness he'd never known he had.

"No."

"I never thought you were a coward, Abbey." He knew he'd put that wariness in her eyes. Could she feel pain over what he'd done if she didn't still love him? He held on to that hope. His only hope. She was hurting and he had to be happy that at least she felt something for him.

"To be honest, Sasha, I don't give a damn whether you think you love me or not. Yours isn't the kind of love I'm looking for so just drop it." Abigail gripped the paddle until her knuckles turned white. She was shaking with fury and if it weren't for the fact that they were on the trail of killers, she would have turned back. But whomever he was searching for had not only killed his friend, they had nearly killed Gene and attempted to murder her as well.

The kayak glided through the rather flat expanse of ocean, Abigail's attention on the shore. As they rounded the point she could make out a small beach in the distance where a group of women, most in billowy skirts and bright purple shirts, raced barefoot into the sea. The wind carried their laughter, a bright happy sound that warmed her.

"Do you see those women, Abbey?"

"They're impossible to miss." She found herself smiling at the bobbing red hats and squinted to try to pick out her aunt among them.

"They know how to live life. They participate and they find ways to be happy. You want to hold on to things that forever will keep us apart. For what?" He paused, turning his head to pin her with his steely eyes. "Tell me why you refuse to allow us to be happy."

"I came out here to help you find your criminals, not to engage in some philosophical debate, Sasha. Did you think you'd climb into my bedroom and I'd just melt into your arms after what happened?" She turned to look at the women racing waves and leaping over white foam. They did look happy and they appeared to be having a wonderful time. Unexpectedly her heart ached. Carol had always known how to have fun. To love and forgive and to enjoy every moment of her life. She cared little what others thought, but stuck to her own code.

"Maybe that's what's wrong with me," Abigail mused aloud. "Maybe I've forgotten my own code."

He reached out and stilled her boat. "Do you see something up above the beach in the rocks, near that small grouping of trees?"

Abigail narrowed her vision and peered at the windswept trees. "I can't really see anything. Was there movement?"

"Possibly. That is your aunt on the beach with the other women, isn't it?"

Abigail took a slow sweep of the rocky cliffs, paying particular attention to the trees and shrubs directly above the beach where the women were piling driftwood for what she very much feared was an illegal fire. She didn't have the prickle of awareness that sometimes came to her through her sisters, and her aunt was joyfully dancing, her arms waving gracefully in the air. Surely Carol herself would feel an alarm were she in danger.

Abigail dug her binoculars out of her pack and took another long look. The women formed a loose circle around the driftwood and, sure enough, small flames began to leap between the logs. One woman, and it was definitely her aunt Carol, stepped out of the circle to snap a photograph with the camera she always kept on a strap around her neck. Abigail centered her attention a second time on the cliff above the beach.

"I see them now," Abigail said, relieved. "Yes, a couple of the local boys and a couple of their friends from Fort Bragg. They're spying on the women. You don't have to worry about them, Aunt Carol will take care of them."

"Do you think she knows they're there?" he asked as he relinquished his hold on her kayak.

"Of course she knows. Aunt Carol is just like Sarah. She definitely 'knows' things. The boys are probably hoping she's going to do some kind of witchcraft for them to catch on film and show all their friends. Who knows, just to oblige them she might. She started the flames. More than likely Inez Nelson, who owns the grocery store in Sea Haven and pretty much runs the town, will box the boys in the ears when she sees them."

"I like your aunt." He was silent a moment. "And your sister Joley, too."

She didn't want him liking anyone in her family. "Come on, let's get around the next point. There are rocks there and we can get closer to shore."

Abigail took the lead, rowing strongly to get them away from the beach. Carol would know they were out on the ocean, watching her just as the snoopy teenage boys were. She didn't want Carol to think she was spying on her.

Around the point several rocks rose out of the water. Aleksandr and Abigial powered the kayaks over the larger swells, timing their move to get closer to land. The small inlet looked promising. Occasionally a large wave would break over the boulders, but the water was much calmer as they made their way toward the shoreline.

Stony cliffs rose up from the ocean. Green and brown vegetation grew in every possible crevice, but the terrain looked bleak, worn and carved through the centuries by the water. One long finger of stone reached out into the ocean as if beckoning to them and as the first set of boulders yielded no caves, they paddled to the larger rock formation.

"There's one here, Sasha," Abigail said, inching her way to the darker entrance. "It's small, more a grotto than an actual cave. I don't think anyone could successfully hide here." White water capped and foamed along the base of the rock and some sprayed into the air.

He struggled to find something genuine between them, a bridge to her. Something to ease the tension and give them a starting point. "It's wild here. Beautiful and wild, Abbey. No wonder you love this place."

"Yes, it is. I've always felt lucky growing up here." It was much easier paddling in the calmer water and Abbey pointed to the shore where the beach sparkled and glittered everywhere he looked. "That's Glass Beach, right in the middle of Fort Bragg. It's very unique and quite beautiful in its own way. It has tons of polished glass and people come to find the right colors they want."

"How can there be a beach of glass?"

"It was originally a dump site. For years, the ocean has pounded the glass, shaping and polishing it until the pieces look like beautiful glass stones." Abigail gestured toward the huge rock formations jutting up along the shore. "I doubt if we're going to find anything here, and in any case it's too close to a popular, well-frequented beach. They'd want a place far more secluded."

They rowed through the hundreds of rock formations strewn along the beach, paddling until their arms were weary. There were shallow channels and several caves, but nothing that would work to hide a boat. The kayaks wouldn't fit into the few small openings and

Abigail was certain they were still too close to shore and the smugglers would never risk being seen. They went around the next point where the cove was. The entire beach was private property.

Abigail immediately began maneuvering around the rocks to make certain there was nowhere a boat could be hidden. "I don't think there are any caves here, Sasha. At least I've never noticed any and I have gone kayaking along this shore many times."

"You're getting tired."

Abigail could feel his voice caress her skin. It seemed to sink through her skin and wind itself around her heart. Not for the first time she wondered if Aleksandr had magic of his own because she couldn't help reacting to him, every single time she heard him. "A little. I haven't done this in a while and I'm out of shape. What about you?" He didn't look tired. He looked as if he were enjoying himself. The spray skirt covered his legs, but she could see the powerful muscles of his back and arms working as he drove the kayak through the water.

"You said you had a code, Abbey. Do you?" The question seemed to come out of the blue and she struggled to find his motive for asking. He knew very well she lived by her honor as best she could. Whatever his reasons, she didn't want to be drawn in.

A touch of wind found them, slipped over her and brushed her cheek so that she almost didn't hear him. It wasn't the words, so much as how he said it. She remembered that voice from Moscow, when she loved him. When she'd do anything for him. When he made her feel as if she were the only woman in his world. Special beyond all imagining. Knowing she would be better off keeping her mouth shut, she nevertheless raised her chin, taking comfort from the touch of wind. "I know that I do. What about you? Do you have a code, Sasha?"

"Absolutely I live by one, Abbey." His gaze slid over her. "You know that I do. You know I will never turn away from a path when I know it is right."

"And it was right to sacrifice me for your career?" Why couldn't she stop? She could hear herself screaming to stop but she wanted to hurt him and she wasn't doing anything but hurting herself.

"No. Never for my career. For the lives of the other children the monster would have murdered. I would not trade lives for my own happiness, or for yours." He spoke quietly but his eyes were turbulent and a deep, dark blue. "I can't change who I am, Abbey. I can't undo the things I've done in my life. I can only tell you I love you and I want you in my life."

She looked away from him, looked away from the conviction in him, the lack of remorse. Abigail swallowed several times before she was certain she had complete command of her voice. "That's the last point before we're at Noyo Harbor. If we don't find what you're looking for, we'll have to try another day, leaving from the harbor and going farther south along the coastline."

"Do you really think I made the wrong decision?"

She stopped paddling and made a show of adjusting her seat. When she looked at him she deliberately met his gaze. "I want to know if you knew about my talent before we actually met." She waited in agony for what seemed a lifetime. In reality it was only a heartbeat of silence.

"Yes, I did."

The pain came out of nowhere, taking her by surprise. She could hear herself screaming with it, deep inside where no one else could hear. She told herself she had been expecting that answer, but it didn't lessen the stabbing, relentless ache. She had given him everything she was, everything she'd ever wanted to be. She had given so much of what she was, she had nothing left when he'd thrown her so carelessly away.

Abigail made every effort to keep him from knowing he'd gotten to her once again. She even told herself not to ask any other questions. She didn't want to know the extent of his betrayal, but she'd always been stubborn and filled with pride. "And my taking your picture was just an added bonus? A way to meet me so you could use me?"

"Yes."

Abigail turned away from him, slipping through the water with sure strong strokes to enter the bay. The screaming inside her rose until it was bile in her throat, until her ears roared and her temples throbbed. Pain ran so deep there were no words in her to tell him . . . or anyone else. She didn't want to feel. Not ever again.

She kept her face averted as she scanned the coastline looking for the arches and darker areas that would indicate openings in the rock.

Tears blurred her vision, but she shook her head to rid herself of them. He didn't need to know she'd never loved anyone before him. Or after him. Or even that he still had the ability to hurt her.

Abigail spotted several caves near the point. "Jackpot." She forced the word past the painful constriction in her throat.

"Stay behind me, Abbey."

"And your reasoning would be what? To protect me?" She quirked an eyebrow, but kept her face averted. "I think it's a little too late for that, Sasha."

"I'm not arguing about this. I'm taking the lead and you hang back." There was steel in his voice and a whip of anger.

Aleksandr was a man very much in control. For him to betray anger meant she was definitely hitting sore spots. She dropped back, allowing him the lead. If someone was lying in wait, Aleksandr had to be thinking about danger, not about being angry with her. Or maybe it was at himself. She gave him room to maneuver and followed him toward the first cave.

The cave was large enough to paddle into and Aleksandr did so with little hesitation, studying the high walls and roomy area. A boat could definitely slide inside and not be seen. With the chamber being so wide, it echoed and boomed as the waves slammed into the rock barrier, and inside the cavern the water was extremely rough. He relied on Abigail to remain outside to warn him of the larger waves coming into the cave that might be dangerous. He tried to find some sign, some small bit of evidence that would indicate the speedboat had been hiding when the coast guard had gone looking for it, but there was nothing at all. There was a light coming through a crack on one side indicating there might be another opening along the series of caves.

Water had poured and pounded the rock formation, widening the holes and smoothing and polishing, over centuries. Aleksandr paddled around the cove to try to find the source of the light, but was disappointed when the crack was too small for the kayak. A speedboat wouldn't have fared any better. There was no way through the cave.

He shook his head at Abigail. She was trying to watch him, watch the ocean, and keep an eye on the surrounding cliffs and cove in case a sharpshooter was positioned somewhere in concealment, watching them. Aleksandr powered the kayak along the bridge of rock to the next cave. This appeared far more promising. The chamber was quite large and could easily hide a speedboat. The water was far calmer, although much more shallow.

"I'm going in, Abigail. The water's about a meter deep, but the chamber goes all the way back and looks as if there's more to it than I can see from here. The water's far calmer in this cave and I don't like you being so exposed out here. Anyone could be sitting up in those rocks. I don't want you getting shot at again."

Abigail didn't particularly care to be a sitting target either, so she followed him into the large chamber, paddling all the way through it to the back where waves crashed into a smaller tunnel.

"We might be able to make it on through," Aleksandr said. "What do you think?"

"I doubt they'd take a speedboat in there." She peered as far in-side as she could. "It looks as if it makes a turn toward the left and narrows a bit. We might make it through, but I don't think they'd risk it. I think this cave is close to the harbor and they more than likely hid out here while the coast guard looked for them. If they had to abandon the boat they could make it back to shore with diving gear."

"If that tunnel goes all the way through to that other cave, they have a handy escape route," he reasoned.

"Let's look around in here first before we try it," Abigail suggested. "If we find anything at all to indicate they might have used the tunnel, then we'll see if we can make it through."

She paddled around the inside of the chamber, peering down into the water while he examined the rocky walls and the few outcroppings and ledges for any evidence that might indicate the men who shot Danilov had been in the chamber. If they'd used it once, there was a good chance they would use it again and Aleksandr would be waiting.

"There are caves over by Sea Lion Cove," Abigail said. "Isn't it more likely they'd use a place close to the mill and the smugglers' route on a more permanent basis? They'd have to have a place to stash the boat when they weren't using it."

"Not necessarily."

Abigail turned sharply and stared at him. "Who are you chasing, Sasha? Are they art thieves? Is Jonas being fed a line of bull?"

"My country has one of the highest ratios for stolen art in the world," he said.

"That isn't an answer."

"You saw the necklace. It is genuine."

Abigail felt the small flutter in the pit of her stomach, the one that always warned her when the truth was something more than what she was hearing. She'd felt that flutter four years ago and hadn't acted fast enough. "Aleksandr, don't send Jonas on a wild-goose chase. He doesn't deserve that."

"His job is to find out who killed Danilov. The murder occurred in his jurisdiction and I'm certain he'll take his job seriously. He's that kind of man. My job is to shut down the drain of artifacts coming out of our country and to recover what I can."

"Then why are we out here paddling kayaks looking for that speedboat?"

He glanced up, his eyes glittering, diamond hard. "It happens to be part of my investigation."

Abigail shivered. He had changed in the last four years. There'd always been an edge to Aleksandr, a side of him she could never quite reach, but it seemed more pronounced now. Jonas had warned her away from Aleksandr, and Jonas was a shrewd judge of character.

Without warning Aleksandr reached over and dragged her kayak close to his so they were facing each other. "Get that look off your face. I may deserve anger from you, but not that."

Her heart jumped wildly and her hand went to her throat in a gesture of defense. "I have no idea what you're talking about."

"*Fear.*" He snarled the word. "You have never had reason to be afraid of me. You're looking at me as if I might whip out a gun and shoot you. I don't deserve that from you and I'm damned sick of seeing it."

She bit back a retort. She *wanted* to fight with him. She wanted to be at odds with him so she could keep him at arm's length, but his behavior was very unusual. Aleksandr didn't fight or argue. It wasn't his way. Abigail didn't like to argue either and most of their time spent together had been either hot and sexual, or lazy and pleasant. Worse than his strange behavior, and the unusual anger that seemed to be smoldering just beneath the surface, was the hurt in his eyes. She didn't want to see it. He didn't *deserve* to have her see it or acknowledge it, but she'd hurt him simply by the flash of fear she'd shown.

"I'm sorry, Sasha." She snapped her teeth together, annoyed that the words had slipped out. "I guess we really don't know one another very well anymore. It's been a long time. I've been through a few traumatic events and I'm not quite as strong as I used to be. Maybe it's the same for you."

She refused to stare into his eyes. She would not be mesmerized by him. She wouldn't believe in him or be dazzled by the strength of his personality or his driving purpose. She had to stay focused on what she could and couldn't live with. Aleksandr Volstov had been a beautiful dream, a figment of her imagination. The man with her now was hard, as tough as nails, and he would sacrifice anyone or anything for his purpose. She had to see him that way and no other or she would lose herself again.

Abigail peered over the side of her kayak, scanning the water. It was darker in the cave and the shadows made it difficult to see below the surface. A hole in the ceiling near the back allowed the sunlight to pour down across the water. She quartered slowly back and forth, keeping away from Aleksandr. Trying not to think or feel. There were so many rocks and nooks and the kelp swayed back and forth with the motion of the waves, making it nearly impossible to see anything.

"What's that?" He pointed to a spot just to her left.

Abigail moved slightly. The kelp alternately covered and revealed an object glinting in the sun. "I can't make it out."

"It's something shiny. Could be metal."

Retrieving the object was going to be a slight challenge. If they'd been in kayaks without skirts, they could hop off and fish around. But with the type of kayak they were using, once they got out in the water, they would have a difficult time getting back in without help. "Do you want it?" she asked.

"I'll get it," he said.

Abigail ignored him and leaned over as far as possible, her paddle locked firmly in one hand while she stretched her other arm toward the object, closed her eyes, and dove for it. Her hand landed clumsily on it, and she made her grab as she set up for the roll and came up dripping wet, the thing in her palm.

"Show-off," Aleksandr groused. "What is it?"

She opened her fist. "A watch." She held it out to him. "Do you recognize it?"

Aleksandr turned it over in his hands. "This was Danilov's watch. The bastards must have taken it off of him before they shot him."

"I'm sorry, Sasha. Why would they take it off of him?"

"We sometimes carry tracking devices. Danilov's was in his watch."

"How would they know that?"

"It may have been a guess."

His voice was distant, as if his mind were somewhere far away. The tight knot inside of her shifted and loosened. And that was frightening. She had lost herself after his betrayal. She could never go through such a thing again and she needed to keep her defenses up. His sorrow, his anger, all of his emotions ate away at her until she could only think of comforting him. She detested that particularly empathic part of her she could never control.

"What was he like?"

Aleksandr was silent for a long time. The ocean boomed against the rocks as the waves washed in and out endlessly. He sighed. "I worked with him, Abbey. I didn't socialize with him. I wish I could have gotten past that part of me, the kid raised by the state to work for the state and never trust anyone, but I've only done that one time." He pushed his hand through his hair, a sign of agitation she had rarely seen him make. "I should have talked with him more. He had a family, people he was close with." Aleksandr swore in his own language and looked away from her.

Abigail thought back to all the time she'd spent in his company. They had been so wrapped up in one another she hadn't considered that he'd never introduced her to friends. Coworkers, many times, but never friends. "You were so wonderful with Joley, Sasha, you knew exactly the right thing to say to her."

"I've had a lot of training, Abbey. I read people."

"Were you ever really in love with me?" The moment the words slipped out she wanted to stuff them back down her throat. Her throat was raw with pain and it came through in her voice.

He swore again. "How can you ask me that?"

"You just told me our meeting wasn't an accident, that you knew about my abilities before you ever met me. I may have been naïve,

Aleksandr, but I'm a thinking person again. You arranged that meeting with me and you pretended to enjoy my company so I'd help you with your case."

"Damn it, Abbey. Children were dying. Do you want me to apologize because I wanted to use every tool available to me? I was fighting red tape, my superiors, parents, other agencies. He'd been killing for over two years. Do you want to know what my nightmares were like?"

For a moment his chest burned and his stomach knotted and churned. He wanted to shake her. He wanted to drag her off where they could be alone and she couldn't get away and would have to listen to him. It was a dark, primitive urge and he was slightly ashamed of it, but he wasn't going to apologize for the things he had to do. She hadn't been the one to examine the little bodies. And she wasn't the one to tell the parents their child wasn't coming home because a sick and twisted monster had taken them. And she wasn't the one fighting day and night to get assistance, *any* assistance, when no one wanted to admit it was happening. Or even that it *could* happen.

She studied his face. His anger turned his eyes a dark blue and put small white lines around his mouth. "Why didn't you just ask me to help you?"

"I didn't know you. I didn't know what you were like. You were from another country and you had a talent I didn't really understand. If I had it to do over again, Abbey, I'd have told you the truth from the start, but even if I wasn't truthful about having prior knowledge of your abilities, believe that my feelings for you were—and are—genuine. You didn't just change my life, you changed *me*. Something inside me is different. I thought I could exist without you, but I can't. I can't and it doesn't make any sense."

"Aleksandr." She tried to stop him but he shook his head.

"No, you did this. You made it impossible for me to be alive without you. The work doesn't matter the way it did. I go through the motions and I get the job done, but it isn't the same. I had purpose and drive and you took that away with you. I've thought a lot about this. God knows I've had enough time to think about it. You're angry and you're hurt and I accept that you have a right to be, but it doesn't change the fact that we're supposed to be together. I'm not willing to just throw away what we had."

A strong wave crashed through the chamber, booming and spraying water high. "We'd better get out of here," Abigail cautioned.
There was no talking to him. If what he said was the truth, it broke
her heart. If what he said was a lie, it was broken anyway. She wanted
to go home and be comforted by the warmth and love of her sisters.
"We still have to get to the harbor, Sasha. It's getting late. At least you
know this is where they hid that night."

"It isn't where they keep the boat. We have to find the boat."

Abigail frowned, trying to remember every detail of the coastline
she'd traveled. She snapped her fingers. "Wait a minute. I don't know
why I didn't think about this before, but there is a place south of
here. It's a distance, but if I were going to hide a boat from everyone,
that's where I'd hide it. It isn't a cave, Sasha, but you see how the tide
comes in and the waves can be rough. This is calm for this coastline.
Hiding a boat in a cave is dangerous even for a short time. I'll bet they
hid here and then moved the boat as soon as they thought it safe."

"They'd want someplace not easily seen from either a beach or
the sea."

"There's a cove just north of the town of Elk. It sits between two
fingers of Cuffeys Cove. The beach is sandy and stays dry at high
tides unless there's a storm. A boat could be hauled back up into the
brush and trees. Sport fishermen might see it, but a coast guard cutter
wouldn't because the cove faces south. Even the highway curves
away from the shore and that would make it possible to hide it there.
Normally they have a caretaker who runs anyone off when they try
to go through private property, but Inez told me a couple of weeks
ago that they found him injured and he's in the hospital."

"Let's go check it out."

"You know we can't do it today. Look at the swells." She gestured
out to sea. "This coastline can be very rough. Let's head in and we'll
do it another day."

"I still need you tonight. I'm heading over to the Caspar Inn and
will need you to go with me."

"Why would I have to go with you? The inn is perfectly safe.
Everyone goes there just to hang out."

"I need you to go with me. I don't have a partner, remember?"

"Take Jonas," she hissed through her teeth, paddling furiously to
try to get away from him.

He easily kept pace. "Everyone knows Jonas. I think I've located Ilya Prakenskii. He works for a man named Sergei Nikitin and I told you, he's a very dangerous man. If you're with me, it might be a peaceful meeting. Without you there, they'll think I've come hunting them and someone could get hurt."

She scowled at him with open suspicion. "I cannot imagine you wanting me with you if there's the least chance of danger."

"Ordinarily, that would be true, but I think your presence will deter violence and there are too many innocents there."

"Do you think Prakenskii and Nikitin are involved in the theft of artifacts?"

"That's what I intend to find out."

Abigail sighed. She should just say no. It should be easy, but instead she shrugged, trying to still her pounding heart. "What time?"

9

ABIGAIL could hear a loud chorus of giggles as she walked down the stairs. Her aunt's voice said something and then a solemn chant followed. Her sisters were definitely casting and not one of them had called her in on the fun. Irritated, she stomped into the living room.

Hundreds of candles flickered, throwing dancing shadows on the walls. Her sisters and her aunt formed a circle in the middle of the floor where seven red candles were arranged, one in front of each of them. Abigail gasped. "Oh, no! What are you doing?" She took a step closer and to her horror a pair of red lace panties lay in the exact center of the circle. "Those had better not be mine!" They looked like hers. They looked *exactly* like hers. "You wouldn't *dare!*"

The women looked up, grinning from ear to ear, dissolving into laughter at her outraged expression.

"I *know* you didn't steal my underwear out of my drawer!"

"Of course not," Hannah said righteously. "We'd never go into your room."

Abigail put her hands on her hips and glared. "I've never worn them. I bought them months ago when I was determined to get over Aleksandr, but I decided I wasn't ready. You can't claim you found them in the laundry."

"We're almost finished." Hannah held up her finger and turned back to the circle. Six of the seven red candles were lit. Only the one in front of Hannah remained. The women intoned the ritual words solemnly.

> *Scarlet lace fans passion's flame*
> *Summons the man of studly fame*
>
> *Lusty love on floor and chair*
> *Tabletop and vixen's lair*
>
> *The fires engulf, set senses aflame*
> *With pulsing desire, he calls your name*

As their voices rose in harmonic accord, Hannah lit the last red candle so that seven flames burned around the sexy lace underwear.

Abigail briefly covered her face with her hands. "I don't believe this. I really don't believe this." She glowered at her youngest sister. "I can understand the others—Hannah and Joley especially and even Aunt Carol—but Elle, you?"

Elle grinned, clearly unrepentant. "You don't have to wear them, Abbey, but just in case, you have them."

Hannah completed the ceremony by rolling a scroll containing the words and symbols of the chant around the red panties and sealing the scroll with a drop of wax from each of the red candles. "Here you go, Abbey," she said brightly. "Just remember to be *very* careful when you wear them. Anything can happen."

Abigail put her hands behind her back. "All of you are in so much trouble. I intend to retaliate. This is so wrong! How did you get my brand-new underwear when I *hid* them even from myself?"

Hannah shrugged. "They floated down the stairs right into the circle."

Abigail scowled at Joley. "*You!* You treacherous witch. You did this with your spell singing. Those things"—she indicated Hannah's outstretched hand—"are lethal *especially* since I'm going out with him tonight."

Hannah dropped her arm to her side, retaining possession of the lace underwear. Laughter faded from her eyes. "What do you mean, you're going out with him? Him? Aleksandr? The rotter who made you cry? *That* him? The ceremony was for when you go on a date with someone else. Not for *him*."

"It isn't exactly a date," Abigail corrected her. "He needs me to go with him to the Caspar Inn."

"Really? Dancing is always fun." Joley raised her eyebrow and glanced at Hannah. "I feel like a night out, what about you?"

"You can't go," Abigail said. "None of you. It might be dangerous. Joley, you were already shot at and forced to swim through an underwater cave."

"I'm totally with Aunt Carol. Memories are great. I'm taking pictures of the cove and journaling the experience," Joley said, winking at her aunt. "I told you I think scrapbooking is the best way to go."

"I'm *forbidding* any of you to go to the Caspar Inn."

"They do have great music there," Sarah pointed out.

"You're supposed to be helping me," Abigail wailed. "What's wrong with all of you? This could be really, really dangerous."

"Which is exactly why we should be there," Joley said. "Aleksandr the Great did not look after you properly so we're going to make certain it gets done."

"It's not like we don't go dancing at the inn all the time," Kate added. "It's normal for us to go. People expect it. Matt will probably suggest to his brother Danny to bring Trudy Garret. They're engaged. I forgot to tell you all that. She'll have to find a sitter for her little boy, Davy, but if I call now, she'll be able to go."

"The more the merrier," Joley said. "What about you, Aunt Carol? Would some of the ladies in your Red Hat Club want to come?"

"That sounds lovely, dear. And I might ask Reginald as well," Carol said.

"Reginald?" The Drake sisters exchanged puzzled looks.

"I believe you refer to him as old man Mars," Carol said, a small bite in her voice.

The silence lengthened and grew. Candlelight flickered. The sisters looked to Sarah. She cleared her throat carefully. "Aunt Carol. Hon. You aren't considering taking a romantic interest in old . . . er . . . Mr. Mars, are you?"

"And why not? He's quite dashing and in his youth he had a wonderful sense of humor. I saw him at his fruit stand and we chatted for an hour. He was quite charming and very happy to see me."

"But Aunt Carol," Kate protested.

"He was extremely interested in Creative Memories and made an appointment with me to host a workshop at his home. He's inviting the ladies of the Red Hat Club and we're going to make up several pages for their albums."

"I didn't know he had a home," Joley said.

Carol smacked her over the head with a rolled-up newspaper. "That isn't funny, young lady. Reginald is a wonderful man and his home is lovely."

"Are you telling us that old man Mars is going to invite a bunch of people into his home and do scrapbooking?" Abigail asked incredulously.

"I don't see why you're all being so silly over this," Carol said. "I dated him years ago, even before Jefferson. I broke his heart, although I didn't mean to. It was a difficult decision which one of them to stay with. I was engaged to both but of course had to make up my mind when my mother found out. I cried for days."

Abigail sank down onto the floor beside Hannah. "You actually dated him?"

"And cried over him?" Joley asked.

"I'm feeling faint," Hannah said.

Abigail took the rolled-up red panties from Hannah. "Maybe we should give these to you, Aunt Carol."

Joley gripped her leg hard. "Abbey! Bite your tongue. Aunt Carol, you cannot sleep with that man. I mean it. He has repressed hostility issues. He could murder you and throw your body into the ocean."

"His hostility is hardly repressed," Sarah said. "He throws fruit at people."

"That hardly makes him a serial killer," Carol said.

"Wait a minute." Libby held up her hand. "You were engaged to *both* men? At the same time?"

Carol sighed and patted her hair. "I know, I know. It was wrong of me, but they were so wonderful. Two handsome, strong men utterly devoted to me. I couldn't resist either of them."

"Aunt Carol." Libby chose her words carefully. "Have you set up any other Creative Memories workshops?"

"Well, Inez wants to have a class at her home and of course so does Donna. I did stop by Irene's just to say hello and Drew was interested in his own small album so I said I'd help him with that. And I ran into Frank Warner." She looked at their faces. "It was purely an accident. He was coming up the sidewalk and it was such a good thing. I stepped in a crack and nearly fell. I turned my ankle, but fortunately he prevented me from falling and helped me hobble down to the Sidewalk Café. We had coffee and chatted."

"Jonas told you to stay away from him," Sarah reprimanded her.

"Should I have been rude when he helped me?" Carol looked pleased with herself. "In any case it turned out superbly. Reginald went by and saw us together and that will definitely get his attention, and Frank invited me to his home to see his collection."

"And why would he do that?" Kate asked suspiciously. "He's never invited any of us to see his collection."

"Well, dear, he knew I shared his interest and he was being polite. I told him my hobby was photography and asked if he'd mind me practicing on his art. It's much more difficult than people think to take great pictures of art objects. I told him I'd give him the photographs in an album along with the negatives. He was very cooperative."

"You know, Aunt Carol," Hannah said, "you think you're safe from Jonas's lectures because you're his favorite aunt, but that won't stop him. He'll be awful. He'll get all snarly and make you feel guilty."

Carol smiled serenely. "That's just not possible, dear. I rarely allow myself to feel guilt. It's such an exhausting and wasteful emotion. It can actually be self-indulgent and some people get caught up in wallowing in guilt. I prefer to move forward and live my life. Jonas can snarl all he likes, but the fact is, I'm reacquainting myself with Sea Haven and I rather like Frank."

Joley put her hand over her ears. "I don't want to hear this. We have to go to his freakin' parties every single time we come home. In fact, I think he only has them when we come home so we can be his celebrities on display. I detest going to those parties. We have to dress up and mingle with tons of people we don't know and will never meet again."

"Your language is atrocious, Joley. And in your business you should be used to dealing with strangers," Carol admonished. "Helping your community is a must for anyone, not just a Drake."

Joley grinned impishly. "Fine, if you want to date the man, go right ahead. I'll show up at his posh open house and poke around a little myself."

"You will *not!*" Carol and Sarah said at the same time.

"Why is it everyone else can play sleuth and have fun, but not me? In fact, maybe I will take those red panties. Abbey doesn't need them." She snapped her fingers and held out her hand.

"Back off, sister!" Abbey found herself laughing again. It was just that way in her family. When they were together, no matter how bad she felt, her sisters managed to make her laugh. "Speaking of the red panties, Aunt Carol, there is *no* way that spell came from a spell book. It's too silly. Where in the world did it come from?"

Carol joined in the laughter as her gaze rested on Hannah. "I'll bet you try new things all the time, don't you, dear?"

Hannah held up her hands. "This time, I'm totally innocent. It wasn't me."

"No, it wasn't you. It was your aunt Blythe. She has your talent and one of our dearest friends was over one night, in tears. Her life was so difficult, you know. She took care of her father, who was quite ill, and she hadn't had a romantic encounter for quite some time. Years, actually. So we wanted to make her laugh and boost her confidence and Blythe came up with the red panty ceremony. Of course we laughed hysterically and made our friend laugh and all in all it was a great evening."

"But it works."

"Well, of course it does. Hannah will tell you she can take something very silly and still make it work. Women need confidence at times; just as many people carry a talisman and think it brings luck, the extra boost made our friend, and anyone using the ritual, as silly as it is, feel beautiful and confident. Every time you put on the red lace underwear you can't help but remember the ceremony and it makes you laugh, so you glow and that's attractive as well. It all works on a woman's confidence."

"Go, Aunt Blythe!" Joley said.

"Hannah, can you really do that?" Abbey asked. "Create spells?"

Hannah shrugged and looked at Joley, and the two burst out laughing. "We do it all the time, but sometimes it backfires." Hannah nudged Abigail. "What time are you supposed to be ready for your big date? It's getting late."

"It's not a date," Abigail insisted. "I'm helping him."

"Is he picking you up or are you taking your own car?" Sarah asked.

"Oh, for Pete's sake, he's picking me up, but we're supposed to look like we're on a date. That's the point."

"Are you sure you want to do this?" Kate asked. "I know it hurts you to be in his company."

"It hurts me when I think about him, which is all the time," Abigail admitted. "I'd rather help him, make certain he doesn't get killed, and get him out of Sea Haven fast. I always enjoy going to the Caspar Inn. I know everyone there and I'll have fun." She glanced at her watch. "I'd better get ready. And all of you stop with the ceremonies."

Hannah held out her hand. "I'll lock those up until he's long gone."

"No, you won't. And none of my other stuff had better start floating through the house," Abigail warned.

"Jonas is coming up the drive," Sarah announced.

"I don't want to talk to him," Abigail said hastily. "He's left a couple of messages and I don't have anything to tell him."

"I'm not answering the door," Hannah said. "Someone else get it."

"Abbey," Sarah protested, "it's Jonas. You can't just ignore him."

"I'm not exactly ignoring him, I'm busy. There's a big difference." She raced back up the stairs as Carol opened the front door. Her sisters stared after her in dismay.

ABIGAIL sat on the edge of her bed for a long time wrapped in a bath sheet after her shower. She slowly broke the seal on the scroll. The spell didn't have to work and she told herself she just wanted to feel beautiful. She *needed* to feel beautiful. She couldn't face being in a roomful of women with Aleksandr, feeling like plain old Abigail Drake.

The Caspar Inn wasn't fancy, she didn't have to dress in elegant clothes, but she wanted something feminine and attractive. The inn was all about great music and dancing, a place where many of the residents from several of the coastal towns met to visit. She touched the red lace with a small sigh. It wasn't as if she and Aleksandr had taken a room at the inn, or anywhere else for that matter.

"Hey!" Hannah poked her head in the room. "Do you want company?"

Abigail nodded and waited until Hannah had firmly closed the door. "Jonas is still down there, isn't he?"

"Oh, yeah," Hannah admitted. "Sarah and Kate diverted him by giving up Aunt Carol. She's handling him quite nicely, but I know if he can't make her do everything he says, Jonas will jump all over me. He always does when he's angry with one of the others. I'm an easy target apparently, so I'm hiding up here with you." She looked curiously at the red lace panties. "What are you doing?"

"I don't know. Sitting here. Deciding if I'm going to be good and dress in blue jeans and a nice, demure top, or wear the red lace and a dress to make him squirm. Should I be the good girl or the bad one?"

"Which do you want to be?"

"Bad. Very, very bad. I want him to look at me and wish he'd never given me up. I want him to dream about me and remember every time he touched me."

"You want to torture him?"

"Absolutely torture him. And I want it to last a very long time," Abigail admitted.

"Torture can be a two-edged sword, Abbey," Hannah counseled. "Are you certain you want to take the chance? What if you fall in love with him all over again?"

Abigail looked around her as if the walls might have ears. She lowered her voice. "I never fell *out* of love with him. I'm so far in love with him it makes me sick, but I'll never admit it to him again."

"Definitely wear the underwear and that really tight black tank with a red lace bra under it. The tank that is open over your tummy. You have a great tummy. All that swimming." Hannah picked up the brush. "Wear your hair down. You never do and he's probably used to you wearing it up. You have wonderful hair."

"I shouldn't be doing this," Abigail hedged.

"Maybe not, but it might make you feel better. And in any case, if he hurts you, he's going to be turned into either a toad or a slug.

I'm leaning toward the slug at the moment." She laughed softly. "That place will be packed. You know Sylvia Fredrickson is going to be there and she'll be flirting like crazy. Gina Farley, you know her, she runs the local preschool now and Patty Granger will probably be there too. They love to dance. A lot of the women like to go there to dance. You'll need to feel beautiful." She paused, allowing Abigail's hair to settle into place. "Is he the type to look at other women when he's with you?"

Abigail laughed. "You know me better than that. I'd hit him over the head."

"You look beautiful, Abbey, and dressed up in your black jeans you'll look awesome. Wear the pair that hugs your hips. Do you have a chain to go around your waist? I've got a great one if you don't."

"I'd love to borrow it," Abigail said bravely. Hannah was always a fashion plate, while Abigail tended to throw on her most comfortable outfit. If Hannah said she needed a chain then she was going to wear one and she was going to knock Aleksandr Volstov's socks off.

"Do you mind if I say something?" Hannah asked. "It's a very personal observation."

"Go for it." Abigail felt reckless.

"Abbey, you've never been the type of woman to have a knockdown drag-out fight. Even when we were kids, you didn't really argue, not with Mom and Dad, not with us, and not with your friends. If you didn't like something you went away. Literally. You close doors on people."

"I know I do." Abbey stared down at her hands to avoid Hannah's gaze. "I survive that way."

"It isn't just survival. It's your way of fighting. You refuse to engage and then you can't lose. You're a very strong woman and you aren't afraid. You do things most people would never do. You're way stronger than I am, but you have to know when you close those doors, you don't leave anything for the other person. Everyone makes mistakes. *Everyone.* I love you very much and all I'm saying is, you wouldn't be letting Aleksandr Volstov into our home, into our lives if you didn't still have *very* strong feelings for him. You'd never admit to Aleksandr for a second that you love him, and you'd *never* consider dressing up for him."

Hannah stepped one foot out of the bedroom, her hands gracefully moving through the air. "I just think if you have such strong feelings for him, you should consider why. What he did was terrible. Or maybe to us it's terrible. I have no idea what it would be like to try to live and work in the turmoil of what's been taking place in his country over the last few years. You've always been good at looking at all sides of an issue, Abbey, but maybe you're too close to this one."

Her fingers snagged a glittering chain of fine gold as it floated through the hall to her. "This will be perfect on you."

"I honestly don't know how I feel about Aleksandr right now," Abigail admitted as Hannah dropped the chain onto her outstretched palm. "I did close that door. Very firmly. I made certain I moved around so there was no chance that he could catch up with me. I returned his letters unopened. There was nothing to say. I don't know him. I thought I did, but I don't. I can't be in love with, nor can I trust a man I don't know."

"You're very drawn to him," Hannah said. "And when he's close to you your auras mix together. They aren't distinct. The house let him in. You say you've closed him out, but you went with him kayaking and you certainly didn't have to do that. You're going with him tonight and again, there's no real reason. What I'm saying is, you aren't a woman to do things you don't want to do. You *want* to be with him. If you didn't, Abbey, he would never get close to you. You'd be in the sea or on the beach or flying off to Australia or Florida or any other place where you go to be with your dolphins. You wouldn't be here with him."

Abigail drew the tank top over her head. "I wish you weren't right, Hannah." She pulled her hair out off her neck and let it settle back into place. "I have no idea what to do with him. I'm so afraid I'll never survive him again."

"Why?" Hannah peered at the earring rack to find the most suitable earrings. "Do you even know why?"

Standing in the red lace panties and black tank top, Abigail looked vulnerable as she pressed the black jeans to her chest. "I don't think love is supposed to be like this, Hannah. I ache all the time. I think about him all the time. I've always been whole without a man, but somehow he changed that and now I look at him, this man who was my world, and wonder if I ever really knew him. He isn't what I thought."

"What did you think?"

Abigail sank onto the bed. "Words like *gentle* and *tender* come to mind. Now I look at him and think *ruthless* and *merciless*. How can that be?"

"We all have many sides. You do. You know you do. Why are you always so careful to hold yourself in check? You have a temper and you're quite capable of retaliating when someone has upset you. That's why you walk away, you're so afraid of what you might do."

Abigail shook her head. "It isn't the same. I thought it was the same, but it isn't."

Hannah sighed. "I'm not certain what you're talking about so I can't help. Would he hurt you? Hit you?"

"No! Heavens no! He would *never* hurt me no matter how angry he got. No." Abigail shook her head adamantly. "Aleksandr would step in front of a bullet for me."

There was a small silence. Abigail looked shocked. "Did I just say that? It's true, but I hadn't thought about it."

Hannah patted her hand. "If you know that deep in your heart, Abbey, I suspect you know he's very much in love with you. Maybe you owe it to both of you to give him another chance, to find out exactly what happened, his reasons, and see if you can live with them."

Abigail pulled on her trousers. "I don't know. I still can't believe he's here. It seems like a dream. And he told me he thinks a man named Leonid Ignatev has put out a hit on him. Ignatev tried a power play using me as a pawn and Aleksandr managed to get me out of Russia and defeat him."

"That's not good," Hannah said and sank onto the bed. "Have you told Jonas?"

"We can't tell Jonas. He'd try to have Aleksandr deported just to get him away from us. You know he would. He wouldn't want Aleksandr anywhere near us." She rubbed her temples. "I shouldn't let him anywhere near any of you, but I know you all so well. It won't matter what I say. You'll butt in anyway."

Hannah laughed. "You're so right, although I am worried about Aunt Carol playing the detective with Frank Warner. None of us really know him that well. Could he be involved in this?"

"He's good friends with Inez and she's a great judge of character.

I don't know. On the surface, it looks like there's some small pointers toward him, but I'm not about to jump to conclusions," Abigail said. She settled the gold chain around her waist. "What do you think?"

"I think you're going to make him crazy," Hannah said. "Don't be surprised when most of Sea Haven shows up tonight at the Caspar Inn."

"I'm expecting everyone. There's no way Aunt Carol and her friends are going to stay away. And it might be worth it to see her Reginald."

"I wish I could attract men the way she does," Hannah said wistfully.

"Hannah!" Abigail hugged her sister to her. "You attract tons of men. You just don't do anything about it."

Hannah shook her head. "No, I don't. No one ever asks me out."

"Do you want them to ask you out? Is there anyone in particular you're interested in?" Abigail asked.

Hannah shrugged. "No. Not really. I just would like to be able to go on a date if anyone interesting did come along."

Abigail studied her sister's face, with its perfect bone structure. Hannah was beautiful with her flawless skin and enormous, heavily lashed eyes. "It will happen."

Hannah flashed a brief smile. "I'll magically be able to talk without stuttering?"

"You can talk to all of us without stuttering. And sometimes Jonas. We're not always helping you when he's around."

"Jonas doesn't count. I have to be able to talk to him in order to defend myself. And I never talk about anything important with him."

"It will happen."

"Abigail!" Jonas's voice boomed up the stairs.

Hannah flinched visibly. "I think I'll go get dressed and see if Joley wants to go with me tonight."

"You're really going to show up in Caspar, aren't you?" Abigail asked.

"I wouldn't miss it," Hannah said.

"Wish me luck." Abigail winked at Hannah and raised her voice. "I'm coming, Jonas, there's no need to wake the dead." She hurried down the stairs to prevent him from coming up and running into Hannah.

"Sorry, Abbey." Jonas pushed a hand through his hair, leaving it disheveled. "I've got too many things on my mind and I think Aunt Carol is going to be the death of me. If the Russian mafia is in any way mixed up with Frank Warner, I certainly don't want her over there with her camera."

"Have you eaten today? You look tired," Abbey said. "Come in the kitchen while we talk and I'll fix you something to eat."

"Thanks, I can pick something up at the Salt Bar and Grill later."

"It's no trouble." She led the way to the kitchen and waved him toward a chair. "You can't watch over everyone, Jonas. We're all responsible for the choices we make."

"I know that, Abbey." Jonas toed a chair around and straddled it, watching her as she waved a casual hand toward the stove. "I have friends in all the small towns up and down this coastline. The mafia plays rough. If they're here, I want to know why. And I want them out of here before anyone else gets hurt."

"Have you talked to Marsha? How's Gene doing?"

"He's still in intensive care. Without you and your sisters, he would be dead. Marsha sends her love and says she'll be in touch when Gene's out of the woods."

"Has he been able to say anything?"

Jonas shook his head. "No, he's still in a coma. The doctors aren't sure he'll be able to remember much, if anything at all, even if he does wake up."

"Poor Marsha. The entire family must be so upset." Abigail sighed. "You'd think, since all the towns are so small, it would be easy to find a group of Russians. Someone must know where they are staying, Jonas. They have to be at one of the hotels or motels or bed-and-breakfast inns. Once you find them, everyone can keep an eye on them." Abigail beat several eggs and poured the mixture into an omelet pan.

"Unfortunately it isn't that easy. I've made inquiries, of course, but my guess is they rented a house through a third party so the house owner doesn't even know who they're renting to." He indicated the eggs. "More cheese. I like a lot of cheese."

"I'm saving room for vegetables. You need good nutrition." Her hands flew over the vegetables as she chopped a variety into small pieces. "Of course, if they're at all like Aleksandr and can speak English without an accent . . ." She trailed off.

"He has an accent."

"Only when he wants to have one. I minored in languages, Jonas, and I speak six fairly well, but nothing like Aleksandr. He speaks with a perfect, native accent whenever he wants to. And depending on the local dialect he can change the sound to blend as well. He's a genius when it comes to languages."

"Then why does he speak with a Russian accent?"

Abigail turned around at a sound in Jonas's voice. He was no longer sitting slumped, but was fully alert, his eyes diamond hard. "I don't know. That's a good question. He spoke with an accent when we were in Russia as well, but I've heard him speak flawless English and he can sound as if he's from the South or a native of California. I wouldn't be able to tell the difference. He said he was trained that way."

"I'll just bet he was." Jonas leapt up. "You have any coffee around here?"

"We don't drink coffee, Jonas, you know that. What's wrong?"

"He's an operative, that's what's wrong. He's probably a spy."

"There isn't a cold war going on—do we still have spies?"

"You know, Abbey, you're not funny. You need to be serious about this. Aleksandr Volstov is bad news any way you look at him."

Abigail dumped a handful of vegetables into the middle of the egg mixture. "I'm well aware of what Aleksandr is and what he isn't. He says he's here on Interpol business, Jonas. I was not-so-subtly giving you a heads-up."

There was a small silence. "Thank you," Jonas acknowledged.

"You're welcome."

"Turn on the tea water." He looked around. "Where's Hannah when you need her? In fact, where is everyone? They all disappeared."

"She was afraid you'd be mean to her." She leaned her hip against the counter and pointed the spatula. "Did you really call her a wire hanger?"

"Damn it, Abbey, let's not go there."

"You did, didn't you? That was cruel, Jonas. Why do you do that to her? Don't you think she has feelings?"

"She knows she's beautiful, Abbey. Hell, everyone knows it. She's on the cover of every magazine from here to hell and back. It would be cruel if it were true. You can't tell me I'm hurting her feelings when I tell her to gain a little weight."

"She doesn't need to gain weight to be beautiful, Jonas."

"No, she needs to gain weight to be healthy. Are you going to stand there and tell me you haven't noticed how pale and fragile she looks lately? A good wind could knock her over. They work her too hard."

Abigail carefully turned the omelet. "Let me get this straight. You observed that Hannah was pale and seemed fragile and underweight and you were upset because you think she's working too hard so your solution was to tell her she looked like a wire clothes hanger?"

"When you put it like that, it doesn't sound very good, but that's not the way I said it."

"Yes, it did sound that way. How else could it sound?" Abigail waved her hand toward the bread drawer and it opened. "You're a moron, Jonas. And all this time I thought you were charming with the ladies."

"I've just been keeping an eye on her lately and she doesn't seem well. I thought about asking Libby to take a look at her while she's here, but then all hell broke loose around here with this murder and I haven't had the chance to catch Libby alone."

"Hannah's fine." Even as she said it, Abigail wondered if it was true. Did she really know? She'd been so caught up in her own problems since she'd arrived home, she hadn't really paid much attention to any of her sisters. It made her ashamed. "We'd feel it if she wasn't."

"Would you? She hides things from people. I didn't know she had asthma until last Christmas. I've known her all of her life. How could I not know that?"

She scooped the omelet onto a plate and handed it to him. "There are a lot of things you don't know about Hannah."

"I'm beginning to realize that. And I don't think I'm alone. I watch her now when she's home. She's always doing for everyone else. Who does for her?" Jonas took a bite and grinned at her. "You can cook. I had no idea."

Abigail found herself laughing. "Amazing, isn't it? Self-preservation. Some of the places I went to do research didn't have fast food or food carts."

"Hey, you two." Hannah came partway into the kitchen, leaning one slim hip against the door.

Abigail studied her sister and for the first time could see signs of exhaustion. She was thinner than usual, although Abbey had to admit, it didn't seem to matter. Hannah was so striking and exotic she looked beautiful no matter what. "You hungry? I'm cooking."

"Just tea for me." Hannah waved toward the kettle and it whistled instantly.

Jonas grinned. "I love how you do that."

Hannah's eyebrow shot up. "I didn't think you loved anything I did."

"You're all dressed up. Where are you going?" Jonas asked.

"I'm wearing jeans and a very comfortable shirt," Hannah pointed out. "Abbey's the one dressed up."

Jonas turned to look at her. "Wow! You look great."

"Thanks for noticing," Abbey said wryly.

"She's going on a date with Aleksandr," Hannah announced.

"He didn't ask *me* where I was going."

"I'm asking now." Jonas glared at Abigail.

"Someone's at the door," Hannah said with a small smirk.

"You just stay right there and I'll get it," Jonas said and marched through the house to yank open the front door.

10

"HARRINGTON," Aleksandr greeted, his features expressionless as he stepped through the door, forcing Jonas to give way. "Is Abbey ready?"

"Yes, I am," Abigail said hastily and attempted to push past Jonas, who stood squarely in her way. She exchanged a look with Hannah, rolling her eyes as she did so. Did men have to posture all the time?

Aleksandr reached around Jonas and caught her hand. "You look truly beautiful, *baushki-bau*." His palm swept her hair as he pulled her in close to him.

His accent was very much in evidence and Abigail immediately felt guilty for having told Jonas about Aleksandr's superb language skills. She felt his fingers curl around hers, his body heat enveloping her, the strength in his muscles as he fit her beneath his shoulder. It was all so familiar. He even smelled like she remembered, clean and masculine and far too sexy for her liking.

His body moved against hers almost protectively as they walked out into the night air. In the distance the ocean boomed and she could smell salt in the air. The sky was clear and the stars sparkled. A perfect night, just what she needed.

"You're pulling away from me, Abbey." His voice was low, his lips against her ear. "Tell me what's wrong."

She waved her hand to encompass her surroundings. "This. You. Me. I'm always so lost around you, Sasha."

He drew her hand to his mouth. "Not around me, not as long as I'm with you, you'll never be lost, Abbey."

Her skin tingled where his lips brushed her knuckles. In all the time she'd known Aleksandr, there had never been awkward silences between them. Now, she felt nervous and edgy. With supreme self-discipline, Abigail drew her hand away from him. "How's the investigation coming?"

There was another small silence and then he sighed with resignation. "It's coming along. I have some leads. The necklace on first examination appears to be authentic, but of course we've sent it to the real experts." He opened the passenger door of his car for her.

"We?" She tilted her head, hesitating before slipping onto the seat. "Do you have someone else working with you?"

"It was a figure of speech."

"Was it?" He closed the door and Abigail felt trapped. That feeling intensified when he entered on the driver's side. His shoulders nearly touched hers. His hands were large, fingers wrapping around the steering wheel and reminding her of too many things. She turned her head away from him to stare out the window. Why was she thinking about his touch, his kiss, the taste and feel of him instead of betrayal and lies? She inhaled, breathing him in, taking him into her body when she should have been stiff and resistant. Immediately she held her breath, trying to avoid the scent and feel of him. Trying not to notice her hands were shaking and, inside, her stomach was curling into tight knots of anticipation.

As the vehicle pulled onto the main highway, Aleksandr reached for her hand again, lacing his fingers through hers. "You're not breathing. If you keep that up, I'll have to give you mouth-to-mouth and you know where that will lead."

His voice was so low and sensual it seemed to vibrate through her entire body. The thought of his mouth on hers was dangerous. She remembered the first time he kissed her. It felt like a brand, as if he'd stolen a part of her and left his mark on her forever. "I'd probably faint," she managed with a small smile. "And then where would I be?"

"In my arms. Safe."

Abigail allowed silence to stretch between them for a few minutes. The thought of being in his arms actually made her feel faint. It *was* dangerous. "What do you want me to do tonight?"

He pressed her hand to his thigh and held it there. She could feel the shape and strength of his muscles beneath the thin material of his trousers. "Just have fun. Nikitin likes music and the Caspar Inn has great live entertainment so it stands to reason he might be there. He'll recognize me, of course, and he'll have bodyguards, so we'll all be amicable. I want to see who he talks to, who is with him. And afterward, I'm going to follow him. They have to be holed up in a house somewhere. They wouldn't risk a hotel. They would have had an intermediary rent them a house."

"My family will probably show up," she warned him. The temperature seemed to be going up in the car, at least straight up her arm and burning over her face.

He shrugged. "That will help with the appearance that we are on a date."

"Will there be any danger to my sisters?"

"Nikitin would never publicly start trouble. He maintains the illusion of being a very upstanding businessman."

"Aleksandr, do you think this man Nikitin is the one responsible for putting out a contract on you? Do you think he'll make a try for you?" There was no way to conceal the anxiety in her voice so Abigail didn't even try.

"Not with everyone around. And Nikitin is a middleman. He takes the money and makes the arrangements, but he never pulls the trigger. He really does conceive of himself as a businessman, not a criminal." He flashed a brief smile. "In my country there is sometimes a fine line."

"In any country there is sometimes a fine line." She found herself beginning to relax, not a good thing when she needed to keep her armor on around him. He was wearing the aftershave she loved so much; it smelled rugged and tempting.

"Leonid Ignatev is behind the contract. Unless I manage to neutralize him, I'll be looking over my shoulder for the rest of my life. I knew that, though, Abbey. It isn't news. He sent others for me, but they missed and I didn't." He shrugged. "That's life."

She shook her head. "No, it isn't. That's no way to live. Sooner or later someone's going to be waiting for you and you won't be ready."

His teeth flashed in a faint smile. "I thought I'd be safe for a while in the United States investigating stolen art, but it seems I walked into a hornet's nest."

"It seems so. I don't believe in coincidences. If there's stolen art from Russia here, they have to be involved in some way, don't you think?"

He nodded as he turned into Caspar off the main highway. "I don't believe in coincidence either, Abbey. In any case, nothing much gets out of Russia without Nikitin eventually knowing about it. And he'd want his cut."

"Aleksandr." Abbey waited until he parked the car in the side lot of the Caspar Inn. "You can speak without an accent, yet you don't. Why not?"

"It is expected of me, *baushki-bau,* and I would not want to appear different in any way."

"No, of course not." She sighed softly. "Why do you call me *baushki-bau?* Where did you ever come up with that?"

For the first time since she'd met him, Aleksandr appeared almost vulnerable, if such a thing could happen. "It's just a term of endearment. There's no translation."

"I know that, but where did it come from? Why do you use it?"

He turned toward her and in the car he seemed to take up all the space. His fingers tightened around hers. "It's silly, really, Abbey."

"Well, tell me anyway."

He swept his free hand through his hair, another gesture of nerves. Aleksandr Volstov, the man with nerves of steel. Now she was really intrigued. She maintained steady eye contact, refusing to allow him to get out of an explanation.

"This is ridiculous, Abbey, it's just a silly name." When she kept looking at him he made an attempt to shrug casually. "When I was in the home where I was raised, there was one woman who was really good to us. She sang us a lullaby at night, or when one of the younger boys was hurt or afraid. She would sometimes use that particular term."

"And that's the lullaby you always sang to me." There was a lump in her throat. For the first time she thought of the difference in how they were raised. A little boy in a home with many other little boys. No parents to dote on them and no house filled with love and laughter. She framed his face with her hands. "I love that song."

Relief flashed briefly in his eyes. "I do too, but I know it's one of those leftover childish things we all try to get rid of."

"It makes you human, Sasha. I think you try very hard not to feel emotion. That's really not a good thing."

"It's sometimes necessary for survival."

She ached inside for him. For both of them. His life was so different and yet, the same as hers. "I'm going to hate it if you were right."

"About what?"

"That we should be together." She nearly clapped her hand over her mouth, but the words had escaped before she could stop them. It had to be the red panties talking. She certainly couldn't be so close to him and not feel his breath on her skin and ache for his body in hers.

"I am right."

A small smile curved her mouth. "You always think you are. Let's go in before I get into any more trouble." She opened her door quickly, sliding out into the cool night air before he could stop her.

He quickly got out, too, and his gaze swept the parking lot, the building, and street, the way it always did. Careful. Meticulous. Noting every detail. Committing the layout to memory. Aleksandr swept his arm around Abigail and drew her to the wall behind one of the many large bushes. His body pressed against hers, his shoulders blocking out the light from the porch. He pinned her wrists to the wall on either side of her head.

She seemed small and light, her soft curves tight against his chest. Memories flooded him. The warmth of her skin, the feel and texture like satin. Her hair pouring over his body like a silken waterfall. Her touch. Her taste. Her mouth teasing his senses into a terrible craving. Her body moving with perfect rhythm under his.

A man had only so much discipline. He'd been too many months without laughter or sunshine. Too many nights without the comfort of her soft body. He couldn't wait until he'd convinced her. He even knew he was rushing her, but it was too late. With a small groan, he bent his head to hers.

Her lips were cool and soft and seemed to melt beneath his. He teased her mouth with his tongue, running over the seam of her lips to coax her to open for him. Need was hot and greedy, clawing at his gut and spreading lower, racing through his veins with a kind of voracious hunger to harden his body into an intolerable ache.

He kissed her again and again, unable to get enough, unable to tear himself away from her. His body pushed aggressively against hers and he gathered her into his arms, dragged her so close there was barely room for clothes between them. He felt starved for her. He shook with desire. With a ferocious need to just hold her to him forever.

"I want time to stop, Abbey. I want everyone to go away and let us just be together." He whispered it against her ear, returned to her mouth. Fire and honey, a combination he could never resist. She turned his world upside down and made him feel as if he had everything. As if everything he did was worthwhile. "How do you do it?" he murmured, bringing her hair to his lips. "How do you make me feel so out of control when my entire life is all about control?"

"Don't talk. Kiss me." Abigail slipped her arms around his neck, her mouth moving over his, back and forth, tiny teasing kisses designed to drive him crazy. "Again, Sasha. Kiss me again."

Her voice slipped past his guard and went straight to his heart. Damn her for her ability to bring him to his knees. He'd always been a strong man, able to stand alone, until he met her. Now he felt incomplete, lost even. He'd never felt alone or had really known the meaning of the word until she was gone from him.

He kissed her with every fiber of his being, every emotion in his heart. Anger and lust and mostly love, all mixed together so he couldn't separate them. Abigail Drake had given him his soul and then she'd walked out of his life and taken it with her.

"Oh, my," Inez Nelson said. "Don't look, ladies. These young people have no sense of decorum anymore."

Abigail pulled back, trying to flatten herself against the wall, her gaze jumping to Aleksandr's. She tried to make herself smaller in the hopes no one would recognize her. A chorus of giggles followed Inez's declaration.

"Abbey! The ceremony is working!" Carol shouted gaily and waved.

Color crept up Abigail's neck into her cheeks. She didn't look away from Aleksandr, even when she knew she looked guilty. "It certainly is, Aunt Carol," she replied and was mortified when she heard whispers and another chorus of laughter, which meant her aunt had explained just what the ceremony was all about.

"What ceremony?" Aleksandr asked.

"You don't want to know," Abigail said. "Do we absolutely need to go in there? You have no idea how bad those ladies can get."

He smoothed back her hair. "I think I'll have to hear all about this ceremony that has you so worried. Come on, let's go in before things really get out of hand."

"Were things getting out of hand?" Abigail was acutely aware of Aleksandr's palm burning through the thin material of her tank top as they walked up the ramp to the wraparound deck leading to the bar entrance. Her lips were swollen from his kisses, her skin tender from his five o'clock shadow. Her body burned, every nerve ending alive. The red panty ceremony was a killer and she was planning on blaming her response to him entirely on that. "I thought things were moving along nicely." With no responsibility she could be as bad as she wanted to be. And she wanted to be very bad.

She went through the door as if in a dream, greeting so many familiar faces, waving at old friends, hugging a couple of the older women, a smile on her face, and all the time fear was creeping into her mind, drowning out lust. She could live with lust. She could live with his kisses and his body and be perfectly happy if she could walk away unscathed, but as she weaved her way through the crowd with Aleksandr so close, she realized she was standing on the edge of a great precipice. One wrong step and she would be lost forever.

She had never stopped loving Aleksandr Volstov. Not ever, even when she hated him and was so angry she lay awake night after night in her bed with her fists clenched, thinking up endless tortures for him. She had known all along if she were alone with him she'd be kissing him, wanting to see his gaze grow hot, feel the heat of his skin. She had thought she was so angry she could wrap it around her like armor and be protected, but her love welled up unwanted and scared her to death.

"Is something wrong?" He worked his way through the crowd, protecting her from the crush with his larger body as they made their way toward the smaller, more intimate tables at the back of the room.

It was impossible not to remember how he did that, the small things, making her feel so safe. So loved. Abigail turned her face away from him, wanting to weep with the memories of what she'd lost.

"Abbey." He curved his arm around her waist. "Tell me."

"I'm too afraid to love you again, Sasha." She made the confession in a low voice. The lump in her throat nearly choked her. "I can't lose you a second time. I can't lose myself a second time. I'm just not that strong." It hurt so much she couldn't explain, couldn't find words to describe the razor sharp cuts still so raw in her heart.

Aleksandr drew her closer, moved onto the dance floor where he could safely hold her. He kept to the shadows. The tears shimmering in her eyes broke his heart. She fit so perfectly, her body moving with the rhythm of his, her face buried in his shirt.

"Let the past go, *baushki-bau,* you have to let it go or we'll both lose. My life is better with you in it. Your life is better with me in it." His chin nuzzled the top of her head as his arms enfolded her close. "If you reach out to me, just a little, Abbey, we can make it."

She shook her head, denying something she knew was inevitable. If she didn't step off the cliff and reach for him, he was already lost to her.

"I'm tired, *moi prekrasnij.* I stopped sleeping the day they took you from me. Do you remember what it was like together? My body curled around yours, holding you as we drifted off to sleep. I thought at first I'd be unable to allow anyone to sleep in my bed. I have no trust, but, with you, it was natural. You belonged with me. The moment my arms were around you, I was at peace. Do you remember the feeling, Abbey?"

His whispered words slipped inside her, hovered there, brushing against the fragile barrier she tried to erect between them. The music was slow and dreamy, a soft blues number that matched her melancholy mood. She could feel the touch of her sisters and knew that they had arrived, worried as they felt the strength of her emotions. She slipped her arms around Aleksandr's neck, trying not to weep for her lost trust in him. He had not only shaken her faith in him, but in herself and her magic. The past wouldn't let her go, not her love for him and not her memories of his betrayal.

"I remember." She choked out the words against his throat. "Can you hear me screaming in pain? Can you, Sasha? It's so deep I can't ever get it out and it's locked inside me forever."

He crushed her to him. "Yes. I'm screaming too." He held her, staying to the shadows, his face buried in her silken hair. He was screaming, deep inside where no one else could hear. Where it hurt so much he couldn't find words to let it out. He had never needed anyone before Abigail had brought love and laughter into his bleak world. His duty had been his life and in that barren existence there had been violence and deceit and even treachery. Abigail had been an unexpected treasure, precious beyond even his understanding until he'd lost her. It hurt like hell to know he was responsible for their pain. "I'm sorry, Abbey."

She didn't respond and he'd spoken the words so softly he wasn't sure she'd heard him. He leaned over her and put his lips against her ear. "Did you hear me?" He couldn't remember a time in his life when he'd said those words to anyone. When he meant them. And now he knew he would say them again and again until he put right what he had made wrong between them. He brushed his lips against her ear. "I'm sorry, Abbey, I'm sorry."

"I heard." Her fingers curled around the nape of his neck, stroked bare skin until he felt her touch burning through his body like a brand. "I heard you."

Lights flickered as the last notes of the song faded away and Aleksandr turned her toward the back of the room and the small tables. Fitting her body beneath his shoulder protectively to prevent others from seeing her poignant expression, his gaze shifted around the room, a slow, unhurried examination, noting the placement of furniture, exits, and most of all the faces in the room. Several fishermen sat at the bar. A group of locals laughed together in a larger group at the far end of the bar near the entrance. Couples held hands, some standing, some sitting. Abigail's sisters sat together right next to the table where Carol and her friends were gathered. Deliberately, Aleksandr chose the small table between Abigail's family members and he took the chair facing the entrance, pulling hers around so she would be sitting beside him rather than across from him.

"Do you see the men at the table behind the partition?" He brought her hand up to his mouth and nibbled on her knuckles, smiling at her as he did so. "Just glance over at them, Abbey, and see if anyone is familiar to you."

She had all but forgotten why they had come to the inn. Abigail rested her head on his shoulder and shifted her gaze. People came from the various surrounding towns, and she might not know them all by name, but she knew their faces. Camaraderie was strong on the coast and she nodded and smiled at those she made eye contact with. Most of the younger men were staring openly at Joley and Hannah. A few strangers hung out at the bar, around the dance floor, and in small groups at a couple of the tables. Behind the low partition a larger group of men sat together and they didn't look as if they were enjoying the music all that much.

"They aren't blending in," she said.

"No, and it's probably annoying the hell out of Prakenskii." There was a wealth of satisfaction in Aleksandr's voice. He opened Abigail's hand and pressed a kiss into the exact center of her palm. "He likes to be the chameleon, never noticed."

"Prakenskii? The man you said was a . . ."

He drew her finger into his mouth, distracting her. Her gaze jumped to his face. She looked wary. Excited. Interested. He smiled at her. "You taste good."

"You better pay attention to your job. Which one is Prakenskii?"

"He's standing up against the wall, one hand in his jacket, very aware I'm in the same room with him. I'll have to go over and acknowledge Nikitin. It would be poor manners not to do so." He kept his gaze firmly on hers, the picture of a man enthralled with his date.

A small crumpled napkin hit Abigail on the side of the head. She turned to see Joley making faces at her.

"Does she need help?" Aleksandr asked. "Is she having some kind of fit?"

Abigail dipped the wadded-up napkin in her water glass and threw it back with accuracy, smacking Joley's cheek. "She's warning me. And she's about as subtle as a bullhorn."

"Warning you about what?"

"Not what. Who. Sylvia Fredrickson has arrived. The resident man-eater. Sylvia doesn't much care for me. I'd much prefer not to go into the details. Suffice it to say my magic went a little wrong and her marriage ended. Not only her marriage, but also her lover's marriage." Abigail sighed.

Aleksandr read her body language easily. He had trained all his life to read the smallest details in expression and posture. Abigail was uncomfortable with the other woman in the room. He glanced at the newcomer, a blonde with a low-cut top and the generous curves to carry it off. She looked brittle, laughed too loud, and touched every man as she worked her way through the crowd.

Aleksandr slipped his arm around Abigail. "I feel sorry for her. She's desperate. Desperation often makes people do things they're ashamed of. Her life can't be easy."

"No, I'm sure it's not. I'd hoped when she married Mason Fredrickson that she'd settle down. Mason's a good man and he really loved her and seemed to understand her need for constant attention, but she cheated on him as well. Unfortunately, along with making her own life difficult, she makes everyone else's life around her the same way."

The band swung into a faster dance rhythm and at once the dance floor was crowed with swaying people. Aleksandr watched as Carol joined the Drake sisters in a small circle where they danced together. His gaze shifted back to the Russians and he frowned as he laced his fingers through Abigail's. "I don't like the way Nikitin is watching your sister."

His chin rubbed across the back of her hand. Abigail found the small gesture sensual. Her awareness of him was so heightened she felt she could feel every breath he took. She tried to look over toward Nikitin casually, as if she were just sweeping the room. All the while she leaned into Aleksandr, wishing she were in his arms again. Wishing she could turn back the clock. If she only had confidence in her magic as a Drake, in herself as a woman, but she was more shaken than she'd known.

Nikitin was staring at the dance floor, even leaning forward in his chair. As she watched, he signaled to someone at his table without ever looking away from the dancers, put a wad of bills in the man's hand, and sat back, still watching. Abigail followed his gaze to Joley.

Her sister was a wild, uninhibited dancer. A true musician, she lost herself in the beat, eyes bright with laughter, her body moving in a sexy interpretation of the rhythm. As Abigail watched, a stranger approached her sister, inserting himself behind her, moving with her in an attempt to "freak" dance. The moment his body touched her, Joley spun around, jarred out of her enthrallment. Beside Abigail, Aleksandr tensed and half rose.

"Joley can take care of herself," Abigail assured him. "And the others are there. She won't want attention when she's having fun. Look, that's the manager." She indicated a man moving through the crowd with her chin. "Joley comes in here a lot just to relax and listen to music. He's not going to allow anyone to mess with her."

As she watched, Ilya Prakenskii came out of the shadows and caught the man accosting Joley and took him away from the floor. He did it without a sound, without fuss, so quickly no one seemed to notice. Joley stood for a moment, watching the two men disappear out the door, and then she shrugged, grinned at the manager, and went back to her dancing.

"What just happened?" Abigail asked. "I swear, two seconds ago, Prakenskii was standing against the wall behind Nikitin. How in the world did he get through the crowd like that and why didn't I notice him?" She leaned her head back to look up at Aleksandr. "You move like that. Like Prakenskii. Sometimes I don't even hear you or see you and you're across the room."

He grinned at her. "We blend. I hope the eager young man is all right. Prakenskii, depending on his mood, can be a little enthusiastic about his work." He nodded toward the wall behind Joley, and Abigail frowned when she saw the Russian had returned unnoticed.

"That's just creepy. He isn't looking at Joley at all, but I still don't like him being so close to her."

"He sees her. He sees everything."

"Great." Her fingers tightened around his. "How do you do this day in and day out? I'm a nervous wreck, worried about my family, you, what the heck they're up to. The man Nikitin gave his money to didn't go to the bar to get drinks; he's up by the band."

"It's possible Nikitin wants a certain song played and he's going to bribe the band. He's reputed to really love music and it is something he would do. Money talks with him. There is no need to worry. Prakenskii has twice acknowledged my presence and indicated they are here peacefully."

"Well, that's just great. As opposed to going into battle?" She toyed with the drink on the table. "At least Aunt Carol and the other ladies are having fun."

As the music ended, the Drake sisters returned to their table. Joley paused and went up to Prakenskii. Abigail held her breath. The man wasn't exceptionally tall, but he seemed to loom over her sister, powerful and looking enormously strong. More than anything he had an aura of danger surrounding him. Her sisters wouldn't fail to recognize it.

"I'd like to buy you a drink," Joley said as he walked with her to the table. "It wasn't necessary to rescue me, but it was very gentlemanly. Thank you."

"You should be more aware of what is going on around you," Prakenskii reprimanded her. "And drawing attention to yourself by dancing so suggestively is utterly stupid for a woman in your position."

"Oh, God." Abigail covered her face with her hands. It didn't help that all the women sitting at Aunt Carol's table overheard and nodded their heads in complete agreement.

Joley tossed her head, sending her hair flying in all directions. Sparks fairly flew from her eyes. "Really? How lovely of you to give me unsolicited and unwanted advice. Take a hike, buddy."

"He had a knife on him and he carried a drug to put in women's drinks."

Joley had turned her back on Prakenskii, but that stopped her cold. She turned back slowly. "Where is he? Did you get his name?"

"Did you know this man?"

"No, but sometimes I get letters. . . ." She trailed off. "Where is he?"

"I suggested he leave before the police were called. His knife and the drugs were confiscated and thrown away. What letters?"

Joley waved the question away. "We should have called the sheriff and had him arrested." She tilted her chin. "Men like that don't need suggestive dancing to do what they do. They're sick perverts."

"That is true, but it does not excuse your deliberately enticing men with your suggestive dancing."

"You are a jerk."

The singer in the band stepped up to the microphone as the music faded away. "I'm certain if we all put our hands together we can persuade Joley Drake to sing for us."

The manager of the bar frantically drew a line across his throat, signaling the band member to stop, but he was ignored.

Abigail swore softly under her breath. "The Caspar Inn is one of the few refuges left to Joley where she can enjoy herself without fear of tabloid reporters or crazed fans. Singing would definitely draw unwanted attention and this place would be lost to her if word got out that she ever dropped in to sing."

"Now we know why Nikitin gave his man money. He wanted to bribe the band to ask Joley to sing." Aleksandr sat back in his chair. "What is interesting is that Nikitin knew it was the band he had to bribe, not management. He knew ahead of time that management wouldn't take the money and sell her out. How did he know that?"

The crowd had gone wild, stomping and clapping in an effort to get Joley to the stage. Abigail could see resignation on her sister's face.

"You can say no," Prakenskii said.

"How?" Joley asked, swallowing hard. She took a breath and moved past him, waving and smiling to the crowd.

"Nikitin has to be using someone local for information, someone that would know a small detail like that. The person would have to know your family and the places you all like to frequent. Do you recognize anyone at all around his table, or someone standing near enough to talk to him?"

The band swung into a blues number, and Joley's voice poured into the room, rich and edgy and evocative. It carried magic and power and passion and flowed into those listening, carrying them away with her.

Abigail kept her gaze fixed on Nikitin. He was staring at Joley with rapt attention, certainly not talking to anyone at his table. When one person started to say something, he held up his hand for silence. The cocktail waitress approached and he waved her off as well.

"I think he's obsessed with her," Abigail said. "Look at him."

"No, look around him. You have to see beyond the obvious. Who do you see that seems familiar?"

"Tim Robbins, a fisherman I see often at Noyo Harbor. He's the older gentleman to Nikitin's left outside the partition. Tim practically

lives on his boat. He comes here or hangs out at the Salt Bar and Grill."
Abigail studied the crowd around Nikitin. "There's Ned Farmer, the
really distinguished man standing just to the other side of Tim. He's an
accountant, has a lot of money, and owns a lot of property. I think he
has his hand in several of the smaller businesses in Fort Bragg and Sea
Haven. He's been around for years and everyone likes him. He's married and has three kids. I went to school with them. All three have
moved out of the area, but they visit often."

"Does he come here often?"

"Everyone comes here, Aleksandr. I've seen him here often. Usually with his wife, but sometimes alone."

"Is she here?"

Abigail looked around. "I don't see her at the moment, but the
crowd seems to be growing."

"Anyone else?"

"Two others. The younger men staring at Joley."

"Everyone's staring at Joley."

"One's in a blue shirt and one's wearing green. The one in blue is
Lance Parker and he does roofing. The other is Chad Kingman and
he works for Frank Warner."

Joley finished the song and the place erupted into thunderous ap-
plause.

"She didn't hold anything back," Aleksandr said.

"Her small revenge on the band. They won't be sounding so good
now the crowd has heard her."

Joley made her way through the crowd, back to the table, but
before she could sit down, Prakenskii was there. "Mr. Nikitin would
like to meet you. He asks that you join him at his table."

Joley flashed a false smile. "Thank you for the invitation, but I
don't think so."

"Mr. Nikitin is not a man you say no to."

"Then tell him to go to hell," Joley said. "I don't appreciate him
forcing me into the position of singing for a crowd when I've come
here with my family to enjoy myself. Run along to your master and
say thanks but no."

Aleksandr's fingers tightened around Abigail's wrist to prevent her
from jumping up to shield her sister. Prakenskii didn't change expression, but turned away to start back toward his boss.

Joley waved her hand at his back, just a small shove of air that should have made Prakenskii stumble. Instead the air crackled and snapped, small sparks arced around her palm, and she yelped, holding it to her.

The Drakes immediately stood, their expressions shocked as they shoved Joley behind them and faced Prakenskii.

11

ALEKSANDR inserted himself between the Drake sisters and Prakenskii, despite Abigail's restraining hand. He had no idea what had just happened, but the tension had gone up significantly. Joley cradled her palm as if she'd been injured.

"Move away from Hannah," Abigail insisted, tugging at him. "Give her a clear line to Prakenskii."

The crowd seemed to swirl around them, people moving continually. Music blared from the stage and dancers gyrated, yet no one touched Prakenskii and no one went near the Drakes.

"The one thing I do know," Aleksandr answered, "is that none of you want to get in a battle with that man. Sit down. All of you. Abbey, come with me. Now's as good a time as any to pay our respects, so to speak, to Nikitin."

Prakenskii didn't turn around and face the eight women. He walked without further incident to his boss's table and bent down to whisper to him.

Abigail had a death grip on Aleksandr's arm, preventing him from following after the Russian while the Drake sisters exchanged long, puzzled looks.

"How did he do that?" Joley asked Hannah.

"Aunt Carol?" Hannah asked.

"I don't know, girls, but this isn't good. I think we should get home as quickly as possible and consult the books. I know there have been rumors about males with our gifts, but I've certainly never run across any other who had our talents." Carol tilted her head to look up at Aleksandr. "What do you know about him?"

Abigail saved him. "We'll talk about it later, when we're at home, Aunt Carol."

"Of course, dear. In the protection of the house. I must be getting old to have made such a mistake. Forgive me."

"That's silly, Aunt Carol. We were all shaken for a moment. None of us has ever had our magic turned back on us by a man before." Libby put her arm around her aunt and reached out to Joley. "Does it hurt bad?"

Hannah pushed her hand away before she could touch Joley. "Not in here. Don't give him anything of us to work against. We should leave now. Abigail, you should come with us. It might not be safe."

"He won't touch her," Aleksandr reassured them. "She'll be safe with me." He caught a movement as Hannah nudged Joley.

Joley met his eyes. "She'd better be safe with you."

Abigail flicked her hair over her shoulder. "I'll be fine. I'm more worried about Joley. Prakenskii wasn't close enough to you to get anything personal, was he?"

"I doubt it. Let's get out of here. My palm hurts like hell and I know I'm going to lose control and slap his face if he comes near me again with a request from his puppet master, the superior arrogant bastard."

"Lead the way, Sasha, I'll be very interested in meeting Mr. Nikitin." There was a whip of anger in Abigail's voice.

Aleksandr picked up his drink and made his way through the crowd to Nikitin's table, his hand firmly clasped in Abigail's. The Drake sisters, their aunt, and her friends followed, waving at friends as they made their exodus. As Joley passed the partition where Nikitin and his party were seated, Prakenskii reached out and caught her damaged hand, his thumb sliding briefly over her palm and then releasing her just as quickly. The moment he touched Joley, the air around them crackled and snapped. The hairs on Aleksandr's arm stood up.

Joley hesitated for a split second, her eyes turbulent, but Hannah and the other sisters crowded her and kept her moving when they could clearly see she wanted to retaliate.

Aleksandr ignored the byplay, not wanting to cloud issues. He had to focus on finding out as much information as possible. The Drakes were well versed in magic. It was their field of expertise, not his. "What a small world it is, Sergei. One never knows where one will encounter acquaintances." He shook the man's hand and turned toward Abbey. "This is Abigail Drake."

"Wonderful to meet you, Miss Drake." Nikitin nodded at her as if bestowing her some great honor. "Would you care to join us?"

"I wouldn't want to interrupt you," Aleksandr said. "I just wanted to say hello."

Nikitin waved two of the men out of their chairs and pulled one back for Abigail. "I insist, Aleksandr. We are far from home and it's good to see a familiar face." He shifted closer to Abigail. "Joley Drake is your sister? She has a wonderful voice. I've never heard anyone better."

"Thank you. I'm very proud of her. I'll be sure and pass on your wonderful compliment to her." Her fingers twisted harder against Aleksandr's.

"Please ask her to forgive my blunder. Prakenskii tells me she was upset that I put her in the position of having to sing. I didn't understand why a great singer was forced to endure another of lesser talent and no one asked for her. They should have been on their feet paying tribute to her greatness."

"She likes to come here to relax," Abigail said with a small smile that didn't quite reach her eyes. "There are so few places left to her."

She risked a glance at Prakenskii. Aleksandr believed Sergei Nikitin was the more dangerous of the two Russians, but she knew differently. Prakenskii wore violence, deceit, and death as a second skin. He showed no emotion, acted as if the entire incident with Joley had never happened, but his gaze was restless in the same way Aleksandr's was. He was aware of every detail of the room, the crowd, even conversations, whereas Nikitin was completely self-absorbed. And Prakenskii had his own agenda, she could read that much. He wasn't as loyal to Nikitin as his boss believed, nor was he in the least bit afraid of the man.

Aleksandr's thumb rubbed across the back of her hand in warning and she sent another smile to Nikitin. "I'm certain you know what that's like."

"Yes, of course. It makes perfect sense. I was told she might come here. It was why I chose this place, but I had no idea she wouldn't be singing."

"Really? She'll be so flattered." Abigail tilted her head, resting her hand on her chin as she leaned a little in toward him. "Where did you hear she comes here? All this time we thought her secret was well guarded."

Aleksandr leaned back in his chair. Nikitin was more interested in talking to Abigail about Joley and that left him free to watch the room and Prakenskii. Nikitin had almost forgotten he was there. The man had narrowed his attention to Abigail, and it occurred to Aleksandr that Nikitin hadn't even been aware of the small exchange between Joley and Prakenskii. It didn't fit with his assessment of Nikitin. The man was reputed to be a shark, not a minnow.

Abigail was a natural at leading a conversation; her voice was pitched just right, her eyes were wide with interest. He resisted the urge to acknowledge her skills by kissing her hand; instead he turned his attention toward the two men who had vacated their seats to allow Aleksandr and Abigail a chance to visit with Nikitin.

"It isn't difficult to get information on your sister. She's a very public figure. One of my friends knew a local woman and he asked her."

Abigail's fingers dug into Aleksandr's hand, but she hung on to her smile as she glanced around the bar looking for Sylvia Fredrickson. She was in a nearby corner talking animatedly with several men including Chad Kingman, Ned Farmer, and Lance Parker. Her hand was on Chad's arm and she leaned into Lance, nearly rubbing her body against his. Occasionally she rested her palm on Ned Farmer's thigh.

Abigail could feel her temper beginning to rise and she struggled not to wave her hand toward the drink in Sylvia's hand. Instead she concentrated on the universal laws and glanced briefly toward the door, hoping it was enough to get a response, before flashing another smile at the Russian. "I'm so pleased you enjoy Joley's voice. We think she's incredible."

"I would really like to meet her." Nikitin raised his empty glass and immediately one of his men sprang up to get him a drink. "Do you think it's possible to arrange such a meeting? I would be very grateful. I'm a man who repays favors."

For one terrible moment Abigail wanted to trade a visit with her sister for the contract on Aleksandr's life. The urge came out of nowhere and hit her hard. The walls of the room seemed to move, nearly crushing her. It was almost impossible to draw air into her burning lungs. She could see the words floating in front of her eyes, bizarre headlines flashing. The urge to speak was so strong she bit down hard on her lower lip, hoping the small bite of pain would help her focus.

Only one other time in her life had such a thing happened. She and Joley had been experimenting, working with a spell to influence others by using a steady flow of power, and it had backfired on them. Instant recognition flooded her. She sat back and clapped her hands together, waving the air around them back toward Prakenskii, openingly challenging him. Her temper had the better of her now and if he wanted war, she was more than ready to do battle. He had secrets. His aura told her that, and his secrets weren't safe with her. He had power, but he wasn't immune from magic any more than she was.

One of the two men Aleksandr was observing leaned over the partition and said something to Chad Kingman, and handing him a lighter, Kingman nodded and slid it into his pocket. Even as Aleksandr watched them, he felt the air around them growing static with electricity. Abigail's eyes glittered as she looked at Prakenskii. Suddenly fearing what she might do, he caught her hand again and squeezed hard. She ignored him.

"Perhaps we should play a little game of truth or dare," she said to Prakenskii. "It's a wonderful game we enjoy. What do you think?"

Alarm flickered in Prakenskii's eyes, then faded, leaving him stone-faced. He bowed slightly to Abigail. "I do not enjoy playing American games. Aleksandr, did you tell me you two needed to leave soon?" His tone was mild, gave nothing at all away.

Aleksandr took the excuse, not understanding what was going on between Prakenskii and Abigail and not wanting to take any chances with her life. He rose to his feet and tugged on Abbey until she was forced to stand up as well. "Thanks, Ilya." He glanced at his watch. "I promised Abbey's sisters we'd be home in time to help with the wedding plans."

"Mr. Nikitin"—Abigail held out her hand—"it was a pleasure to meet you. I'll certainly pass on your compliments to Joley." She kept her eyes on Prakenskii every moment.

"I'm staying in the area for a few more days and hope we can arrange a meeting."

"I'll let Joley know." She allowed Aleksandr to lead her to the door. As they approached it, the door swung open and Mason Fredrickson walked through. Abigail looked behind her in time to see Sylvia stiffen with shock. The left side of her face was covered in a rash in the shape of a bright red handprint as if someone had slapped her. Abbey glanced again at Prakenskii. He gave her a faint smile and a brief salute.

"What in the hell was going on in there?" Aleksandr demanded as they hurried down the ramp into the parking lot. Before she could reply, he pushed her behind the large bushes, his arms going around her and his head bending to hers so his lips were a breath away. "He's out here."

"Who is out here?"

"Chad Kingman, one of the men you pointed out to me. He borrowed a lighter from one of Nikitin's men and he's out here smoking. I want him to go back inside before we get in the car."

"I'm not going to make out with you like a teenager behind the bush, for heaven's sake," Abigail said. "Although the idea does have merit. What I'd really like to do is become Hannah for just a few minutes and send Prakenskii a little warning."

"What did Prakenskii do to Joley that had all of you so up in arms?" He pulled her closer, fitting her body tightly against his, his hands sliding down her back to the curve of her spine. "I never saw him touch her."

"He didn't touch her, not physically. He's like us. He has power, magic, talent, whatever you want to call it."

That gave him pause. He stared down at her, not comprehending what she was trying to say. "Prakenskii? As in, speak the word *truth* and everyone reveals secrets?"

She shook her head. "Not exactly like my talent, more like Hannah's or Joley's. Maybe even Elle's. I hope not Elle's. That would be bad."

"Why?"

"Elle can do it all. She has to carry all the gifts to pass on to the next generation. I saw him brush Joley's palm when she went out the door. I have no idea if he took away the pain, but if he did, that definitely makes him a very powerful adversary because he's adept at more than one thing."

He turned his head slightly to keep a better eye on Chad Kingman. The man crushed his cigarette butt beneath his shoe, looked around, and ambled back up the ramp to the wraparound deck. Instead of going inside, he leaned over the railing and stared up at the stars.

"Let me get this straight. You're telling me that Ilya Prakenskii, the man I've known since he was a child, is able to use the same kind of magic as you and your sisters."

"He had to have been born with the talent, Sasha. What do you know about his background? Did you ever see him do anything different? Anything you thought was strange? As a child did he tell you he was different?"

Aleksandr tried to remember what Ilya Prakenskii had been like in the days before they were separated. "He kept to himself. We all did. He was fast and strong and at the top of the class so in a way we competed, but we were friends. He once told me he had brothers, but the children were all sent to different homes. I have no idea whether or not he ever found them and contacted them."

Aleksandr murmured a warning to Abigail when he saw the same Russian who had given Chad the lighter walk out onto the deck. The man looked around, shoved his hands into his pockets, and shifted closer to Chad. Chad pushed himself up from the railing as the Russian stopped beside him.

"Thanks for the use of your lighter, man," Chad said as he handed an object back.

The Russian shrugged and took whatever it was, concealing it in his hand as he turned and walked rapidly toward the entrance of the bar. Chad made his way to a car in the parking lot. Aleksandr caught the flare of a match just before Chad slid behind the wheel. A cigarette glowed briefly and then the car pulled out of the lot.

"That was a very sloppy drop," Aleksandr said, puzzled. He kissed Abigail lightly and stepped out of the bushes. "Why would Prakenskii get me out of there just in time to witness a drop?" He shook his head as he opened the door of the car for her. "It doesn't make sense. Ilya would know I would see the handoff."

"Maybe getting me out of there was more important to him than you seeing Chad do whatever he was doing," Abigail said. "He tried a power play on me, trying to get me to trade a visit with Joley for the contract on you. I had to fight hard against the impulse."

"And you think Prakenskii put the impulse in your head?"

"I know he did. And he couldn't risk being susceptible to my talent. He has too many secrets, not the least of which is that he isn't exactly enamored with this boss. He isn't working for Nikitin. I'm not certain he's capable of working for anyone but himself. His aura is very dangerous and violent. Death was very close to him, surrounding him." She glanced at him. "Your aura is very similar to his."

"He doesn't have to like who he works for." Aleksandr turned the car around at the end of the road and backed it behind a shed before turning off the lights to wait. "He wouldn't want Nikitin to know what he thought of him, but would that be enough for him to give up their local contact?" He paused for a moment, glaring at her. "And my aura, whatever that is, is *nothing* like his."

She flashed a brief smile at him. "If he had very strong feelings one way or the other, it might. I had the impression he detested the man. In fact, I'd go so far as to say Prakenskii is a very real threat to Sergei Nikitin. And yes, you do."

"How could you read all that in him?"

"He used power a couple of times in there. He uses it when he moves through the crowd too. I didn't catch it at first because it's so subtle. He's very strong and very disciplined. But power has a distinct fingerprint. I know when my sisters are casting and which sister did which spell. The use of magic leaves the caster somewhat vulnerable."

"This is so out of my realm of expertise I can hardly comprehend it." Aleksandr picked up her left hand and stroked the bare fingers where his ring should have been. "I'm trying to remember Ilya as a child. Looking back, there might have been one or two odd things. Once I was talking to him and his drink was sitting on the table several feet away. I turned my head and when I looked back, it was in his hand. I had been working on noticing details. It was an exercise I not only enjoyed, but prided myself on. I knew the drink had been on

the table and I couldn't figure out how he'd gotten it." He brought
her hand up to his mouth and rubbed his lips across her knuckles, his
tongue tasting her skin. "And you can't possibly be all that good at
reading auras because mine is filled with a rainbow of colors and
Prakenskii's is black."

Abigail burst out laughing. "You don't know the first thing about
auras. For all you know, black is good and rainbows are bad." She
tugged at her hand but Aleksandr refused to relinquish his hold on
her. "I'm the one having a difficult time believing Prakenskii really
could have the ability to use such strong magic. Other than my family, I've never known anyone else born with the same kind of strength.
I guess it was rather arrogant to think we'd be the only ones."

"His coffee was always hot. It never cooled down." Aleksandr
suddenly grinned at her. "We used to go on field trips. Our trips were
to learn to tail someone without being seen, to make a drop or rendezvous with a contact under the eyes of our instructors without
their knowledge."

"How could you do that if they were watching you?"

"That was the point of the exercise, to learn to be skilled enough
to make a handoff or follow someone who knows they might be followed without being caught. When we were training together, no
matter how long the stakeout or how cold the night, Ilya's coffee was
always hot. I wondered how he did that."

"I know you think he's dangerous because of his skills as a trained
operative, but Sasha, with his powers he can do incredible things and
that makes him far more dangerous than you can imagine. He can
slip in and out of places using suggestions to have those he wants to
remain hidden from look the other way. It doesn't mean it will work
on everyone, and sometimes it's dangerous even to wield magic, but
he's an adept user, I can tell just by how subtle he was."

"What did he do to Joley?"

Abigail sighed. "We all have silly childish retaliations when we're
angry. It's better than to lose control of our tempers. Joley intended to
make him stumble as he walked back to his table, but he felt the push
of her magic and he retaliated with a virtual power slap. The energy
turns back on the user. In all honesty I think he shoved a little harder
than he intended and it hurt her hand. We didn't let Libby touch her
because he would have felt Libby's 'fingerprints.'"

"You don't think he was really trying to harm Joley?" Aleksandr leaned forward to look out the window. "There they are. They have two cars. I'm going to hang back because I'm guessing they'll have a sleeper car as well."

"I don't know what that is."

"Sometimes a third car waits to see if the principal—in this case, Nikitin—is followed. Ilya is driving the second car." He stayed still as the two cars turned out of the parking lot. "It's a gamble waiting for a third car, but I can't imagine Ilya, if he's responsible for Nikitin's security, not taking the precaution knowing I'm here."

"You trained together, Sasha. He'd have to know you would be waiting to follow them. If there is a third car and it leads you to the house where they're staying, he's deliberately letting you find them. And you'd better worry about a trap, especially if you think Nikitin is the middleman for Leonid Ignatev."

"I have reliable sources telling me Ignatev put out the hit and Nikitin brokered it for him."

"And Ilya Prakenskii works for Nikitin. You said he's reputed to be a hit man." Abigail sighed. "I know you well enough to know there's respect and even admiration in your voice when you talk about him."

"I had few childhood friends, Abbey."

That simple statement tore at her heartstrings. Damn him for doing that. There was no way to have single-minded resolve when she ached for him. She rubbed her temples, trying to ease the beginnings of a headache. "He isn't a friend if he's trying to kill you. You have to listen to me, Aleksandr. If he can wield magic the way I suspect he can, he has a tremendous advantage over you."

"We've had several battles. I have scars. He has scars. If he had such an advantage, why hasn't he used it against me? We fought with fists, with knives, even took a couple of shots at one another."

"I have a hard time believing that you shot at him and didn't hit him."

"I did hit him." He turned on the engine. "There it is, the third car."

"You didn't kill him, Sasha. And that could be anyone leaving the bar, not necessarily one of the Russians."

"I have a feel for these things. It's the sleeper."

"You didn't kill him," she repeated. "Was he using magic to

deflect your aim or . . ." She paused to study his averted face. "You deliberately wounded him rather than kill him, didn't you?"

He muttered a Russian curse under his breath. "I don't look at things that way. I wasn't after him. He wasn't my job. It wasn't personal and it wasn't business. We got in each other's way." He shrugged. "It happens. I hurt him, though. If he really had the same ability to use magic as you and your sisters, would I have been able to do that?"

"If he had my talent, or Libby's. In my opinion, Hannah would be the most difficult to harm, unless someone surprised her, came at her unexpectedly."

"Why not Elle?"

"Hannah's powers are very concentrated in one or two areas. Elle carries all elements so she's not quite as strong. And Hannah uses her gifts daily and she works at strengthening them. She'd make a powerful adversary. Libby uses hers as well, but I'm not certain with her gift she would be capable of harming someone."

"You think Prakenskii is like Elle?"

"He exhibited signs of tremendous control with several talents, not just one. I can do several things, all of us can, but we're not *great* at all of them."

"I don't suppose I should venture the hypothesis that he's male and maybe stronger because of that."

"Not if you want to live through the next few minutes."

"That's what I thought." He flashed a small grin at her. "The idea wouldn't enter my mind."

"Good thing." She caught his arm as he went to make a turn off the highway onto another road, following the sleeper car. "Wait! Don't take that road. Keep going. There aren't any houses for rent down that road. It makes a loop back to the highway. Just drive to the bluff up there"—she pointed—"and park. We should be able to see if they continue south or turn back on us and go back north."

Without hesitation, Aleksandr did as she said. He had hung back far enough that he was certain on the main highway, even with the small amount of traffic, the driver wouldn't be able to spot him. He turned off the lights. "Were any of the men with Nikitin familiar to you? Could any of them be the men who killed Danilov?"

Abigail frowned. "No. And I injured one of the men with my punch stick. If I didn't break a bone, I gave him a whopping bruise and he'll be limping for a few days. It has a very powerful blow. Just punching a shark with your fist isn't all that effective, so I use a small trigger device and it really packs a wallop. If you see someone limping, check him out."

Aleksandr tapped his fingers on the dashboard. "What are we looking for? We know someone is bringing in artifacts and art from Russia via freighter and dropping them off to a fishing boat off this coast. There's a good chance the items are being smuggled through Warner's gallery. Either he's aware of it or he's not, but it's a great route. He ships items to the city all the time and it would be a very slim chance that someone would open one of his crates."

"And if they did, would they even know what they were looking at? He ships art and sculptures all the time," Abigail said. "I wouldn't know the difference."

"He's one of the owners of the fishing boat we suspect is being used. But so is Ned Farmer. I recognized his name the minute you said it."

She smiled. "You've always had the best memory for details. I meet people and can't remember their name five minutes later. How do you do that?"

He shrugged. "Partly training, but I always have had a talent for names and places. I can read text and not forget it. It's a tremendous asset when I'm given so much data to cross-check." He leaned forward to peer out the window. "There it is. See the headlights? One is just a little bit off. He's going south."

"Wait just a minute. The highway has switchbacks and twists and turns, and we'll be above him. We'll catch glimpses of him on the turns."

He nodded his agreement and waited until the car had gone around a sweeping turn before pulling out onto the highway after it. "It would be useful to know if Chad Kingman works in shipping."

"Jonas would know. And Inez Nelson. She knows everything. If you go into her grocery store and just hang around a few minutes and listen, everyone tells her everything. She's like the local counselor. It isn't that hard to lead the conversation where you want it to go, but she's sharp, Sasha. Very sharp. Don't let her fool you. If you think you're going to put anything over on her, you won't."

"She must know Warner and Ned Farmer. She's a part owner in the fishing boat as well."

"Don't even think Inez would do anything illegal. She was born and raised in Sea Haven. Her husband was a wonderful man, born and bred there as well. Donald Nelson was a leader in the community and when he died five years ago, Inez stepped into his shoes and took over helping small businesses grow and neighborhoods thrive. She was behind the small library and theater and even the park. There is absolutely no way she would be involved in anything illegal."

"You have such faith in people, Abbey."

She looked at his expressionless face. It didn't matter what she said about Inez or Frank or any other of the town's inhabitants, Aleksandr reserved judgment. The things people did never seemed to shock him. She shrugged, slightly annoyed. "You can look at her if you'd like, but it's a waste of your time."

"I look at everyone. Did you know your aunt Carol had coffee with Frank Warner the other day?"

"Yes, I did. Does that make her a suspect? For heaven's sake, she just got back to Sea Haven. Do you suspect me?"

"Don't be so sensitive, Abbey. I have to be thorough in any investigation."

"Well, what about your friend Prakenskii? Don't you think he's up to his eyebrows in this?"

"Not necessarily. Nikitin is here for a reason. It could be as simple as the fact that he admires Joley's singing and heard this was her hometown and hoped to meet her. I know he's a huge music buff and he definitely has a sense of entitlement. He would think he should be given extra privileges. It could be Ignatev took a contract out on me and gave it to Nikitin. He did a little research, realized I was coming here, and got here first to set up shop. That's highly unlikely."

"Why?"

"Because Nikitin wouldn't want to be in the vicinity when the hit went down. He likes to look clean."

Abigail allowed her head to fall back. She was suddenly tired and the headache that had been pushing so close all evening had become a throbbing pain. "What are you not telling me?"

"I think Nikitin is here for an altogether different reason that has nothing to do with you or with me. I think it's a lot worse than that."

A chill went down Abigail's spine. "Worse than trying to kill you? What would be worse than that?"

"Killing a lot of people."

"Why would Nikitin want to do that?"

He shook his head, slowing the vehicle. They were catching up to the sleeper car and he didn't want that. He signaled and pulled onto a side road, killed the lights, and made a U-turn to bring them back to the entrance. "I told you, Nikitin is a businessman. You have to think like him. He has no reason to kill a large group of people. In his mind he simply brokers deals. We know that much of the stolen art leaving Russia is coming to this coast. That means the route has been open for some time and most likely Nikitin would be aware of it. He probably has a hand in the thefts."

"So he is involved in the stolen artifacts."

"As long as he gets his percentage, he's happy. Why would he have Danilov killed over a smuggling route? When a route gets hot you just close it and move to another until things cool down again. No one should get killed over it unless they can't shut down the route for a reason. And it would have to be *big* reason and worth a great deal of money to take a chance on killing an Interpol agent, especially since they know I'm here."

"Some art is worth millions." Abigail placed a hand on his wrist and indicated for him to go past the street the car had turned onto. "Keep going, this is another loop. Several of these houses are rentals and we can enter from the other side. We'll be able to see him getting out of his car and going up to the house."

Aleksandr did as she suggested, setting the car back in motion. "Art can be worth a great deal of money, but it isn't time sensitive. Why wouldn't they change the route? They could easily rendezvous in San Francisco or anywhere along this coast. It would take a little time to set it up, but it could be done. So they're bringing in something that *has* to use *this* route because everything is already set."

"Like what?"

"Nikitin deals in violence, Abbey. He has ties to a dozen terrorist groups and he'd take money from any of them."

"There's a coast guard station just a few yards from where your partner was killed. If they were going to do anything involving terrorists wouldn't they choose a better place to do it?" Abigail was appalled. "Why would you make such a leap between art and terrorists?"

"Because I know Nikitin and I'm certain Prakenskii didn't know about the hit on Danilov. There're only one or two things Nikitin wouldn't use Ilya for. It's fairly well known in the business he holds terrorists in contempt. He thinks they're cowards. Nikitin deals with them, but never through Prakenskii. I heard a rumor once that Nikitin sent him to a meeting and when the police showed up there were explosives everywhere, guns, and several dead terrorists, but no Prakenskii. How true the story is, I don't know, but if Nikitin didn't use Prakenskii to kill my partner, whatever Danilov found out that night involved terrorists." He didn't even glance at the house as they drove past and back out onto the main highway.

"It seems strange that Nikitin would have someone working for him who wouldn't do everything he wanted. Nikitin seems to be a self-absorbed, very violent man who insists on instant cooperation."

"He's all of those things, Abbey."

He sounded tired. She turned her head to look at him. "Are you taking me home?"

"I want you to come to my place." He reached for her hand, his thumb sliding over her skin, sending a small shiver down her spine. "I'm renting a small home almost right on the beach."

She shook her head. "I can't do that."

He tightened his grip on her hand as if she might slip away from him. "I was telling you the truth when I said I hadn't been able to sleep. I get up every hour all night long. Some nights I don't bother going to bed. I pace around the room and think about calling you and what I'd say when you answered. Sometimes I write you letters I don't bother to send because I know you won't read them. I'm tired, *baushki-bau,* and I can't sleep without holding you. At least lie down with me. I swear I won't do anything you don't want me to do."

"You know exactly what I'll want if I'm alone in bed with you. I've never been able to resist you, Sasha."

"I'm being very honest. Ask me. Ask me how often I've slept without you. I need you, Abbey. Come home with me."

12

ABIGAIL paced through the house. What was she doing there? It didn't make sense that she'd allowed Aleksandr to take her somewhere they'd be alone. She couldn't resist him when they were alone. She closed her eyes briefly and stepped out the sliding glass door leading to the lower deck where the hot tub was. The ocean view was spectacular. She could see white spray arc into the air as waves hit long fingers of rocks. It was cool outside, but the stars glittered overhead. She stood for a moment, contemplating whether or not she was strong enough to make love with Aleksandr, hold him all night, and walk away the next morning.

"What are you doing out here?" Aleksandr came up behind her. "It's cold, Abbey."

"But beautiful. Look at the moon." She indicated the dazzling silver ball. "We've had incredible weather lately."

He wrapped his arms around her from behind, nuzzling her hair out of the way so he could kiss the nape of her neck. "Are we going to talk about the weather?"

She shivered with his touch. "No, I just wanted you to see the night and listen to the ocean. I can hear the singing of the whales sometimes even in the dark." She turned in his arms and clasped her hands behind his neck. "Do you remember the night you took me up to the roof of your apartment? You said the city appeared to be a place of lights and color, a palace with a thousand secrets like in the Arabian Nights. You wanted to share that with me."

His hands stroked over her silken skin, his body and brain imprinted with the memory of her soft curves, her tight heat, her soft cries of surrender. "I remember laying you down on my blanket under the stars and making love to you for most of the night. And it started to rain just before dawn. I picked you up and ran for the stairs, wrapped up in the blanket and nothing else."

"We were laughing so hard we were afraid the neighbors would come out." She turned to gesture toward the sea. "This is my world. The place I want to share with you." She looked into his eyes and found them mesmerizing. "I've never wanted to share it with anyone else, Sasha."

"You're shivering."

"Am I?" She really hadn't noticed. His skin was hard and hot and he smelled fresh and clean and masculine. She had needed him for so long, hurt for so long, she almost couldn't comprehend that he was with her. Having him there with the ocean booming endlessly in the background, with the stars overhead, seemed such a gift, surreal, a dream she wanted to live in forever. The past and future seemed far away. Reality was his arms and little else.

"You are." He left a trail of kisses along her neck. "Let's go inside."

Abigail shook her head as her fingers tangled in his hair, as she smoothed the silken strands and laid her head against his chest. She wanted him to hold her like this, out under the stars where she could hear the call of the sea and feel the cleansing breeze on her face. She didn't want to feel afraid. She didn't want to remember anything but his touch and his body and the way he loved her.

Abigail pulled out of his arms and reached for the hem of her tight tank top. She drew it over her head and tossed it aside. Aleksandr thought he'd remembered every line of her body, every generous curve, but the sight of her soft breasts encased in her lace bra, the cool air tightening her nipples into inviting peaks, brought a rush of desire so strong it shook him.

"Let's make a bed out here," she suggested, her voice low and sensual. She raised her arms toward the sky, embracing the night, her long hair flowing around her like a silken cloak.

"Are you certain, Abbey? It's cool out tonight."

She half-turned her head, her exotic eyes and hair lending her a fey appearance in the light spilling down from the moon. "I'm certain. It's very sheltered out here. We can use the hot tub and the shower's right inside."

"Abbey . . ." His throat constricted. "If you want me to just hold you tonight, I'll keep to that. I meant what I said. I'm in this for the long run."

She sent another one of those smiles he couldn't interpret, slow, seductive, and just a little bit out of reach. "I want tonight. Give me tonight, Sasha, and we can sort the rest of it out later."

Aleksandr turned up the temperature on the hot tub and went back inside to return with the mattress and sheets. While Abbey made up the bed, he brought out several comforters and large bath sheets.

"This is a wonderful house," Abigail said. "A brilliant design. So many of the houses along the coast fit so nicely with the setting."

"You love living here, don't you?"

She sent him a faint smile. "It's home. Of course I love it. The sound of the ocean comforts me and every time I look at it, I feel peace. It doesn't matter if it's calm or turbulent, there's something soothing about the sea."

He reached for her, pulled her closer. "That's how I feel about you. You remind me of your sea. So often fishermen will say the sea is their mistress and she's in their blood." He kissed her neck, stroked his hands from her breasts to her belly. The golden links of the chain around her waist were already cooling in the night air but served to fuel the growing heat in his groin. "You're in *my* blood, Abbey. I don't even want to get you out."

He heard the soft hiss of a zipper as she stepped away from him. The hungry ache intensified to an agonizing fullness. She slid the pair of black jeans slowly over her hips and down the length of her legs, stepping out of them so that she stood on the deck wearing only her red lace bra and panties and a pair of black high heels.

"You're killing me, Abbey," he admitted softly, dropping his hand to the rock-hard bulge straining against his slacks. "I've dreamt of you coming to me, but my fantasies don't quite live up to the real thing."

The light from the moon surrounded her so that her skin appeared to be a glowing pearl. Her mass of thick red hair fell below her waist, drawing attention to the curve of her bottom. His world of violence and betrayal was a way of life. He understood it. Trusted no one. And then there was Abigail with her laughter and warmth, with her soft, melting body and secret haven of pleasure beyond his wildest dreams. She stood there, holding out her hand to him, not recognizing what she meant to him.

A roaring started somewhere in his head and consumed him. Tears burned behind his eyelids. He'd held himself in check for so long, refused to feel or think or dream, and now the dam had burst and the floodgates were wide open. He was damned if he was going to give her up. She thought she was offering a night of solace. He could feel her holding a part of herself back from him, but it wasn't going to happen. Abigail Drake was his, and every single cell in his body belonged to her. He had one night to make her admit that and he wasn't going to blow his chance.

He enveloped her hand in his and tugged until her body was against his. He had waited four years for this moment and he couldn't wait a moment longer. His fist clenched in her hair, his mouth found hers to catch that first small moan of surrender she always made. He reveled in that sound, that moment when he knew she would give herself to him. There'd been too many nights when he'd awakened alone, his body as hard as a rock, that small breathy sound filling his mind and bringing an ache to his heart.

Her hands slipped to his shoulder, fingers digging into his muscles as his tongue sank deep into the sweet heat of her mouth. He pressed his aching groin against her soft belly, allowing the sensation of her skin and lush curves to push him to the edge of control. Every memory of touching her, the endless pleasure, the unbelievable love that had crept into his heart and soul so slowly he hadn't recognized it in time to protect himself. It had been too late by the time he knew what was happening. He needed her when he had never needed anyone.

Her mouth was velvet heat, her tongue tangling with his, heightening his pleasure. He could barely breathe as he skimmed his hands possessively over her.

"You have too many clothes on, Sasha," she complained.

Reluctant to break their kiss, his teeth teased at her lower lip. He raised his head, taking just enough time to pull his shirt over his head and toss it aside. Before he could reach for her again her palm slid over the front of his slacks. His body shuddered at the sudden heat and friction as she rubbed him through the material.

"Way too many clothes," she emphasized, looking up into his eyes.

He was lost and he knew it. How many times had he drowned in her gaze? Abbey was a craving he'd never be over. He had stopped fighting the fact that he needed her. It was only a matter of making her realize she needed him just as much. He rid himself of his clothes, carelessly dropping them as he reached again for her, lowering her to the bed.

He found the warmth of her neck, kissing and biting gently, teasing her ear, her throat. Her nipples pressed into the hard muscles of his chest, only the lace separating skin. She was making soft sounds of pleasure, her nails digging into his back and her hips moving restlessly beneath him.

His body burned with a fever of desire. He kissed his way over the swell of her breasts to find the tight hard buds peaking through the red lace. "You're so beautiful." He could only stare at her while the moonlight caressed her body. He bent his head slowly and licked a curling heat over each nipple. Her body reacted, muscles contracting, hips jerking wildly. She moaned with the intensity of her pleasure.

Abbey never held anything back from him, always showing him how much she wanted him. The knowledge helped him to hang on to his control when he wanted her so much. He was determined to go slow and bring her to the same agonizing intensity that held him in its grip.

She arched into him, pushing her breast toward his mouth in invitation, her fists clenching in his hair. He lowered his head, his mouth closing hotly over her nipple, suckling with greedy lust. His hand moved up her leg to her thigh. He could feel her heat, the dampness on the red lace barrier between them. She said his name, a breathy, aching sound, pleading with him.

He stroked her silken thighs as he switched his attention to her other breast, his teeth taking tiny nips and his tongue flicking hotly over her skin as he kissed his way to her abdomen and the little golden chain. Her breath came in gasps, her fingers biting deep into his shoulders. His hands were everywhere, shaping every curve, finding every shadow, tugging on her nipples and stroking her until she was spiraling out of control right along with him. There was a plea in her voice as her hips shifted continually beneath him.

"I love this red lace," he whispered against her belly. His hands parted her thighs as his chin rubbed the damp lace. He inhaled her scent. Her fragrance enveloped him. He remembered it so vividly, the taste and scent uniquely hers. His teeth teased the lacy fabric over her pulsing mound.

"Sasha!" Abigail sounded hoarse with need.

His tongue slipped through the lacy holes and stroked deep. She bucked hard beneath him, nearly coming apart in his arms.

"What are you doing? It's been so long. I want you inside of me."

He smiled at the demand in her voice. "I want to have all of you. Even the parts you don't want to give me. Everything." His tongue slid deep again, a foray through lace, robbing her of breath. "It isn't my fault these panties are in the way."

Her hands pushed at them frantically. "Get them off. Hurry. Take them off." She kicked her feet until her high heels went flying.

Aleksandr stared down at her face, the glazed look in her eyes, the way her breasts heaved through the lacy bra. Her skin was flushed and sensitized, so beautiful his heart ached. He ripped the lace with one smooth motion, giving him full access to her body. He stroked his palm over her, sank his finger into the intriguing dampness. Her muscles clenched hard as he widened her thighs, slipping between them. "I've missed the taste of you."

He lowered his head to her, his mouth finding her most sensitive spot. He took his time, suckling, licking, driving her to the very edge of control and holding her there. Her body pulsed with arousal. She pleaded with him, fists back in his hair, tugging at him as fire raged through her bloodstream and her body wound tighter and tighter.

Abigail was on the verge of insanity. He was making hot sensual sounds of pleasure as he ate at her, licking and biting gently. He sounded desperate for her, yet he didn't take her, didn't fill her or allow her to come when she needed release. His eyes were so dark they looked black. He looked so hungry, a dark desire etched deep into the lines of his face. His fingers replaced his tongue as he bent forward and rubbed his face along her stomach. Her womb clenched and another cry escaped.

Aleksandr shifted positions, rising above her onto his knees. His body was hard, muscles defined, his shoulders wide. She'd forgotten how large he was. Kneeling between her legs the way he was, even with her body pulsing with need and damp with welcome, she had that one moment of uncertainty.

"We've done this many times," he reminded her as he pressed the large head of his erection against her.

He pushed into her tight folds, stretching her slowly. He gasped. "You're so damned tight, Abbey." His breath was ragged, matching hers. She was tight and so damned hot he wasn't certain if he was in paradise or hell. He had never wanted her so much and the sensation was somewhere between sheer ecstasy and pain as he drove deeper into her body.

Heat and fire lashed at her body, spread and consumed her. Abigail felt tears on her face and wondered how she'd ever lived without him. She had wanted to hold part of herself safe, but he was taking everything she was, demanding it all, and she couldn't stop the wealth of need pouring through her. Her body melted around his, became part of his. Skin to skin they rocked, hips finding the perfect rhythm, his body surging hard and fast and deep into hers. She rose to meet him, tightening her muscles around him to hold him to her. She was certain she wouldn't survive, that she would die with him buried deep inside of her as her body wound tighter and tighter with the need for release.

He plunged into her with hard desperate strokes while her body pulsed and throbbed around his. His hands gripped her hips, allowing him to drive down into her, fierce thrusts that sent shock waves through her body. Sensations poured into her, through her, building and building until there was only Aleksandr in her world. She felt her body tightening, reaching in a frenzy of lust and need, higher and higher.

He didn't stop moving, thrusting harder and harder and taking her so high she was afraid she could never get back. It didn't matter, he held her with his strength, his face a mask of dark intensity, as his furious rhythm increased. She heard herself scream as he rubbed against her most sensitive spot, throwing her over the edge so that her womb convulsed, sending shock waves ripping through her. She felt the hot jet of his release filling her, heard his throaty cry mingling with hers. He lay over her, his body shuddering, hot, beads of sweat dampening his hair, his heart pounding through his chest.

She lay beneath him fighting to breathe, her body not her own, but then it hadn't been since the first time she'd lain with him. Tears leaked out of the corners of her eyes.

"*Lyubof maya.*" His voice was gentle, sensual. "You'll tear out my heart again if you cry." His fingers threaded through hers. "I love you more than life. Is there no hope for us? I had nothing until you came into my life and when you left, you left me with nothing." He kissed her eyes, his tongue taking her tears. "Try for me, Abbey."

"I am trying." Her body was still pulsing around his, little aftershocks rocking her, sending tiny electrical charges through her bloodstream.

"You're trying not to love me." He kissed her throat, pressed another kiss between her breasts. "I know you so well. You don't want to love me."

She hated that he knew that. That he knew her so well he could tell what she was thinking and feeling. She touched his face. His beloved face.

"We were so right together. We fit, Abbey. We belong."

"I had to work so hard to find myself again, Aleksandr." There was pain in her voice. "I was so lost without you. You left me raw and wounded and trapped in a dark place with no windows or doors. I didn't know how to live without you. I didn't know how to smile or feel or *be*. It took almost two years before I really accepted that it was over and I had to find a way to go on. I made myself strong. I'm alive again. I can wake up some mornings and be happy. I can look at the ocean and find peace again. Now you're asking me to risk everything all over again and I'm not certain I could survive if it all came crashing down."

He lay on her, her soft body imprinted on his hard flesh. He was still buried deep inside her and they had just had earth-shattering sex. She was looking up at him with a mixture of love and fear and he couldn't even pretend he didn't know why. He had mishandled things through arrogance, his confidence that he was so powerful no one would think to try to take him down. He had been wrong and Abigail had been the one to pay the price.

"I know, *rebyonak,* I'm so sorry. I know I'm to blame for what happened to you and I know the price you paid for my mistake. But I swear to you, I won't let it happen again." He kissed the corners of her mouth. "I don't make the same mistake twice."

She smoothed back his hair. "Give me time."

"I'll go get us something to drink. Do you want something hot or cold?"

"Something cold. I'm going to take a shower and get in the hot tub."

Aleksandr kissed her again, long and slow, trying without words to show her how he felt. He reluctantly slipped out of the haven of her body. He had such a precarious hold on her and he didn't want to leave her even for a moment, afraid she would manage to slip away from him and leave him alone again.

Abigail wrapped her hair up to keep it from getting wet and allowed the hot water to pour over her body. It had been a long time since she'd made love and she was somewhat sensitive, her body slightly sore. Aleksandr had always been so ravenous for her. He made love to her often, sometimes several times in a day. The things they'd done, she'd never do with anyone else. With him it always seemed right and natural. Her body stilled throbbed for his. She could feel the pulsing of her womb, wanting more.

Naked, she walked out onto the deck. Aleksandr had already removed the hot tub's cover and he took her hand, helping her into the water. The contrast of the cool night air and the heated water made her gasp as she sank down into the depths. She sat, her head pillowed on the cushion, looking up at the stars and listening to the boom of the ocean as he took his shower.

Abigail sat up and watched him walk toward her when she heard the slide of the door. He was carrying two champagne glasses filled with golden liquid. He stepped into the hot tub and handed her a glass. She set the flute on the edge of the tub and cupped his sac in her palm, gently squeezing as she came up on her knees. Her breasts floated in the hot water as she leaned toward him. "You're such a gorgeous man."

At her touch, he was coming alive even in the coolness of the night. She wrapped her fingers around him, felt him grow longer and harder in answer. "Just stand there, Sasha, and drink your champagne. I want to touch you."

He had explored her body thoroughly, but she had only managed to anchor herself by digging her nails into him and holding on when the sensations became too much. Now she had time for a far more leisurely exploration.

Aleksandr closed his eyes as her warm breath moved over his body. Her hands slipped over his skin, traced lines and muscles, returned to brush lightly over his suddenly raging erection. He raised the glass to his lips and took a small sip of the champagne just as her mouth closed over him. He nearly dropped the glass and choked. His free hand settled in her hair.

"I love your mouth." He was once again agonizingly hard and throbbing heavily.

She didn't respond. Moisture was already pooling low and her womb clenched again, rippling and pulsing with need. Both hands came up to grip his thighs, her fingers digging into the heavy muscle there as he filled her mouth with his fullness. She began to suckle strongly, her tongue dancing and teasing while he groaned in pleasure.

Aleksandr threw back his head and looked up at the sky. The moon bathed them in light while the ocean played a strong melody in the background. The heat of the tub was nothing in comparison to the fire of her velvet mouth. He had no idea what he'd done in a former life to deserve a woman like Abigail. He had never conceived of having a woman who would share herself so completely, so honestly. One who would enjoy his body with such complete abandon. She could do amazing things with her mouth and seemed to love doing them to him.

His legs trembled and he felt like he was strangling with pleasure, his breath coming in ragged gasps, lungs burning for air. He thrust deeper into her mouth, his hips picking up the ebb and flow of the sea. His sac was so tight he was afraid he would burst. "I want to come inside of you, Abbey. I'm close, so close."

Her body was pulsing with such need she reluctantly gave up the pleasure of driving him out of his mind and allowed him to pull free of her mouth. He reached down and gripped her waist, lifting her without preamble to her feet and turning her toward the pillowed headrest. With the flat of his hand on her back he forced her to lean forward. She found herself staring out at the pounding sea as his hand slipped between her legs, his fingers seeking her dampness.

He groaned. "You're so ready for me. Do you have any idea what that can do to a man?" It could bring him to his knees. Abigail had no idea what she'd done for him, how she'd changed his life, how she'd changed him as a person. He wouldn't go back to what he'd been without her. He drove into her hard, needing the pounding pleasure pulsing through his body to drive his demons away. They rose up so unexpectedly. Abigail had confessed how difficult it was to get her life back and go on without him, but she had managed. He hadn't been able to do it.

He had poured his heart into his letters and she had sent them back unopened. Before Abbey it had never mattered if he was happy as long as he did his duty. He pursued criminals and he dodged bullets and went home to an empty apartment. He trusted no one and cared for no one. He had been able to live in the labyrinth of deceit and treachery, skillfully maneuvering through the minefields of his world, but she had taken that from him. He had lost himself just as surely as she had lost who she was. He couldn't think about losing her again; he doubted if he'd survive it either.

His fingers bit into her hips. She was hot and tight and a miracle of pleasure driving the dangerous thoughts from his head. He could feel her body bathing him in hot liquid, her muscles gripping him hard, squeezing and massaging, the friction incredible as he thrust into her. Abigail pushed back against him, rocking her bottom against his tight sac with each deep stroke, sending his pleasure spiraling out of control. He felt her body spasm around his, convulsing, contracting tightly. Her soft cry rose up into the night.

A hoarse cry escaped his throat as he emptied himself into her, his arms circling her waist, his mouth finding the nape of her neck. He pressed a trail of kisses down her spine to the small of her back as he slipped out of her. He turned her, helping her to sit back down in the hot tub when both had shaky legs. She was looking at him with such a mixture of pain and pleasure he felt his heart jerk in his chest. There was so much sadness in her he couldn't stand it.

He caught her chin, and his other hand went to his chest. "*Baushki-bau,* you're breaking my heart. Can't you see what I feel for you is real? That I love you more than anything in this world? I'd do anything to take away the pain I caused you. Tell me what I can do. Please, Abbey, you can't hurt like this anymore."

She sent him a faint smile, touching the small lines around his mouth. "It isn't just my pain. It's yours as well. I feel you in the same way you do me." She pressed her hand over her heart in a gesture nearly identical to his. "We'll get through this. It will just take time. I never thought to see you again and I'm still in a state of shock."

"You deliberately seduced me tonight."

Her smile widened. "It doesn't take all that much to seduce you, Sasha. You think when I look at you I'm seducing you."

He shrugged his shoulders. "That's true."

Abigail reached for her champagne. "It's a good thing I'm on the pill. We'd be in big trouble. Just because Elle is the one destined to have seven daughters doesn't mean the rest of us can't get pregnant. You should have thought of that before you got so wild."

He took her flute and tilted it just slightly so a few drops ran down the slope of her breast. "I did think of it," he murmured as he bent his head to lick the champagne from her skin. "I'd hoped you'd forgotten."

His tongue sent little electrical charges pulsing through her center. He sat back, his head against one of the cushioned pillows, and drew her to his lap. "Lie back and look at the stars. It's an incredible night and I just want to hold you."

Abigail relaxed, wiggling her hips until she could feel his groin along the seam of her buttocks. She allowed her head to rest on his chest. Immediately his hands came up to cup her breasts. "You can't possibly."

"No, but I can hold you. I missed touching you." His fingers massaged her breasts, tugged at her nipples. "I loved waking up in the middle of the night and finding you next to me naked. Your body was always so receptive."

"You're a sex maniac." There was a smile in her voice and one creeping into her heart. Maybe she was a sex maniac. When she was with him, she was always damp and ready, her body pulsing and throbbing. It didn't matter what he asked, when he asked, she wanted him. He liked touching her body and he'd done it often. Even when they were out she remembered how his hand would accidentally brush across her nipples or her bottom. Once they'd been in a club late at night and his hand had crept up her thigh beneath the table. She'd been so hot for him by the time they left, they'd barely made it to his apartment before she was stripping his clothes off.

He never minded when she reciprocated, as she often had, deliberately arousing him when she knew he could do nothing about it. She loved the look in his eyes, hot with promise, and he always followed through.

Aleksandr nibbled on her shoulder, his teeth nipping her skin playfully as his hands wandered over her body. She allowed champagne to slip down her throat and passed the flute to him once more. He took a drink and then pulled her head back to kiss her, tasting of champagne and sex.

"Do you want to go to bed?" Abigail asked.

He gave her back the flute and slipped both hands back under the water, seeking her thighs. "Yes. With you. I want to eat you all night."

"I thought you wanted to hold me all night."

"That too." His hands parted her thighs and he rested his palms on either side of her mound, thumbs moving with slow persuasion through her tight curls. "I want tonight to last forever."

She sighed and shifted just a little bit more to accommodate his stroking fingers. "I want tonight to last forever too." He was making her hot all over again with his teasing kisses and his fingers sliding deep inside of her, stroking and dancing with an expertise that came from all the nights he'd made love to her.

"Come for me." He whispered the temptation. He pushed his fingers deeper, filling her, stroking her clit and murmuring explicit fantasies in Russian in her ear.

She pushed her hips forward, riding his hand, her breath coming in gasps and her breasts heaving with the excitement of her building pleasure. He kissed her again and again, stealing her breath, stimulating her breasts with one hand while the other stroked in and out of her tight sheath. In between his kisses he whispered in Russian. She could only catch some of what he was proposing she was so lost in the rising tide of heat. She lifted her hips to meet the rhythmic thrust of his fingers, wanting more, desperate for more.

Aleksandr bit at her collarbone, a small bite of pain he eased with his tongue. He pushed deep inside her with his fingers, rubbing at her most sensitive spot. Excitement flared through her, hot and needy. She could feel her body winding higher and higher.

"You're so tight," he whispered. "So hot and tight."

She exploded, the orgasm coming at her fast and hard and shaking her with its strength. Heat rushed through her body and she actually felt faint. "I'm going to have to get out of here," she said. "But I don't think I can stand up."

Aleksandr picked her up easily and stepped out of the hot tub. He set her on the edge and dried off her body with a large bath sheet. "Thank you for being here with me tonight, Abbey."

"No matter what happens later, I'm glad I did, Sasha."

Her voice betrayed her exhaustion and he carried her to the bed and laid her down, smoothing back her hair from her face. "Stay under the covers while I put the cover back on the hot tub. I don't want you getting cold."

She curled beneath the thick down comforters. "I'm so sleepy I don't think I'd notice. Hurry and come to bed."

Aleksandr cleaned up the deck and returned her, staring down at her for a long time, amazed that she was actually with him. He was very aware she hadn't given him a single commitment and he knew she was going to walk away from him in the morning. But he had her with him now and it was more than he had ever expected.

Aleksandr crawled into the bed beside Abigail and curved his body around hers. "What do you know of Jonas Harrington?" He wrapped his arms around her and pressed a kiss against the nape of her neck.

"What do you want to know?" There was a note of wariness in her voice.

He smiled in the darkness. "You are so protective of this man."

"He wouldn't think so. He's our family. I love him. My sisters, my parents, even my aunts love him. He's a pain in the butt most of the time, but he'd walk through fire for us."

"I have learned much about him and he seems to be very good at his job and has an excellent service record."

"How'd you find that out?"

"These are modern times and even backward Russian Interpol agents use laptops and the Internet to send and receive files. Interpol is rather renowned as an agency for information." He nuzzled her hair. "I love the way your hair smells."

"I use an herbal shampoo my sister makes. It's great stuff."

"Tell me about Harrington as a person. A man. Is he rigid about rules? Does he go strictly by the book? Would he back up his partner when it got rough?"

Abigail opened her eyes and turned over to look at him. Her soft body moved against Aleksandr's with a sweet fire that shook him. It was one of the things he missed the most, lying in bed with her, feeling her simply move against him.

"Don't you dare use Jonas for anything dangerous."

"He seems to be very much on top of the investigation and he's brushing a little too close to Nikitin and Prakenskii. I don't want them to target him. I don't think Prakenskii would take Harrington down except in self-defense, but Nikitin's answer to anyone in his way is usually some sort of violence. I thought I might better be able to protect Harrington if I worked with him."

"Jonas takes his job very seriously and he'll find out who murdered your partner. If you're asking me would he be an asset to you, then yes. And if you're worried that he'll get so close to the truth that whoever is behind this will want him dead, he's tenacious and he'll find the killer. I'd be very grateful if you'd watch over him." She yawned. "I'm so sleepy."

He kissed her neck again. "Go to sleep then. We have tomorrow to talk."

"Sasha . . ." Her voice was drowsy again. "I have to be at the cove first thing in the morning to give the dolphin antibiotics and then I have a meeting with my sisters. I'm supposed to be helping them plan a double wedding and so far I've contributed absolutely nothing toward the plans. There's also that thing." She made a noise of disgust.

"What thing?"

"Frank Warner is having his party for all the bigwigs and we received the royal summons from Inez, which means we have to go."

"Are you giving me the brush-off?"

She stiffened at his tone. "No. I'm telling you I have plans tomorrow and won't be able to see you. I do have a life, you know. And I thought you were here on business. Don't you have an investigation to run?"

"My investigation is going fine. I'm able to juggle more than one thing in my life at a time."

She looked at him with her vivid green eyes. "Am I one of those things?"

"You're everything."

13

"**ABBEY!** You're late!" Hannah glared at her sister. "And you're dripping all over the floor."

Abigail stood in the doorway for a moment, looking like a guilty child caught with a hand in the cookie jar. Her usually vivid red-gold hair hung in damp tails, dripping water down her neck and shoulders. There was even water on the tips of her feathery eyelashes.

Hannah regarded her with amusement. Abigail had stripped off her wet suit somewhere before coming home, but her mask still hung from her fingertips as if she'd forgotten she carried it. She was barefoot and wearing only her modest one-piece and a pair of very wet sweatpants.

"I know, I know. I'm sorry." Abigail Drake slammed the kitchen door closed and looked longingly over toward the kettle. "I'm desperate for a cup of tea."

Hannah couldn't resist Abigail's enormous puppy-dog eyes and she glanced at the silver kettle sitting on a burner. As if on cue, the burner sprang to life, flames hissing softly beneath the kettle. "I'll make you a cup while you shower, but *hurry*." She glanced at her watch. "We're already half an hour late."

Abigail ran for the stairs, Hannah following behind her. "I couldn't help it. I had to give antibiotics to Kiwi this morning and then the other dolphins were in the cove and they were so responsive I couldn't resist a swim. It was so peaceful that I completely forgot the time." She grinned at her sister over her shoulder. "If you had a choice between sweet, entertaining dolphins versus making an appearance at Frank Warner's gallery, which would it be? Besides, Frank avoids me pretty much like the rest of Sea Haven if he can help it. I hate these things."

"They don't avoid you, Abbey," Hannah said.

"Sure they do, they're all afraid I'm going to blurt out the wrong thing and they'll tell the world a deep dark secret. I'd rather be under the sea with the dolphins."

"You have a point, but you also missed the meeting about Sarah and Kate's wedding plans. Even Aunt Carol was in a huff over it and you know she adores you."

Abigail paused at the entrance to the tiled bathroom. "I know." She shoved back the mass of wet, salty hair from her face. "I shouldn't have done that. It's just that . . ." She trailed off with a small sigh.

"Is it Jonas or Aleksandr that you're avoiding?" Hannah asked.

Abigail stiffened, a slight reaction, but Hannah caught it right away. Abigail's expression was immediately wary. "Both. Did either of them call?"

"Yes." Hannah put her hand on Abigail's shoulder to prevent her escape into the bathroom. "Jonas has been calling all morning. Why are you upset with him?" She watched her sister closely for a reaction. Shadows moved in Abigail's eyes, veiled her expression.

Hannah pressed her hand over her heart. It actually ached and she knew she was feeling her sister's pain in spite of the fact that Abigail smiled at her. "Abbey, I wish I could help."

"I know you do, honey. I have to work things out on my own. I'm so mixed up right now and it doesn't help with Jonas calling and demanding I talk to him about things I really don't know about. He should just talk to Aleksandr and leave me out of it. I came home to help plan my sisters' wedding and to research my dolphins. I don't want to know anything about stolen artifacts or murders. I just wish they'd all leave me alone."

Hannah regarded her sister with solemn eyes. "You slept with him, didn't you?"

A faint smile touched Abbey's mouth. "Well, yes."

"And it wasn't good?"

"It was great. Aleksandr and I are very compatible. It isn't the sex. It's how much I need him. How he can get to me. I want it to be just sex—it would be so much safer that way, Hannah."

"Abbey, any woman who spends her life in the sea doesn't play it safe. I'm not saying go after him, because I don't honestly know what he's like. His aura is very mixed and indicates conflict, violence, and danger, but also protection and a lot of other great qualities."

"I ache for him. I can't get him out of my head."

"I'm sorry, hon, I know you're hurting. And he's called every hour for you. I know he thinks I'm lying when I tell him you aren't here." Hannah indicated the bathroom. "Go take a shower. You're dripping all over the hall. I'll make you a cup of tea. You'll need it to go to this party." She made a little face.

"I know how much you hate them."

"I feel like I'm two people inside, Abbey." Hannah looked down at her hands. "I'm the real me, the way I am with my family, outgoing and strong, and then I go out into a public situation and I can't talk without stammering. It's so frustrating. I believe in myself. It doesn't matter to me what others think of me." She paused. "Well, my family and maybe that rat Jonas, although why he matters, I have no idea."

Abigail studied her sister. She was always slightly shocked at how beautiful Hannah really was. She was tall, fashionably thin, but managed to still have full, natural breasts. Her hair was white-gold, thick and long, and held an incredible shine. Everything about Hannah was elegance and class, from her large, heavily fringed eyes and high cheekbones to her wide, full mouth. There was power in Hannah's slender body, and a mischievous nature hidden beneath her ice cool exterior. Few ever saw that side of Hannah. The larger the gift, the stronger the power, the more drawbacks nature counterbalanced with, and Hannah's talent was extreme. And Jonas was right. She looked tired and drawn and far too thin in spite of her beauty.

"Don't." Hannah blinked back tears. "I'm fine."

"I'd hug you, but I'm all wet," Abigail said. "You could always turn him into a toad. That would solve both our problems."

"I've been considering it. Or better yet, every time he opens his mouth to say something mean to me, a nice loud croak comes out."

They both burst into laughter.

The kitchen door banged just as the kettle began to whistle. "Hey!" Sarah Drake called up the stairs. "I can hear the two of you cackling like a couple of witches, but I sure don't see either of you at the gallery where you belong. Just what are you up to?"

The two sisters exchanged a long, guilty look.

"Save me," Abigail mouthed and rushed to the bathroom to wash the sea salt from her hair and body.

Hannah raced down the stairs to intercept her oldest sister. "Sarah! I thought we were meeting at Frank's gallery."

Sarah lifted an eyebrow as she examined Hannah's flawless face. "I'll just bet you did. Were you and Abbey thinking of sneaking off and accidentally missing it?"

"I was making a quick cup of tea for Abbey," Hannah hedged.

"You did consider it, didn't you?" Sarah poked her sister in the ribs. "You look beautiful all dressed up in that elegant outfit. Where else would you go in Sea Haven dressed so nice?"

"I was thinking of my old flannel pajamas, a good movie, and some popcorn," Hannah said. Her hands moved gracefully as she spooned tea leaves into a small teapot.

"Abbey just got back, didn't she? Kate said she and Matt dropped by the old mill to make a few changes in the plans and she saw Abbey's skiff out in Sea Lion Cove. Abbey spent the day playing with the dolphins."

"It isn't playing, Sarah. She works. She's a marine biologist."

Sarah gave an inelegant sniff. "Not here, she's not. You're a model, Hannah, but when you come home, you're our sister and you're here to plan a wedding. A double wedding. Abbey's out every day in the ocean instead of working with us."

"I know." Hannah ducked her head. "She's worried about the dolphin who was injured and she went out to take care of him. You know how the dolphins always congregate and call to her when she's around."

"She's hiding the way she always does," Sarah said, a mixture of concern and exasperation in her voice. "She slept with that man, didn't she?" She glanced toward the stairs. "Has she said anything at all about the other one? We need to know what we're up against."

"I haven't asked her yet, but I was going to over tea."

"I want to know just how dangerous he is. And if Jonas knows about him."

"Jonas doesn't need to know anything about that other man. He can't handle someone with that kind of power," Hannah said. "Did you feel the electricity gathering in the air with that small push he sent Joley? He really zapped her hand and yet, just brushing her palm with his thumb took the pain away."

"Joley was furious. I've never seen her that way," Sarah said. "I was actually afraid she'd start some kind of battle with him right on the spot."

"You have a lot of connections. Can you find out anything about him?"

"If we get his name, I'll start inquiries."

Hannah nodded and glanced up the stairs. The water in the shower had turned off but Abigail would be upstairs a few minutes longer. "I'm worried about Abbey. She's been really unhappy for years and with Aleksandr coming back into her life she's more upset than ever. Her solution is always to disappear. She goes off to another part of the world researching and doesn't have to interact with us at all. She just withdraws."

Sarah studied the shadows in Hannah's eyes. "You're *really* worried, aren't you?"

"Aren't you?" Hannah countered.

Sarah nodded, her shoulders sagging a little. "The truth is, I've been scared for Abbey. I was hoping I was just being paranoid. But she lets you closer to her than any of the rest of us. Don't lose her, Hannah. I know it's a burden for you because you're so empathic and she's so troubled right now, but you've got to hang on to her until the rest of us can figure out how to bring her back to us." Sarah flicked a glance toward the stairs, then forced a smile. "What about you? How are you doing? How'd the shoot in Africa go?"

"The photographer was a genius. I'd like to work with him again. I enjoy the traveling and Africa was beautiful. I hired a guide and stayed three weeks just to try to take everything in. I can't even begin to tell you the awe I felt out in the wild." Her eyes sparkled. "It was like being free. The strange thing was, I didn't have a single panic attack out in the wild, with just the guide and me. I didn't stammer. I could actually talk to him. Mostly I just listened. He had such wonderful stories to tell me."

"I'm so pleased for you, Hannah," Sarah said. "I wondered why we didn't receive an SOS from you."

Hannah poured a cup of tea, added milk, and handed it to Sarah before pouring a second cup. "I know it must get old for everyone to have to help me when I'm on jobs. It's so draining for all of you over such a long distance." She turned with perfect timing and handed the cup of tea to Abigail as she came up to them dressed in a sleek pin-striped pantsuit that was more feminine than either sister had ever seen her wear.

"Nice, Abbey. Are you expecting to go out on a date with Frank?"

Abbey made a face. "As if. I'll leave that to Aunt Carol. Is she already there?"

"She helped oversee all the details with the caterers and the party planner along with Inez. They want this to be a huge success. Aunt Carol ordered me to come and collect you," Sarah explained. She glanced at her watch. "We're already late so a few more minutes won't matter that much. I haven't had a chance to ask you about the other Russian, the one with the magic. Who is he?"

"His name is Ilya Prakenskii. He was raised in the same state-run home that Aleksandr was raised in. I asked Aleksandr if he remembered anything different about Prakenskii and he did recall a few things that indicates the man may have been born with the same gifts we have. He's definitely adept at them. He tried to subtly push me to say something I didn't want to say, and when I realized it, I challenged him to a game of truth or dare." She smirked. "He definitely didn't want to engage."

"Does Aleksandr think he's dangerous to us?"

"He says he's a dangerous man, has the reputation of a hit man, and that he works for Sergei Nikitin, who just happens to head up one of the Russian mafia families. Nikitin absolutely loves Joley's music and wants to meet with her."

"She attracts the worst people. I think she needs a stamp on her forehead that says, 'If you're a psycho, apply here.'" Sarah sighed and looked at her watch again. "We have to find out as much as we can about this Prakenskii. And all of us need to keep a watch on Joley.

She can be a bit psycho herself if anyone pushes her too hard. We'd better get to the party. After all, Frank let the press know Hannah would be there."

"Not just Hannah," Abigail said. "Poor Joley and Kate as well. He did a lot of name-dropping to bring in a crowd. He'll get it, too, dangling the three of them like that."

"Inez is proud of him for that. She wants this event to be a huge success and for the townspeople to fully support him," Sarah said. "She thinks he brings culture to us."

Hannah put up one hand in surrender. "Fine, I'll go, but I wish he wouldn't have so many of his famous fund-raisers. He seems to time them so coincidentally when I happen to be back in town."

"He does, doesn't he?" Abbey said.

"Clever man," Sarah added. "Free press for him."

The town, usually quiet and homey, was alive with people. Several limousines were parked along the wooden sidewalks and various top-of-the-line models of cars lined the streets. Teenage boys hung around in groups to admire the more exotic cars while the young girls tried to catch glimpses of celebrities as they entered the fashionable art gallery.

Frank Warner had been in Sea Haven a good ten years and his gallery was classy, spacious, and filled with interesting antique artifacts and paintings. Sarah had been to his home once with Inez and she said his house was filled with beautiful artifacts from around the world. Old and much-revered paintings were kept in special rooms where the sun never touched them.

The gallery featured sculptures from modern times as well, art forms in several types of material, all pleasing to the eye and carrying a hefty price tag. Only a couple hours' drive from San Francisco, the town's quaint beauty, with its theater and culture, had appealed to Warner and he'd stayed, making a surprising success out of his gallery.

He often featured some of his own paintings of the local area, the harbors and cliffs, the crashing waves and windswept landscapes. The Drake sisters found him talented, eccentric, and a bit of a coward, using their fame but not wanting to get too close to the strange, magical gifts they shared.

Hannah waved to a crowd of teenagers and Abbey sent a brief

smile, stepping close to her younger sister. Hannah always looked poised and confident, even a bit haughty as she swept through a crowd with her elegant, exotic beauty, yet she was painfully shy and often had panic attacks. Whenever she made public appearances her sisters aided her by binding together so she could speak and breathe without problems. It was draining on all of them, but they were so used to it, they did it automatically.

"You look beautiful, Abbey," Sarah said as they entered the gallery. "I like that pinstripe on you. And you've done something different with your hair."

Hannah burst out laughing, the sound turning heads. "She's wearing it down and it isn't soaking wet and dripping saltwater."

"Hey now!" Abbey protested. "I'm not always soaking wet."

Sarah made a derisive sound. "Yes, you are. I think you'd live in the sea if we let you. Kate thinks you're evolving into a mermaid. Don't you, Kate?" she added as Kate approached them.

Kate Drake laughed at Abbey's expression. "You know it's true, so don't bother denying it. I'm getting married in a couple of months and you haven't contributed so much as a preference for colors or flowers."

"I said I thought a scheme of coral reef would be pretty as a centerpiece on the tables," Abbey pointed out.

Kate nearly snorted the sip of wine out her nose. She waved Abigail away. "Go mingle so Inez will be happy with us. She's looked at her watch fifty times in the last ten minutes and she's upset because Joley made a comment about one of Frank's goddess sculptures looking a little anorexic."

"That's our Joley, stirring the pot," Sarah said. "Come on, Kate, we'll do damage control. You two stay out of trouble."

Hannah caught sight of Joley weaving her way through the crush of the crowd and nudged Abbey. "There's Joley. Let's do a fast run through and make our way to her. Maybe we can get out before Inez asks us to do something like stand on our heads for everyone."

"Good idea." Abbey drifted around the room, murmuring greetings to people she knew and acknowledging introductions quickly to protect Hannah as much as possible.

"There's so many people," Hannah said. "Isn't there a fire code? Where does he find all these people?"

"There's Aunt Carol. Take a look at the man hanging on her arm"—Abigail pointed rudely but she was so shocked she didn't care—"that's old man Mars."

Hannah laughed. "You mean Reginald. He's all cleaned up and wearing a suit. Aunt Carol is snapping pictures like mad. Hopefully she'll get one of him because if any moment in time is worth recording, this would be it. I've never seen him in anything but his overalls and a scruffy face."

"He's actually good-looking."

Abbey smiled and waved at Frank Warner as he swiftly, but very politely, moved through the crowd in the opposite direction. Amusement put a smile on her face as she waited for Hannah to sign another autograph. Over in the corner Kate was signing a book she'd written and Joley scrolled her name across a baseball cap.

"Abbey?" Hannah gripped her wrist hard. "I'm having trouble breathing in here." Her voice was so low Abbey could barely hear her.

Immediately Abbey slipped her arm around Hannah's waist "You're all right, baby, as long as you stick by me. You know how everyone is afraid of me. Especially Sylvia. Is she here?" She wanted to make Hannah laugh and she succeeded, although it was a brief wheezing response.

"I think she's more afraid of me," Hannah admitted. "You never retaliate."

Abbey laughed aloud and the sound turned heads in the room. "So you admit it! You'd better be glad I'm not Sarah or you'd get a lecture."

Hannah shrugged. "Someone has to be the bad girl."

Abbey hugged her sister a little closer. "You have the proverbial heart of gold, Hannah. Joley's the wicked one. You're a sweetie."

"Hey! I heard that," Joley came up behind them, slinging her arm around Hannah so she and Abbey guarded her from either side, protecting her from the crush of the crowd. Unfortunately Joley was too big of a star to make it across the room without a dozen people stopping her to ask for her autograph.

"I'm so glad I'm not a rock star," Hannah whispered.

Joley winced. "I am *so* not a rock star." She tossed her head and assumed a haughty expression. Hannah naturally looked haughty but Joley could pull it off beautifully when she wanted.

"I also *so* want out of here, but Sarah and Inez and Aunt Carol will tear strips off us if we take off too early."

"I've got an idea," Abigail said. "It's really, really bad and we'll probably get into a lot of trouble. You want to hear it?"

"I'm in," Joley said. "Lead the way. I don't have to hear it."

Abigail threaded her way through the crowd toward a door marked Employees Only. "Chad Kingman works in the back. Do either of you remember him?"

Joley made a face. "You aren't thinking of dumping your Russian hottie for Chad, are you? Do you remember him in school? He was totally obnoxious."

Hannah burst out laughing again. "Everyone was obnoxious in school, Joley. We all grew up, even Chad."

"Well, the hussy can't sleep with one and rush off to be with the other."

"I know you're not calling me a hussy, Joley!" Abigail glared at her. "You have no idea whether or not I slept with Aleksandr."

Joley grinned at her. "Hannah told me you wore the red panties. You had every intention of sleeping with that man and you stayed out all night. I don't need confirmation that you're a hussy. I already know!"

Abigail tried to look innocent but the blush was creeping up her neck and into her cheeks and her sisters were giggling like schoolgirls. "Well, fine, maybe I did," Abigail conceded. "But I'm not going off to find Chad Kingman, for heaven's sake. He would never talk to me even if I did think he was hot, which I *don't*. There was this little incident at a party when he was a junior in high school. Very bad. I've never been his favorite person since."

She glanced around, shoved open the door, and waved her sisters through. It was dark and gloomy in the back room. Boxes cluttered the floor and tables. Sculptures of various sizes littered the room.

"It's a little spooky in here," Hannah said.

"What are we doing?" Joley said. "Although, this isn't bad. At least we don't have to smile at Frank and watch him flirting with Aunt Carol. She's deliberately leading that man on so she can spy for Jonas."

"Aunt Carol loves drama. And it doesn't hurt to have two men hanging on her every word," Hannah said. "I don't know how she does it. I've even gotten close to her to see if I can feel the flare of magic when she's flirting, but I can't. It's really her appeal. She makes everyone feel so good."

"She brightens the world," Joley said. "Abigail, you should sneak back to the buffet table and get us food and something to drink and we can have our own party right here."

"We aren't partying, you slacker, we're spying."

Hannah gripped her arm in excitement. "Spying?" She lowered her voice and looked around. "We need Aunt Carol's camera."

"Fine, you two wait here and I'll go get the camera and some food." Abigail slipped through the door again and joined the throng wandering through the gallery.

Carol was in the corner laughing with Reginald Mars. Abigail caught up a plate, filled it with finger foods, and made her way to her aunt. "Hello, Mr. Mars," she greeted. "You look absolutely wonderful."

Carol ran her hand up and down Reginald's arm. "Isn't he handsome?" She beamed at the man, her eyes bright and her smile genuine.

Old man Mars shook Abigail's hand politely and flashed a charming smile. He had eyes only for her aunt. "Nice to see you, Abbey."

"I hope the two of you are having a great time. Aunt Carol, would you mind letting me borrow the camera for a few minutes? Joley wants a few shots for her scrapbook."

"Well, dear, of course not." Carol removed the camera and handed it to Abigail. "But I did take several pictures of all of you girls as you moved around the room. Would you like me to show you how to use it?"

"I'm good, thanks." Abigail tried to look as innocent as possible. The smile was slowly fading from her aunt's face and that was a bad sign. "You two have fun!" She hurried away before Carol could get a good "reading" on her.

"What did you bring for us to eat?" Joley greeted her as Abigail slipped through the door. "I'm starving."

"How can you be starving? You hung out at the buffet table," Abigail objected. "I brought a camera. The food's just a cover in case anyone was watching."

"Then we may as well eat it," Joley said. "It's only practical."

Hannah rolled her eyes, but she grabbed a black olive. "What are we looking for, Abbey?"

"You wench, you took my olive!" Joley smacked her sister's hand. "Eat the cucumber thingies. I hate those."

"Something that could be a Russian artifact. Packing maybe might have come from Russia. Anything at all that might indicate something illegal is going on here."

Joley stood in front of a naked statue of a man, turning her head this way and that to study the rather smallish endowments. "Pathetic if you ask me. Seriously, this thing should be illegal. Where the heck would you put it? In your garden?"

Abigail dragged her away from the statue. "You're such a pervert, Joley. You would find the only naked man in the room."

Joley hung back. "I think I'm in love. Well, almost. I'll need Frank to do a little work on him. Can you imagine Frank's face if I asked him to add to the proportions?" She snapped her fingers. "Give me the camera."

Abigail exchanged the camera for the plate of food. "What have you found?"

"I'm going to give Aunt Carol a preview of what her life might be like if she chooses the wrong man." Joley began snapping pictures of the statue. "You never know, Frank may have used himself as a model, in which case Aunt Carol should definitely give old man Mars, as fruity as he is, a chance."

"Joley!" Abigail tried to sound stern. "This is serious business. Aleksandr says a shipment of stolen art from Russia was off-loaded from a freighter to a fishing boat. It had to go somewhere and Frank's name came up a couple of times. Chad works here unloading freight and packing boxes to ship to other places."

Joley skirted around two opened crates on the floor, peering into them to see what they contained. "I don't get any respect," she groused. "I'm learning to be an art connoisseur. Do you know how many times some man has asked if I wanted to see his etchings?"

Hannah stifled her laugh with her hand. "You're going to make me choke."

"You wouldn't be choking if you weren't stealing my olives, you thief." Joley peered under the table. "There's a lot of packing stuff here, Abbey. Some of it has watermarks on it. If they were taking something off one ship and putting it on a fishing boat, it would probably get wet, wouldn't it?"

Abigail hurried around several boxes to look under the table. "Even if we find evidence, how are we going to know if it's Chad or Frank or if both are involved?" She crouched down to get closer to the paper. "It definitely has watermarks, but it's just a plain brown wrapper." She took a picture anyway, zooming in on the stain. "This is probably a total waste of time, but it gets us out of the party for a few minutes."

"You didn't bring us anything to drink," Joley complained. "Looking at art stuff that isn't deemed good enough to be on display is hard work."

Abigail turned around and looked at her. "Why isn't this on display? Is it being shipped? Did someone purchase it already? Frank must have ordered it, right?"

"Maybe someone commissioned him to sell this stuff."

"Abbey," Hannah said, "come over here. It feels different."

Abigail immediately crossed the room. She wasn't nearly as sensitive as Hannah to changes, but even she felt the strange shifting surrounding a small corner of the room. Her heart began to accelerate and her mouth went dry. "What do you think it is?"

"Can't you feel it? Violence. Not death, but definitely violence." Hannah searched the floor and walls, careful of her clothes. "Look around, see if you can see anything that indicates a recent fight. It has to be very recent to be so strong."

Joley stood beside Hannah. "In the last couple of hours." She shivered. "It was definitely a physical fight of some kind. Did either of you get a look at Frank's knuckles?"

"Frank has to be in his late fifties. I can't imagine him in a fistfight an hour before the press and a roomful of people and celebrities show up," Abigail said. "He just isn't the type."

"Chad is," Joley said. "In school, any altercation with anyone he wanted to settle with his fists."

Abigail crouched down to examine the floor. "There's blood here. Spots of it. A few on the table legs." She ran her hand over the floor, "feeling" for the aftermath of a violent encounter. "There's even blood on the cabinets." She pulled open the bottom one and stared at the four paintings inside. They were stacked upright, the frames facing her. "Hannah, look at these."

Hannah, using two of the napkins Abigail had provided from the buffet table, carefully removed one of the paintings from the slot it was in. "This is no forgery, Abbey. This is the real thing. I don't know an awful lot about art, but I can feel the age of the canvas. What do you think, Joley?"

Joley held her hand inches from the canvas. "I think Frank Warner is a swine of the first degree and he better keep his greedy paws off of my aunt."

"It still could be Chad." Abigail focused the camera and took several shots, indicating Hannah remove the next one. "I'll show these to Aleksandr and see if they've been stolen."

"There's no way these paintings don't belong in a museum somewhere," Joley said. "And I'd have a difficult time believing Chad has the brains to sell hot paintings from other countries."

"He drinks too," Hannah pointed out as she held the third canvas. "He talks about everything and anything when he's drinking. Wouldn't he slip up and brag?"

"He's got to be making big money off of this if it's him," Abigail said as she photographed the last painting. "Do either of you know what he drives, or if he owns a house?"

"I've heard he's a gambler." Hannah slipped the last painting back into its slot and closed the door to the cupboard. "Inez has mentioned it a couple of times. Once she said if he wasn't careful he was going to get his legs broken."

"What about Frank?" Abigail retraced their steps toward the door. "Does he gamble? What have you heard about him?"

"Strangely, not very much. He seems to lead a quiet life," Hannah said. "He likes theater and is very supportive of the community. I don't know, he just doesn't seem the type to do anything illegal like this."

Joley caught at Abigail before she could open the door. "Someone's coming," she hissed. "Hurry, we have to hide."

Abigail didn't question the decision but made a dive to get behind a modern art fountain that had been relegated to a dark corner. Hannah sank down beneath a table surrounded by a fortress of boxes and Joley squeezed into a small space behind one of the largest statues. The door swung open and Sylvia Fredrickson crept into the back room, tugging on a man's hand. Aleksandr Volstov followed her, closing the door behind him.

"Hurry," Sylvia said. "I know you'll find this so interesting. My friend Chad works back here and I've visited him dozens of times." Her eyes darted around the room, searching out the corners. She gave a small disappointed sigh and plastered a flirtatious smile on her face.

"Are you certain we're allowed back here?"

Abigail swallowed hard as she watched Sylvia drag Aleksandr into the center of the room. Aleksandr appeared smooth and interested, but there was no doubt that he didn't want the other woman stroking him with intimate fingers. His aura held itself away from Sylvia's, retreating each time she stepped closer. The brazen woman kept a firm grip on his hand and batted her eyelashes at him.

Aleksandr's gaze was restless, taking in the details of the room, seeking out every secret in every dark corner. Abigail knew him well enough to know he was alert and uneasy. He twice looked toward the fountain where she crouched, trying not to breathe.

"It's no big deal." Sylvia halted and turned toward Aleksandr. "I told you I'd show you something amazing." Her hands went to the buttons of her blouse.

"You said art." He stopped her by placing his hand over hers.

"I am a work of art," she answered, her smile seductive.

Abigail sucked in her breath sharply, her stomach knotting with a terrible anger. She glanced toward her sisters. She needed to leave, get away quickly before the building rage turned into something she couldn't control.

Aleksandr moved around Sylvia to track around the room. Abigail could see he was drawn to the corner where she found the blood. He crouched down, just as she had, and examined the floor. "I don't think we should be here," he objected again.

Sylvia had gone back to opening the front of her blouse. "Don't be silly. We won't get caught. Everyone is busy asking for autographs of our resident celebrities." There was a bite in her voice.

Hannah raised her hands and a breeze stirred dust through the room. Sylvia immediately began to sneeze, a violent onslaught that wouldn't stop. Aleksandr was forced to do up the buttons on her blouse and lead her out of the room. As he went through the door, he glanced back toward the fountain.

14

JOLEY and Hannah slipped out of their hiding places, both trying not to laugh. They hurried over to Abigail and dragged her out from behind the fountain.

Joley popped another black olive into her mouth. "I thought we were going to be caught for sure. Or worse, that Sylvia was going to strip all the way down to her bare skin right in front of us."

Hannah rubbed her hand down Abigail's arm in an effort to soothe her. "Aleksandr didn't look very interested in her artwork. I'd say she's definitely visited with Chad here in the back room."

Abigail looked around the room, anywhere to avoid looking at her sisters. She was furious. *Furious*. She wouldn't have sent dust flying. Hannah had been kind. Her temper was roiling in her stomach and had she been able to grow claws, she might have considered raking Sylvia's face. "Next time she lays a hand on him, she's going to find herself in a pit somewhere very wretched."

Her sisters exchanged a small look of alarm.

"She probably saw you with him the other night," Joley said. "You know Sylvia, she'd take her revenge by seducing your man. Let's just get out of here while we can." She hurried through the doorway, stepping aside to allow Hannah and Abigail through.

The crowd seemed to have swelled in numbers. It was a crush just fitting into the room. Abigail tried to draw air into her suddenly burning lungs. Sylvia might have tried to seduce Aleksandr, but he hadn't been in the least interested. So why had he gone with her into the back room? He was using Sylvia just as certainly as Sylvia was using him. And what did that mean?

She knew how far Aleksandr would go to solve a case he was working. Did it include seduction? The thought crept into her mind. Tightened like barbwire around her heart. Would he sleep with another woman he wasn't the least interested in? He had allowed Abigail to be interrogated, incarcerated, and deported to keep his position as a detective. If Sylvia could get him information on Chad Kingman and the only way she would impart it was for him to cooperate sexually, would he?

Abigail looked up and her gaze collided with a pair of dark, almost midnight blue eyes. Aleksandr and Sylvia were only a foot away. Close enough to reach out and touch. Abigail's heart nearly stopped then began to pound. For a moment she couldn't breathe, couldn't think, even her vision blurred. She told herself he wouldn't stoop to sleeping with another woman for information, but Sylvia's hand was curled possessively around his arm. *And what else would he do to solve his cases?*

Hannah turned her head and looked at Abigail. The smile faded from Joley's face. There was no way to stop the connection from leaping from one Drake sister to the next. The emotion was too strong and even across the room, Sarah and Kate went on the alert, turning to see what had caused the disturbance.

Aleksandr's gaze held Abbey's, compelled her to keep her gaze locked with his, a captive, though she desperately needed to look away, to regain her composure. There was a strange roaring in her head.

"Hello, Sylvia," Joley said, "how are you?"

Sylvia cleared her voice. "Hi, Joley, Hannah, Abigail." Her voice went tight as she said Abigail's name.

Abbey flicked her a glance, was driven to look back at the familiar face. Familiar eyes. Her heart clenched hard. Her stomach contracted and she felt a punch, an actual physical punch to her stomach. Pain swept through her, shaking her, spilling out of her so that it swept through the room and filled every space. Laughter ceased as the intensity of her emotions hit the others in the room.

"Abbey," Joley whispered in warning, her fingers biting deep into Abigail's waist.

Sarah arrived, flanked by Kate. "How lovely to see you this evening, Sylvia," Sarah said, appearing calm, but her expression, as she looked at Sylvia, was murderous.

Aunt Carol took the camera out of Abigail's limp hand.

Abbey took a breath and tried to regain control of her emotions. Her pain was so strong, the memory of betrayal, fear, and bone-deep pain when she had realized Aleksandr had traded their love to save his job. She hadn't wanted to think that he might have killed someone in order to get her out of Russia, but she knew he was capable of anything when he felt he had justification. Seeing him with Sylvia and realizing he might very well betray her in other ways crushed her fragile hope that she could make things work with Aleksandr. They were too different. Far too different.

Hannah's hands moved gracefully and the room was clear of all but laughter and merriment.

"Abbey," Aleksandr murmured, recognizing the pain in her eyes. He held his hand out to her.

She made a small sound, much like that of a wounded animal, and stepped back, avoiding contact with him so that his hand fell to his side.

His features hardened perceptibly and a muscle ticked along his jaw. His eyes went flat and ice cold. "Let's go somewhere and talk," he suggested and stepped closer to her.

Abbey felt the heat of his body right through her clothes. She took another step back, hating herself for being a coward. Her hand itched to slap his handsome face, but it was really herself she was upset with. Aleksandr couldn't help being who and what he was, but she knew better.

Aleksandr moved again and this time it was a clear act of aggression. Kate stepped in front of Abbey, cutting off his access to her.

"I'm going to be sick," Abbey whispered to Hannah, her voice so low it was nearly inaudible, or maybe it was through the telepathic connection the sisters shared. "Get me out of here." She had been so incredibly stupid, thinking she could live with Aleksandr's way of life.

He had no compunction about doing things she believed were utterly wrong. To him, the end justified the means.

Hannah and Joley immediately turned and shielded her with their bodies as they hustled her out of the room.

Aleksandr took a step after them, ignoring Sylvia's tug on his arm. Sarah stepped smoothly into his path, shoulder to shoulder with Kate, so that he was forced to halt. She smiled at him, but her eyes were flat and cold as she looked at Sylvia. "I've heard you've been visiting Lucinda Parker over in Point Arena, Sylvia." She kept her voice bright, a conversational tone, but there was nothing friendly in her steady gaze.

Sylvia turned pale and drew back from Sarah.

Sarah kept her smile. "You should be very careful of experimenting with forces you don't understand, Sylvia. It can backfire on you and then you're in a real mess."

Sylvia's breath hissed out and her hand crept to her cheek. "I'm not doing anything, honest, Sarah. I just wanted to get rid of this rash I sometimes have." She glanced at Aleksandr, but he was staring after Abigail. "I have to get rid of it. I can't stand it anymore."

"Then do the right thing." Sarah turned on her heel, suddenly aware of Kate's restraining hand on her elbow. She shook her head and walked away.

"You were threatening her," Kate said, shocked. "You've never done that in your life."

"I was warning her. There's a difference." Sarah's soft features hardened perceptibly. "Did you feel Abbey's pain? It terrifies me. Sylvia had better not be dabbling in black magic. She has no way of understanding what can happen. If she harms Abbey in any way, I will retaliate."

There was a grimness in her voice Kate had never heard before. Sarah was always the steady, practical one. "Sylvia's been visiting the black magic queen?" she asked. "Lucinda is nuts. Everyone knows that. She makes it all up and mixes all the practices. It isn't real."

"Yes, but she can stir things up that are better left alone. Lord only knows what she told Sylvia. She may have a voodoo doll that is supposed to be Abbey."

"Sarah! Wait!" Sylvia rushed through the crowd and caught at Sarah's arm. When Sarah's gaze collided with hers she let go immediately. "I know you see things ahead of time. Are you saying something is going to happen to me? What did you mean?"

Sarah glanced up at Aleksandr, who had followed them. For a moment she stilled, everything inside her rebelling at his presence with Sylvia. His aura always blended with Abigail's when she was close to him. Everything she had learned of her gift, of her craft, told her he belonged with Abigail. It seemed obscene that he would be with Sylvia. Sarah could *feel* Aleksandr's reluctance to have physical contact with Sylvia. Right now an aura of danger surrounded him and twice he shifted subtly to keep Sylvia from clinging to him. Sarah looked from his hard-edged features to Sylvia.

Sylvia craved attention, any man's attention. She needed it to feel good about herself. If she could take Abigail's man she would be ecstatic.

Power clung to Aleksandr. It was in the set of his wide shoulders and defined muscles of his arms, the thickness of his chest, and the fluid way he moved. Sarah had spent a great deal of her life as both an athlete and a bodyguard, and she recognized a dangerous man even without her heightened abilities. Sylvia only saw his rough good looks. His strong sexual appeal. She would never see past that to anything else.

"Be careful, Sylvia," she advised. "Know your real friends." She turned away to follow Kate out of the gallery.

"What does that mean?" Sylvia wailed. "I don't understand. Sarah. You have to tell me what that means." She trailed after Kate and Sarah, outside in time to see Abigail's pale face flash by as Joley pulled their car onto the highway. Aleksandr swore as the car went past them.

"TELL us," Hannah said. "What happened, Abbey?"

Abbey rocked back and forth, curled away from her sisters in the backseat, her face staring out toward the sea with its rolling waves. The roaring in her ears seemed louder. How could she explain? What could she say? That she was so weak she loved a man she knew she could never be with? It sounded so pathetic. When had she become pathetic? And why were her emotions so amplified, so out of control? She felt pain a thousand times worse than she'd ever remembered.

"Abbey?" Hannah was as gentle as possible.

"Stop the car. Hurry. I'm going to be sick," Abbey said in desperation.

Joley slammed on the brakes, guiding the car toward the narrow ribbon of shoulder along the cliff. Before the car had completely stopped, Abbey leapt out, bending over as her stomach protested. She hated being sick, had always fought it, but nothing could stop her body's reaction to the acute pain she felt on recognizing that familiar ruthless streak in Aleksandr. There was no room for someone like her in his life. He needed a woman who would take second place, a back seat to his job and his tremendous drive and need to succeed at whatever he was doing. Someone who would never question him too closely about his methods of investigation.

Hannah handed her a small cloth and Abbey wiped her mouth as she stared down below her to the waves crashing against the rocks. Her heart ached so severely she pressed her hand hard against her chest to ease the pain. Out in the surf, several dolphins leapt into the air, spinning before diving back into the sea. A whale poked his head above the water, spy-hopping as if looking for her. She heard the music of the sea creatures carried to her on the wind. Calling to her. Easing the ache in her heart.

"Abbey!" Joley caught her around the waist and jerked her away from the edge of the cliff. "What are you doing?" There was alarm in her voice.

Abbey blinked to bring her into focus. "They're calling to me."

"I don't care what they're doing. I'm taking you home. You can't possibly think Aleksandr had the least bit of interest in Sylvia Fredrickson, do you?" Joley was horrified at that thought. "He could barely stand her touching him. You had to have felt that."

"Of course I did." Abigail rubbed at her pounding temples.

"Did Sylvia touch you? Could she have gotten a hair or anything at all personal of yours?" Joley guided Abbey back to the car.

Hannah yanked the door open. "Have you gotten anything strange in the mail?"

Abbey slid into the warmth of the backseat. "You both think Sylvia put some kind of spell on me?"

"You just nearly walked off a cliff, Abbey," Joley said, wrenching at the wheel to get the car back on the highway. "That's not normal."

Abbey stared down at her hands. They were shaking. "Sylvia doesn't have the power to disrupt my life at all. She has nothing to do with this."

"She'd better not," Hannah said. "She tried to make our lives miserable in school. It would be just like her to try to seduce a man she thought one of us was interested in. I swear, I thought she was trying to get back with her husband."

"I was hoping she'd try to get back with him," Abigail said, struggling for control of her emotions. It was unfair to her sisters to be so wild with her feelings. "I'm sorry. I can't imagine what Sarah and Kate are thinking."

"Libby's in the house and I want her to do a psychic healing on you," Hannah said firmly. "You have to let her. The pain is getting worse, not better."

"You could have stepped off that cliff," Joley pointed out.

Hannah and Joley looked at each other. "Prakenskii," they blurted out simultaneously.

"What was this about?" Joley inquired.

Abigail shrugged. "I feel so stupid. I was looking at Aleksandr with Sylvia and I realized he might very well sleep with her, not because he was at all attracted and had the impulse to cheat, but because he can be cold-blooded enough to use whatever tool he deems necessary to further an investigation. I was responsible for a man's death, or at least played a part in the tragedy of his death, while I was in Russia. All this time, I've wondered that Aleksandr might have killed someone, maybe more than one man, in order to get me out of Russia. I couldn't face it. I wanted to pretend he'd never do such a thing. And I didn't want to feel responsible for any more deaths. But he could have. He could have done such a thing if he thought there was no other way."

"Abigail, you don't know that," Hannah protested.

She wiped at the tears on her face. "But he did. I know he did. He can be utterly ruthless. And if that's what it took to get me out of Russia, he'd do it. The moment I saw the truth and I had to admit what he did for me, I realized I love him just as much or more than I did four years ago. That I'm never going to stop and I can't live with him." She covered her face. "I can't live with him." She raised her head to look at her sisters with haunted eyes. "And I don't know if I can live without him."

Hannah wrung her hands together. "It has to be Prakenskii. Who else has the power to amplify your emotions to such a state?"

"Abigail's always felt things strongly," Joley said. "Although I'd like to meet Prakenskii one more time without everyone around."

They arrived home and parked. In the doorway to the house they found Libby waiting for them, one hand pressed to her stomach. "I think she's feeling both of their pain," she told Hannah, "Aleksandr's as well as her own. I'm wondering if he feels it too."

"Their auras mix," Hannah said.

"I noticed that." Joley glanced down the long drive. "I expect that he'll show up here very soon. He isn't the type of man to let his woman walk away from him like that." She narrowed her gaze as she looked in both directions. "I still think Prakenskii has something to do with this."

"I think we'd recognize his fingerprints all over the magic." Hannah was practical. She handed Abigail over to Libby. "Let's make up the circle and be ready for when the others return home."

"I'd like to take a shot at matching magic with that man." Joley rubbed her palm up and down her trousers, scowling at her sisters. "I swear I still feel him touching me."

Hannah glanced at her sharply. "You didn't tell us that. You should have said so right away, Joley. Prakenskii's a total unknown. We have to be very careful until we know exactly what we're dealing with."

Abigail sat on the floor in the middle of the living room while her sisters drew a circle of protection around her using wooden staffs. She rested her cheek on her raised knees, feeling worn out and thin. "Hannah, we weren't looking for magic at the party. We were looking for evidence of smuggling. Would we have recognized Prakenskii's magic? Except for when he turned Joley's magic back on her last night at the inn, his power has been very subtle. I'm not certain I would know if I were being influenced—would you? Except that my reaction to seeing Sylvia with Aleksandr is so unnatural."

"I honestly don't know," Hannah admitted. "It's outside my realm of expertise. Other than the aunts and Mom and Grandma, I've never encountered anyone else using magic, and certainly not directed against us."

"And if he is directing it against us," Libby said, "I think the question would be—why? What are we doing that is interfering with what he's doing?"

There was a sudden abrupt silence as they all looked at one another, trying to come up with an answer. Sarah and Kate burst through the door, followed by their aunt and Aleksandr Volstov.

He walked in without hesitation and, ignoring the warnings of circles and protection, went straight to Abigail.

The sisters shared a long look as he simply stepped over the wooden staffs on the floor and nothing happened.

"What happened, *baushki-bau*? I felt the pain hit you and when I looked into your eyes, it hit me."

Abigail shook her head, tears welling up. "What are you doing here? You shouldn't be here." She waved her hand indicating the wooden staffs laid out in a circle. "This doesn't concern you."

"Everything about you concerns me. Tell me what happened." When he didn't get a response, his gaze swept around at the women in the room. "Tell me." There was hard authority in his voice.

"We don't know," Joley answered. "We think it's possible Prakenskii used magic to amplify her feelings of pain and despair."

A mixture of bafflement and anger crossed his face. "Why would you be having feelings of pain and despair? You certainly didn't believe for one moment that I was in the least attracted to that woman, did you?"

She shook her head.

"Did anyone see Prakenskii at the party?" Joley asked. "Sergei Nikitin was there earlier, following me around and generally making a complete ass out of himself."

"What did he want?" Sarah asked.

"To be my boyfriend, I gather," Joley said. "I told him I don't date. He wasn't very happy about it."

"I doubt if he's used to being turned down by a mere woman," Aleksandr said as he sank down onto the floor in the center of the circle and pulled Abigail onto his lap. "I, however, have firsthand knowledge of it on a regular basis."

Abigail lifted her head and looked into his eyes. There was hurt there. Love. Pleading he probably didn't even realize he was revealing. She sighed and leaned into his chest. "I didn't turn you down."

"You've been turning me down for years, Abbey," he said.

"Actually," Aunt Carol commented as she fussed with the protective circle, making it just right and adding several candles at various points, "Prakenskii was at the gallery earlier. He spoke with Frank about Mr. Nikitin attending the party and then I thought he left, but instead, he went into the back room. He and that young man you went to school with, the one always getting into fights, must have had some kind of argument."

"Why do you say that, Aunt Carol?" Sarah asked.

"Light those candles on the mantel, dear," Carol instructed. "What was that obnoxious boy's name?"

"Chad. Chad Kingman," Kate supplied.

"Yes, of course, Chad. His mother was a very hard worker, but his father was a mean drunk. He believed in settling everything with his fists. I saw Prakenskii talking to him. Chad seemed rather heated, although Prakenskii didn't at all."

"Aunt Carol," Sarah reprimanded, "were you in the back room witnessing this?"

"I promised Frank I'd be the official photographer at his event. As a matter of course I took preparation photos. Naturally they included shots of the back room."

"Naturally." Kate glared at her. "You must have driven Grandma and Gramps crazy, Aunt Carol. You know perfectly well you shouldn't have been in that back room."

"You can make all the excuses in the world," Sarah added, "but you know you were spying. It's far too dangerous for you to be doing that kind of thing. Jonas told you not to do it."

Aleksandr's eyebrow shot up. He crooked his little finger at Sarah. "You have smears of white resin on your jacket and Kate has them as well. I saw that very powder in the back room where there was broken statuary."

Sarah hastily dusted off her jacket. Kate did the same. Hannah, Joley, and Abigail exchanged a long look of complete and utter guilt.

Libby burst out laughing. "That back room must have been a very popular place. Aunt Carol, all of you, and even Aleksandr all went snooping. I stayed home and read a book with my feet up, missing all the fun."

"We brought home pictures," Joley assured her. "Aunt Carol, do you think Prakenskii and Chad were in a fistfight? We found blood in one corner and the area carried the feel of violence."

"Oh, there was a terrible brawl. Chad swung a statue at Prakenskii's head. I think he meant to kill him. They had exchanged words, but I couldn't hear. I was in the small closet near the door leading to the alley where the delivery trucks come. Prakenskii hardly seemed to move, but he tore up Chad. If I hadn't seen Chad attack Prakenskii first, I would have felt sorry for him."

"What happened to Chad?"

Carol sighed. "I thought I could take a picture of the fight, but I must have knocked into the door because it squeaked. Prakenskii didn't look toward me, but he did grab Chad in one of those policeman holds and force him out the back door. I decided it best not to follow them and to allow them to settle their argument in private."

Joley burst out laughing. "We could have had a Drake family convention in the back room of the art gallery. What does that say about us?"

"It says you're all foolish and take chances," Aleksandr said.

"Well, you were there too," Joley said. "And we were almost treated to the traumatic, forever-stamped-on-our-memories, take-to-the-grave vision of Sylvia baring her breasts, thank you very much."

"Before we do anything else, I want to perform a healing ceremony on Abigail and we may as well see if it helps Aleksandr too," Libby said, pinning him with her gaze. "He wasn't invited, but it doesn't look as if he plans on leaving soon."

Aleksandr watched with interest as Libby unwrapped several beautiful stones and set them carefully within the circle. The stones were round and blood red. "Those aren't genuine rubies, are they?" he asked.

Carol nodded. "They've been in our family for generations and we purify them when needed with the elements of earth, air, fire, and water. The ruby is a strong stone and can be used for protection as well as healing. This is a star ruby and particularly powerful. We'll use a second ruby outside the circle placed beside a red candle to aid our energy in the healing."

Aleksandr shook his head. "I can't imagine Prakenskii doing any of this."

Carol flashed him a quelling look. "If you are going to be disparaging about our practices, young man, now is the time to leave."

"I'm sorry, I didn't mean it that way. It's just that Prakenskii is one of those men who is very action oriented. I can't see him trying to manipulate energy in crystals and stones." He indicated the stone in Libby's hand. "I've never seen anything like that before—what is it?"

Libby held it up. It looked almost like an orange-gold opal, with fiery flashes of many colors when held up to the light. "It's a very rare type of feldspar stone from India, called sunstone."

While Abigail's sisters and her aunt prepared for their protective cleansing, Aleksandr swept back Abbey's hair and pressed a kiss against the nape of her neck. "What were you thinking? Why would you be so upset at that party?"

"I realized things about you. About me. Do we really want to discuss this now?"

"I don't want you hurting like this. Give me something to work with, Abbey. Don't just shut me out." His lips moved up her neck to her ear. "If you feel things, you must feel how much I love you. If you can hear truth in voices, you have to hear it in mine." He kissed her neck, his teeth teasing her skin seductively. "You have to believe in me just a little."

Was she just being stubborn, holding on to her hurt and anger, believing he betrayed her? Was she so terrified of living with his ruthless streak, knowing what he was capable of doing, that she would rather lose everything? Was she such a coward that she couldn't let go of the past? "What would you do to solve a crime, Aleksandr? Would you sleep with another woman to get information? Would you go that far?" Her throat felt constricted and raw with pain when she asked. Her heart thudded so hard in her chest she feared it might burst through the walls. She couldn't ask him if he'd killed someone to set her free. The words pounded in her head, but she couldn't force them past the constriction in her throat.

Aleksandr stiffened, his arms slowly releasing her. She could see by his face she didn't have to ask the real question. He knew. He knew what she feared the most. "Can you really think so badly of me? I spent close to three *years* tracking that child killer. For the first year, I did it alone—my superiors refused to even admit the possibility that there could be a serial child killer in Mother Russia. Twice they relieved me of duty for seeking help from agencies outside of our country. And all the while he was out there, luring children to him."

"Aleksandr," she protested.

"No, Abbey. Let's get this out in the open. I fully admit I made mistakes. I told the clerk to send you into the interrogation room. I thought he'd follow orders. I had no idea Ignatev was working behind the scenes to bring me down and that he had his men in place. When everything went to hell, I weighed my options. In my mind I thought you'd be perfectly safe, my men would hand you a drink, walk you out, and it would be over."

She rubbed her chin on her drawn-up knees, hugging herself as she rocked back and forth. "But it didn't work out that way."

"No. Ignatev took the opportunity to strike at me. His men, not mine, were in the interrogation room with you. You weren't safe, although I didn't know that at first. I was scrambling to do damage control. I was so close to solving the case and didn't want to get yanked. When I found out what happened, and that Ignatev's men had you in their control, I had to move fast to get you out. At that point I couldn't come forward about what had happened because if I had taken the blame for everything, not only would I have been off the case, but I wouldn't have been able to get you free."

Abigail looked at him. "What did you do?"

"Whatever was necessary to get you out of there. They would have killed you. Ignatev wanted to strike at me, you weren't cooperating, and he wanted the violence against you stepped up. It was only my reputation that kept it from happening in the beginning. And yes, Abbey, if I had to sleep with another woman to save your life, I damn well would have done it. I would have done anything to save you. Is that what you wanted to know about me?"

His eyes blazed fire at her. Aleksandr, always so calm and in control, looked as if he wanted to shake her. She studied his face, the lines that hadn't been there four years earlier, the edge to his mouth and his strong jaw. What was it she was really so afraid of? Would she have wanted him to abandon the dead children? Would she have wanted him to abandon her? He had probably saved her life, just as he had saved other children from a madman.

The realization was slow in coming, but Abigail knew she loved him for those very qualities, his single-minded determination to bring a killer to justice, his protective instincts that made him aggressive in his search for a serial killer. So many good traits, so what was it she feared so much?

"How did you get me out of Russia?"

His gaze hardened. "I did what I had to do. That's my life, Abbey. That's who I am. You're the only person I've ever loved. Do you think I'd do less for you than I would for those poor children? Damn you for asking me that." He leaned close to her, his face inches from her. "I have a lot of things to apologize for, I know that, but getting you out of Russia, saving your life, is not one of them. If I had to sleep with forty women, kill forty men, or trade my life for yours, I would have done it and I'm not about to ask for forgiveness for it. If you want to pass judgment on me, go ahead."

"Where is there a future for us, Sasha? I can't be in Russia. I don't know if I can live with the extremes you're willing to go to. What are we doing?"

"There *has* to be a future for us. We have to find a way. Are you happy without me? Can you truthfully say you've been happy hiding in the sea with your dolphins, living your life without me, Abigail?"

Abigail sat up and brushed back her hair. "Grab your tea before it spills."

She pointed vaguely at a spot ahead of him and when Aleksandr turned his head the mug of tea nearly hit him in the face. It seemed to be floating in the air. Her sisters and aunt had disappeared, leaving them sitting in the middle of a circle made of a type of wood he couldn't identify and what seemed like hundreds of lit candles. He took the mug of tea right out of the air and watched Abigail do the same.

When they had been together in Russia, Abigail had always kept the use of magic in their lives to a minimum. He hadn't thought much beyond her gift of getting others to speak the truth. Her abilities and those of her sisters were obviously far more than he had ever conceived. The wielding of magic seemed effortless, an everyday occurrence in the Drake sisters' lives. It would always be a part of Abigail.

"I'm not willing to live my life without you, Abbey. I've tried it. I tried burying myself in work. I took every dangerous case, every interesting case, anything I could think of, but nothing worked. I want you back. Tell me what I need to do to get you back."

"It isn't that I don't love you, Aleksandr. I loved you with everything in me. I admire your strength of resolve and respect your determination that is so much a part of you. I know it's what makes you successful at the things you do. But at the same time, I don't think I can live with them."

"That's a cliché, a ridiculous thing to say when you aren't willing to talk something out, and I'm not about to accept it from you. I do what I have to do to survive and to keep others alive. I'm not some maniac running around with a gun shooting people for no good reason. Hell yes, I took out Ignatev's men. Every one of them I could get my hands on. I would have killed him if I could have gotten to him, but he had already melted into the shadows. That's why I have a price on my head. He was going to have you killed, but first he wanted to torture you. It wasn't going to happen. Can you understand that much about me? *It wasn't going to happen. Not to you.*"

"I just feel I'm in way over my head." Loving him. Afraid of losing him. Fearing his very strength. She was so mixed up. How had she gotten so pathetically fragile when it came to loving him?

"You're not a coward, Abbey. You wouldn't swim in the sea with dolphins if you were. You wouldn't have pulled that fisherman out of the water, or even attacked the shooter when you had the opportunity. You can do all those things, yet you're afraid to let yourself be with me. If I leave, will you love me less? Will it take away the pain of what you consider a betrayal?" He put his tea on the floor and caught her chin, forcing her to look into his eyes. "I'm condemned either way. I'm condemned for *not* protecting you when I didn't know you were in trouble, and I'm condemned for getting you out of a very dangerous situation. Which is my real sin?"

"Making me love you." The truth spilled out of her. She pulled away from him. "I don't want to love you."

"Well, welcome to the club, sweetheart. I didn't want to love you either. My life was a hell of a lot easier before you came into it."

She sighed softly. "I've never had to live the way you've had to live. You can be ruthless if the circumstances call for it. How do we live together when our lives are so different? When we come from two such different cultures and backgrounds?"

"Do you even understand the choices I made? Would you have done it differently?"

"I don't know. I honestly don't know. You nearly destroyed me. When I thought you'd betrayed me it felt as if you'd torn out my heart and the wound just wouldn't heal. I hate saying that. It's so melodramatic, but it's the truth. Do I want you to have that kind of power over me again? Someday you'll be working on something terrible, some hideous crime, and you'll have to make decisions I'm not certain I can face. What do I do then?" Tears shimmered in her eyes. Her throat was raw. "You can't be anything but who you are. I wouldn't love you the same if you stopped being you. How do I change enough to accept that ruthless streak in you?"

"I don't know, Abigail. You have to decide if you love me enough. You think that I have all this power over you, but in reality it's the other way around. *You* walked away from me and you didn't look back. You can call it self-preservation if you want to, but in the end, you didn't love me enough to live with what I have to do. And yes, it isn't always pretty and wrapped up in a neat bow. In order for me to track the kind of criminals I normally track, I have to get down in the filth and slime with them. There are evil people in this world, truly evil, Abbey. I chase them. And I do my best to bring them to justice. It isn't always possible to use acceptable civilized rules in order to stop them. When you go after evil or sick people who have no rules, you have to do whatever it takes. There are times I have to do things I'm not proud of. And there are times I have to take a life. And if it is for you, Abigail, there will never, at any time, be a question of whether I'm willing or not to do *anything* it takes. That's who I really am. The real question is, can you love the real me? Not the perfect person you want me to be, not that image you had of me, but who I really am."

15

ABIGAIL sighed softly. "I'm struggling to understand all of this, Sasha. I had no idea what happened in Russia, why you let them haul me away from you, and maybe I should have opened all those letters from you. . . ."

"You cut out my heart when you sent them back," Aleksandr said.

"So we both ended up hurt. Do you really want to go there again?"

"Have you wondered why I haven't asked you to 'talk' to Nikitin or even Chad Kingman or Frank Warner? We'd know immediately who was doing what if you had a conversation with them."

Abigail spread her hands out in front of her. "I made a horrible mistake and it cost a man his life."

"That's bullshit and you know it, Abbey. That man died because he was overwhelmed with grief and one of the officers all but handed him a gun. It had nothing to do with you. I watched the tape over and over before it was destroyed and you were trying to tell us he wasn't guilty. There was nothing wrong with your magic or the way you used it. I haven't asked you to help me because I was wrong to use you. In the beginning I wanted every tool possible. I heard a rumor about a woman psychic and did a little research and decided to meet you to see if you could help, even if what you could do sounded as wacky as hell."

She ducked her head, unable to answer him. She had nightmares of that poor man, so distraught over the death of his daughter. She should have known, sensed what was going on, put aside herself and her ego to divine the truth. Aleksandr absolved her of guilt, but she had been raised to believe that with her gift came ultimate responsibility.

"I don't want to use someone I love as a tool or a weapon or for any other reason. I love you, Abbey." He put his hand over his heart. "I don't know how else to get you to believe me other than saying it a thousand times."

She could only look at him, a mixture of pain and love swirling in the depths of her eyes. She wanted him. Wanted to reach out and start all over again, but the past was there, a raw ugly wound that terrified her.

Aleksandr sought for a way to comfort her, to reach beyond the past and wipe that look of fear from her eyes forever. When he couldn't think of anything to say, he changed tactics, seeking a distraction. The thick staffs of wood making up the circle were unlike anything he'd seen before. He touched one. "What is this?"

Abigail pushed his hand away. "Don't touch that. You're always touching things. The wood is very, very old and came from Italy. It's been in our family for centuries and it possesses great power. What if you'd gotten zapped? You should have gotten zapped when you entered the circle without permission."

He ran his finger over the polished wood one more time. "But I didn't. Your house seems to like me."

Carol trailed after the Drake sisters as they came back into the room. Abigail could tell they'd heard every word of the conversation and, worse, her emotions were so strong, so out of control, that they could feel the deep soul-searing love that she felt for him. She could tell by their faces they were sympathetic toward his cause. And he could see it as well.

Aleksandr appealed to them. "If you all know magic, don't any of you know a good love potion? If you'd just slip it into her drink, we'd work this out."

"What makes you think we haven't, dear?" Carol asked, winking at him. "She hasn't finished the entire cup of tea yet."

"These things take time," Joley added.

Abigail looked up, alarmed. She carefully set the cup of tea in the middle of the floor. "You wouldn't dare. Aleksandr, don't drink that."

"If it helps, I'm drinking it." He drained the tea mug and held it out to Joley. "More, please. It was very good."

Joley laughed. "She's the one who needs to drink the tea, not you. I think you're just fine the way you are."

"Don't encourage him," Abigail said.

"Someone has to encourage me." Aleksandr set the mug on the floor and regarded her with a faint smile. "You certainly don't."

"It isn't like she goes around sleeping with lots of men," Hannah pointed out. She set out a small table and placed a mortar and pestle on it just outside the circle. "I'd say you should be very encouraged."

"We are *not* discussing whether or not I sleep with men on a regular basis," Abigail objected.

"Well, dear, it isn't like there's much to talk about," Carol said. "By the way, I dropped the film at that one-hour shop in Fort Bragg and Jonas is bringing it by this evening so he'll probably be here any minute."

"Great. We can talk about my sex life in front of him too," Abigail said. "Hurry up, Libby. I can't sit here forever."

Kate handed several herbs to Libby. "She's getting very irritable. Must be all that talk of sex and she's stuck here with all of us around and can't do anything about it."

"Are you saying she's frustrated?" Aleksandr asked. "And we're not supposed to leave this circle?"

"No, not until Libby does her thing," Kate advised.

A huge grin spread across Aleksandr's face. "I think the tea is working, *baushki-bau*. Come here, my little dumpling."

She fended him off with one hand. "What do you think you're doing?"

"I can't help myself. Your aunt put something in the tea and I can't keep my hands off of you."

"There was nothing in the tea and it doesn't work that way anyway," Abigail protested, trying not to laugh as he gathered her into his arms.

"It works that way on me," he said, pulling her close to him. He bent his head until his lips were a mere breath away from hers. "I need you to kiss me."

"I can't kiss you in front of everyone."

Joley snickered. "Sure you can. We won't watch."

Libby chose several herbs and began to prepare them for the cleansing and protection ceremony. "I'm watching. Break it up, you two."

Abigail grinned at her. "Finally, someone on my side."

"I didn't say I'm on your side. I'm just not going to watch you get all lovey-dovey and then blow it because that Prakenskii put some kind of whammy on the two of you."

"Do you think he really did? Real hexes are very rare."

Libby ground the herbs together in the small bowl made of polished agate. "He did something. Look at the difference in you already, Abbey. You were in such emotional pain, ready to throw Aleksandr away, and yet now, inside this house, inside the circle, you're laughing with him again. You're much calmer and you're not hurting the way you were before."

Joley gave a little sniff. "I told you Prakenskii was a rat bastard."

"You think all men are rat bastards. I believe you even called Aleksandr a rat bastard."

Aleksandr gasped. "Joley!"

She waved her hand. "She dragged me out of bed before noon. Everyone is a rat bastard before noon."

"What would be the point of Prakenskii enhancing my feelings?" Abigail asked.

Aleksandr reached for her hand. "To keep us apart?"

She drew her hand away. "We are apart."

"Now, Abbey"—Aleksandr's voice was a teasing caress—"I thought we settled this when you went to bed with me."

"We did not." Abigail glanced up to see her sisters and her aunt pausing in their preparations to listen. "Don't you all have something to do?"

"Well, he does have a point, Abbey," Joley said.

"What point would that be?" Abigail demanded.

"Well, really dear," Carol said. "You shouldn't just sleep with a man if you have no intentions of taking him back. It really isn't polite to lead him on that way."

"No, no, Aunt Carol," Joley defended her sister helpfully, her eyes wide with innocence. "They're engaged. She isn't exactly leading him on. It's official and everything. She has a ring."

"A *ring!* You didn't show us a ring," Kate said. She leaned over the wooden staff to peer at Abigail's hand.

Abigail covered her bare fingers with her other palm and glared at her younger sister. "Joley! You're *such* a rat. All of you stop looking at me that way. Libby, hurry up. I've never seen you so slow at this."

"Sorry," Libby murmured, a small frown creasing her face. "I'm just thinking about why this Prakenskii would do this. If he was going to attack one of us with magic, why not do something that would really harm us?"

"What are the laws of magic?" Sarah asked. "Let's go back to basics."

Hannah shrugged. "I know what you're getting at, but saying magic can be used as a defense but not an attack is worthless if he's doing it. Magic is natural and *should* be used for good and not self-gain, but you know very well it can be turned around."

"But he hasn't harmed anyone," Libby persisted.

Joley rubbed her palm along her thigh. "He hurt me."

"Maybe it wasn't on purpose. You pushed magic at him and he shoved back. That's using magic as a defense, not an offense. Maybe he didn't intend to shove so hard and you got zapped. He healed your hand, didn't he? Why would he do that if he seriously intended to harm you?"

Joley scowled at Libby. "Do not even sound interested in him. Sheesh, Libby. He's probably stirring a cauldron right now and conjuring up some demon from hell." She rubbed the pad of her thumb over the injury and shuddered. "I still feel him. It's as if he left behind his fingerprints on me or something. I hate it."

"Let me see." Libby held out her hand toward Joley.

Joley took a hasty step back, cradling her hand against her heart. "That's okay, it's nothing. We're supposed to be concentrating on Abbey."

Sarah gave a small groan. "Jonas is coming up the steps."

She'd hardly given the warning when the front door was flung open and Jonas came striding in. He halted abruptly, observing the hundreds of lit candles, the small table set up facing north with Libby's equipment for a ritual, and the long wooden staffs made of ancient wood from Italy forming a circle with Abigail and Aleksandr sitting in the center. A scowl settled on his face when his gaze fell on Aleksandr.

"You're not going to be killing any chickens, are you?" he greeted the Drake sisters, closing the door with his foot. "I've been to Point Arena three times in the past month checking out complaints against Lucinda and I sure don't want any of that going on here."

"You're so funny, Jonas," Joley said. "Ha ha ha. As if we'd harm an animal." She gave an indignant sniff.

"Hannah's always harming my hats," Jonas pointed out. "I've taken to buying them in bulk." He put his hands on his hips and regarded Aleksandr with some amusement in spite of his obvious wariness. "You're a brave man, Mr. Volstov."

Aleksandr flashed a brief smile. "My fiancée insists on these strange ceremonies." He shrugged. "What can I do?"

"How's the investigation coming?" Jonas asked. "You any closer to finding your stolen art?"

"I'm getting there. I wanted to consult with you on a couple of details. Maybe you could give me a few minutes after we're finished here. And you could fill me in on how your investigation is coming along."

Jonas eyed him with suspicion. "Sure. Gene Dockins, the fisherman Abbey pulled out of the water, is out of the coma, but he doesn't remember anything at all about the shooting or what led up to it. The doctors say he probably never will."

"That's not uncommon," Libby said. "I'm so pleased to hear he's recovering."

"Yeah, apparently he made some pretty miraculous progress after you went to visit him this morning."

"Libby!" Sarah glared at her. "That's why you didn't attend Frank's party. You must have been totally exhausted. Why didn't you tell us?"

"I was fine. I promised Marsha I'd check on him. The doctors had given him a very poor prognosis and he wasn't showing any signs of coming out of the coma, so it was the least I could do."

"We could have helped you," Sarah said.

"I spent the evening resting with my feet up," Libby said. "Let's get started."

"Are you certain you aren't too tired?" Elle asked. "I can take over for you. I'm just eating all the cookies Hannah made this afternoon."

"Cookies?" Jonas echoed. "Did you put some aside for me, Hannah?"

"Doesn't she always?" Joley answered. "It's the only thing keeping her out of jail. You're always threatening to arrest her for something."

Jonas winked at Hannah. "It's the only way I can stay in cookies." He gestured toward the kitchen. "I brought Aunt Carol's pictures with me. I'll go have a look at them and eat Hannah's cookies while you all do whatever it is you're doing—and don't tell me, because I don't really want to know."

"What herbs are you using, Libby?" Elle asked.

"Ague root for protection; mallow, just in case Prakenskii is using black magic. It's a very effective aid. And of course vervain. Would you like to watch what I'm doing and see how I prepare everything?"

Elle nodded and stepped closer as Libby stood at the north-facing round table she'd set up as her altar. They didn't consider their practice a religion; however, their work platform was always addressed as an altar. Libby placed the mixture of herbs in the center of the table with candles on either side. "I'm using purple, white, and blue candles because I want to give Abbey protection and healing," she explained. "I'm also going to align the vibrations of the plants to increase their effectiveness."

"I can sometimes see the vibrations as a comet. Is it always like that?" Elle asked.

Libby shook her head. "Sometimes it can be jagged lines or sort of a spiral. Once you see them or feel them you can energize the herbs." She signaled the others and at once the room went still.

Aleksandr felt a sudden rush of adrenaline pumping through his body. He was acutely aware of every detail in the room. The darkness. The flickering candles all around them. Anticipation heightened his awareness. Electricity crackled and snapped through the room. Libby's voice filled the silence, a harmonious chant calling on the power of the earth, the wind, fire, and water. The Drake sisters and their aunt stood with hands touching, eyes closed, just outside the circle, surrounding Abigail and Aleksandr. The air was charged with so much electricity their hair seemed to stand out.

Aleksandr took a deep breath and inhaled the combination of strange fragrances coming from the herbs, candles, and incense. The air grew heavy. Small golden sparks arced from the Drake women's fingertips, glowing first white and then yellow.

Aleksandr's heart accelerated. Teacups floating and people speaking the truth were one thing, but this ceremony was something altogether different. Power was building in the room. He drew Abigail's hand against his heart and held it there as the house creaked and shifted as if coming alive. He felt the floor shudder and the walls seemed to expand. Small comets of purple and blue streaked across the ceiling, then faded away, only to reappear, merging into shades of the two colors, to pulse with a vivid intensity.

The pictures of the Drake sisters and their ancestors on the wall began to shake slightly. The chant swelled in volume and Aleksandr was certain other voices had joined in. A far-off sound like the tinkle of chimes in the wind could be heard, the notes striking such an oddly discordant tone the hairs on his neck and arms raised.

Colors spun faster, blurring together, the tails of the comets leaving behind sparks in the air. The chimes grew louder and more distinct. A call. A summons. Persistent. Reverent. Anticipation tightened the knots in his stomach. In the entryway, over a detailed mosaic, movement caught Aleksandr's eye. Shadows swirled, rising up out of the tiles, taking shape as they emerged. Women. An army of women.

Seven by seven they came out of the tiles swirling together in a shapeless gray mass and then separating into distinct individuals. They were transparent one moment and solid the next. More and more joined them, filling the room, standing solidly behind the circle of the Drake sisters. The women crowded in, voices swelling, candles flickering, power growing, packing the room until it seemed as if it was impossible any more could fit inside.

The shadowy women lined up directly behind each of the Drake sisters. Those behind Libby had their arms raised toward the moonlight spilling in through the windows, just as she did. The others held out their hands to one another and the same sparks arced from their fingertips as from the Drakes'. The last group formed a protective circle around all of them.

Libby dropped her arms and all the shadows behind her followed suit. A hush fell over the room. Aleksandr held his breath. The woman closest to Libby stepped forward, crowding her impossibly, overshadowing her, merging until they disappeared, leaving only Libby behind. He glanced around. The same process repeated itself with each of the other women until there were only the seven sisters and Carol left in the room.

Again there was that moment of expectation. The Drake women raised their arms toward the moonlight and the surge of power was tremendous. It brought whips of electricity that danced white-hot through the room. A bluish flame outlined each whip. The tails of crackling light swirled through the air and slithered across the ceiling and down the walls of the house, sliding across the floor toward the circle. The whips left behind a luminescent film, a thin coating of bluish purple over everything they touched. The color spread across the floor toward the circle of wooden staffs and for one moment he felt the electrical charge rushing *through* him and over him. He looked down to see his fingers, entwined with Abbey's, glowing with that same colorful light.

The chimes faded away. The color faded. The candles flickered in silence. Aleksandr forced air through his lungs. The tension began to seep out of him and he forced his muscles to relax. He'd been unaware he had partially covered Abigail's body with his own in an effort to protect her from the unknown. She hadn't made a sound, but one arm was wrapped around his neck.

Jonas flicked a switch on the wall, flooding the room with light. He leaned one hip against the doorjamb and grinned at Aleksandr. "Welcome to the Drake family." He held out a handful of cookies. "You hungry?"

Abigail came up on her knees and framed Aleksandr's face with her hands. "This is who I am, Sasha. This is my heritage."

"Those women?" He had faced many killers in his lifetime, many dangerous situations, but none of them had put fear in him the way that ceremony had. He didn't know what to think or feel. Looking around the room, it seemed almost normal again. No colors flashing.

No electricity arcing. The wooden staffs were gone, the candles no longer lit. Even the small round table had been whisked away.

"My ancestors."

"When you said the house was protected, you really meant literally," he said, feeling slightly dazed. Even seeing it, Aleksandr felt it was impossible to fully comprehend what had happened.

"You look a bit pale," Jonas said and crossed the room pull Aleksandr to his feet. "Don't try to figure it out," he advised. "Just accept them."

Aleksandr drew Abigail up and fit her in close to his body. He needed the reassurance of her real and solid against him. "That was incredible. I'm not sure I believe what I saw." He waited a heartbeat. "What I think I saw."

"Do you feel different, Abbey?" Libby asked. "Is the emotional pain gone?"

Abigail nodded. "It lessened inside the circle and is gone now." She smiled at Aleksandr. "What about you? Do you feel better?"

"I knew I was feeling your pain. I don't know how I knew it, but it overwhelmed me. I think the thought that I could do that to you, cause you so much hurt, was more distressing than anything else. That and thinking you wouldn't give me a another chance." He bent his head to kiss the tip of her nose. "It was very distracting."

Sarah spun around. "What did you say?"

Aleksandr looked up. "I wanted another chance with Abbey."

Sarah waved the explanation aside. "Right. Right. But you were distracted. From what? What were you doing?"

Joley snickered. "Staring at Sylvia's works of art in the back room of Frank's gallery. Just what were you doing back there anyway? That room was off-limits."

"To everyone but the Drake family?" Aleksandr raised his eyebrow.

Jonas looked from one to the other. "Why were you all so interested in Frank Warner's back room?"

"I wanted to take a look around," Aleksandr admitted. "Sylvia offered and I took her up on it."

"You mean you planted the suggestion," Abigail corrected.

He shrugged. "She was angry with you for some reason. Something to do with her ex-husband. Apparently she's been trying to get back with him. He was at the party and he saw her talking innocently to Ned Farmer. She wasn't making much sense. She claimed her ex-husband hated a rash on her face that Abbey was responsible for and talking to Farmer had somehow brought out the rash. I didn't see a rash."

"Ned's married," Hannah said. "And she had to be flirting if the rash came out."

"I think she flirts as a standard way of talking with men, Hannah," Sarah said. "So Aleksandr went into the back room with Sylvia looking for something. What?"

"Well, Sylvia saw her ex go into the back room. He didn't come out so eventually she wanted to see what he was up to. She kept talking about it so it wasn't all that hard to give her a little nudge. I thought I might get a few answers."

"He was looking for stolen paintings," Joley volunteered. "We found them. At least we think they were stolen. We found four in a cupboard and took pictures of them. They should be in the photographs Jonas brought back."

"You have pictures?" Aleksandr asked.

"Those photographs are of stolen art?" Jonas asked and turned back to the kitchen where he'd spread the snapshots over the kitchen table. The rest began to follow him.

"Jonas!" Carol's voice reprimanded from the kitchen. "You dropped cookie crumbs on them."

Sarah stopped Aleksandr before he could follow the others. "Once you felt Abigail's pain, you stopped investigating the back room, didn't you?"

"Abbey or one of the others stirred up the dust in the room. Sylvia had a sneezing fit. I knew they were in there. Not *them,* the Drakes, at first. I just knew we weren't alone and when the dust swirled around us and Sylvia began sneezing uncontrollably, I took the opportunity to get out, but I intended to go back in myself later to have a look around."

"Because you suspect Frank?"

"I know he's involved and also the man working for him, Chad Kingman. I wanted to find proof and if Abigail did manage to take pictures of stolen paintings and the pictures can lead us to the thieves, I've got them nailed. Frank will give it up. He isn't a tough guy."

"Could Prakenskii have been deliberately keeping you from that back room?"

That stopped him. Abigail had been listening and she turned fully around. "There was a fight. I know you saw the spots of blood. We could all feel the vibrations of violence. And we're certain those paintings are real, they *felt* old, not that Frank couldn't have acquired them legally."

"If Prakenskii had already left, and your aunt Carol told me he had, how would he have known I was in that room, or that I was going back to it?" Aleksandr asked.

"Sarah sometimes knows things."

"Not like that, though, Abbey," Sarah told her. "It doesn't work that way. I don't think Prakenskii could have known without being present. He must have seen you going into the room and used Abbey to distract you from returning."

"We know he's good at moving through a crowd without being seen," Abbey said. "I want to know what happened to Mason Fredrickson. Do you think it was his blood and not Chad's? If Sylvia saw him go in earlier, but none of us saw him, where did he go? Aunt Carol said she saw Prakenskii give Chad a beating, but Mason was nowhere around. Had he been there earlier, saw something he shouldn't have and was hurt? Or could he be involved?"

"There's a door that exits out into the alley where the delivery trucks come," Aleksandr said.

"And Mason's good friends with Chad. They went to school together," Sarah added. "I'm more concerned that Prakenskii seems to be subtly influencing everyone."

The three entered the kitchen and Aleksandr reached past Abigail to snag the last of the cookies on the plate ahead of Jonas. "Prakenskii follows his own rules. I have no idea what his agenda is, but I can tell you, whatever he's doing here isn't exactly what Nikitin thinks it is."

"What is this?" Jonas picked up a photograph of a naked male statue and thrust it at Hannah. "I suppose this is your idea of a stolen painting."

She nodded, taking the photo from him and passing it on to her aunt. Carol laughed. "Joley, you took these, didn't you?"

Joley widened her eyes innocently. "I can't imagine why you'd think it was me, Aunt Carol. Abbey and Hannah were both there as well."

Abigail glanced over the pictures spread across the table and her heart suddenly began to pound. She stared down at one of them un-believing, certain her eyes were tricking her. The face and body were familiar, the stuff of nightmares, she was certain of it. She leaned closer, almost afraid to touch the photograph.

"Abbey?" Aleksandr slipped his arm around her. "What is it? You look like you've seen a ghost."

Abigail reached past Hannah to grab the picture and wave it at Jonas and Aleksandr. "This is one of the men who shot Gene and Danilov. I know it's him. I'm certain of it."

Aleksandr took it out of her hand. "Who took this?" There was shock on his face and in his eyes.

Carol peeked under his arm. "I did. The ladies from the Red Hat Club decided we were going to visit a few of the private beaches as a sort of defiant statement of owning beaches. I'm fairly certain he was staying at the old Hogan place. I saw him start down the deck stairs and knew he was going to run us off. I took a couple of snapshots of him using the zoom lens. It's such a great feature, don't you think?"

"You *trespassed,*" Jonas emphasized. "And you darn well did it on purpose, Aunt Carol. You knew the murderers were outsiders and that they would probably be renting one of the more secluded beach houses, didn't you?"

"Well, dear, it may have occurred to me. If I were going to rent a house and not want the law to catch me, I'd use someone else to do the actual renting. How in the world would you be able to find them? The ladies loved the idea of invading private beaches. We danced and sang and ran barefoot into the sea! It was so much fun. And of course I took lots of pictures for all of our scrapbooks."

"Carol, you can't be doing that kind of thing. You aren't a spy, for God's sake. And you can't take Inez and the others along on your little adventures." Jonas raked his hands through his hair. "Stay out of this."

"Just say thank you, Jonas," Joley said. "She got you the address."

Abigail heard the half teasing, half bickering that often went on between Jonas and her family as if from a distance. Her attention was on Aleksandr. "What is it? Who is this man?"

"Leonid Ignatev. He's here, in the United States."

"What does that mean?" Abigail's heart began to pound.

"He wouldn't be here for stolen art." He looked up at Jonas. "I think your murder investigation and my stolen art investigation have just crossed paths."

"Who is this man?"

"He was a high-ranking member of the police department with aspirations for political office. When Abigail and I met, four years ago, my career had surpassed his and I unwittingly, in the course of several investigations, stepped on his toes. I knew he was dirty and that he had a hand in shaking down businesses in the city." Aleksandr shrugged. "It can be a way of life, and there are so many like him, I didn't give it much thought. I would have left him alone even knowing he was in deep with the mafia if he stayed out of my way."

"But he didn't," Jonas prompted.

Aleksandr drew Abigail to him. "No, he didn't. He went after both my career and Abigail. I had no choice but to take him down. It was the only way to save Abbey's life. His men would have killed her when they got what they wanted out of her."

"What did they want?" Sarah asked.

"For her to give me up. If she once gave them my name, I would have lost everything, but she held out and when I found out what was going on, I moved quickly to free her and destroy him. Several of his men were killed and evidence against him was discovered. He had to run in order to survive. He put out a hit on me using Nikitin as the broker. We know Nikitin is very violent and mafia, but we've never been able to get anything at all on him. Several times agents have been sent in and they turn up dead."

Jonas rubbed his jaw. "We've been keeping an eye on this Nikitin. I've got a file on him a few inches thick, but he hasn't made a single misstep and you're right, there's nothing to charge him with. He's acting as if he's on vacation and just enjoying the coast. He's frequenting the best restaurants and he's shopping in all the stores."

"And making contacts," Aleksandr pointed out. "He can be very charming, but there's no question he's a shark." He tapped the picture. "This one is up to something very bad. He'd never bother with stolen art. What we have here is a takeover of an established route and whatever they're bringing into the country via that route is hot and it's coming in soon. They're willing to kill to protect whatever it is. Nikitin is up to his neck in this, he's most likely the advance man, but Ignatev is almost certainly the man in charge."

"Are you certain the man in that photograph was one of the men in the speedboat?" Jonas asked. "It was dark."

Abigail nodded. "Absolutely. It was a full moon and they weren't all that far away from me."

"If Ignatev was there to pick up something and there was a problem, even a small one, he would have been angry. He has no patience and he solves his problems with violence."

"What would they be bringing in that would be so important?" Carol asked.

Aleksandr's gaze shifted to Jonas. Their eyes met over Carol's head. Jonas nodded ever so slightly. Aleksandr let out his breath. "Ignatev was involved with a group that used terror tactics to try to overthrow the government. I know that he was trained in Africa and has ties to several terrorist groups. I would guess he's returning a favor for someone and getting very rich while he's at it. To get out of Russia safely, he had to use his connections and those kinds of favors always come with strings. He'd need money to rebuild."

Abigail looked from one grim face to another. She turned to Sarah. Sarah looked frightened. "Sasha, do you think he's bringing in a bomb of some kind?"

His arm swept her closer and he brushed a kiss on top of her forehead. "I think he's bringing in a dirty bomb. Ignatev is here to receive it and pass it on to a mole. He'd never use it himself, but he'd be in a position of having no choice if they asked him to get it here. Nikitin knew about the route for stolen art, it's been going on for years, so when Ignatev approached him, naturally he chose it. Unfortunately, we were in the middle of our investigation and Danilov was already in position undercover. They didn't know about him or that Interpol was looking hard at this coast."

"You don't know that for certain," Joley said, her hand to her throat.

Hannah made a small distressed sound and Jonas reached out and ran his hand down her arm in reassurance. "We'll stop them, now that Volstov is working with me." He frowned. "Why are you working with me? You've been stonewalling me this entire time. Why the sudden change?"

"After Abigail and I are married, I'm going to need a job and someone on my side," Aleksandr said.

Abigail made a face and rolled her eyes at her sisters, but she remained silent. Aleksandr may have had a trace of amusement in his voice, but he was being serious.

Jonas regarded him for a long moment. Abigail could hear the clock ticking in the silence of the room while Jonas weighed his reaction. "A job, huh? You do have a few skills that might be useful."

"A few," Aleksandr agreed.

Joley and Abigail exchanged a quick smirk. Men always seemed to growl and sniff around each other, bristling over nothing, and just as suddenly become buddies at the least likely moments.

"Aunt Carol." Jonas turned his attention to the older woman. "You really have to listen to me this time. I don't want you spying on anyone else. This is far too dangerous. You can see from everything we've said that you were in danger whether you realized it or not while you were playing at James Bond. You need to give me your word you won't be skulking around with your camera poking into the hornet's nest."

"I never skulk, dear," Carol said.

"Aunt Carol," Sarah persisted, her voice stern. "Jonas is right this time."

"This *one* time," Hannah muttered under her breath as she stared down at one of the photographs.

Jonas scowled darkly, snatching the picture of the naked statue from her and crumpling it into a small ball. "You don't need to be looking at this crap." He looked exasperated. "And I mean it, Aunt Carol, no more poking around."

"I'm certainly not about to do anything so silly." Carol grinned at him. "But you have to admit, I broke the case!"

Relenting, Jonas slipped his arm around her and dropped a kiss on her head. "You did do that. I now have gray hair, but you definitely gave us a very important piece of information."

"I'll get back to my house and send off some inquiries immediately and see what data Interpol can give me on recent movements of materials needed for a bomb. I'll also check the freighters coming close to the coast in the next few days," Aleksandr said. "Harrington, don't go after these people alone. Nikitin is dangerous and he has a few people working for him that are even more so. Ignatev is a venomous snake."

"I can't move until I have something concrete," Jonas said. "Right now, it's all speculation."

"I'm taking Abigail home with me," Aleksandr announced to the Drake sisters. "When she comes back, ask her to see the ring."

16

"DID you mean what you said to Jonas?" Abigail asked as she tossed her purse on the soft leather sofa and whirled to face him.

Aleksandr closed the door to his rented beach house and locked it. "I usually mean what I say, *baushki-bau*. What exactly are you referring to?"

"The part about when we get married you'll need a job."

"It isn't as if I'm independently wealthy and I'm certainly not planning to live off of you. I like working," he replied.

Her gaze was on him. Bright, half hopeful, half afraid. She looked so beautiful to him, standing there waiting. He could see the rise and fall of her chest, the way her breasts strained against her thin silk top. She looked an elegant lady, still in her clothes from the party. He wanted her the way he always did the moment they were alone. It always hit him that way, the need raw and intense and so strong it shook him. He never bothered to hide it from her, what would be the point? She held such power over him, over his body, over his heart.

She licked her lips, that little flick of her tongue making him groan. "Here? You'd be willing to come here and work?"

"I believe you're persona non grata in my homeland," he pointed out. "We can live anywhere you want, but I think this is where you're happiest."

Her lips curved, trembled, but she held back the smile, still too afraid to believe. "I travel a lot with my work."

"I like to travel."

Her mouth trembled and she pressed her fingers to it. "Are you serious?"

"*Ya lyublyu tibya.* I love you in any language, Abigail. Wherever you are is home to me."

"But you love your country so much."

"That will never change. Because I live here or on an island somewhere doesn't change who I am or where I'm from. I'll always love my country, but that doesn't mean I can't love another one as well. You're the most important person in my life, Abbey. I tried living without you. I didn't like it."

"Are you certain, Sasha? Very, very certain?" The color washed out of her face. "I couldn't go through losing you again. I mean it. Think about this before you answer. We're so different. And you can be so ruthless sometimes. I'm not certain we're capable of living together for any length of time."

"I'm not capable of living without you, Abbey, so we'll find a way to make it work. That's all there is to it."

She studied his face as if trying to see through his expression to what lay deeper. He'd spoken the simple truth and he was counting on the fact that she was a woman who knew the truth when she heard it. It took a few moments to believe. His heart jerked in his chest and he felt the familiar knots gathering in his gut. And then joy lit her face, her eyes, and he could breathe again.

Abigail launched herself at him, crossing the distance separating them with a couple of leaps. Aleksandr caught her, laughing, his mouth meeting hers, hands tearing at her clothes. He dragged the jacket over her arms and popped three buttons on her silk blouse. Abbey was worse, ripping his shirt even as all the buttons went scattering in every direction. He wanted to touch her, touch that soft satin skin that drove him so wild. She always made him hotter just by the way she was so eager for him, sliding her hands up his belly and chest, her mouth frantic on his, small little frenzied sounds escaping her throat.

Aleksandr stripped the classy pin-striped trousers from her hips, urging her to step out of them. She kicked off her heels and allowed him to move her away from the clothes. He whirled her around and backed her up to pin her body between his and the wall. Her white silk shirt gaped open, giving him tantalizing glimpses of her full breasts peeking through flesh-colored lace. A tiny black thong covered only a fraction of her red tight curls and three V-shaped straps cuddled the top of her buttocks.

Aleksandr's mouth was rough and greedy with hunger on hers. She was giving herself to him, but it wasn't enough. A part of him was angry with her, furious with her that four long years had gone by and she'd left him alone. *Forced* him to be without her. That she could just walk away and not look back. That he had been alone in a living hell without her, while she went around the world doing whatever it was she did. He tore the artfully placed combs from her red hair so that it tumbled down in wild disarray, just the way he loved it.

"Tell me you love me." He ordered it gruffly as his mouth left hers to find her throat, licking and sucking at her soft skin. He trailed kisses lower until his teeth found her sensitive nipple and he had her arching against him, her head thrown back and her breath coming in small gasps.

It wasn't enough, her surrender, her offering. She had been his, her body given to him and then mercilessly taken from him. He licked and sucked at her nipples, his hand sliding over her stomach to the thatch of red hair. Tiny beads of moisture welcomed him. "Damn it, Abbey, tell me. Say it out loud and you'd better mean it this time."

She cried out when his mouth took possession of her breast, suckling, teeth scraping her nipple gently, little nips and teasing bites. His fingers sank into her waist as he held her pinned against the wall. She tried to tear at his clothes; her hands at the zipper of his trousers and the feel of her fingers brushing against him, her throaty cries, and moist sheath nearly drove him mad. Only Abbey could destroy his control this way. It was only *her* body that made him crazy with need.

He was desperate for her, desperate to bury himself in her hot, tight sheath, to feel her so wet and ready for him. To *know* she needed him every bit as much as he needed her. He wanted to see her eyes glaze over with lust as he drove her body to the point of release over and over again. He wanted to know her little desperate cries were for him alone.

"Hurry, Sasha." She could barely get the words out, panting as she tried to drag his clothes from his body. "I can't wait to feel you inside of me."

He loved the little thong, but it had to go. He yanked the thin strip of material from her body and dropped it carelessly aside as he dropped to his knees and shoved her thighs apart. "Damn it, Abbey, do you have any idea how much I missed you? Missed the taste of you? The feel of you wrapped around me? The other night wasn't enough. A lifetime will never be enough."

Her fingers tunneled in his hair, tried to yank him up where she could get to him, but his hands caught the soft curves of her bottom and his tongue swept over and into her. She screamed, her body jerking in his hands, but he held her firmly, fingers massaging while he lapped at her heat and fire. He had dreamt of this night after night, waking with his body raging at him and the taste of her still in his mouth. She came, her orgasm rocking her, so that her legs buckled.

Aleksandr caught her around the waist and lifted her in his strong arms, bracing her against the wall, and drove into her hard, without preamble, burying himself deep inside her throbbing, pulsing sheath. She was fiery hot. Hotter than he'd ever felt her before. His hands were rough, his demands rough, but Abbey took him into her, panting, crying for more, her nails digging deep, head thrown back and breasts swaying with each hard thrust of his hips.

There it was, the glazed look of complete surrender, of ecstasy that captivated him. She burned for him, matching his ferocious needs with her own, offering him her body as a refuge, as a playground, as an instrument of intense love. She gave him everything and no one would ever match that for him.

The walls of her sheath pulsed and gripped tightly, as greedy for him as he was for her. He bent forward, taking her mouth, his kiss as hungry as his shaft, his need so great he was brutal in his thrusts. She screamed again, flooding him with hot cream, the walls of her sheath milking and gripping, but he refused to come.

He took her to the floor, buried deep inside her body, riding her hard and fast and deep, his face etched with lines of strain, with excitement and pleasure.

"*Sasha.*" She panted his name, rose to meet each thrust with one of her own. She couldn't get her breath as orgasm after orgasm ripped through her. The sensation tore through her body, through her vagina, her womb, and up through her belly to her breasts. Her entire body seemed to pulse and throb and fracture.

"More. I need more from you." He bit the words out between his teeth. He had no idea what would assuage the terrible ache in his heart. But he wanted her coming completely apart in his arms, submitting to his every demand, screaming his name over and over and admitting she loved him.

Coming up on his knees between her thighs, he thrust her legs wider, watching the way they came together, watching his body moving in and out of hers. She was so wet, so hot, her breasts heaving and her nipples incredibly erect. He drew her knees even higher so he could angle himself to press tighter against her clit.

Her body shuddered with pleasure, nearly taking his with it as she went over the edge again, the orgasm was so strong, but he held back, stilling his body, holding her against him so he could feel the tightness in his balls as they lay up against the curve of her buttocks. He stroked with his fingers, felt her jump in response. Her fists tried to dig into the floor, desperate to find something to hang on to. She writhed under him, moaning softly, pleading with him.

He bent forward to whisper to her, hot passionate words, all the things he'd missed doing with her, all the things he intended to do to her. All the ways he would take her. How he wanted her mouth, so beautiful, so hot and tight on him. Each erotic word sent shudders of anticipation through her body so that her muscles clamped all the tighter around him, so that the walls of her sheath pulsed with fire and hot liquid.

"Tell me you love me, Abbey," he said again.

She wanted to hold out. She knew what he would do, exactly how he would react to her stubborn refusal. He was very demanding in his lovemaking, and she loved it the most when he was like this, rough and insistent and inventive. He was thick and long and so damned hard she felt stretched and full. He was hitting every nerve ending she had. His fingers were busy, stroking juices over her body, delving deep, teasing and tormenting even as he occasionally bent over her to use his teeth to deliver a series of small bites, his tongue following to ease the tiny pinpoints of pain.

He thrust into her so deep she could feel the large thick head of him bumping against her womb. His face was lined with intent, with desire, his powerful body thrusting hard and deep, over and over, driving her closer and closer to the edge.

"Tell me," he bit out, his expression turning savage.

She couldn't stand the pain in his eyes. His face was rough and dark and his eyes were twin storms. He needed her. It was raw and plain and so intense she couldn't deny him anything. Not even the truth. "It terrifies me how much I love you," she admitted.

He stilled. Buried deep inside her, her silken sheath a tight fist gripping him, her body soft in surrender beneath him, he stared down into her eyes. Her lips were swollen from his kisses, her breasts rose-colored, the nipples hard peaks, and her eyes were half dazed with desire, but he saw beyond the wild frenzy of heat and lust they shared. He saw it clearly in the depths of her eyes.

"Abbey," he whispered her name.

She shook her head. "I want you so much sometimes I can't breathe, or think properly. I don't care what's right or wrong. I forget about the future, the past, about everything because I want you. I want you buried so deep inside of me you'll never get out. I want to be stretched and full and fall asleep with you kissing and holding me and wake up to you eating me like candy, like you'll never get enough of me. It's the most terrifying thing in the world to love you, Sasha, because I don't know what you'll do."

He bent his head and found her mouth, kissing her over and over, trying to take the pain out of her voice and the fear out of her heart. Her tongue tangled with his, a dance of love that quickly grew hot with need. His hips began a slow, seductive rhythm again. He straightened up and pulled her ankles over his shoulders. "You're safe with me."

Abigail closed her eyes as his body slid almost out of hers and then slammed deep again in one hard stroke. Heat began to build, spreading like wildfire, her body winding tighter and tighter as his hips drove downward and he angled her body to stroke her most sensitive spot. Pleasure mounted until she thought she would have to scream for release. It built and built, higher and higher, tighter and tighter, and her body was no longer her own, but his, completely under his command.

"I can't come again, it's too much," she gasped, her head tossing from side to side. But she *had* to, she needed release more than she needed anything at that moment.

"You'll come for me," he decreed. "Again and again. It's never too much to bring you pleasure. Feel us, *lyubof maya*." He was harder and thicker than he'd ever been, swelling within the hot glove surrounding him. She was like a fist, holding him tight, rubbing and milking and demanding more. Always more. He didn't want it to end. He didn't want her breathless, eager pleas to stop.

She whimpered, a soft little sound he'd been waiting for, knew would come when he pushed her past the point she thought she could take. She was mindless with pleasure now, writhing beneath him, lifting up to meet the hard surge of his body into hers. He reveled in the feel of her muscles rippling and gripping, so desperate for him. He began to drive into her, clamping her ankles to his shoulders so he had that perfect angle and he could piston into her faster and faster.

He felt her body shudder, shatter, implode around him, taking him with her, her vaginal walls clamping around him like a tight fist, so hot he thought he'd go up in flames. His hoarse cry mingled with hers and he felt his knees go as he emptied himself deep inside of her. Letting go of her ankles, he helped her legs to the floor and allowed his own body to settle over the soft cushion of hers.

He held her pinned to the floor, his body deep in hers feeling every ripple, every electric shock. He loved that, the aftermath when the slightest touch to her nipples or neck, cupping her buttocks or flicking his tongue over her skin, sent another shudder of pleasure through her so that her muscles convulsed around him.

Abigail lay under him, the floor hard against her back and her body melting around his. There were lines etched into his face that had not been there before and she reached up and traced them with the pad of her finger. She stroked his chiseled lips and ran her palm over his shadowed jaw. Even now, after they had shared so much, he could look so lonely. It never seemed to matter how much of herself she gave, she could see the loneliness in him. It was so much a part of him, he didn't even seem to realize it was there.

"Why are you crying, *baushki-bau?*" There was a throaty growl of displeasure in his voice. He leaned forward and flicked at the tears on her face with his tongue. The simple movement had her muscles fluttering and tightening around him.

She turned her head away from him, but not before he caught the flash of pain in her eyes. His heart jerked. Immediately he eased his body from hers and went up on his knees to lift his weight from her as he glanced around, taking a quick assessment of the room. Their clothes weren't the most salvageable. He was going to be making a run early in the morning to get her something to wear, but more important, there was no comfortable spot to sleep.

He picked her up, cradling her against his chest. "You're so beautiful."

"I'm a mess," she protested, turning her face against his heavy muscles. He felt the touch of her tongue on his skin and his nerve endings jumped with pleasure.

"You're *beautiful.*" He carried her through the house to nearest bedroom and followed her down to the feather mattress, kissing her face, her eyes, the corners of her mouth and teasing at her lower lip with small little nips before settling his body around hers, his arms holding her close. "Tell me why I make you cry."

"Maybe I'm really happy." She swallowed and attempted a watery smile.

"Truth seekers make terrible liars." He kissed the tip of her nose, took a small bite of her chin and kissed her there too. "Why do you look at me that way sometimes after we make love? I've seen it before. You look so sad, yet I know you're happy with me."

She turned in his arms so she could look up into his face. "But are you really happy with me?" She retraced his rough features, exactly as she had earlier, and the memories of her doing the same thing flooded him. The way the pads of her fingers stroked over him as if brushing something away.

"I came halfway around the world to find you. I poured my heart and soul into letters that I painstakingly wrote. I had to mail the damn things from all over Europe because I was so paranoid some-one would read them. I even set up a box in France rather than my country when I realized you were going to keep sending them back. With all that, I still persisted. Why would I do that if you didn't make me happy?"

She shrugged, her gaze shifting away from his. Aleksandr caught her chin. "Abigail, *tell* me. Just say it out loud. Let's get everything over with so we can live together the way we should have been all this time."

"You like my body."

He stared down at her face for a long time, trying desperately not to cry. He *loved* her body. What man wouldn't love the lush curves and silky softness? He loved the way she was so responsive to him, the way she trusted him so utterly and completely. She was a haven to him, a secret place of absolute beauty in a world where he found most things bleak and ugly. Right now she lay nearly under him, pinned by his weight, her soft breasts pushing into his chest, nipples raking his skin, one leg tangled with his. His hand was cupping the round curve of her bottom, fingers caressing, and she never once shifted away from him. Never said enough. Never protested anything he wanted to do. She *gave* herself to him utterly and completely.

The lump in his throat burned. "I love your body, yes. I love every-thing about you, Abbey. Even your stubborn streak, although I think next time you turn it on me I'm going to turn caveman and be unpo-litical and insensitive. Don't you want me to love your body?" His hands slid down her spine and cupped the globes of her bottom, bring-ing her damp curls tight against him. "Every time I touch you, each time I take you, no matter how I do it, I'm telling you in the only way I know how just how intense my feelings are for you. There's no real way to express in words the way I feel for you."

"But afterward, when we stop, when it's over, you look so lonely. I never want it to end because I know that look is going to creep back no matter what I do."

There was an ache in her voice. Tears swam in her eyes. His heart did a funny little melting thing he'd never experienced before. "*Ya lyublyu tibya*. Always. There'll never be enough time in the world to spend with you. To touch you and make love to you. I love you al-ways, Abbey. When we're skin to skin and my body is inside of yours

I know I'm home and I'm safe and I'm loved. I've never had that and maybe a part of me doesn't trust it yet. I know I don't just want to be dominant when we make love, I know a part of me *needs* it. I need to have you give yourself to me."

Her hands framed his face. She kissed his throat, his chin, and he felt her tears on his skin. Her body moved beneath his, a small subtle shift, pliant and welcoming. She was killing him. How could he ever show her what she was to him? His hands tangled in her hair, pulled her head back to look into her eyes. "Don't leave me again, Abbey. Don't do that to me. I'm never alone when I'm with you. *Never*. No matter how I look, I don't feel alone when you're with me."

"I love you so much it hurts, Sasha. I don't think I could go through another separation."

"You satisfy me completely, Abbey, never think that you don't." Aleksandr nuzzled her neck as he wrapped his arms around her, his body fitting around hers protectively. "I love the way you smell after we make love."

She smiled in the darkness. "I think you're primitive. You want your scent all over me."

"That too." He pressed his body closer, wanting to crawl inside of her skin. "After you were gone, I would lie awake at night and re-member you, the curves of your body and how soft you were." His hand cupped her breast, his thumb sliding over her nipple. "Like this. Full and round and so damned soft you feel like heaven." He closed his eyes and burrowed his face into her wealth of silky hair. "I remem-bered every detail. And when I couldn't sleep I'd think about how your body curved, every valley, your hips and ass. I love your ass."

"You were obsessing, Aleksandr. That's not a good thing."

"Maybe not, but it kept me sane." He kissed a spot between her shoulder blades. "Before I met you, I had a satisfying life. I got up in the morning and had my coffee and went to work. Whatever case I was working on consumed my morning, afternoon, and evening. Sometimes I worked until two or three in the morning. Looking back, I realize I didn't have friendships. I didn't dare. Betrayal is a way of life and getting too close to anyone is dangerous business. When I met you, the first thing that really hit me was the way you smiled at me. It was so genuine. It lit your eyes and your face and seemed to be coming from somewhere inside of you. You didn't want anything at all from me."

His teeth nipped her skin, his tongue flicking the small mark. "I wanted something from you and I was ashamed. I'd never felt shame before. It was a new and very unpleasant experience for me. I wanted our chance meeting to be real."

"I was hurt when you first told me," she admitted, "but now it doesn't seem so terrible. At least we did meet. I loved the way you touched me. Very strong, very sure, guiding me through a crowded street." She smiled at the memory. His face has been so strong, remote, so completely bleak, yet confident. He had been a puzzle to her. The more she was in his company, the more layers she discovered. The first time he laughed, her heart had soared and she'd known he was the one. That he'd always be the one.

She had loved being the person to put that laughter in his eyes. He smiled, but rarely with his eyes and when he'd laughed, her entire being had responded.

"I didn't know people like you existed," he confessed. "I grew up in a school. A place where they trained us. We didn't have mothers and fathers, we had teachers. We worked at skills all the time and that was our playtime. We didn't know others had different lives, because it seemed natural to us."

Her heart ached for him. She shifted position again, her back to him, pressing her buttocks tightly against his groin, her face buried in the pillow. If she cried, he would stop talking about his past. He always stopped if he thought she was upset and as much as it hurt to hear his childhood, she wanted to know. He was always so matter-of-fact. It was never a bid for sympathy. He had known no other way of life and it seemed natural to him. Duty. Work. Acquiring necessary skills. She knew his teachers had shaped a weapon, sharpening his mind and building on his natural athletic ability and his reflexes.

His hand stroked her silken hair. "We had to ask for our food in at least three languages. We were never allowed to just use one language when we spoke. If I said anything to a teacher, or to anyone else, I had to say it three times." He lifted the hair from the nape of her neck, his lips trailing over her skin. "I didn't mind. It was a chal-

lenge to be able to do it, but not all of the others had a gift for languages and it was harder on them."

"What was hard on you?" His teeth and mouth were driving her
slowly crazy. He nibbled and licked and sucked and her body was
beginning to respond to the stimulation with a slow burn.

She felt his smile against her neck. "I didn't like anyone telling me
what to do. If I thought I had a better way to accomplish something,
I did it my way."

"Did you get into trouble?" She closed her eyes as his hands
cupped her breasts and his strong fingers began a slow assault on her
sensitive nipples.

"I often was reprimanded. I think it was considered part of the
training. We weren't allowed to make a sound or answer back when
they beat us. I think it set the stage for working as an operative in the
event we were captured and tortured."

His erection was growing against her, hardening into a persistent
bulge. She felt a small drop of moisture on her cheek. His hips moved
in a slow, languorous rhythm, almost lazy, almost as if he couldn't
help trying to burrow into her softness.

"You were just children," Abigail protested. "It wasn't right." She
couldn't stop from pushing back against him, rubbing her bottom
over him in a slow glide, resting her head back against him so she
could arch her breasts into his hands.

"We didn't know any different," he said again. "How the hell do
you get so soft?" His hands were calloused and rough yet she never
protested. Abigail never stopped him from touching her and that
meant everything to him. Sometimes he felt starved for touch. For her
hands on him, for his hands on her. He massaged her breasts, tugged
on her nipples, his mouth at the nape of her neck.

"You need to sleep," she said, but her body slid against his in invitation.

He closed his eyes briefly, savoring what a miracle she was. Her
invitation. Her acceptance. The way she seemed to know what he
needed. "I can't sleep. My mind won't shut off."

It was often that way. Most nights he got up and paced when he
couldn't sleep, or brought out his case files or studied the data on the
computer. Lying in bed holding Abigail usually allowed him enough
peace to rest, but not tonight. Tonight there were knots in his guts.

Fear that she might disappear still stabbed through him. Fear that she wouldn't be able to accept him the way he really was. He had been shaped at a young age to be ruthless and cold when needed, to do whatever it took to get the job done. There was a dark side to him, one that Abigail had glimpsed before. And he knew that part of him scared her. Maybe would always scare her.

"I'm not going to give you up again, Aleksandr."

"You said you were terrified of me."

She laughed softly. "I said I'm terrified of how much I love you. There's a huge difference." She pulled out of his arms, shoving the heavy comforter off of them as she knelt beside him. Her long red hair fell in a silken cascade and brushed intimately over his stomach. "You need to sleep."

"You sound like a little dictator." His body was all at once fully erect, stiff and hard and aching. He slid his hand over his pulsing shaft. He wanted her again and again. There was no end to it. Right now he fought the urge to catch a fistful of hair and drag her head down to his full, painful erection.

She licked her lips, watching him with her mysterious green eyes, eyes that had gone slumberous and sexy. Her breath came faster and her breasts lifted enticingly with each drag of air she took in.

"I am. You don't need to be thinking about anything right now."

Her hands reached for his pulsing erection and his breath left his lungs in a long rush. She looked so sexy rising above him, her breasts full and rounded and swaying as she moved over him. The curve of her butt enticed him and he brought up his hands to stroke her rounded cheeks.

She suddenly bent her head, her hot mouth taking half of his erection deep into her mouth. "Oh, hell, Abbey," he gasped, his hands coming up to tangle in her hair. Her mouth was pure hot silk, tight and moist and gliding over him with wicked intent. One hand stroked his tight sac and the other gripped the base.

He angled his head to get a better view of her lips sliding up and down him. Her mouth was wet as it slid over his shaft, leaving behind a gleaming trail of moisture. She was so beautiful he wanted to weep, so sexy a part of him felt nearly animalistic in his need for her. The sight made his heart pound ferociously and drove every sane thought out of his mind. Her tongue did some kind of swirling dance and need knotted his belly. He'd just had her yet he was ready to erupt with the heat of her mouth and her tongue doing a wild tangle. She breathed and he felt it vibrate right through his shaft. She worked her throat and his entire body jerked.

"You have to stop. You're going to make me come too fast and I want to be inside you again." His fists tightened in her hair, his thought to drag her head away from him, but his body had other ideas and he held her to him as his hips thrust deep. He could feel the silken heat of her mouth, tight like a glove, and a hoarse moan escaped before he could stop it. "Again," he ordered, his voice unrecognizable. "Do that again."

He swore she laughed. Sensations rippled through him and need clawed at his gut and tightened his groin until he was certain he would explode. He took a deep controlling breath and pulled back, wanting the haven of her body again. He dragged her head back and caught her around the waist, lifting her. "Straddle me."

Abigail widened her thighs and settled over him with a slow, seductive wiggle that sent deep shudders of pleasure through his body. She was hot, hotter than he'd ever known her to be, so tight he had to work through the velvet soft folds, and each push sent a roaring through his head and tightened the knots in his stomach. His fingers bit into her waist and he began to force her body to ride him hard and fast, setting the brutal rhythm with his surging hips. Her muscles convulsed around his almost immediately. She cried out, her head back, long hair brushing his thighs.

He slammed into her, driving deeper, that edgy need claiming him, taking him over, as she arched back, giving him better access to her most sensitive spot. Her muscles clamped down on him like a vise; liquid heat surrounded him. His entire body felt the building hunger, a painful contraction of every muscle, waiting, anticipating.

She climaxed again, so hard this time her body shuddered and her small muscles gripped him like a hot fist, milking him dry, taking everything from him until there was no choice but to lose his control and empty himself into her.

Abigail collapsed over him, her head on his shoulder, her hair everywhere in a wild tangle of red silk. Her breath came in the same rasping gasps as his did. He could feel her heart pounding through her soft skin. Aleksandr brought up his arms to enclose her, to wrap her tightly against him. "I need to hear you say it, Abbey."

"I just showed you." She licked his throat, a small flick of her tongue.

He was enjoying the aftershocks rippling through her body and that little flick only heightened his pleasure. His fingers shoved her hair aside. "I still want to hear you say it."

"You're so greedy. You want everything."

He loved that drowsy, sexy note in her voice as she teased him. He reached down and pulled the comforter over their bodies. This was how he remembered so many nights with her. Making love so many times, so many ways they were both exhausted and covered in sex and each other. Neither could move. Neither wanted to move. They could only lay wrapped in each other's arms trying to find a way to breathe and calm their pounding hearts.

"Say it," he insisted. "I tell you all the time. I think there should be a rule you have to tell me at least once every time we make love."

"Then you'd be spoiled." Her eyes were closed. He could see the dark fringe of lashes on her cheek and the faint smile curving her mouth.

"I need to be spoiled."

She yawned and snuggled closer to him. "I love you very much, Sasha."

Satisfaction swept through him. He held her to him, feeling the rise and fall of her breasts against his chest. His body had slipped from hers, but he lay snug in her nest of curls. He shifted her gently until she was on her side with him curled around her, his favorite position to sleep. And he knew he would sleep. She'd managed to calm his mind and soothe whatever demons had held him in their grip.

He held her to him, listening to her breathe. When she was almost asleep he whispered into her ear, "If I touch you again, will you come alive for me? Will you let me have you, Abbey?" He slid his hand between her thighs and cupped her feminine mound. "As tired as you are, will you still give yourself to me?"

She turned her head toward him, smiling, her green eyes looking straight into his. She reached behind her with one hand to cup his neck, to arch back and find his mouth with hers, kissing him with every bit of passion and hunger and surrender she'd shown earlier. "Do you think anything has changed in ten minutes?"

She was laughing at him. He bit down on her lower lip, tugged for a moment, then wrapped his arms around her and rested his chin on her head. "Go to sleep."

"Will you be able to sleep?"

"Yes."

"If you wake up in the middle of the night . . ."

"I already know exactly how I'll wake you," he promised.

17

THE pounding on the door of her family home brought Abigail to her feet, and the research paper she was writing slid to the floor and the notebooks scattered in all directions. She knew something was wrong before she opened the door, but the last person she ever expected to see was Sylvia Fredrickson.

Abigail stared at the woman, shocked by her appearance. Sylvia's eyes were red and swollen from crying. Her clothes were disheveled and she sobbed wildly. "Sylvia!" Unable to think what else to do, Abigail drew her into the house. "What is it? Were you in an accident?"

"I didn't know where else to go." Sylvia's eyes were wide with shock as she stared around the living room, as if afraid something would jump out and attack her. "I had nowhere else to go."

"Let me call Libby. Do you need an ambulance? The police?" Abigail could see the red and black aura surrounding Sylvia. "Sit down. Are you going to faint?"

"No! Don't call the police. Whatever you do, don't call them. You have to help me. I don't know what to do." She began wringing her hands together. "I don't know what to do. You're smart. All of you are really smart. You have to tell me what to do."

Abigail glanced down at the torn nails, the bruising on Sylvia's wrists and arms. "All right. Just sit down. Take a deep breath. I'll help you. I will, Sylvia. Please sit down." She could feel the woman trembling as she assisted her into a chair. "Just tell me what happened and we'll figure it out together."

Abigail waved a careless hand toward the mantel to light several candles and aromatic diffusers and fill the air with the scents of roman chamomile, geranium, and lavender to aid in comforting Sylvia.

"I know you hate me, and I shouldn't have come here, but there's nowhere else to go. I don't know what to do and you always do." Sylvia took the tissue Abigail handed her and blew her nose. "You won't believe me, but I really love Mason. I do. I would never have cheated on him, but we had this terrible fight and I was angry with him and Bruce was at the bar complaining and we both got drunk. I was just so drunk."

"What happened tonight?" Abigail prompted.

"They're going to hurt him." Sylvia leapt to her feet and began pacing, twisting her hands together again in agitation. "They might even kill him. You have to help him. You have to do something."

"Who's going to kill Mason? Why?"

"Chad Kingman." Sylvia spun around. "He's doing something terrible. Illegal. And he's mixed up with some very bad people. Chad looked awful, his face all black and blue and swollen."

"Sylvia, is Mason in trouble right now? Where is he?" Abigail hung on to her patience. "I know you're upset, but if you don't calm down and tell me everything, I can't help either one of you."

"Sylvia," Libby greeted the woman as she entered the room, the other Drake sisters following. Libby took the woman by the arm and led her back to a chair. "Please sit down. I've brought you a cup of tea. Take a couple of sips and you'll feel much more able to tell us what happened."

"You can't go to the police," Sylvia said anxiously. "I know if you go to the police they'll kill him. I overheard them talking. They want the Russian, Aleksandr Volstov. Abigail knows him. She was with him all evening at the Caspar Inn." She reached out again to Abigail and gripped her hands hard. "Please talk to him. Tell him he has to go and get Mason back."

"Why do they want Aleksandr?" Abigail made eye contact with Joley, who nodded and left the room to make the call.

Sylvia took the teacup from Libby and inhaled the soothing aroma. She was obviously struggling to get her breath back. Libby sat beside her and very gently wrapped her fingers around Sylvia's wrist. The trembling lessened and Sylvia dragged air into her lungs.

Abigail crouched in front of the disheveled woman. "Tell us what Mason's involved in." She wanted to keep Sylvia calm until Aleksandr arrived.

"Chad called me at home yesterday and told me Mason was going to the big party at the art gallery. He knows how I feel about Mason. We've always been good friends and he knew I wanted to patch things up with Mason." She touched her face. "I ran out and bought a new outfit and went, even though I knew it would be awful and no one would talk to me. I just wanted Mason to see I was serious about being with him, but everything went wrong."

"And you were angry with me," Abigail said.

Sylvia nodded. "I thought it was your fault. He found out about the affair because of you and every time he saw the rash on my face it just reminded him of what I'd done." She ducked her head. "I was so desperate to get rid of it I even went to see Lucinda, the voodoo lady over in Point Arena, but nothing she did worked. I was talking to Ned Farmer and the stupid rash was suddenly all over my face and I turned around and Mason was standing there. I could see his disappointment in me. He walked away without saying a word." Tears filled her eyes all over again.

"I'm sorry, Sylvia," Abigail said gently, "but where is Mason now? You have to tell us what happened to him. What happened to you?"

"I'm trying to." Sylvia took another sip of tea. "Mason went into the back where Chad works. I waited and waited for him to come back out so I could talk to him, but he didn't. And then I ran into the Russian, the one you were with at the Caspar Inn." She swallowed convulsively several times. "I was so angry with you. I wanted you to hurt the way I was hurting and I asked him to go in the back room. I though Mason would be there, but he wasn't."

"It's all right, Sylvia," Abigail soothed. "I understand."

Sylvia shook her head. "No, you don't. Mason never went home.

I sat on his porch all night and he never came home. I went by his boat and he wasn't there either so I decided to go ask Chad where he was. They're such good friends." Her voice broke. "I thought they were good friends."

"I'm sure Aleksandr will help," Abigail offered. She'd known Sylvia since the third grade and she'd never seen her so broken.

"Mason really loved me. He didn't think I was stupid or a slut, or any of the other things everyone else thinks. I can't believe how stupid I was to ruin everything over a dumb fight."

"Sylvia, where is he? What happened to you?"

"When he didn't come home, I went down to Chad's place to ask him if he'd seen Mason. Chad was just getting into his truck and he didn't see me waving him down. I followed him to that old abandoned barn just past the turnoff to Caspar. You know the one that looks like it might fall down any minute? It's overgrown all the way up to the house. I parked my car a distance away and sneaked up on him."

"Why?" Abigail looked at Sylvia's dirty jeans, the knees torn and black.

"I don't know. He was acting strange and he was beat up like he'd been in a terrible fight. He kept looking around like he expected to be followed and I was afraid. I thought maybe he'd gotten into a fight with Mason. I hid in the grass and crept up on the barn until I could look through one of the cracked boards."

"Sylvia!" Abigail was horrified. "You could have been killed. What were you thinking?"

"I don't know. I just wanted to find Mason."

"Aleksandr is here," Joley said softly. "He'll help, Sylvia."

Sylvia gasped in horror as she saw Jonas follow Aleksandr through the door. She began shaking her head violently.

Abigail rescued the teacup. "Jonas isn't in uniform, Sylvia. You know he's friends with Mason. He would never do anything to jeopardize Mason's life."

"I was with Aleksandr when Joley called," Jonas explained. "I couldn't help but overhear. I know this coastline better than most, Sylvia, and nobody is going to kill Mason if I can help it."

"Sylvia was just telling us she followed Chad out to the old run-down barn just past the Caspar exit. She was hoping to find Mason and thought Chad was acting funny," Abigail said. "So she followed him."

Sylvia nodded. "I looked into the barn and there was a man standing there holding a gun to Mason's head." She broke into sobs again, choking, pressing her palm to her mouth to muffle the sounds. "They were going to shoot him right there. Right at that moment in front of me." She looked up at Abigail. "I was so scared. I was afraid to move."

"Of course you were. Anyone would be."

"Before he could pull the trigger another man came out of the shadows. I hadn't even noticed him, but I could tell everyone was afraid of him, especially Chad."

"Chad was going to let them shoot Mason?" Jonas swore and turned away. "I would never have thought that of him."

"Maybe he didn't have a choice," Abigail said. She glanced questioningly up at Aleksandr, reading the answer in his eyes. He believed, as she did, that the man coming out of the shadows was Prakenskii. It stood to reason that Chad would be very afraid of him.

"The man said they could use Mason. He said Volstov or the cops didn't have a clue what was going on and why should they take the chance. Chad could transport it and they'd hold Mason until he returned. I didn't know what *it* was, but Chad kept shaking his head and looked like he was going to cry."

"They referred to something as *it,* but they didn't say anything at all that would help you identify what it was?" Jonas asked.

Sylvia shook her head. "They talked about what a threat Volstov could be. Even Chad said so." She looked at Aleksandr. "They must be afraid of you. Can't you do something? *Please* do something."

"This man, the one they were all afraid of, did he talk with a Russian accent? Was his hair worn fairly long?" Aleksandr asked.

Sylvia nodded. "He said something to Mason I couldn't hear and Mason kicked out at him. The man seemed to get mad and he told Mason if the police came anywhere near the barn, he w as a dead man. Mason spit at him. He shoved his gun against Mason's head and I couldn't help myself, I screamed."

"That doesn't sound like Prakenskii," Aleksandr said.

"Yes! That was his name. The other Russian man called him Prakenskii. It sounded different when he said it, though." She took the tissue from Joley and blew her nose. "He came out of the barn and I ran as fast as I could. About halfway to my car, he caught up with me, grabbed my ankle, and I fell down. I kicked and scratched him and fought until I was free. I was frantic. I ran back to my car and he shot the gun once and missed me. He called out to me that if I went to the police, he'd kill both Mason and Chad and hunt me down."

Aleksandr sank back on his heels. "You were able to get away from Prakenskii? He shot at you and missed?"

"I kept kicking until his hands slipped off of me," Sylvia said. "Jonas, if he sees me with you and knows you're a cop, he'll kill Mason."

"Sylvia," Libby said, "I want to help you calm down a little. Jonas and Aleksandr will get Mason back and I'll give you a mild sedative. You can stay here with us until they bring Mason to you. It won't help him if you make yourself sick."

Sylvia touched her face. "Can you take away the rash?"

Libby glanced at Hannah, who shrugged and lifted her hands palms up in a gesture of surrender. "Only you can do that, Sylvia," Libby said. "You have to do the right thing."

"You've said that before," Sylvia wailed. "I don't know what the right thing is."

"Apologize to Abbey for slapping her." Joley fought to keep the exasperation from her voice. "I don't think that's too much to ask. She didn't intentionally use the word *truth* and you were the one who screwed up and was having the affair. You should never have hit her."

"It doesn't matter," Abigail said.

"It does," Joley insisted. Hannah nodded her head in agreement. "It's the only way to get rid of it."

"All I have to do is apologize?" Sylvia asked incredulously. "I'm sorry a thousand times. You have no idea how sorry I am."

Libby drew her out of the chair. "Come with me. We'll get you cleaned up and you can rest."

Sylvia touched her face. "Will it really go away now?"

"Yes," Joley confirmed.

"And you two will get Mason?" Sylvia asked the men.

Jonas nodded and waited until Libby had led her away. "You don't think she got away on her own? Do you think she's lying?"

"It's possible, although I don't know why she would." Aleksandr frowned as he tried to puzzle it out. "There's no way she could have gotten away from Prakenskii. And he'd *never* miss."

Abigail cleared her throat. She took a deep breath and let it out. "She's not lying." She had promised herself she'd never divine the truth again, not for law enforcement, but she couldn't let them think Sylvia was in some way trying to deceive them. Sylvia's fear and her concern for her ex-husband were very genuine.

Aleksandr reached out to her and laced his fingers through hers, knowing how difficult it was for her to give them that small piece of information. "So Sylvia did get away. Then it couldn't have been Prakenskii. He never misses and no woman, especially an untrained one, could have fought him off."

"Could he have let her go on purpose?" Abigail asked.

They all fell silent. Jonas drummed his fingers on the small end table until Hannah leaned over and put her hand over his to stop the irritating noise. When he glanced at her, she snatched her hand away. "That's s-s-so annoying."

"How nice that Barbie doll is speaking to me today," Jonas said.

Hannah made a face at him.

"*Don't* start!" Abigail commanded. "I don't like any of this and I want clear heads while we all figure it out. If it was Prakenskii and Aleksandr's right about him, then he deliberately allowed Sylvia to escape. He *wanted* her to find Aleksandr."

"I'd have to agree with that," Jonas said as his fingers began to drum on the end table again. "A setup, Aleksandr? Are they deliberately drawing you into a trap?"

Aleksandr shrugged. "It isn't Prakenskii's style. If he was going to kill me, he'd sit outside of Abbey's house and nail me through a window or as I was coming out. I'm not ruling it out, but it seems rather elaborate. He isn't a man who would leave things to chance. What if Sylvia went home and hid under her covers? What if she went to the police? There are too many variables for a man like Prakenskii to use her to set me up for a kill."

Carol sank into a chair. "Nail you through a window? You mean shoot you?"

"I'm sorry," Aleksandr said, observing that she was pale. "I didn't mean to upset you. Would you like me to get you a glass of water?"

Carol waved her hand toward the kitchen at the same time Hannah did. She flashed Aleksandr a faint smile. "You're a good man. I hope my niece decides to forgive you and give you another chance."

"We shouldn't have been discussing something like this in front of you, Aunt Carol," Jonas said.

"I'm not upset talking about murder and murderers. I just realized that someone was looking through our window through something that reflected light. Binoculars maybe, or a scope. Jefferson was a hunter before we married and he kept rifles. That first day, when Abbey had the run-in with killers, I was taking snapshots of the girls, mostly to make them laugh. It was at night and I was facing the large picture window and there was a glare on the camera. I snapped the shot and have the photograph in the other room." She shuddered. "Just the idea that someone could have been looking through our window, holding a gun on one of us, is terrifying."

Abigail tightened her fingers around Aleksandr's. "That was the evening you came to my room. I remember Aunt Carol taking pictures. We were sort of joshing Jonas about being spies and she got out the camera. She told us there was some kind of light in the window. It made all of us nervous and we closed the drapes and added to the protection binding the house. You told me you ran into Prakenskii that night. Could he have been here the entire time waiting to get a clear shot at you?"

"I like the spying part of the job," Carol admitted, "but not the danger. I think my blood pressure is climbing."

Joley sat on the arm of her aunt's chair. "Shall I get Libby?"

"No, of course not." Carol fanned herself. "Jonas, do you really think Frank is involved in something illegal? Maybe he doesn't know about the stolen paintings in his back room. Couldn't Chad have hidden them?"

Aleksandr touched her shoulder gently. "I'm sorry, Carol, if he is your friend. We've been tracing his shipments for some time."

"But Chad's the one who crates everything and sends the artwork all over the country," Carol protested. "Couldn't he be doing it without Frank's knowledge?"

"Are you interested in Frank?" Joley asked. "As more than a friend?"

"Not me," Carol said. "But Inez has been for some time. I personally think Reginald is the hottest ticket in town. Frank has no sense of humor and I think a person has to have a sense of humor or they just don't have fun in life. I want to have fun."

Jonas looked confused. "Reginald?"

"Aunt Carol is dating old man Mars," Abigail confided in a solemn whisper.

"He's a lovely man."

Jonas had a coughing fit. Hannah helpfully slapped his back. "On that note, I think Aleksandr and I are going to push off," Jonas declared. "We have to go get Mason back for Sylvia. Not that I'm certain he isn't better off where he is. That woman may genuinely love him, but she'll never change her ways. If they have a fight, he'd better look out."

"You *can't* go," Abigail said, clinging to Aleksandr. "You said yourself Prakenskii had to have let her escape. They'll be waiting for you. They've laid a trap for you and you can't just walk into it."

"I'll be with him," Jonas pointed out.

Her eyes flashed, going a deep blue-green, turbulent and stormy. "How arrogant. I should have expected it. The contract is out on Aleksandr, not you, Jonas. Just how do you think you're going to keep him alive?"

Aleksandr bent close to her, brushed a kiss along her temple. *"Baushki-bau."* His voice was low and intimate, touching her nerve endings and sending little butterflies swirling in the pit of her stomach. "You worry far too much. This is my field of expertise. I don't walk into these situations blindly. We cannot leave this young man to his death."

She balled her fists. "For all you know he's already dead. Why would Prakenskii keep him alive? And they wouldn't stay in that barn. They've moved him. You know they have. They'll have a sniper waiting to kill you and Mason will be dead anyway."

"Actually, Abbey makes a very good point," Jonas agreed unexpectedly. "Why would they keep Mason alive? If they need a mule for anything, they have Chad. If Mason isn't a part of this, why not put a bullet in his head and be done with it?"

Hannah shivered and Carol made a small sound of dismay. Abigail glared at him. "You said that deliberately, Jonas Harrington. You wanted us to see a very vivid image of Mason with a bullet in his head. I see an image of Aleksandr or *you* lying on the ground dead."

Abigail was trembling and Aleksandr drew her into his arms and rocked her back and forth, murmuring soothing phrases in his own language to her. He tried not to be too happy over her concern for him. She was obviously distressed and rather than wanting to reassure her, his first reaction was elation that she cared enough to be worried about him. "I'm too mean to die," he said, nuzzling her ear. "You know that. And Jonas has my back. It isn't like we're going in there without checking things out first."

"I just don't like it, Sasha. Something stinks about the entire setup. I think you're getting too close to whatever it is they want to hide and this is a way to draw you out where they can get rid of you," Abbey insisted. "Does it make sense to you that Prakenskii would let her go? He *has* to move Mason. If Sylvia goes to the police—and how could he know she wouldn't?—the police would simply surround the barn and get a negotiator. He'd lose."

"Prakenskii doesn't lose."

"My point." She pounced on that. "He doesn't. They want you dead and he's finding ways to lure you out into the open where he can kill you."

"Maybe," Aleksandr mused, "but for me, it still doesn't add up. Prakenskii just isn't a man to play games. He'd be more likely to walk right up to the front door and shoot me than do something like this." He glanced at Jonas over Abigail's head. "I know him. This isn't his way of doing things."

"We'll be careful, Abbey," Jonas added. "Jackson will come along with us and you know what he's capable of with a rifle. I'll have him covering us."

"I'm g-going too," Hannah announced.

Jonas snorted. "Not a chance in hell, so don't even think about it."

Abigail pulled out of Aleksandr's arms. "Hannah's right. Prakenskii works with magic and the three of you can't possible combat that."

Hannah lifted her chin. "I can."

"I don't give a damn what you can do." Jonas pointed a finger at Hannah, his gaze a dark warning. "You either do it from here, up on the captain's walk, or you don't do anything at all. I'm not even going to argue about this. And if you do go up there, Hannah, you stay the hell back from the railing; you nearly fell over it the last time you collapsed."

He straightened and stalked toward the kitchen. "Sarah, I'm holding you responsible. You know damn well what we're walking into. I'll have Aleksandr and Jackson out there, that's it. Anyone else is an enemy."

"No one will leave the house," Sarah said. "We do our best work from a power source and this house holds tremendous power. We'll be up on the walk. You'll feel the wind on you and that will be us."

Aleksandr framed Abigail's face with his large hands and bent his head toward hers. "I won't be careless, Abbey, you know me better than that. When I come for you, be wearing that ring. I miss seeing it on your finger." He kissed her as tenderly as possible, trying to pour as much love into it as he could convey. "I'm not about to lose you again," he added, pressing small kisses from the corner of her mouth to her eyes.

"We'll go out the cliff-side door into the backyard," Jonas decided. "Just in case someone is watching the place. Keep Sylvia here. She's liable to try to get a gun and launch a rescue herself."

"Libby's with her," Sarah assured him.

Abigail walked with Aleksandr to the door, her fingers tangled with his. "You come back to me."

"I will."

There were no lights on in the kitchen and Jonas exited the house in darkness, sliding quickly to the cover of the shadows and waiting for Aleksandr to join him. They made their way through the thick brush to the waiting car. Jonas examined the area around the car carefully while Aleksandr checked all the high positions where a sniper might lie in wait. When they were certain they were in the clear, they slipped into the car and took off, Jonas using the radio to call his deputy, Jackson Deveau, a man who had served as a Ranger with him and, more importantly, a sniper with a deadly accurate aim.

"We don't want to be using a marked car," Jonas said. "Jackson will bring his. He knows the highway and his car can take the road fast if we need speed."

"They won't be there. They'll have moved him," Aleksandr said.

"Yeah, they'd be idiots not to, and I don't think they're that stupid. But we might pick up a few clues. Jackson is hell on wheels with tracking. He'll be able to read who was there and what was going on.

He'll also be able to see where Sylvia was and if it was possible for her to get away from Prakenskii." Jonas glanced at Aleksandr. "I take it this Prakensii is a badass."

A brief, humorless smile curved Aleksandr's mouth. "You could say that."

They met Jackson just north of Caspar and exchanged vehicles on one of the many back roads. "The road the barn is on is narrow and sweeps around in a big loop. There's only a couple of houses off of it, so if someone is waiting, the minute they see the headlights, they'll know we're coming," Jonas warned.

Jackson shook hands with Aleksandr briefly. "Drop me a distance out and let me work my way into position to cover you. I'll signal you when I'm secure and then drop Volstov a little closer so he can go through the grass to the barn."

"I'm the decoy," Jonas said. "Great."

"I've already gotten rid of the overhead lights and I'd advise driving without headlights," Jackson said.

Aleksandr watched the deputy's hands smooth over his rifle. It was a sniper's rifle and well kept. Earlier in the car, Jonas had told Aleksandr a little bit about his deputy. Jackson Deveau had served with Jonas as a Ranger and then gone on to do other things. Aleksandr was fairly certain those "other things" involved being dropped into "hot zones" and completing a lone mission before being extracted. Jackson Deveau didn't seem too far removed from Ilya Prakenskii, a man with his own code, lethal, loyal, and a good man to have on your side when going into battle.

Jonas grinned at his deputy. "If anything happens to me, move out of town. The Drakes will most likely turn you into some kind of really ugly toad."

"They'll give me a medal," Jackson muttered as the car slowed. He opened his door and rolled out onto the grass.

Aleksandr scooted over into position. Jonas kept the vehicle at a slow pace as they drove up the winding, narrow dirt road. Even so, Aleksandr hit the ground hard, the breath slamming out of him, his body jarred as he rolled into deeper grass. He lay a moment trying to catch his breath and assess his body for any damage. When he was certain there were no broken bones, he began to crawl through the vegetation toward the old rickety barn.

Jonas and Jackson had given him detailed information of the terrain and he knew there were several large areas that had once been garden beds. The weeds and wildflowers were thicker in those spots and he made his way to the first of them as quickly as possible. When he was certain he was well covered, he paused to get his bearings straight and listen to the night sounds.

The moon spilled light across the meadow. Several deer grazed a hundred yards to his left. Crickets sang to one another and frogs called out in a steady symphony. He had to move carefully not to spook the insects. The lack of sound was a dead giveaway to any accomplished sniper. He was very aware that Jackson Deveau was moving to higher ground and there wasn't a single change in the night noises. That told him more than anything else he needed to know about the deputy.

Aleksandr listened for sounds coming from the barn, but there were none. He moved a few inches at a time over the uneven ground, gaining feet, then yards. He knew Jonas had intended to park the car at the entrance to the dirt road, back behind some trees, and would hoof it in from the other direction.

An owl hooted once, the sound carrying easily and naturally across the meadow. Jackson had found high enough ground to cover them and had signaled an all clear. Aleksandr felt some of the tension ease out of his body. There were more eyes and ears in the night than his own. His brain told him Prakenskii was long gone, that he'd never stay in the area once Sylvia was gone, but still, the man had to know Aleksandr would take the bait. How could he not? How could he leave Mason Fredrickson to be killed without at least trying to save him?

Nothing about the entire setup made any sense to him and Aleksandr was a man who preferred logic. He was familiar with treachery and deceit. It never surprised him, but there had to be logic, even if it was twisted. Prakenskii was too well trained to make such an error, unless he was banking on the fact that Aleksandr preferred to work alone. It might not occur to him that Aleksandr would hook up with the local sheriff.

Aleksandr dug his elbows in the dirt and scooted closer to the barn. The building rose up in the night, boards old and cracked, paint chipped and peeling. The entire barn tilted as if it would slide to the ground on one side any moment. There was a rustling in the bushes close to the barn. Aleksandr froze, his breath catching in his lungs. A spot between his shoulder blades itched. He eased a knife out of his belt and waited.

The owl screeched out frustration and rage at missing prey. Aleksandr allowed his breath to leave his lungs slowly at the warning, careful not to make a single sound. Jackson was amazing with his bird cries, so close to the real thing, it had taken a moment to figure out that it hadn't been an owl. He waited, motionless, listening for another telltale rustle or whisper of movement.

A frog croaked somewhere to his left and almost immediately he heard a noise, the brush of something against wood inside the barn. Aleksandr levered himself another foot forward through the grass on his belly like a lizard. He was a big man and it wasn't easy to move without sound. He lay motionless again, sweating, waiting for the bite of a bullet in his back.

A frog croaked again, much closer this time. His tension eased a little more when he realized Jonas was approaching from the opposite side of the barn. He rolled toward the entrance. There was no door, just a burlap sack tacked over the gaping hole where it should have been. Moonlight spilled through the cracks in the ceiling, but left far too many shadows where someone could hide. There was that rustling again, this time sounding a little more frantic. Something large bumped against the back wall of the barn. There was a muffled swearing. Aleksandr didn't have animal noises to make to warn Jonas, so he had to hope the man was close enough to hear.

Aleksandr lay at the mouth of the barn, right beneath the burlap sack at the entrance, and studied the darker areas in the interior. He could see Mason Fredrickson, bound and gagged and thrashing to free himself almost directly ahead. It was a tempting sight. Get in, slash the man free, and get out. He smiled to himself. Surely Prakenskii had more respect for him. This was a juvenile plan. *It had drawn him there, so it had worked.* The thought came unbidden. He froze, his heart accelerating.

It was an old ploy. The simplest of traps. A basic game of cat and mouse. Movement caught the eye and he wasn't about to move. Jackson might be able to protect them outside the barn, but once inside, once he made his move to free Mason, Aleksandr was on his own. He lay in the entrance, belly down, breath barely moving through his lungs in complete silence, waiting. Time passed. Five minutes. Fifteen. A half an hour.

Insects rustled the leaves near his ear. The wind touched his face and he felt Abigail close to him. Why would Prakenskii go to so much trouble to bring him out to an old barn to rescue Mason Fredrickson? The question turned over and over in his mind with no concrete answer. But he waited, because in a game of cat and mouse the first one to move was dead.

In the far corner, up in the rafters, there was a rustle of clothing. "You tied him too tight, he isn't making enough noise." The voice was American.

"Shut up!" Aleksandr didn't recognize the Russian. It wasn't Prakenskii, but he knew where the killers were now.

A frog croaked just outside the far corner of the barn and relief swept through him. Jonas was fully aware of the men with guns trained on Fredrickson. They desperately needed a distraction.

Immediately, on the wings of that thought, came the wind, not the light touch of earlier, but a rush that brought with it the scent of the sea and carried the faint far-off chant of female voices. Almost at once came an answer. An eerie rush of wings, high-pitched pulsing sounds, filled the air. Aleksandr allowed his gaze to sweep upward and saw the night sky filled with bats. Wings pumped as the bats wheeled and dived and flowed in a spiraling circle toward the barn. The air was heavy with the migration as more bats arrived, dancing in the air, darting at insects as they flew toward the barn.

The frog croaked a friendly sort of greeting. It took a split second to register that the sound had come from *above* rather than on the ground. Jonas was in position on the sagging roof, directly over the two killers. From the edge of the tree line nearest the barn, the owl gave a soft inquiring hoot. Jackson had moved closer to them, abandoning his high position to give them more coverage for the rescue.

The bats swarmed into the barn, using every crack in the boards, the gaping hole in the roof, and the opening around and under the burlap sack. Aleksandr rolled into the barn with them, straight across the floor to Mason Fredrickson.

18

THE bats filled the barn with the sheer weight of numbers, going high into the rafters, wings beating against the two gunmen sitting up in the beams. Chad Kingman dropped his weapon and grabbed the rotten wood, swaying precariously as the small furry bodies hit his chest and face. The Russian fought off the onslaught of bats, striking out with his hands blindly to get them away from him. His arm slammed into Chad, knocking him off the beam onto the dirt floor below. Chad hit hard, the breath slamming out of his lungs.

Above them, Jonas leaned through a particularly large crack and shoved his gun hard against the Russian's neck. "Drop your weapon," he ordered. "This is the sheriff and you're under arrest."

Aleksandr used his knife to slice through the ropes binding Mason Fredrickson. The man had been tied for so long his arms and legs were leaden. He tried to move but could only glare at Chad. Aleksandr peeled the duct tape from his mouth in one smooth motion. Mason yelped, his gaze furious as he stared at his longtime friend.

Chad lunged for the gun that was only a few feet from where he lay. "I wouldn't." Jackson Deveau stood to one side of the door, his rifle trained on Chad. He stepped forward and kicked the gun out of the way, glancing toward Aleksandr, who had his arm back for the throw, his knife in position. "Not a smart move, Kingman."

Chad sat on the ground cursing as Jackson cuffed him and then carefully searched him for weapons while Jonas did the same with the Russian.

A small breeze blew through the barn, taking the bats outside into the open air and leaving the men to face one another. Aleksandr frowned, uncomfortable over the ease with which they'd retrieved Fredrickson. He didn't recognize the Russian, but when the man climbed down from the rafters, he was limping. Jonas examined the man's calf and found a huge bruise. "Looks bad. How'd you manage to do that?"

The man mumbled something unintelligible.

"I don't suppose a woman did that to you? Nailed you with her little shark stick?"

Aleksandr studied the Russian. "You must be Chernyshev."

The man looked startled and turned his face away. Jonas and Jackson hustled Chad and Chernyshev to the car in handcuffs.

"Wait!" Mason protested, his voice hoarse with distress. He looked at Aleksandr with desperation. "They shot a woman, my ex-wife, Sylvia Fredrickson. I heard her scream, I heard her pleading with Prakenskii. She sounded so scared and then there was a shot fired. They must know what happened to her."

Aleksandr patted the man's shoulder a little awkwardly. "She got away. She's at the Drake house. She went to them to get help for you."

For a moment tears glimmered in Mason's eyes but he blinked them away. "Are you sure she's all right? She's never liked the Drakes. I can't believe she'd go to them."

"I think nothing mattered to her but that you were rescued. She was certain they were going to kill you and the Drakes are powerful women. I think she thought they were your best chance for survival. She was very brave."

Mason ducked his head, but Aleksandr caught the dawning realization in his eyes. "Yeah, she was, wasn't she?"

Aleksandr helped Mason Fredrickson into a sitting position. "Did they harm you in any way?" He was still uneasy. Nothing about the incident seemed right to him.

"Chernyshev knocked me around a little bit. Chad stayed away from me." Mason licked his dry lips. "You don't have any water, do you? After the other Russian left, no one would give me a drink."

"Prakenskii?" Aleksandr kept his voice casual.

Mason nodded. "Yeah, that was his name. He pretty much ran everything. Chernyshev wanted to kill me right away. I went into the alley behind the gallery and they were out there with Chad. I thought they were shaking him down, so I went to help him.

"I heard Chad say he wanted a hundred thousand dollars for transporting the bomb. The next thing I know, Chernyshev slams a gun against my head and is going to kill me right there and then. Chad doesn't say anything but this guy Prakenskii steps out of nowhere and stops them. He says they can use me. Chernyshev started to argue with him, but not very much. I could see they were all afraid of him."

"Did Prakenskii hurt you?"

"No, he gave me water and food and when Chernyshev got pissed about something and walked over and kicked me, Prakenskii told him to do it again and see what happened. He said it really low, no inflection, but it scared the hell out of Chernyshev. He didn't touch me after that."

"Let's get you on your feet. Just hang on to me and let's see if your legs will work."

Mason gritted his teeth. "Man, it hurts like hell. It feels like a thousand bees stinging me."

Aleksandr helped him up, keeping a firm grip when Fredrickson staggered and broke out into a sweat. "Where did Prakenskii go?"

"I don't know. He told Chad and the Russian guy to wait here for you and then to meet him after they'd taken care of you."

"What *exactly* did he say?"

Jonas returned, and propped Mason up on his left side. "Can you walk?"

Aleksandr halted. "I really need to know what Prakenskii said. It's important." He met Jonas's gaze. "I think this is a stall. Keep us looking in one direction while they go in another. Prakenskii knew I'd never fall for this. With or without you, there was no way I'd be taken by rank amateurs. He sent us out here to get us out of the way. And that means they're bringing in the shipment tonight."

Fredrickson shook his head. "No way. They were going to use Chad to transport the bomb."

Jonas met Aleksandr's eyes and reached out to take Fredrickson's arm, walking him to the car where he could sit comfortably and wait for the deputies.

When he returned, Aleksandr cleared his throat. "I was afraid they might be trying to bring in a dirty bomb. It wouldn't have to be much larger than the size of a suitcase." He raked his fingers through his hair. "We have all sorts of rotten waste material scattered everywhere left over from the nuclear age. I could tell you stories of dumps you wouldn't even believe. Nikitin is probably heavily involved in the smuggling. It isn't my jurisdiction, but I've heard the rumors. He's very violent and it is a known fact that the uranium smugglers are very nasty."

He looked at Jonas. "It wasn't very long ago that the deputy minister issued a warning stating that dirty bombs and biological substances made of fissile material and radioactive isotopes would be the most likely weapons terrorists would try to obtain. He knew what he was talking about. We've had information for some time that terrorists were trying to acquire the materials. Our power stations and the nuclear and biological institutes are vulnerable in Russia, just as they are here in the United States. The deputy minister has been working to improve the security."

Jonas swore under his breath. "Why would they bring it here? Why not Florida or southern California?"

"Because no one would suspect this area and they had a viable route. It was just their bad luck that a fisherman noticed and sent the word to Interpol and we stepped up our investigation." Aleksandr let out his breath slowly. "They have to be rendezvousing with the freighter tonight. Cherynshev and Kingman are sacrificial pawns. Most likely, Prakenskii thought they'd be killed."

Jonas glanced at his watch. "The other deputies are here to transport the prisoners and we'll let them take Fredrickson as well. We'll want Jackson with us."

"Your coast guard is going to want to handle it. You'll have to notify them and give them a list of the names of the freighters we've been tracking," Aleksandr said. "If any of the freighters are in the area, that's your ship. The freighter will either drop to the fishing boat, or directly to the men using the speedboat." The moment the words escaped, his head jerked up.

Jonas flashed him a look of inquiry, but Aleksandr glanced toward the deputies and prisoners and shook his head.

Aleksandr waited impatiently while the sheriff and his deputy made the transfer of prisoners to another vehicle and notified the coast guard of their suspicions. He provided the names of several freighters known to Interpol as ones used by smugglers or terrorists that might be in the area. A second sheriff's car took Mason Fredrickson from them. Jonas told the driver to take Fredrickson to the Drakes. The man seemed more concerned to see his ex-wife than a doctor.

The moment they were alone in the car, Jonas turned to Aleksandr. "Why do you want the coast guard to intercept the drop without us? They'll never stop them."

"That's why. I think it's too late. There are too many names, too many places they can be out on the sea. Even with all the technology, how are they going to find them in time? When Abigail and I were checking caves, she told me about one that could be used to hide a speedboat. She specifically mentioned it was facing south and the coast guard wouldn't be able to see into it as they passed by. She said that the small beach could be reached by land, but a caretaker was vigorous in stopping people from using it. Apparently he recently met with an accident."

Jonas and Jackson shrugged, puzzled. "There are hundreds of little coves along this coastline."

"Somewhere near Elk?"

"She isn't talking about Cuffey's Cove, is she?" Jackson asked. "Quite a few campers use that. There wouldn't be any privacy."

"She mentioned Cuffey's Cove, but it wasn't that. It's a cove north of Elk and has no public access."

Jonas drummed his fingers on the steering wheel. "Wait a minute. I know what she's talking about." He glanced back at Jackson. "Do you remember a few years back when that gray whale washed up onshore?"

Jackson nodded. "People came out of the woodwork, hiking across private property, tearing up fences to get a look at it."

"It was a mess," Jonas agreed. "I'll bet that's the cove Abbey was referring to. The caretaker, with our help, ran them off. It's a beautiful piece of land, but private property. Abigail's right. They could easily hide a small Zodiac there." He pulled out a cell phone. "I'll double-check with Abbey and alert them to where we'll be going. If they're that worried about Prakenskii, I'll want them standing by to help us."

"Abigail's not telepathic," Aleksandr said. "How do they know when we need help?"

Jonas shrugged, a faint smile on his face. "With the Drakes, you just don't ask questions. I told you, you have to accept what you see and hear with them. And even if Abbey isn't telepathic, a couple of the others are."

"Great." Aleksandr sighed. "Let's just get to the cove. Talking about the Drakes gives me a headache."

Jonas laughed softly. "That's because they are a headache."

"Well, call them and get it over with."

"You're on the coast, Aleksandr. There are only a couple of places around here that a cell phone actually works."

Aleksandr admired the way Jonas drove along the highway, maneuvering the switchbacks and twists and turns as fast as it was safe to go. He didn't like relying on the coast guard to try to intercept the drop, but the truth was, he didn't believe they'd made the call in time. Prakenskii's delaying tactic had certainly worked. They had been forced to make a slow approach to the barn in order to assure safety. The entire plan had been conceived to burn up as much time as possible.

Jonas glanced at him in the rearview mirror. "Think out loud."

Aleksandr shrugged. "I have more questions than answers."

"Let's hear them."

"This still doesn't make any sense to me." Aleksandr laid his head back against the seat, trying to shut everything out of his mind but the puzzle. "Prakenskii deliberately sacrificed both Chad Kingman and Chernyshev. Why? Just to buy time? What if Sylvia hadn't gone to the police? What if she hadn't gone to the Drakes? Abbey says he's like they are, that he's capable of using magic. Is it possible that he planted the suggestion in Sylvia's mind to go to the Drakes? Was that how he was able to set up his ruse so successfully?"

Something nagged at the back of his mind and he suddenly leaned forward in his seat. "Why in the hell is Prakenskii working so hard to bring a dirty bomb into the United States? If the rumors are true, he despises terrorists. Nikitin deals with the terrorists, but he keeps Prakenskii around for personal protection. Everyone fears Prakenskii. Especially the terrorists. The word is, Nikitin keeps Prakenskii far away from them."

"He must be a valuable man for Nikitin to keep him," Jonas mused.

"Prakenskii has sources no one else can come close to. There isn't much going on he doesn't know about." As soon as he said the words aloud another thought that had been niggling at the back of his mind leapt to the forefront. "Is it possible he handed Kingman and Chernyshev to us? Gave them up?"

"Why would he do that?"

"I ran into him earlier at the Drakes. I thought he was there to kill Abigail or waiting for me to show up, but he denied it. And he denied killing Danilov. Prakenskii is a lot of things, but he isn't a liar."

Jonas snorted. "Believing a hit man isn't a liar is a good way to get yourself killed. Why would he tell you the truth? What other reason would he have for being at the Drakes other than to case the place and set up to kill you or one of the women?" He didn't like the idea of a killer lurking anywhere close to the Drake family and it showed in the snarl in his voice.

"Carol was taking pictures of the sisters at one point and she claimed there was a light in one of the windows. Suppose someone else, such as Leonid Ignatev, was planning on killing Abigail, and Prakenskii was looking out for her. It's something he would do."

"Why would Ignatev want to kill Abbey?" The suppressed anger was becoming something much stronger and much more lethal.

"In order for me to get Abigail out of Russia, out of harm's way, I had to take Ignatev down. He would have killed her. He had his men beating her to get her to give me up. I took out his interrogators and produced enough hard evidence against him to force him to run with a price on his head. He put out a contract on me and I'm certain he'll do his best to kill Abbey just to get to me."

"How do you plan to stop him?"

"You're the sheriff. I don't think discussing that with you is the best plan," Aleksandr said. "Especially since I really do plan on hitting you up for work when Abbey and I are married."

"Just make certain you get the job done," Jonas said.

"I don't leave loose ends." Aleksandr watched the coastline fly by as they drove swiftly along the highway. The ocean swells were large and powerful as they rushed toward the cliffs, capping white and sending spray high into the air as water hit rock formations.

"Why would Prakenskii protect Abigail?" Jackson asked.

It was one of the first sentences Aleksandr had heard him utter. He was obviously a man of few words. "That's a good question. I can't quite figure him out. We grew up and were trained together. He went one way and I went another. We've met a few times since and battled it out, both licking our wounds afterward."

"Would he protect you?" Jonas asked.

Aleksandr's first thought was to deny it, but who really knew what went on in the mind of Ilya Prakenskii? He often did the unexpected. There were always larger-than-life rumors about him. He was nearly a legend in some places in Russia, his name whispered rather than spoken aloud. "I don't know. Why would he? He shot me once and he cut me another time, put me out of commission for a couple of months."

"Is he good enough to wound you without seriously harming you?" Jonas asked.

"Depends on what you mean by seriously harming me. I wasn't exactly feeling wonderful after he shot me." But he had known Prakenskii had chosen not to kill him. Prakenskii just didn't miss. He hit exactly what he was aiming at every time. Had he been going for a kill, Aleksandr would have been dead. "He deliberately missed."

"And you deliberately missed him." Jackson made it a statement.

Aleksandr was uncomfortably aware of Jonas glancing at him in the rearview mirror. He didn't have answers they wanted. Something deep within him made him spare Prakenskii. Or maybe it was misplaced loyalty. Or possibly it was Prakenskii's magic. That was still a difficult fact for Aleksandr to swallow. Could Prakenskii have been manipulating him just as he was certain the man had manipulated Sylvia?

He swore. "I don't know. It just doesn't fit with everything I know about Prakenskii. I can't see him getting involved with terrorists. There are stories about him I know aren't true, but many are, and some worse than anything told. Nikitin sent him to meet a group of terrorists who were believed to be placing bombs along the railroad tracks. Bombing the trains is a tactic used to make a political point. That was in the early days when Nikitin didn't know Prakenskii very well and had no idea about his views on terrorists. All of the terrorists were armed, all were well trained and seasoned. I saw photographs of the scene afterward. They were all dead and they'd died hard. He walked away without a scratch."

"It's a wonder Nikitin didn't have him killed," Jonas said.

"I thought that at the time. I worried about him." Aleksandr rubbed the shadow on his jaw. He let out a slow breath, weighing how much he should say. Abigail trusted Jonas implicitly and it was obvious Jonas trusted Jackson. "I've heard a very soft rumble about an antiterrorism unit formed. Several countries are rumored to be participating. The information is collected in one clearinghouse"—he hesitated again—"much like Interpol, and once it is determined they have found a terrorist cell a hit team is sent in. The team members are totally anonymous; they go in quietly, get in and get out. They execute everyone on-site. My understanding is they are totally anonymous so that they can operate in safety, as the terrorists would certainly go after their families."

Jonas looked at him with flat, cold eyes. "How are they going to get information if they don't take at least one prisoner?"

Aleksandr shrugged, returning the expressionless gaze.

"Damn it. You know a hell of a lot more than you're willing to admit."

"I'm telling you there's a possibility this team exists and that Ilya Prakenskii is a part of it. When I saw those photographs, it occurred to me that Prakenskii would be a perfect recruit for such an international force."

There was a small silence. Jonas broke it first. "And it follows that if he were on that international force and was here, he'd be working undercover. That's where you're leading with all of this, isn't it? You've suspected for some time, but you don't know."

"No, I don't know. If I'm wrong and he's really Nikitin's muscle, I've wasted several opportunities to kill him."

"And if he is following a cell of terrorists and he's come here, then that means my county has a major problem." Jonas hit the steering wheel with the palm of his hand. "And if he's undercover, he handed me Chernyshev because he found out Chernyshev murdered Danilov. Chad Kingman was worthless to him."

"And he got us out of his way."

"Does he have backup?" Jackson asked.

"I doubt it. I've never known him to work with anyone. He wanted me to get Abbey out of the bar the night we went to the Caspar Inn. She challenged him to a game of truth or dare and he was very uncomfortable." Aleksandr peered out the window. "We must be getting close. We don't want them to see us if they have a guard."

"Don't worry. I know the area," Jonas said. "Let's say, just for the hell of it, that you're right and Prakenskii is on some hotshot international antiterrorist team that he can't admit to. He wouldn't be out at sea watching them make the drop, would he?"

"No, he wouldn't." Aleksandr's voice was grim. His gaze was already searching the high places above them. "He'll be sitting up somewhere above that cove with a scope and a rifle and he'll take them all out."

Jonas pulled the car into a tangle of overgrown brush on a small side road. "We walk from here."

"I'll go high," Jackson said. "You'll have to give me a few minutes to work my way into position, especially if I have to worry that he's out there."

"In my country, a knife blade is often coated with poison so a single cut, even a shallow one, will kill you." Even with the cover of the brush, Aleksandr crouched down and kept his voice low. "Prakenskii can attack with equal skill with either hand. I've seen few expert enough to go up against him in close fighting."

"I'm not hunting him," Jackson said. "I'm protecting you and Jonas."

"If you have to shoot, he'll see the flash and track it right back to you." Aleksandr didn't know how to shake the deputy up, to make him aware just how dangerous Prakenskii really was. Jackson's eyes were black, flat and cold and empty. There was no expression on his face and nothing the Interpol agent said seemed to alarm him. Aleksandr recognized the look all too well. When Aleksandr looked in the mirror, those same dead eyes stared back at him.

"Jackson knows what's he doing." Jonas handed him night glasses. "You might need these."

"Thanks."

"I'm going to hit them with the light when they're all well away from the boat," Jonas said, holding up a powerful floodlight. "Wait for me to identify myself and tell them they're under arrest."

"I have no problem with that."

"Let's go, then," Jonas said.

Jonas knew the terrain, so Aleksandr dropped back to allow him the lead. They stayed in the shadow of the foliage, keeping out of the moonlight as they made their way over the uneven ground to the fence. They went over the wire one at a time, keeping their actions slow and fluid, trying to blend with the moving shadows. The wind accompanied them, riffling the vegetation, keeping it in constant motion to help confuse the eye of any watcher.

Jonas crouched low as the ground began to swell, moving faster now to cover more terrain and get into position. Aleksandr split off and went left as they dropped down on the other side of the small hill. The cove came into view, nestled between two rising cliffs. Windswept cypress covered the tops of both cliffs, although one rocky shelf fingered out toward the sea, sheltering the cove from prying eyes. The entire area was wild with an explosion of flowers and shrubs and trees. Waves washed up onto the sandy, rock-strewn shore. Twisted pieces of driftwood lay scattered across the sand, taking on dark, malevolent shapes. The boom of the sea was loud and echoed through the small well-protected cove. White water sprayed high along the sides of the cliff.

Aleksandr hunkered down, crawling as close to the edge of cover as he could get. Two boulders crowed together just at the vegetation line and he used them to his advantage, lying flat behind them, the hole between them perfect to see through. He had a good view of the cove and the sea. The idea of Prakenskii lying in wait with a scope and rifle somewhere up above him gave him an all too familiar itch between his shoulder blades. He didn't move, didn't make the mistake of looking for more cover, but kept his eyes trained on the sea.

Minutes passed. Fifteen. Thirty. An hour. The night air was cold on his skin. He glanced again at his watch. He might be wrong. There was every chance that they were in the wrong cove. Or that it was the wrong night, that he'd completely misread the signs. He remained still and was grateful for Jonas's professionalism. The sheriff didn't make a sound.

The wind grew stronger, ruffling his hair and the grasses surrounding him. He heard a soft song, feminine voices riding on the sea breeze. The words were incomprehensible, but the notes slipped into his mind in warning. He slid his gun out with a slow, careful movement and eased it into the wide hole between the two rocks. He had a good angle on the beach and could cover almost all of the shore.

Aleksandr felt the wind touch his face, and he strained to see past the long plateaus of rock. The sound of an engine carried over the boom of the sea. He let his breath out slowly and slipped his fingers inside his shirt to warm them.

The Zodiac swept into sight, coming in fast, rolling over the waves and straight toward shore. Aleksandr lifted the night glasses to his face, focusing on the incoming boat. There were four men, two standing and two seated. He recognized three of the men with AK-47s nestled in their arms. They'd been sitting at Nikitin's table at the Caspar Inn. The fourth man was a stranger. He held what appeared to be a small suitcase. The driver took the boat right up onto the sand, riding a wave as far up the shore as possible. Two of the men jumped out and dragged the boat farther up onto the beach.

The others leapt clear and began hurrying toward the cover of the denser brush. Aleksandr kept his eye on the man with the suitcase. He was the last to get out of the boat and lagged behind the other three men, who now had the AKs up and ready for action as they fanned out and moved up the sand toward the wilder terrain. They were obviously protecting the man with the suitcase.

Aleksandr willed him to move away from the boat. Every few steps he halted and looked around, clearly wanting the others to reach the brush before he ventured too far from the safety of the boat. The three men were within feet of cover. Aleksandr swore to himself. Jonas was going to be forced to hit them with the light and the man with the suitcase was still too close to the Zodiac and could possibly escape.

The wind shifted slightly. He heard the catch in the voices of the women. Alarm. It was the only warning he had. The man with the suitcase sagged to the ground, lay sprawled only feet from the boat, the case beside him in the sand. Staring through the night glasses, Aleksandr saw the stain spreading out like a halo around his head.

Even as Jonas hit the other three men with the floodlight, temporarily blinding them, a second man went down and then the third without a sound. The remaining man threw himself to his right, but Aleksandr knew it was too late. Someone had to be using a Russian-made VSS Vintorez sniper rifle with a silencer and subsonic rounds. The range of subsonic rounds wasn't nearly as far as regular ammunition so if the sniper was Prakenskii, he had to be concealed on the finger of rock just above them.

The sniper had fired one, two, three, four rounds, just that fast. Squeezing the trigger, moving to the next target, and repeating the action. Four quick rounds and four lay dead in the sand. There were no flashes to give his position away. The sound carrying across the water wasn't that of a gun, but more like a soft rat-tat-tat that was nearly lost in the boom of the ocean and the shift of the wind. Aleksandr kept his glasses trained on the four men lying in the sand, but none of them moved at all. Four shots. Four kills.

Aleksandr could hear Jonas swearing a blue streak. "What the hell am I going to do with this mess now? Damn it." He raised his voice. "Damn it! You just can't do that kind of thing in the United States! I would have arrested the bastards. They've got the evidence on them. Now if I find anything to connect you with these kills, I'm going to have to charge your ass with murder."

Silence met the outburst. Jonas didn't move. He stayed away from the light, obviously waiting for a signal from Jackson. It was a long time coming. The deputy had to work his way around to the finger of rocks where the shots had come from. It occurred to Aleksandr that while they waited to ensure they were in the clear, they were giving Prakenskii time to get away. He had to make his way through the brush in silence, avoiding Jackson, avoiding leaving a trail, and make his getaway.

There would be no evidence. There was never evidence of Prakenskii's passing. Just the dead bodies left behind. Aleksandr was certain the shooter was the Russian, but he would be long gone and impossible to find. Even if Jonas got lucky and got his hands on the man, there would never be proof. They wouldn't find the rifle. It was probably already in the sea. There would be no residue, no sign of him. That was Prakenskii. The phantom, more legend than real.

The owl hooted. Once. Twice. Three times.

Jonas swore again. "Jackson can't find him. We have no idea if he's around so I'll go out and examine the bodies for signs of life. You stay out of sight and shoot the son of a bitch if he kills me."

The wind rushed in off the sea. Aleksandr felt the light touch of reassurance. "He's long gone." How the Drake sisters knew and could convey the information to him, he wasn't entirely certain, but he knew Prakenskii had melted away into the night.

Jonas came out of the brush cautiously. "You'd think one of the Drakes would be able to track him if he's really like they are. They always seem to know when there's trouble with each other." He made his way down to the first body. "I'd say he was dead. He shot him in the left eye. Each kill was made that way. This guy's good."

He raised his voice. "Jackson, we'll need to work the crime scene. You have a camera on you? We'll have to do it from a distance. I don't want to go anywhere near that bomb."

"In the car. Gloves too." Jackson was still above them. "There's no sign at all, Jonas. He's a ghost."

"What was he using?"

Aleksandr answered. "A Russian sniper rifle. Probably a VSS Vintorez SP-6 with a built-in silencer and subsonic cartridges. It was designed for special ops. The newer bullets can defeat most military-issue body armor, depending on the distance."

"That would be my guess as well," Jackson agreed.

"Is that what Prakenskii favors?" Jonas demanded. "This is going to be a damned headache to sort out. He should have left it the hell alone. We had it under control."

"Prakenskii doesn't favor any one weapon. And you have absolutely nothing on him and you won't either. If you haul him in to interrogate him, he'll have an ironclad alibi and it won't be with someone you don't trust. It will be someone like Aunt Carol. He probably plants the suggestion they've been together the entire time and the person will believe they have been." Aleksandr pushed himself into a sitting position, the gun still ready in his hands. "No wonder there are so many rumors about him."

"Before we do anything else, let's get a call in to the bomb squad and the FBI," Jonas said. He skirted driftwood and dead bodies to reach the fourth man, where he crouched down, taking care not to disturb the scene or get too close to the bomb. "We can let them handle it. I plan on having children someday. Radiation poisoning isn't my idea of fun."

Jonas glanced in Aleksandr's direction. "Do you recognize any of these men?"

"The three with the AKs worked for Nikitin. They were sitting at his table at the Caspar Inn. The fourth man, and I'm guessing here, is likely to belong to whatever terrorist group wanted the bomb brought in. He's the deliveryman. They were going to kill Kingman all along. Prakenskii gave him to us, figuring he had a fifty-fifty shot at making it with us and none with Nikitin."

Jonas had crouched down beside the suitcase. "Chernyshev could certainly identify Prakenskii."

"Not as our shooter," Aleksandr told him.

Jackson handed Jonas gloves and the camera he'd retrieved from the car. "I wouldn't count on Chernyshev identifying anyone. I just got off the radio. Dispatch said someone ran Tom's car off the road before he could reach Ukiah with the prisoners. The deputy's in the hospital but the two prisoners are dead. Both took a bullet in the throat."

Jonas swore again. "We don't have this many dead bodies in a year." He flashed Aleksandr a dark, suspicious look. "You don't seem too shocked."

"I can't say I am. Nikitin is known for his penchant for killing anyone who might betray him. Kingman and Chernyshev could identify him. It was a matter of time."

"You might have warned me. I could have lost a good deputy. As it is Tom is injured."

"I had no way of knowing Nikitin would strike so fast."

Jonas straightened up and moved around with care as he took pictures of each body from several angles. "It could have been Prakenskii."

"You know it wasn't." Aleksandr spread his arms out wide to include the entire cove. "This is Prakenskii's work. We've got the bomb and that's what counts."

"And I've got a bunch of dead bodies," Jonas groused. "We're going to be here all night securing the scene and most of the day tomorrow waiting for the feds."

"I'll get coffee," Jackson said.

19

ABIGAIL tightened her fingers around Aleksandr's and dragged him behind the large bread rack, ducking down in an effort to hide. The grocery store was fast filling up with early morning customers. "I thought we'd be safe," she hissed. "Who gets up this early?"

"Apparently everyone." He couldn't help but grin at her antics.

"You think it's funny now." Abigail glared at him. "You won't in another minute or two. I have to get to the cove today. I can't let the dolphins go another day or they'll head out to sea and I'll spend ninety percent of my time trying to find them."

Voices drifted back to them: "Inez, that can't be. I heard there were at least thirty bodies strewn around on the beach. The bomb exploded. We've all probably been exposed to radiation. Believe me, cancer is going to run rampant here in Sea Haven."

Abigail peered through the open bread shelves to see Clyde Darden clutch his wife tightly as he delivered his message of doom in a loud, carrying voice. Several residents gasped in alarm.

Behind the counter, Inez Nelson shook her head. "That's just silly, Clyde. Jonas was right there and he took care of everything. The bomb squad came and they handled it with no problem. The bomb certainly didn't explode. There were only four men killed, not thirty, and if you ask me, good riddance. They shouldn't have been bringing bombs into our country." She gave a little sniff and banged the cash register a little harder than necessary.

Clyde leaned over the counter as he picked up his two bags of groceries. "Frank Warner was involved. His gallery is closed and he was hauled off to jail. They took several paintings out of his place as evidence. Some hotshot Interpol agent was watching him all this time."

Abigail dug her thumb into Aleksandr's ribs. "That would be you," she whispered. "The hotshot."

"Is it true, Inez?" Gina Farley, the local preschool teacher, asked. "Was Frank really arrested? He was such a nice man."

"And so quiet," Mrs. Darden added.

"He had shifty eyes," Clyde said. "I always suspected him of being a spy."

"He's an art thief, not a spy," Inez corrected with a little sigh. "He had nothing to do with the bomb. Chad Kingman was involved in that, along with the Russians who were in town."

Clyde shook his head. "It's the cold war all over again. They've invaded and are spying on our coast. I told those young punks at the coast guard station they needed to be on the alert, but they didn't listen."

"We haven't been invaded," Inez corrected him again, a small, unusual bite in her voice. "Really, Clyde. We had an unfortunate incident and we lost a really great businessman. Frank Warner did a lot for our town. Please remember that when you start talking about him." She ducked her head, concentrating on ringing up the next customer.

"What's going to happen to him, Inez?" Gina asked.

"I don't know." Inez's voice was strangled. "I just don't know."

Abigail pressed her hand over her heart. "She really cares about him, Sasha. My heart hurts for her. I think I'll ask Libby to drop by and just ease her suffering a little."

Aleksandr leaned down to brush a kiss across her temple. "You hate to see anyone unhappy."

"That's not necessarily true," she demurred. "At least she's running the customers through fast. That means we might be able to get out of here without questions."

He twirled her ponytail around his finger. "You know we have to be careful, Abbey. You don't want to think about it, but that's how people die when they have someone like Ignatev after them. We have to be aware every minute."

"I know." She met his gaze. "No one has seen him and the police raided all the houses they rented. You know he had to have fled the area. It isn't as if he wouldn't stand out here." She lowered her voice even more. "Small towns are very gossipy. We know each other's business. Clyde Darden even keeps a pair of binoculars right next to his porch chair so he can watch all his neighbors. He claims he's bird watching."

"I don't want to know these things."

She rubbed her head against his arm. "You're such a baby. You should have seen your face when Sylvia Fredrickson hugged you after you brought Mason back. All this time I thought you had a poker face."

Aleksandr caught her left hand to him and stroked her bare finger. "You are still not wearing my ring."

His eyes darkened into a midnight blue, the gathering of a large storm. Abigail felt her heart jump and the race of excitement that always came when he turned a little wild on her.

His grip tightened on her hand as he brought her fingers to his mouth and bit gently. "I'm not happy about it. And don't give me excuses. I can see it in your eyes. You were supposed to go home and put it straight on your finger."

She tilted her head. "Was I? I thought the man put it on the woman's finger."

He frowned at her. "I put it on once. You took it off."

Inez raised her voice. "The two of you can quit skulking behind the bread rack and come out now. It's safe for the moment."

Abigail would have charged to freedom, but Aleksandr held her back, leaned close, and whispered against her ear, "You may have gotten a reprieve, but it is a very short one."

She made a face at him and hurried over to Inez. "How are you?" Deliberately she touched the older woman's hand. She wasn't Libby with her miraculous healing skills, but she could at least ease Inez's depression in a small way.

"Busy." Inez attempted a small smile. "Scandals are always good for business."

"I'm sorry about Frank, Inez. I know you two were very good friends."

Inez lifted her chin. "We're still very good friends. I'm going to help him all I can and if possible, keep his gallery open. Most of his business was legitimate. Unfortunately I think his love of art and his need to have it overcame his good sense. He needed to own the paintings, even if he never could share them. And to finance his need, he sold paintings to other collectors like himself." She sighed. "I think it's an addiction, much like gambling or drugs." She met Abigail's gaze for the first time. "He didn't have anything at all to do with bringing that bomb into our country. He would *never* do something like that."

Aleksandr refrained from reminding Inez that Frank Warner was responsible for opening a smuggling route that enabled the terrorists to take advantage of the vulnerability. The woman obviously was very loyal to her friend and was tolerant of any of his mistakes. She was in distress and he didn't want to add to it, but Frank Warner would certainly have been responsible had the bomb been exploded in a crowded area.

"Has Aunt Carol been in to see you?" Abigail asked.

"Yes, she was the one who told me about Frank being arrested. She didn't want me to hear it on the news." Inez swallowed hard and gave a small sniff she covered quickly by ringing up their items. "I really appreciated her coming by personally."

"Aunt Carol has always been very thoughtful. We're heading out to Sea Lion Cove. I've been taking care of one of the dolphins, although I think he's much better."

"How are the wedding plans coming?"

"We haven't had much of a chance to really work on them, but we're going to pull it together," Abbey assured her.

"I've heard rumors that you are engaged." Inez looked pointedly at Abbey's finger and then at Aleksandr. "It is customary to give a woman a ring if you've asked her to marry you."

"I did give her a ring," Aleksandr said and brought Abigail's fingers to his mouth.

She snatched her hand away and put it behind her back as she glared at him. "You have an oral fixation." She turned back to Inez with a smile. "I think we have everything, Inez. Maybe a couple of your famous mochas to keep us warm while we're at the cove?"

Inez smiled for the first time since they'd entered the store. "You Drakes with your men." She shook her head as she began to make the mochas for them. "Carol's giving Reginald a terrible time. She has the poor man dancing through hoops for her. He's shaved and cut his hair and is wearing very nice clothes."

"Did you know they were engaged at one time?" Abigail asked over the sound of the espresso machine.

"Of course. It was a dreadful scandal at the time. Reginald was so heartbroken and over time, he withdrew so much he wouldn't allow us to remain close friends. He became very solitary. I told Carol to be very careful with his heart this time. I don't think he could take rejection a second time from her."

"I had no idea," Abigail said. She took the two mochas as Aleksandr picked up the small bag of groceries. "Thanks, Inez. I'll see you soon."

Aleksandr put his hand on Abigail's shoulder before she could walk out the front of the store. "Inez, would you mind if we went out the back?"

The older woman looked up alertly, but nodded without asking questions.

"Do you really think this is necessary?" Abigail asked as she followed him through the store toward the back.

"Until we catch Ignatev, yes, it's necessary. Jonas may think he's gone, but I know better. I have no doubt this recent turn of events not only cost him a great deal of money, but got him in trouble with his terrorists friends, and he'll want vengeance. I've interfered with his plans too many times for him to just let this go. And unlike Nikitin, who's probably long gone now, Ignatev likes to do his own killing when he can."

Abigail shivered as she watched him put their purchases on the back seat of the car. "At least we'll be safe in the cove."

He shook his head. "The harbor's dangerous, too many buildings and boats. We're vulnerable there. We should be safer in the cove. If we're in the middle of it, a shooter, even a marksman, would have trouble hitting us from that distance."

"Is he a marksman like Jackson?"

"Abigail . . ."

She yanked open the driver door. "What do you want me to do? Stay in the house all the time?" He barely had his seat belt on before she started the car and turned onto the main highway.

"Yes, if you want the truth. It would be safer until I find him."

"I'm sure it would, but it won't help my dolphin and I doubt if you'd be hiding in the house with me. You'd be running around trying to draw him away from me like some hero in a novel."

He leaned over to nibble on her neck. "I am your hero."

She pushed at him, but it was halfhearted. "You're going to make us wreck." She fended him off for the rest of the short drive to the harbor and was laughing by the time she parked the car.

As they loaded the food and drinks and Abigail's equipment into the boat, she realized he was shielding her body with his own. "Are you going to keep this up the entire time we're out at sea?"

"No. Just when we're in the harbor."

Abigail shook her head over his stubbornness. It was impossible to argue with him when he was set on something so she just stowed her gear and took the boat slowly out of the harbor, ignoring the way he hovered over her. Once they were out in open sea, he relaxed and leaned back, drinking his mocha and staring at their surroundings through his dark glasses. She felt the familiar peace of the ocean began to steal into her and hoped it was affecting him the same way.

"So how soon can we get married in your country?"

Abigail dropped her mocha. He snatched the cup off the floor of the boat before the liquid leaked through the lid. "That's not funny, Sasha."

"I wasn't being funny. I'm very serious. I'm not going to take any chances this time around. Your sisters are planning this elaborate wedding that looks as if it's going to take place a year from now and I don't want to wait that long."

Her eyebrow shot up. "Really? How long do you want to wait?"

"Not at all. Do we have to have a huge wedding? Can't we get married quietly and skip all the fuss?"

She increased the speed so the boat bumped rather viciously over a couple of waves and shot his mocha over his thighs. "Fuss? You think a wedding ceremony is fuss?"

He poured the rest of the drink into the sea and crumpled the cup, shoving it into a small bucket. "I think the only thing that matters is making you officially my wife. And you're damned lucky that coffee had cooled off."

She tried to look innocent but a slow smile tugged at her mouth until she was laughing. "You think that when I'm married to you, you'll have more control over me, don't you?" Her eyes sparkled at him. "Why on earth would you think that?"

He stretched his legs out in front of him and stared at her from behind his dark glasses, keeping his face expressionless. It would be impossible for her to miss the hard bulge in his jeans or the way his hand brushed suggestively over it.

Abigail tossed her head, her eyes dancing. Sunlight gleamed in her red hair and the wind pressed her clothes lovingly against her body as she drove the boat over the water. She was so sexy his body ached just looking at her. When she was teasing him, laughing the way she was, when the warmth in her was pouring over him, she was irresistible.

"I don't think so," she warned, but her breath caught in her throat and her gaze slid with evident interest over his groin. "Don't you get all amorous on me. I'm *working*. The only reason I brought you along was because you wanted to see what I do."

"I want to swim with your dolphins," he corrected as she slowed the boat and guided it into the middle of the cove. "You promised me the adventure of a lifetime. For me, that includes sex. Not just *any* sex. Wild, out-of-control sex."

She laughed again, just as he knew she would. He loved the way she threw her head back, exposing the beautiful line of her throat. In the sun she seemed to glow. At times, like now, he could barely conceive of his luck, that he could be with her. That she was willing to give herself to him. That she loved his company as much as he loved hers.

The sound of her laughter played over his skin like a caress. He felt her touch on his body, *inside,* deep, where he knew he could never get her out. He would never tire of talking to her. And he would never tire of making love to her.

"Not here!" Abigail shook her head adamantly. "I don't care if

you're wearing dark glasses or not, I know that look in your eye." She held up a warning finger. "You are not going to touch me. I guarantee my sisters are out on the captain's walk right this minute watching over us. You've got them so worried about me that they haven't let me go anywhere by myself since you arrested Frank and we discovered Nikitin and Ignatev were missing. I haven't had a moment's peace."

"Neither have I." He stood up and reached for her, pulling her against his body, fitting her smaller frame tight up against his, his hand under her chin. "I at least get to kiss you."

Abigail opened her mouth to protest. There was no such thing as just kissing with Aleksandr. He would set her body on fire and she would lose all control. She would forget that they were standing in her boat in the middle of the cove and that her sisters could see every move they made. She'd forget everything but the mastery of his mouth, his taste and scent, the need that rose up like a craving.

He cradled her head in his hand with exquisite gentleness and lowered his lips very slowly toward hers. His hands were tender, intimate, and loving as he held her. His lips brushed hers, a slow sweep, back and forth, a touch only.

Abigail felt the tug of his teeth on her lower lip, the glide of his tongue on the seam of her mouth, the soft leisurely kisses at the corner of her mouth. He seemed to be everywhere, driving her mad with longing, yet never quite settling his mouth over hers.

She caught his face in her hands to still it, rising up on her toes until she could take control, capturing his lips with hers, her tongue sweeping into the dark, velvet recesses. She closed her eyes and savored his taste. He moved, a subtle shift that brought her more completely against him, aligning their bodies as he took control of the kiss, deepening it, enfolding her into his arms.

The wind carried feminine laughter like strains of music fluttering around them. Aleksandr heard the sounds drifting around them, teasing at his ears, the wind touching his face and brushing his shoulders. He lifted his head. "I don't suppose teasing us will make your sisters so weak that they'll have to stop watching us, will it?"

"Not a chance." Abigail brushed another kiss over his tempting mouth. "But we have company anyway. Look." She pointed toward the mouth of the cove.

For a moment the sun sparkled over the water so he didn't see anything even with his dark glasses in place. Then he saw them, the dolphins rocketing beneath the water, mere blurs of mottled shadows as they sped toward the boat. They were only feet apart and swimming in formation, curving first one way and then the other at the same precise moment. His heart leapt. He peered over the side of the boat, gripping the rails.

"They're beautiful."

"Hurry. Let's get ready," Abigail advised. "They won't stay long."

Aleksandr went down into the small cabin and donned his wet suit. He'd heard Abigail tell stories of her dives with dolphins, but he'd never had the experience of actually swimming with them himself. Just seeing them in the water, so many, leaping and spinning, joyful in their exuberance, was an adrenaline rush. He couldn't wait to get into the water. He shared a long, slow smile of anticipation with Abigail. She was obviously pleased by his reaction.

"Remember everything I told you about swimming with them, Sasha. Never, and I mean *never*, approach a dolphin broadside or at a right angle. You have to let them approach you and keep an oblique angle. Be smooth about it, nothing sharp. Head butts are very aggressive behavior, so any headfirst approach toward them is a threat."

"I've got it. And I won't give in to the temptation of touching them," he added before she could repeat the warning.

They'd discussed possibly swimming with dolphins, but he hadn't really considered how it would feel to be surrounded by the creatures. "You're giving me an incredible gift few people ever receive in their lifetime."

She grinned at him, her eyes sparkling. "We're *working*; just remember that so you can tell me your observations when we come back to the surface."

He slipped into the water, exhilarated by the wild dolphins zooming through the blue water, flashing by so fast he could barely make out anything but a blur. They sliced through the sea at tremendous speeds, making him feel bulky and awkward. Abigail joined him, a large video recorder in her hands, and swam into the midst of nearly a dozen dolphins.

Up so close, Aleksandr could see how big the beautiful creatures were, weighing close to or over a thousand pounds. They were strong and powerful and looked threatening beside Abigail's more fragile body. His heart accelerated. He had never really considered that she might be in danger from the dolphins. Sharks maybe, but not the dolphins. Why had he always considered them joyful, fun creatures? He'd heard her stories, knew orcas were really a genus of the dolphin family. He swam toward Abigail, intending to signal to her to rise to the surface, but one of the larger dolphins swam past him, coming in at an oblique side angle, which Abigail had stressed continually was the proper way to swim with dolphins.

The dolphin nearest Aleksandr seemed to be issuing an invitation. It dove down, a slow performance rather than the earlier, much more threatening fast speed, and came up below him so they were belly to belly. He glanced to his right and another dolphin had joined them. A third approached from his left. He swam in a large loop, amazed at how close they were to him and to each other. The dolphins matched his speed as he curved around. He could see their round, dark eyes, intelligence plain as they watched him.

Aleksandr glanced toward Abigail. She was following one dolphin, obviously recording his every move with her video camera while others surrounded her, swimming in long sinuous circles. The dolphins seemed much more intimate with her, touching and vocalizing, always approaching in slow slanting angles, occasionally emitting what she had referred to as a "click train." The dolphins, rather than feeling threatening as he had first perceived them, now seemed playful and social; curious, intelligent creatures studying him as much as he was observing them.

Elation filled him as the dolphins swirled around him and Abigail, keeping the two humans in their group as if they were accepted members. Abigail was focused on her filming, leading a long curving circle while Aleksandr deliberately changed directions to see if his contingent would follow him. They did and the two trails of dolphins moved in slow opposite circles.

Abigail jerked her thumb toward the surface. He shook his head, unwilling to leave the amazing creatures. She pointed to her watch and when he glanced at his own, he was startled to find that, although the strange ballet with the dolphins seemed to have lasted only a few short minutes, in truth, it was far longer than he realized. Several of the dolphins were breaking their formation and beginning the ascent. He nodded his agreement to Abigail.

Humans and dolphins rose together to the surface. Aleksandr nearly leapt out of the water, unable to stop grinning. He caught Abigail around the waist and kissed her, leaning in over the top of her video recorder. "That was—indescribable!" He put his hand over his heart. "Thank you, *lyubof maya*. What an incredible feeling!" He spun around to watch as the dolphins took a breath and dove deep, one after another, two sliding in close to Abigail as if inviting her for another round of dancing.

Abigail swam to the boat and started to muscle her camera onto the deck. Aleksandr took it from her and set it carefully aside. "Are we through?" There was disappointment welling, but it couldn't stop the excitement of the experience or the grin on his face.

"The indication was, they were heading out to sea, but sometimes when I swim to the boat, they come back. Particularly Kiwi and Boscoe." She shoved her goggles onto her head and threw her head back, laughing with joy.

"Which ones are Kiwi and Boscoe?" He wanted to drag her to him and kiss her until neither of them could breathe. She was beautiful. The day was beautiful.

"They're two of the largest males. Kiwi was the dolphin that was injured and he's used to me handling him. That's what I was doing that day in the cove when we were shot at." She wiped droplets of water from her face. "I checked him the other day and he's fine again."

"What are those scars on some of them?" He was scanning the water, hoping for another encounter.

"Those are called rakes. The distinctive scars actually help us identify individuals. When dolphins are aggressive with one another they 'jaw,' or bite without grinding down, and they leave a rake mark. Almost all of the dolphins have them. The less serious rakes will heal in time and disappear, but many times the injury is deep enough to cause a permanent scar."

"Let's go back down and see if any of them will come back," Aleksandr suggested. He was reluctant to leave the cove when he might never get such a chance again.

She laughed softly and touched his cheek. "I'm so pleased you love my world. Just don't be disappointed if they're already gone."

"Nothing can make me disappointed. That was truly wonderful."

They dove together, seeking the darker depths, hoping for another encounter. Abigail hung back and let Aleksandr take the lead. She wanted to cry she was so happy. She'd never seen that particular expression on his face, as if she'd given him a gift beyond measure. He had given her one by embracing her world with the same love and excitement and joy she felt every time she encountered the wild dolphins.

As she swam behind Aleksandr, the water around her unexpectedly erupted, churning and bubbling, coming up from the ocean floor like a great geyser. The water boiled into a frenzy of white froth, cutting off her vision of Aleksandr for a few seconds, but the bubbles were icy cold, as if she'd entered an underwater stream that rose upward. She knew immediately her sisters were warning her of impending danger.

Abigail swam out of the bubbles, using fast hard kicks to fight her way through the water toward Aleksandr. To her horror a darker shadow rose up out of the kelp bed, falling in behind Aleksandr, gliding through the water straight at him. If she could have screamed a warning to Aleksandr, she would have, but he was too far ahead of her and they were underwater. She could only watch in horror, her heart in her mouth, as the diver lifted a speargun.

The warning bubbles burst around Aleksandr just as the spear was triggered. Aleksandr jerked to a halt, half turning back toward Abigail as the cold froth enveloped him in warning. The spear sliced through the water and slammed through the back of his shoulder, driving him forward. The white froth around him ruptured into a volcano of red. Pain and fear for Abigail mixed together, as Aleksandr recognized Leonid Ignatev.

With sure, powerful strokes, Abigail closed the distance between her and Ignatev. She could see him fitting another spear into his gun with calm precision, his attention centered on Aleksandr.

As if he knew she was no threat to him.

Her heart thudded in alarm. She whirled around just as the blade of a knife slid past her. A second diver plowed into her. She caught his wrist with both hands and brought up her foot, kicking with all her strength at her assailant's groin. He doubled over and the momentum carried her backward, giving her time to reach for the knife in her belt. She went around him, slicing at his air hoses and pushing off of him to put distance between them as he swung around.

The man came at her again, his face twisted with determination. Fish, thousands of them in a tight school, swam between them, another barrier thrown up by her sisters to protect her as the man slashed wildly with his knife. Abigail's assailant was running out of air and he was forced to begin his ascent to the surface. She fought her way through the screen of fish toward Ignatev, the knife clutched in her hand.

Through a haze of pain, Aleksandr used his legs, kicking hard and fast in an effort to rush Ignatev. The sharp point of the spearhead had gone completely through his muscle and stuck out the front of his shoulder. His arm was useless and it was awkward trying to swim, but he kept using his legs, kicking powerfully as he tried to reach Ignatev before the man could trigger a second spear.

Ignatev settled to the bottom of the cove in the middle of the kelp bed, taking his time with his aim. He knew Aleksandr had no hope of reaching him and there was a satisfying red stain growing in an ever-widening circle around the wounded man. As he raised the speargun, the ground buckled, shook, rippled in a series of small quakes that threw Ignatev to his knees. Sound carried through the water. Feminine voices rose in a melodic chant, the words foreign, but relentless, the volume rising and falling with the swell of the water. Each time Ignatev attempted to take aim, the ground rolled and heaved, throwing him forward onto his chest. He gripped the spear hard, silently cursing as the kelp tangled around his ankles and legs.

Aleksandr clawed his way through the kelp to try to reach Ignatev. Abigail was nearly on the man and, to his horror, Aleksandr could see Ignatev turning toward her. Ignatev was a big, strong man and he was skilled at killing. Aleksandr's arm lay leaden at his side, refusing to help propel him through the water. The kelp hampered his movements further. He called up every reserve of strength and determination he possessed, throwing himself forward to reach Ignatev.

Ignatev launched himself at Abigail, slamming into her as she reached for him, striking toward her head with his fist, the speargun still clenched tightly. She pulled her head back just in time and flicked her wrist over, slicing his arm with the blade of her knife. He whirled around, firing at Aleksandr, timing it just as his enemy was nearly on him. The spear caught Aleksandr low in the side, slicing through skin and muscle and bone, driving him back.

Abigail attacked again, coming in low and mean with her knife, catching Ignatev around the neck with her arm and slamming the small blade into his belly with as much force as she could muster.

He caught her wrist and tore the knife from her hand, stabbing at her several times as she tried to backpedal. The blade was small and the wounds were shallow, but Abigail felt the sting of each and knew she had very little time. As Ignatev loomed over her, arm raised, Aleksandr caught him from behind, spinning the man around and driving forward with all of his weight and strength, embedding the spearhead that had torn through his own shoulder, deep into Ignatev's throat.

There was one moment of shock, as if the ocean itself had ceased all movement. Abigail saw Aleksandr reach for her and then his arm dropped and the two bodies, held together by the spear, rolled to the ocean bottom.

Libby! Help me! Oh, God, Libby, I need you! Abigail screamed and screamed over and over in her mind for her sister. Raw pain clawed at her throat and belly as she tore the two bodies apart and hooked her arms under Aleksandr's shoulders. She was not telepathic, but her sisters were connected. They knew. They were aware. She began to drag Aleksandr through the water, rising toward the surface as she did so. It was impossible to fight the pull of the sea, drag his weight, and hold his regulator in place. It kept slipping out no matter how many times she tried to keep it in his mouth. She was closer to the shore than to the boat and in any case it didn't matter. He was bleeding out in spite of the cold water. And he was drowning, his lungs filling with water as she dragged his unconscious body to the beach.

Her sisters poured their strength into her, giving her aid even over the distance, all the while attempting to control the sea creatures scenting the blood in the water. It was a long battle, fighting the swells and trying to ride the waves in with Aleksandr in tow.

Exhausted, terrified of losing Aleksandr, Abigail remembered, too late, the second man. The one who had gotten to the surface and was lying in wait. Her heart jumped, then began to pound out an alarm.

She found her feet, staggering as she dragged Aleksandr's dead weight to the wet sand. The man waited for her in complete confidence, a small, infuriating smile on his face. He watched her fight to get the body to higher ground. She dropped to her knees, fighting for breath, throwing off her mask and tearing off Aleksandr's, and placing both hands over his wounds. It was impossible to stem the flow of blood.

She put her lips against Aleksandr's ear. "Don't you leave me." She began CPR, willing him to breathe again, willing him to cough and get the seawater out of his lungs.

The man took a step toward her, drawing her attention. She glanced up to see him hold up a wicked-looking knife. He smiled as he took a second step toward her. The bullet hit before she heard the shot. It tore through the man's left eye, snapping his head back so that he crumpled like a rag doll.

Abigail put her head down on Aleksandr's chest briefly, then looked around her. "Prakenskii! Hurry up. He's dying. I can't heal him. My sisters are as exhausted as I am. I know you're there."

The wind touched her face. Her sisters. Always with her, as afraid for Aleksandr as she. "Please." She whispered it. "Please." She called it out as loud as she could, tears clogging her throat.

A single voice rose on the wings of the wind. Soft. Melodic. Alluring. Joley's voice was incredibly beautiful, a smoky blend of sensual persuasion and emotional outpouring. Her spell singing was mesmerizing and irresistible.

Prakenskii came out from behind the rocks, his gun already broken down. He sent it spinning out into the depths of the cove as he crossed the sand to Abigail's side. "It has to be bad for your sister to give me the path to trace her magic. Let me see."

"You have to help him." Abigail wiped at the tears streaming down her face. Her sisters' exhaustion weighed just as heavily on her as it did on them. She was drained of her physical strength. "I can't save him, but you can."

"If I do, I won't have the strength to get away from the police." Prakenskii should have been walking the other way fast, but instead he crouched down beside Aleksandr. "I tried to warn him. I did everything I could think of to keep him out of this. He's a stubborn son of a bitch."

"I know you can save him. I'll help. My sisters will help. And we'll throw up a cloak of protection between you and the police so you can slip away." She squared her shoulders. "I know you care about him. Save his life."

"You'll owe me. All of you will owe me. When I come back asking, I'll expect you to aid me."

Abigail nodded, unsure if she was making a deal with the devil, but uncaring. All that mattered was that Aleksandr live.

20

ALEKSANDR heard Abigail's voice calling to him. The door slammed downstairs. She called out a second time. He loved the sound of her voice calling out his name. There was such a note of eagerness, of joy, that warmed him.

There was always that moment on waking when he still believed he was in Russia, or somewhere in a bleak hotel, alone, without her. He still had nightmares of Abigail being slapped around and worse in Ignatev's interrogation room and he woke with sweat pouring out of him and her name echoing through the room.

He pressed his hand to his heart and stared out over the railing of the balcony to her beloved ocean. He had always been at home in the city with the crush of people, its strange beauty of light and buildings and the underbelly of deceit and crime. Her ocean soothed him and brought him peace. He suspected it was because he couldn't separate her love and need of the ocean, such an integral part of her personality, from Abigail.

"Where are you, Sasha?" There was a breathy catch in her voice.

He smiled at the note, that small sign of caring. "Out here, on the deck." She had moved in with him to take care of him once he was allowed out of the hospital and, although he was renting the beach house on a very temporary basis, Abigail made it feel like a home.

She raced through the open sliding glass door to his side. "You aren't supposed to be wandering around." She tried to sound severe but couldn't hide her relief at finding him settled in a chair.

"I wanted to look at the ocean." He laced his fingers through hers and brought her hand to his mouth to kiss the ring there. "I think the sound puts me to sleep. I dozed off like a two-year-old."

"You'll get your strength back. I know it's difficult for you to be patient. Libby says you're gaining ground every day."

"What about you?" He pushed her tank top up to examine the raw scars on her stomach. "What does she say about you?"

Abigail leaned over to brush a kiss over his lips. "I'm fine. I told you I was perfectly fine. The stab wounds were shallow. I can have all the babies you want us to have. All two of them."

"At least seven. Elle's little girls have to have someone to play with." His hands caught at her waist and drew her forward so he could press small kisses against each shiny purplish mark marring her skin. "When I saw him going for you, I swear, Abbey, I never thought I could feel such rage or such fear." It had given him the necessary strength to slam his mortally wounded body so hard into Ignatev's, allowing him to kill the man. "I still don't know how you managed to get me out of the ocean."

"I wasn't going to lose you again." She said it matter-of-factly, cradling his head in her arms while he pressed another kiss into her intriguing belly button.

His grip tightened on her and he shifted her until she was standing wedged between his thighs. "Did Prakenskii really save my life?"

"You've asked me that three times. Without his help, you would have died right there. He shot the second man to keep him off of me and then he worked on you. He has all the gifts, no doubt about it, just as Elle does. He carries all the genetic code necessary to pass on each of the gifts to another generation. I wish we knew more about his background." She stepped closer to him, leaning into him because his tongue was doing a little dance along her belly button, teasing at the small gemstone there and making a foray lower.

Aleksandr unzipped her slacks, sliding them over the curve of her hip, down her thighs to her calves. She obligingly stepped out of her shoes and kicked the slacks aside. "Take off your top."

Abigail didn't hesitate, drawing the clingy material over her head and letting it drop to the deck.

"Let your hair down."

"You're definitely feeling stronger. You're turning bossy on me." She dragged the clip from her hair, allowing the mass of red hair to tumble free to her waist.

"I don't have much to do but think about you while I'm here all alone."

Abigail glanced at the tray beside the chair. "Aunt Carol was here."

"With her Reginald. They stayed a couple of hours. He's an interesting man."

She eyed the basket of fruit beside his chair. "Hannah stopped by, too, didn't she? And the magazines are from Joley. Kate must have brought the collection of books. I know Libby checked on you."

He smiled as his hands slid over her bare skin, shaping her hips. "Sarah and Damon stopped in as well. And Jonas." His smile widened to a boyish grin. "Inez and the Red Hat ladies came by and they left dinner in the fridge. They said just to heat it."

"When did you have time to think about me?" She shook back her hair, knowing he loved the feel and look of it.

"Every damn minute. And it was hell hiding my hard-on from everyone. I had to have a lap blanket. I dreamt of you, just like this, standing in front of me with your hair glowing like a halo in the sun. You are so damn beautiful."

"I think you're delirious. Maybe too much sun." But she couldn't help the lick of excitement and pleasure curling through her.

"You don't see yourself at all the way I see you." He leaned back in his chair and feasted his gaze on her. With the sun behind her, she looked more beautiful than ever. "I love you more than I can ever express, Abbey. Why is it I'm always feeling like you're slipping through my fingers and I can't quite catch you?"

"I have no idea." She perched on the edge of the hot tub in her black thong and bra, her skin pale looking rose petal soft. "You might remove the lap blanket so I can see what I'm getting myself into." Her shapely leg swung back and forth. "I dragged you out of the ocean and made a bargain with the devil to save your life. What more do you need me to do to show you I'm not going anywhere?"

"I'm not certain Prakenskii actually qualifies as a devil." Aleksandr threw off the blanket, revealing his nudity without a hint of modesty. "Jonas was very suspicious that you helped Ilya escape. He told me the footprints led into the sea, but it looked more like a setup than reality. Jonas questioned me again about it. Fortunately I was unconscious when Prakenskii was there, so I didn't have to lie."

"I didn't lie to Jonas," Abigail said, her gaze growing hotter as it dropped from his bandaged torso to his full groin. "I hope you kept that blanket over you when all your visitors were fussing over you."

"You told him Prakenskii was long gone, that he saved your life and then mine."

"Which was the absolute truth." She dropped to her knees in front of him. "I love the way you miss me, Sasha." She cupped his aching sac in her palm, fingers caressing the base of his shaft. "You always make me feel beautiful."

"You are beautiful."

"And that you need me desperately."

"I do need you desperately." He closed his eyes at the sheer pleasure coursing through his body at her touch. She had magic fingers. A magic mouth and body. And when she was touching him the way she was now, she made him feel as if she loved him more than anything in the world.

"I want to make love to you properly," he said, looking down at the top of her head. Her hair shone, a vibrant red that never failed to make him want to touch the silky strands. He wrapped his fist in the mass. "I want to be inside you, Abigail."

"You're so impatient." Her tongue flicked out, her warm breath engulfing him.

Aleksandr trailed his fingers over her breast. He smiled when she shivered in reaction. "When are you going to marry me?"

"I thought we agreed we wouldn't talk about marriage when we were making love." She teased him with a gentle scrape of her teeth, another slow lick of her tongue. "We agreed it was unfair to cheat like that."

"No, we didn't. I want to get married immediately." He nearly came out of the chair as her hot mouth closed over him and she sucked, flicking her tongue back and forth. *"Immediately."*

Abigail laughed, the sound vibrating right through his heavy erection and sending waves of pleasure rolling through his belly. "I couldn't possibly marry you until my parents come home. They'd never forgive me."

"You're enjoying the fact that I'm supposed to let you do anything you want to me and I can't retaliate, aren't you?" he asked.

"Oh, yeah," she said, lifting her head, eyes dancing, her grin wide. "I love this."

"I have news for you, *baushki-bau,* I am feeling quite strong again."

She laughed again and flicked her tongue back and forth, hot little licks that sent electricity sizzling through his veins. "I don't think so."

"I do. Come here." He gripped her waist in strong hands and tugged.

Abigail made a face at him. "You're spoiling all my fun."

"Not all." His hand cupped her fiery curls over the black satin. His fingers dipped into soft, moist folds. "I don't think we need this." He dragged the thong from her body and tossed it somewhere behind him. "Straddle me, Abbey. I have to be inside you right now. I can't wait another day. Not another minute."

Abigail circled his neck with her arms, careful not to lean against his bandages as she widened her stance to straddle his thighs and with deliberate slow motion, settled her body over his.

Aleksandr threw back his head as the pleasure poured over him. She sank down so slow, her sheath, a tight hot fist, her folds velvet soft, gripping him as he pushed his way deeper and deeper inside of her. His breath left his lungs in a gasp of pleasure. Joining with Abigail was unlike anything else. The sweet, hot rush, the addiction of her body, the way she moved in perfect rhythm, no matter how hard, how fast, or how slow he went. He always felt as if he'd crawled inside her skin and found paradise.

"I love how you always want me, Abbey. Do you have any idea what a gift that is to a man?"

Her fingers caressed the hair on his neck. "Do you have any idea what a gift it is to have a man look at me the way you do?" She rode his body with a slow, easy glide, covering him inch by slow, excruciating inch, heightening his pleasure, ever careful of his wounds. She rose away from him, gripping with her muscles, creating friction that robbed him of breath.

"I know what I feel every time you touch me, *rebyonak*, each time you walk through the door and your eyes light up when you see me." His hands pinned her hips with unexpected strength, fingers digging into her, holding her still as he thrust hard and deep and fast.

Abigail cried out, unable to stop herself, the pleasure bone deep, tightening every muscle in her body. It was always the same with Aleksandr. She started out in control and he took it away with his body filling hers and bringing her such ecstasy she thought she might shatter into a million pieces. He held her still while he began to surge into her with sure hard strokes, her body pulsing around his, melting into intense heat and with mind-numbing, clawing desire ripping through her until she was chanting his name.

She wanted release. She needed release. She was right there, right on the edge, so close she could feel every muscle tighten in anticipation. In need. But it never quite came. She knew he shouldn't be exerting so much energy but she found herself pleading with him anyway. He was killing her, forcing her to wait. Holding her right on the edge of the precipice.

"Promise me."

"Promise you what?" She could hardly think with her body wound so tight, crying out for release. "Sasha! What do you want?" She moved her hips urgently, trying to force him to give her relief.

"Promise you'll marry me as soon as your parents return."

She was nearly sobbing with pleasure. "You're *killing* me. I can't take any more. I thought you were at death's door."

"You thought wrong." He moved again, a long slow glide driving deep into her, and pulled back, holding her hips so she couldn't follow him down. "When your parents come back you will marry me. Say it."

"Fine. Anything. I promise. You are such a dictator." She wasn't about to tell him her parents wouldn't be home until her sisters' double wedding and that was several months away. Her body was shuddering with the need for release and she deliberately tightened her muscles around him as he surged into her again, desperate for relief.

He thrust again, this time almost brutally slamming into her body. The breath left her body, the fiery sensations engulfed her. "More!" she commanded, feeling his powerful thighs bunch under her. She could actually feel him filling her, pushing through the soft muscles of her vaginal wall, while she gripped him tightly, holding him close to her, holding him in her.

Abigail looked into his eyes, was caught and held by the intensity of the emotions swirling in the dark depths. She could see his love of her, the need and desire that washed through him with the same strength of passion it did her. She'd been so afraid to feel this way again, the tearing, gut-wrenching love that filled her and refused to let her go. It was there in his eyes.

He drove hard, seeking to be as deep inside her as possible. She felt him moving through her, thick and hard and oh so hot, driving all the way to her very womb. She felt his body jerk as her muscles tightened like a vise, refusing to give him up. As her muscles rippled and convulsed, hard mind-numbing spasms that left her breathless, tears glittered in her eyes. His hot release poured deep into her and she pressed her forehead against his good shoulder, savoring the small aftershocks that kept her body shuddering with pleasure.

"I do love you, Sasha. More than anything. It scares me how much I love you."

"You aren't alone, Abbey. I couldn't live without you. You managed without me. You were able to shut me out so completely. That terrifies me."

"It's the only form of self-preservation I have."

"Look at me, Abigail." He pried her fingers from around his neck and shifted her back. The action sent another ripple through her body and around his.

She stared into his eyes and felt her heart jerk wildly. He always seemed to affect her that way.

"I love you. I'm not leaving you. *Ever*. Read my letters. You'll know I desperately need you in my life and you won't have to be afraid again."

Abigail kissed him. She'd already read the letters. She'd read them again and again during all those long hours and days when he was fighting for his life. She treasured every one of them and had cried more than she ever had over the way he poured out his heart to her. "I love you, Sasha. I do."

The wind rushed off the ocean surface to the deck, bringing sea spray, salt, and the muted sound of feminine voices. Distant. Musical. Laughing.

Abigail stiffened, pulled away from Aleksandr in alarm, her eyes enormous. "Oh, no." She looked around frantically. "My clothes. Where are my clothes?"

Aleksandr snagged her shirt and watched as she jerked it over her head. She leapt off of his lap, throwing the blanket over him. "Quick, you have to get in the house and get dressed. Come on, *hurry*."

The wind retreated, then returned, throwing leaves and twigs into several whirling mini tornadoes. From several corners of the house the wind rocked the musical chimes into a strange melody.

"What is it, Abbey?" He pulled a gun from under the tea towel on the tray beside him. His gaze shifted in all directions, looking for danger, assessing their options.

She caught up her slacks and dragged them up her legs. "It's my *mother*. And my father! I can't believe this. They've come back home. This is awful. Where are your clothes? They'll be here any minute. And *don't* say anything outrageous."

He smiled at her and reached for her hand, visibly relaxing. "This is wonderful. I've wanted to meet your parents. You're blushing."

She swiped at her face as if she could remove the stain of color. "I'm not. I cannot believe those rotten sisters of mine didn't warn me *immediately*. Of course they'd come home. Aunt Carol must have told them Ignatev stabbed me." She reached down to help him to his feet. "She said she was going to, but I told her not to breathe a word of it to them. She probably told the entire family. We'll be lucky if all of my aunts, uncles, and cousins don't show up as well."

Aleksandr staggered and that steadied her. She took a deep breath. "It's okay. We'll be okay." She stopped abruptly and glared at him. "You knew. You rotten, deceitful bastard, you knew all along my parents were coming, didn't you? Aunt Carol told you."

He arched an eyebrow, unperturbed by her accusation. "She may have mentioned it when she was here earlier."

"The *only* reason I'm helping you into the house instead of pushing you off the deck is that you're still hurt. Any promises are negated."

"Not a chance, Abbey. I'm holding you to the promise." He sat on the bed and wiped small beads of sweat from his forehead.

"It was made under duress and you tricked me." She brought him a washcloth. "Here, this will help. You're trying to do too much, Aleksandr. You can't recover from wounds like you have this fast. You have to stop pushing yourself so hard. You almost died. You would have died without Prakenskii's magic. I shouldn't have allowed you to make love like that. We just get so carried away."

He pulled her to him. "I love you, Abbey. We didn't get carried away. We just need each other. There's a difference."

Abigail kissed him. "I love you right back, Aleksandr Volstov, but I have no idea why. You're bossy and you insist on thinking you're invincible." She washed him quickly and helped him into a pair of sweatpants and a soft shirt. "You look pale. Do you need something for the pain? Libby is going to kill me for this."

"Stop, Abbey," he said, his voice tender. "Libby isn't going to know. We didn't do any damage. If anything I feel much better." He wrapped his arms around her and nuzzled the top of her head.

She looked up at him. "And did I mention bossy?"

"I think more than once. Let's go into the living room. I'd rather meet your parents for the first time there than in the bedroom." He took a deep breath, felt the instant rush of pain that always came when he forgot and inhaled too deep. He smiled at her anyway. He'd had enough of resting and healing. If she knew just how weak he really was, she'd have him back in bed in a heartbeat and there'd be no more of her teasing mouth and hot body to drain his strength. She'd be feeding him chicken soup.

Abigail looked at him with suspicion, but obligingly helped him stand. "I guess there is a certain disadvantage to meeting parents for the first time in the bedroom, but they'd never think you were weak, Sasha. They aren't like that at all. They're very loving and giving people."

He laughed softly. "I don't want to be in the bedroom, thinking about you in my bed and what I'd like to be doing with you the moment we're alone, when we have company."

She growled, actually growled, scowling up at him with a fierce, no-nonsense expression. Aleksandr burst out laughing, jackknifing pain through this entire body, but it didn't matter. "You have no idea how much I love you."

Abigail helped Aleksandr sit in the most comfortable chair just as the doorbell rang. "They're here," she announced unnecessarily. She wanted her parents to love him. To see him through her eyes. To see the real Aleksandr, not the hard, ruthless man he presented to the rest of the world.

As she crossed to the door, she realized she had nothing to worry about. Her parents trusted her, loved her, and they would embrace Aleksandr into the family.

Her heart pounding with joy, she flung open the door.

Keep reading for a special look at

WATER BOUND

The first in the new Sea Haven series
by Christine Feehan
Now available from Jove Books

FLAMES raced up the walls to spread across the ceiling. Orange. Red. *Alive.* The fire was looking right at her. She could hear it breathing. It rose up, hissing and spitting, following her as she crawled across the floor. Smoke swirled through the room, choking her. She stayed low and held her breath as much as possible. All the while the greedy flames reached for her with a voracious appetite, licking at her skin, scorching and searing, singeing the tips of her hair.

Chunks of flaming debris fell from the ceiling onto the floor, and glass shattered. A series of small explosions detonated throughout the room as lamps burst from the intense heat. She dragged herself toward the only exit, the small doggy door in the kitchen. Behind her the fire roared as if enraged by her attempt to escape.

The fire shimmered like a dancing wall. Her vision tunneled until the flames became a giant monster, reaching with long arms and a ghastly, distorted head. It crawled after her on the floor, its hideous tongue licking at her bare feet. She screamed, but the only sound that emerged was a terrible choking cough. She turned to face her enemy, felt its malevolence as the flames poured over her, trying to consume her, trying to devour her from the inside out. Her scream finally broke past the terrible ball blocking her throat, and she shrieked her terror in a high-pitched wail. She tried to call out, to beg for water to come to her, to save her, to drench her in cool, soothing liquid. In the distance the shriek of the sirens grew louder and louder. She threw herself sideways to avoid the flames . . .

Rikki Sitmore landed hard on the floor beside her bed. She lay there, her heart racing, terror pounding through her veins, her mind struggling to assimilate the fact that it was just a nightmare. The same old familiar nightmare. She was safe and unharmed—even though she could still feel the heat of the fire on her skin.

"Damn it." Her hand fumbled for the clock radio, her fingers slapping blindly in search of the button that would stop the alarm that sounded so like the fire engine from her dreams. In the ensuing silence, she could hear the sound of water flowing, answering her cry for help, and she knew from experience that every faucet in her house was running.

She forced herself to sit up, groaning softly as her body protested. Her joints and muscles ached, as if she'd been rigid for hours.

Rikki wiped her sweat-drenched face with her hand, dragged herself to her feet and forced her aching body to walk from room to room, turning off faucets as she went. At last only the sink and shower in her bathroom were left. As she went back through the bedroom, she turned on the radio and the coastal radio station flooded the room with music. She needed the sea today. Her beloved sea. Nothing worked better to calm her mind when she was too close to the past.

The moment she crossed the threshold of her bathroom, cool sea colors surrounded her with instant calm. The green slate beneath her feet matched the slate sea turtles swimming through an ocean of glossy blue around the walls.

She always showered at night to wash the sea off of her, but after a particularly bad nightmare, the spray of the water on her skin felt like a healing wash for her soul. The water in the shower was already running, calling to her, and she stepped into the stall. Instantly the water soothed her, soaked into her pores, refreshed her. Her personal talisman. The drops on her skin felt sensual, nearly mesmerizing her with the perfection of their shape. She was lost in the clarity and immediately zoned out, taken to another realm where all chaos was gone from her mind.

Things that might ordinarily hurt—sounds, textures, the everyday things others took for granted—were washed away like the sweat from her nightmares or the salt from the sea. When she stood in the water, she was as close to normal as she would ever get, and she reveled in the feeling. As always she was lost in the shower, disappearing into the clean, refreshing pleasure it brought her, until abruptly the hot water was gone and her shower turned ice-cold, startling her out of her trance.

Once she could breathe without a hitch, she toweled off and dragged on her sweats without looking at the scars on her calves and feet. She didn't need to relive those moments again—yet night after night the fire was back, looking at her, marking her for death.

She shivered, turned up her radio so she could hear it throughout the house and pulled out her laptop, taking it through the hallway to her kitchen. Blessed coffee was the only answer to idiocy. She started the coffee while she listened to the radio spitting out local news. She dropped into a chair, stilling to concentrate when it came to the weather. She wanted to know what her mistress was feeling this morning. Calm? Angry? A little stormy? She stretched as she listened. Calm seas. Little wind. *A freaking tsunami drill?*

Not again. "What a crock," she muttered aloud, slumping dejectedly. "We don't need another one."

They'd just had a silly drill. Everyone had complied. How had she missed the report in the local news that they had scheduled another one? When they conducted drills of this magnitude, it was always advertised heavily. Then again . . . Rikki sat up straight, a smile blossoming on her face. Maybe the tsunami drill was just the opportunity she'd been looking for. Today was a darned-perfect day to go to work. With a tsunami warning in effect, no one else would be out on the ocean, and she would have the sea to herself. This was the perfect chance to visit her secret diving hole and harvest the small fortune in sea urchins she'd discovered there. She had found the spot weeks ago but didn't want to dive when others might be around to see her treasure trove.

Rikki poured a cup of coffee and wandered out to the front porch to enjoy that first aromatic sip. She was going to make the big bucks today. Maybe even enough money to pay back the women who'd taken her in as part of their family for the expenses they'd incurred on her behalf. She wouldn't have her beloved boat finished if it weren't for them. She could probably fill the boat with just a couple of hours' work. Hopefully the processor would think the urchins were as good as she did and pay top dollar.

Rikki looked around at the trees shimmering in the early morning light. Birds flitted from branch to branch, and wild turkeys walked along the far creek where she'd scattered seed for them. A young buck grazed in the meadow just a short distance from her house. Sitting there, sipping her coffee and watching the wildlife around her, everything began to settle in both her body and mind.

She'd never imagined she would ever have a chance at such a place, such a life. And she never would have, if not for the five strangers who'd entered her life and taken her into theirs. They'd changed her world forever.

She owed them everything. Her "sisters." They weren't her biological sisters, but no blood sister could be closer. They called themselves sisters of the heart, and to Rikki that's exactly what they were. Her sisters. Her family. She had no one else and knew she never would. They had her fierce, unswerving loyalty.

The five women had believed in her when she'd lost all faith, when she was at her most broken. They had invited her to be one of them, and although she'd been terrified that she would bring something evil with her, she'd accepted, because it was that or die. That one decision was the single best thing she'd ever done.

The family—all six of them—lived on the farm together. Three hundred plus acres, which nestled six beautiful houses. Hers was the smallest structure. Rikki knew she'd never marry or have children, so she didn't need a large house. Besides, she loved the simplicity of her small home with its open spaces and high beams and soothing colors of the sea that made her feel so at peace.

A slight warning shivered down her body. She was not alone. Rikki turned her head, and her tension abated slightly at the sight of the approaching woman. Tall and slender with a wealth of elegant blonde hair untouched by gray in spite of her forty-two years, Blythe Daniels was the oldest of Rikki's five sisters and the acknowledged leader of their family.

"Hey, you," Rikki greeted. "Couldn't sleep?"

Blythe flashed her smile, the one Rikki thought was so endearing and beautiful—a little crooked but providing a glimpse of straight white teeth that nature, not braces, had provided.

"You're not going out today, are you?" Blythe asked, and nonchalantly went over to the spigot at the side of the house and turned it off.

"Sure I am." She should have checked all four hoses, darn it. Rikki avoided Blythe's too-knowing gaze.

Blythe looked uneasily toward the sea. "I just have this bad feeling . . ."

"Really?" Rikki frowned and stood up, glancing up at the sky. "Seems like a perfect day to me."

"Are you taking a tender with you?"

"*Hell* no."

Blythe sighed. "We talked about this. You said you'd consider the idea. It's safer, Rikki. You shouldn't be diving alone."

"I don't like anyone touching my equipment. They roll my hoses wrong. They don't put the tools back. No. No way." She tried not to sound belligerent, but she was *not* having anyone on her boat messing with her things.

"It's safer."

Rikki rolled her eyes. How was having some idiot sitting on the boat while she was under the water not diving alone? But she didn't voice her thoughts, instead she tried a smile. It was difficult. She didn't smile much, especially when the nightmares were too close. And she was barefoot. She didn't like being caught barefoot, and in spite of Blythe's determination not to look, her gaze couldn't help but be drawn to the scars covering Rikki's feet and calves.

Rikki turned toward the house. "Would you like a cup of coffee?"

Blythe nodded. "I can get it, Rikki. Enjoy your morning." Dressed in her running shoes and light sweats, she managed to still look elegant. Rikki had no idea how she did it. Blythe was refined and educated and all the things Rikki wasn't, but that never seemed to matter to Blythe.

Rikki took a breath and forced herself to sink back into the chair and tuck her feet under her, trying not to look disturbed at the idea of anyone going into her house.

"You're drinking your coffee black again," Blythe said, and dropped a cube of sugar into Rikki's mug.

Rikki frowned at her. "That was mean." She looked around for her sunglasses to cover her direct stare. She knew it bothered most people. Blythe never seemed upset by it, but Rikki didn't take chances. She found them on the railing and shoved them on her nose.

"If you're diving today, you need it," Blythe pointed out. "You're way too thin, and I noticed you haven't gone shopping again."

"I did too. There's tons of food in the cupboards," Rikki pointed out.

"Peanut butter is not food. You have nothing but peanut butter in your cupboard. I'm talking real food, Rikki."

"I have Reese's Pieces and peanut butter cups. And bananas." If anyone else had snooped in her cupboards, Rikki would have been furious, but she just couldn't get upset with Blythe.

"You have to try to eat better."

"I do try. I added the bananas like you asked me. And every night I eat broccoli." Rikki made a face. She dipped the raw vegetable in peanut butter to make it more edible, but she'd promised Blythe so she faithfully ate it. "I'm actually beginning to like the stuff, even if it's green and feels like pebbles in my mouth."

Blythe laughed. "Well, thank you for at least eating broccoli. Where are you diving?"

Of course, Blythe would have to ask. Rikki squirmed a little. Blythe was one of those people you just didn't lie to—or ignore—as Rikki often did to others. "I've got this blackout I found, and I want to harvest it while I can."

Blythe made a face. "Don't speak diving. English, hon, I don't have a clue what you mean."

"Urchins, spine to spine. So many, I think I can pull in four thousand pounds in a couple of hours. We could use the money."

Blythe regarded Rikki over the top of her coffee mug, her gaze steady. "Where, Rikki?"

She was like a damn bulldog when she got going. "North of Fort Bragg."

"You told me that area was dangerous," Blythe reminded.

Rikki cursed herself silently for having a big mouth. She should *never* have talked about her weird feelings with the others. "No, I said it was spooky. The ocean is dangerous anywhere, Blythe, but you know I'm a safety girl. I follow all dive precautions and all my personal safety rules to the letter. I'm careful and I don't panic."

She didn't normally dive along the fault line running just above the Fort Bragg coast because the abyss was deep and great whites used the area as a hunting ground. Usually she worked on the bottom, along the floor. Sharks hunted from below so she was relatively safe, but harvesting urchins along the shelf was risky. She'd be making noise, and a shark could come from below the shelf. But the money . . . She really wanted to pay her sisters back for all the expenses they'd covered for her in helping with her boat.

Blythe shook her head. "I'm not talking about your safety rules. We all know you're a great diver, Rikki, but you shouldn't be alone out there. Anything could go wrong."

"If I'm alone, I'm only responsible for my own life. I don't rely on anyone else. Every second counts and I know exactly what to do. I've run into trouble countless times and I handle it. It's just easier by myself." And she didn't have to talk to anyone or make nice. She could just be herself.

"Why go north of Fort Bragg? You told me the undersea floor was very different and the sharks were more prevalent there and it kind of freaked you out."

Rikki found herself wanting to smile inside when just seconds earlier she'd been squirming. Blythe saying *freaked out* meant she'd been spending time with Lexi Thompson. Lexi was the youngest of their "family."

"I found a shelf at about thirty feet covered with sea urchins. They look fantastic. The fault runs through the area, so there's an abyss about forty feet wide and another shelf, a little smaller but still packed as well. No one's found the spot. It's a blackout, Blythe, uni spine to spine. I can harvest a good four thousand pounds and get out of there. I'll only go back when no one's around."

Blythe couldn't fail to hear the excitement in Rikki's voice. She shook her head. "I don't like it, but I understand." And that was the trouble—she did. Rikki was both brilliant and reclusive. She seemed to take her talents for granted. Blythe could ask her to program something on the computer, and she'd write a program quickly that worked better than anything else Blythe had ever tried.

Everything about Rikki was a tragedy and Blythe often felt like holding her tight, but she knew better. Rikki was very closed off to human touch, to relationships—basically to anything that had to do with others. She had allowed each of the other five women into her world, but they could only come so far before Rikki shut down. She was haunted by her past—by the fires that had killed her parents and burned down her foster homes. By the fire that had taken her fiancé, the only person Rikki had ever let herself love.

"You had another nightmare, didn't you?" Blythe asked. "In case you're wondering, I turned off the three other hoses around your house."

Blythe didn't ask how the water had gotten turned on. The entire family knew that water and Rikki went hand in hand and that strange things happened when Rikki had nightmares.

Rikki bit her lip. She tried a causal shrug to indicate nightmares were no big deal, but they both knew better. "Maybe. Yes. I still get them."

"But you're getting them a lot lately," Blythe prodded gently. "Isn't that four or five in the last few weeks?"

They both knew it was a lot more than that. Rikki blew out her breath. "That's another reason I'm going out diving today. Blowing bubbles always helps."

"You won't take any chances," Blythe ventured. "I could go with you, take a book or something and read on the boat."

Rikki knew Blythe was asking if there was a possibility she would get careless on purpose, if maybe she was still grieving or blaming herself. She didn't know the answer so she changed tactics. "I thought you were going to the wedding. Isn't Elle Drake getting married today? You were looking forward to that." Another reason why the ocean would be hers and hers alone. Everyone was invited to the Drake wedding.

"If you won't go to the wedding and you need to go to the sea, then I'll be happy reading a book out there," Blythe insisted.

Rikki blew her a kiss. "Only you would give up a wedding to go with me. You'd throw up the entire time we were out there. You get seasick, Blythe."

"I'm trying gingerroot," Blythe said. "Lexi says there's nothing like it."

"She'd know."

Lexi knew everything there was to know about plants and their uses. If Lexi said gingerroot would help, then Rikki was certain it would, but Blythe was *not* going to sacrifice a fun day just because she feared for Rikki's safety. Rikki's life was the sea. She couldn't be far from it. She had to be able to hear it at night, the soothing roll of the waves, the stormy pounding of the surf, the sounds of the seals barking at one another, the foghorns. It was all necessary in her life to keep her steady.

Most of all, it was the water itself. The moment she touched it, pushed her hands into it, she felt different. There was no explanation for it. She didn't understand it, so how could she explain to someone else that when she was in water, she was at peace, completely free?

"Blythe, I'll be fine. I'm looking forward to going down."

"You're spending too much time alone again," Blythe said bluntly. "Come to the wedding. All of the others are going. Judith can find you something to wear if you'd like."

Rikki had a tendency to go to Judith for advice on what to wear or how to look if she was going to an event where there would be a large group of people. Blythe obviously mentioned her on purpose in the hopes that Rikki would change her mind.

Rikki shook her head, trying not to show a physical reaction, when her entire body shuddered at the horror of the thought of the crowd. "I can't do that. You know I can't. I always say the wrong thing and get people upset."

She had met Blythe in a group grief-counseling session, and somehow, Rikki still didn't know how or why, she'd blurted out her fears of being a sociopath to the others. She never talked to anyone about herself or her past, but Blythe had a way of making people feel comfortable. She was the most tolerant woman Rikki had ever known. Rikki wasn't taking any chances when it came to doing anything that might alienate Blythe or any of her other sisters. And that meant staying away from the residents of Sea Haven.

"Rikki," Blythe said, with her uncanny ability that made Rikki think she read minds. "There is nothing wrong with you. You're a wonderful person and you don't embarrass us."

Rikki tried desperately not to squirm, wishing she were already at sea and as far from this conversation as possible. She adjusted her glasses to make certain she wasn't staring inappropriately. Sheesh. There were so many freakin' social rules. How did people remember them? Give her the ocean any day.

"And you don't need to wear your glasses around me," Blythe added gently. "The way you look at me doesn't bother me at all."

"You're the exception, then, Blythe," Rikki snapped, and then bit down on her lip hard. It wasn't Blythe's fault that she was completely happy or completely sad, utterly angry or absolutely mellow. There was no in between on the emotional scale for her, which made it a little difficult—whether Blythe wanted to admit it or not—for her to spend time with other people. Besides, everyone annoyed the hell out of her.

"I'm different, Blythe. I'm comfortable being different, but others aren't comfortable around me." That was a fact Blythe couldn't dispute. Rikki often refused to answer someone when they asked her a direct question if she didn't feel it was their business. And anything personal wasn't *anyone's* business but hers. She felt her lack of response was completely appropriate, but the individual asking the question usually didn't.

"You hide yourself away from the world, and it isn't good for you."

"It's how I cope," Rikki said with a small shrug. "I love being here with you and the others. I feel safe. And I feel safe when I'm in the water. Otherwise . . ." She shrugged again. "Don't worry about me. I'm staying out of trouble."

Blythe took a swallow of coffee and regarded Rikki with brooding eyes. "You could be a genius, Rikki. You know that, don't you? I've never met anyone like you, capable of doing the things you do. You can memorize a textbook in minutes."

Rikki shook her head. "I don't memorize. I just retain everything I read. I think that's why I seriously lack social skills. I don't have room for the niceties. And I'm not a genius. That's Lexi. I'm just able to do a few weird things."

"I think you should talk about the nightmares with someone, Rikki."

The conversation was excruciating for her, and had it been anyone but Blythe, Rikki wouldn't have bothered making an effort. This conversation skirted just a little too close to the past—and that was a place she would never go. That door in her mind was firmly shut. She couldn't afford to believe she was capable of the kind of thing others had accused her of—setting fires, killing her own parents, trying to hurt others. And Daniel . . .

She turned away from Blythe feeling almost as if she couldn't breathe. "I've got to get moving."

"Promise me you'll be careful."

Rikki nodded. It was easier than arguing. "You have fun at the wedding and say hello for me." It was so much easier being social through the others. They were all well liked and had shops or offices in Sea Haven—all were a big part of the community. Rikki was always on the outside fringe and was accepted more because she was part of the farm than for herself. The residents of Sea Haven had accepted the women of Rikki's makeshift family when they'd moved here just a few short years earlier, all trying to recover from various losses.

She forced a smile because Blythe had been the one to give her a place to call home. "I really am fine."

Blythe nodded and handed her the empty coffee cup. "You'd better be, Rikki. I would be lost if something happened to you. You're important to me—to all of us."

Rikki didn't know how to respond. She was embarrassed and uncomfortable with real emotion, and Blythe always managed to evoke real emotion, the heart-wrenching kind better left alone. Rikki felt too much when she let herself feel, and not enough when she didn't. She pushed out of her chair and watched Blythe walk away. Rikki was angry with herself for not asking Blythe why she was out running so early in the morning—why she couldn't sleep.

Blythe, of all the women, was an enigma. Rikki was an observer, and she noticed how Blythe brought peace to all of them, as if she took a little bit of their burdens onto herself.

Rikki sighed and threw the rest of her coffee out onto the ground. Sugar in coffee. What was up with that? She glanced up at the clear sky and tried to concentrate on that, to think of her sea, the great expanse of water, all blues and grays and greens. Soothing colors. Even when she was at her stormiest and most unpredictable, the ocean brought her calm.

She went back into her house, leaving the screen door closed but the back door wide open so she wouldn't feel closed in. She quickly polished the cupboards where Blythe had touched them, leaving undetectable prints, washed the coffee mugs and carefully rinsed off the sink around the coffeepot.

Rikki hummed slightly as she packed a lunch. She needed a high-calorie meal, lots of protein and sugar. Peanut butter sandwiches, two with bananas, even though there was an old saying that bananas were bad luck, and a handful of peanut butter cups and two bags of Reese's Pieces would keep her going. Her job was aggressive and hard work, but she loved it and reveled in it, especially the solitary aspects of being underneath the water in an entirely different environment—one where she thrived.

Extra water was essential, and she readied a cold gallon while she prepared and ate a large breakfast—peanut butter over toast. She might not like sugar in her coffee, but she wasn't stupid enough to dive without taking in sufficient calories to sustain her body functions in the cold waters.

She ate, toast in hand—she didn't actually use her dishes. Her sisters had given her the most beautiful set with seashells and starfish surrounding each plate. She carefully washed the entire set on Thursdays and her wonderful set of pots and pans on Fridays—and she always had them displayed so she could look at them while she ate her sandwich.

She'd washed and bleached her wet suit the night before, and made certain that her gear was in repair. Rikki repaired all her own equipment religiously, waiting for that one moment when all her senses would tell her there'd be a calm and she could go diving. Her gear was always ready and stowed at all times, so the moment she knew she could make a dive, she was ready.

Her boat and truck were always kept in pristine condition. She allowed no one except the women in her family to step onto her boat—and that was rare. No one but Rikki touched the engine. Ever. Or her baby, the Honda-driven Atlas Copco air compressor. She knew her life depended on good air. She used three filters to remove carbon monoxide, which had killed two well-known locals a few years earlier.

She knew the tides by heart thanks to the *Northern California Tidelog,* her bible. Although she'd committed the book to memory, she read it for fun daily, a compulsion she couldn't stop. Today she had minimal tide ebb and flow with hopefully no current, optimum working conditions where she wanted to dive.

Despite Blythe's concerns, Rikki really did consider safety paramount. Rikki stowed her wet suit and gear in the truck along with her spare gear—divers, especially Rikki, generally kept a spare of every piece of equipment on hand just to be safe. Rikki kept hers in an airtight locked container, which she checked periodically to make sure everything was in working order. Moments later she was driving toward Port Albion Harbor, humming along to a Joley Drake CD. The rather famous Drake family lived in the small town of Sea Haven. The Drakes were friends with her sisters, particularly Lexi and Blythe, who was actually a cousin, but Rikki had never talked to any of them—especially not Joley. She loved Joley's voice and didn't want to chance making social mistakes around her.

Strangely, she'd never been bothered by others' opinions of her. Friendships were too difficult to manage. She had to work too hard to fit in, to find the right things to say, so it was easier just to be herself and not care what people thought of her. But with someone she admired—like Joley—she was taking no chances. Better to just keep her distance entirely.

Rikki sang along as she drove down the highway, occasionally glancing at the ocean. The water shimmered like jewels and beckoned to her—offering the peace she so badly needed. She'd had a few months reprieve from her nightmares, but now they were back with a vengeance, coming nearly every night. The pattern was familiar, an affliction she'd suffered many times over the years. The only thing she could do was weather the storm.

Fire had destroyed her family when she was thirteen. Definitely arson, the firefighters had said. A year and six months later, a fire had destroyed the foster home she was staying in. No one had died, but the fire had been set.

The third fire had taken her second foster home on her sixteenth birthday. She had awakened, her heart pounding, unable to breathe, already choking on smoke and fear. She'd crawled on her hands and knees to the other rooms, waking the occupants, alerting them. Everyone had escaped, but the house and everything inside had been lost.

The authorities wouldn't believe she hadn't started any of the fires. They couldn't prove it, but no one wanted to care for her after that. No one trusted her and in truth she didn't trust herself. How had the fires started? One of the many psychologists suggested she couldn't remember doing it, and maybe that was the truth. She'd lived in a state-run facility, apart from the others. Fire starter, they'd called her, and the death dealer. She'd endured the taunts, and then she'd become violent, protecting herself with ruthless, brutal force when her tormenters escalated to physical abuse. She was labeled a troublemaker and she no longer cared.

The moment she turned eighteen she was gone. Running. And she hadn't stopped until she'd met Daniel. He'd been a diver too.

Rikki turned her truck down the sloping drive leading to the harbor, inhaling the fragrance of the eucalyptus trees lining the road. Tall and thick, the trees stood like a forest of sentinels, guarding the way. The road wound around and the Albion Fishing Village came into view. She drove on through to the large, empty dirt parking lot and then backed up to the wooden guard in front of the gangway connecting to the dock.

As she unpacked her gear, the last remnant of her nightmare faded. Now, in the daylight beside the calming influence of the ocean, she could almost be grateful for the nightmares. They always heightened her awareness of safety measures on the farm, and the recent spate reminded her it was time to check all the fire alarms, sprinklers and extinguishers. She could never risk growing complacent again.

Even if she was not the one who had somehow started the fires, someone else had. It seemed clear to her that someone wanted her and everyone near her dead. She'd almost run from Blythe and the others in order to protect them, but Rikki had been so beaten down, so close to the end of her rope, she couldn't have survived without them. And despite everything, Rikki wasn't ready to die. Thankfully her newfound sisters had realized how important fire safety was to her, and they had spent the extra money on everything she'd asked for.

Rikki walked along the dock until she came to her baby—the *Sea Gypsy*. She didn't buy clothes or furniture, her home was stark, but this—this boat was her pride and joy. She loved the Radon, all twenty-four feet of her. Everything on her boat was in impeccable condition. No one touched her equipment but her. She even did her own welding, converting the design of the davit to make it easier to haul her nets on board.

The river was calm and the boat rocked gently against the bumpers. There was a soothing mixture of sounds, water lapping and birds calling back and forth. There was one lone camper trailer in the park and no one in sight. The harbor was nearly deserted. She went through all her checks and started the engine. Rikki untied the lines and cast off. A familiar eagerness raced through her veins as she pushed the *Sea Gypsy* from her dock.

For Rikki, no feeling on earth matched the thrill of standing on the deck of her boat with the powerful engine, a 454 MerCruiser with a Bravo Three sterndrive and two stainless steel propellers, rumbling under her feet and the river stretching out in front of her like a wide blue path. The wooden bridge spanning the river, with a sandbar and rocks on either side, was her gateway to the ocean. The channel was narrow and impassable in low tide or heavy swells. With the wind on her face, she maneuvered the boat out of its slip and kept a low throttle as she moved along the channel. The sandbar to her right could present problems, and she kept to the center as the *Sea Gypsy* swept around the curve to enter the actual sea.

Double-crested cormorants vied for space on the closest sea stack, a small island made of rock where the birds nested or rested. She sent them a smile as she judged her mistress. She never fully trusted the weather reports or tide books—she had to see for herself exactly what mood the ocean was in. Sometimes, in the protection of the harbor, the sea felt and looked calm, but the waters beyond the land mass could betray her angry mood. Today, the ocean was calm, the water smooth and glistening.

The *Sea Gypsy* swept out into open water and Rikki relaxed completely. This was her world, the one place she was truly comfortable. Here, she knew the rules, the dangers, and understood them in a way she could never understand social situations and human interactions. As the boat rushed over the water, the sky overhead was blue and clear, the surface below as smooth as the California coast ever managed to be. She had a great engine, built for speed—a gift from her sisters and one she could never begin to thank them for.

She rushed past caves, sea stacks and cliffs—from here the coast appeared a different world altogether. Pelicans, cormorants and osprey shared the skies with seagulls, sometimes diving deep, their bodies sleek and streamlined as they plummeted into the depths after fish. Little heads popped up here and there as seals surfaced close to shore, hunting for a meal. Two seals played together somersaulting over and over in the water.

Spray burst up the cliffs in a display of power as the sea met land. She lifted her face to the salt air, smiling at the touch of water on her face. She began to sing, one hand weaving a dancing pattern in the air as she maneuvered the boat with the other. Singing was almost a compulsion, each time she found herself alone where no one could see or hear her. An invitation. A language of love. The notes skipped over the surface to the sides of her boat as it rushed over the water.

Tiny columns began to form, sparkling tubes that danced over the surface like mini cyclones. The sun gleamed through them, lending them colors as they twisted and turned gracefully. Some rose high, leaping above the boat in thin rainbows to form an archway. Laughing, Rikki shot through it, the wind and water on her face and ruffling her hair like fingers.

She played with the water, out there in the safest place she knew, with the shore in the distance and the water leaping all around her boat. Water was drawn to her in some mysterious way she didn't understand, coming when she beckoned, saving her life numerous times, making her feel at peace when everything and everyone she loved had been taken from her. Under her direction the water plasticized, forming shapes. The joy bursting through her there on the water where she was so alive could never be duplicated on shore where, for her, there was only vulnerability and emptiness.

She anchored the *Sea Gypsy* just off the shelf but gave herself plenty of scope just in case a large wave did come at her out of nowhere. She checked her equipment a final time. Eagerness rose inside her, unmarred by any hint of fear. She loved to be in the water. Being alone was an added bonus. She didn't have to try to adhere to conventional social customs. She didn't have to worry about hurting someone's feelings, embarrassing her chosen family or having people make fun of her.

Out here in the water she could be herself and that was enough. Out here she couldn't hear the screams of the dead, feel the scorching heat of a blazing fire or see suspicion on the faces around her.

After rubbing herself down with baby shampoo, she warmed her suit by pouring hot water from the engine in it before putting it on.

Once again, she checked her air compressor—her lifeline. She'd spent a great deal of money on the Honda 5.5-horsepower engine and her Atlas Copco two stage air compressor with the three extremely expensive filters, two particulate filters with a carbon filter on top. Divers had died of carbon monoxide poisoning and she wasn't about to go that way. She had a non-locking Hanson quick release on her end of the main hose so she could detach quickly if necessary. She carried a thirty-cubic-feet small bailout—her backup scuba tank—on her back. Some of the divers dove without one, but since she usually dove alone, she wanted the extra protection. Rikki didn't care to be bent by an emergency ascent. She wanted to be able to come up at the proper speed should anything happen, such as a hose getting cut by a boater who did not see her dive flag.

Donning her weight belt and then her bailout, she put on the most important instrument, her computer, which kept track of her time so there was no chance of her staying down too long. She had a compass to know where she was and where she wanted to go. Grabbing her urchin equipment, she slipped into the water, taking four five-hundred-pound-capacity nets with her.

The massive plunge into the water felt like leaving earth and going into space, a monumental experience that always awed her. The cool liquid closed around her like a welcome embrace, bringing with it a sense of peace. Everything inside of her stilled, made sense. Righted. There was no way to explain the strange sensations she experienced that others obviously didn't feel when being touched. Sometimes fabrics were painful and noises made her crazy, but here, in this silent world of beauty, she felt right, her chaotic mind calm.

As she descended, fish circled her curiously and a lone seal zipped past her. Seals moved fast in the water, like small rockets. Normally they would linger, but today, apart from a few scattered fish, the sea seemed empty. For the first time, a shiver slid down her back and she looked around her at the deserted spot. Where had all the fish gone?

The San Andreas Fault was treacherous. A good nine hundred feet deep or more, it was a long black abyss stretching along the ocean floor. At around thirty feet deep, a high shelf jutted outward, and the extensive jagged line of rock was covered in sea urchins. The drop-off was another good thirty feet across where a shorter shelf held an abundance of sea life as well.

Rikki touched down at the thirty-foot shelf and immediately began to work. Her rake scraped over the urchin-crusted rocks along the shelf wall, the noise reverberating through the water for the sea creatures to hear. She worked fast, knowing that sharks could hunt her from below, whereas normally when she worked on the ocean floor she wasn't in as much danger.

Her feeling of dread increased with each stroke of her rake. She found herself stopping every few minutes to look around her. She studied the abyss. Could a shark be prowling down there in the shadows? Her heart rate increased, but she forced herself to stay calm while she went back to work, determined to get it over with. The sea urchins were plentiful and large, the harvest amazing.

She filled her first net in a matter of twenty minutes, and as the weight increased, she filled the float with air to compensate. In another twenty minutes she had a second bag filled. Both nets floated just to one side of her while she began working to fill the third net. Because she was working at thirty feet, she knew she had plenty of bottom time to fill all four five-hundred-pound nets, but she was getting tired.

After finishing the last bag, she hooked all four bags to her hose and stayed on the bottom while she let the bags go to the surface, holding the hose to slow the urchins' ascent and to keep the air from leaving the float once it reached the surface. She climbed her hose a foot a second until she hit ten feet where she stayed for five minutes to be good and safe before completing her ascent.

Working in the water was exhausting because of the continual flow of the waves. The wash could push forward and back against a diver, and exposed as she was and having to be careful not to fall into the abyss, harvesting the urchins had made her arms feel like lead. At the surface she hooked the bag lines to the floating ball and climbed on board. Using the davet, she hauled two full nets aboard and stored them in the hold. Exhausted, she sat down to rest and eat two more peanut butter sandwiches and a handful of peanut butter cups, needing the calories before bringing in the last two nets.

The strange dread that had been building in her seemed to have settled in the pit of her stomach. She sat on the lid of the urchin hold and ate her sandwiches, but they tasted like cardboard. She glanced at the sky. It was clear. Little wind. And the sea itself was calm, yet she felt threatened in some vague way she couldn't quite comprehend. As she sat on her boat, she twisted around, looking for danger. It was silly, really, the feeling of impending doom. The day was beautiful, the sea was calm and the sky held no real clouds.

She hesitated before she donned her equipment again. She could pull up another four nets filled with sea urchins, bringing her total to four thousand pounds, enabling her to pay a good amount of money toward the farm. She was being silly. This part of the ocean had always given her a bad feeling. Resolutely Rikki put on her weight belt and hooked her hose to her belt before reaching for her tank.

The air around her suddenly changed. It was charged, and pressure pushed on her chest. She was still reaching for her tank when she felt the tremendous swell building beneath her. Rikki turned her head and her breath caught in her throat. Her heart slammed against her chest as she stared at the solid wall of water rising up out of the sea like a monstrous tsunami, a wave beyond anything she'd ever witnessed.